AUTHOR

CLASS F

TITLE

NEW WORLDS 2

New Worlds 2

Brian W. Aldiss
Stephen Baxter
Jim Burns
Warwick Colvin Jnr.
Jack Deighton
Philip K. Dick
Paul Di Filippo
Peter F. Hamilton
Simon Ings
Marc Laidlaw
David Langford
Ian McDonald
Michael Moorcock
Ian Watson
Paul Williams

Edited by David Garnett

New Worlds 2

Edited by David Garnett

Consultant Editor: Michael Moorcock

VGSF

First published in Great Britain 1992 by VGSF,
an imprint of Victor Gollancz Ltd
14 Henrietta Street, London WC2E 8QJ

With thanks to Michael Moorcock, Richard Evans and Ian Craig.

New Worlds is a Registered Trade Mark of Michael Moorcock
New Worlds Vol. 62 No. 218   05392793

The right of David Garnett and the contributors to be
identified as authors of their individual contributions
has been asserted by them in accordance with the
Copyright, Designs and Patents Act 1988.

A catalogue record for this book is available from the
British Library

ISBN 0 575 05145 0

Designed by Peter Guy
Typeset by CentraCet, Cambridge
Printed and bound in Great Britain by
Mackays of Chatham plc, Chatham, Kent

Contents

The second is for my parents
Florence and Desmond Garnett

Without Whom I Would Not Have Been Possible

Introduction

David Garnett

The first volume in this new series of *New Worlds* was published in September 1991, exactly twelve years after *NW*'s last appearance.

In Britain, there were a few reviews in the sf press.

If you lived abroad, you could have turned on the radio and heard BBC World Service interviewing Michael Moorcock, Storm Constantine (who had the lead story in the volume) and myself about the relaunch.

But in Canada, there was a whole half hour television programme devoted to *New Worlds*.

Before the third season of TV Ontario's weekly science fiction show, *Prisoners of Gravity*, a film crew spent a week in London interviewing almost every sf author in Britain for future programmes. They were at the *NW* launch party; the following day they returned to Canada; and the programme devoted to *New Worlds* was transmitted three months later, in December 1991.

Michael Moorcock, Brian Aldiss, Storm Constantine and Ian McDonald, each of whom contributed to the first of the new volumes, were all featured on the show — and so was I. I talked about short stories and how important they are to the development of science fiction, and as I compared them with novels, I came up with the image of bricks and pebbles.

Publishing is a commercial enterprise, and what it produces is books. But every book is different. Each has a different plot, different characters; for the publishing industry, however, everything would be far simpler if all novels were identical.

There is some debate over whether this is what readers also want. Do they buy 'bestsellers' because that is what they wish to read, or because advertising and promotion makes such books seem so attractive? Is the pressure for 'more of the same' from the publishers or the readers? Readers can't buy what publishers don't publish; but publishers won't produce what they believe readers don't want to buy. In between lie the bookshops, and it is they who decide what to stock on their shelves.

56,000 different titles were published in Britain during 1991, but books cannot sell unless they are in the shops. If the country's largest book chain decides not to stock a certain title, a huge slice of the market is immediately denied and potential sales are reduced. The book may make a loss instead of a profit – and the publisher will not be so willing to publish an 'uncommercial' book next time. In the USA, the book chains are even more powerful than in Britain. Publishers sometimes seek the advice of the major retailers before issuing certain titles. If there are not enough advance orders, such books will not be published. The chains are no different from any other stores, they just happen to sell books instead of groceries. That is their sole function: to sell, to make profit. And the safest 'product' for a publisher to bring out is a book by a 'brand-name' author, or a sequel to a previously successful book; better still, a whole series. Familiarity breeds.

(Books by 'celebrities' are another safe bet. It doesn't matter who they are, it's assumed that anyone who has ever been in a film or appeared on television in any capacity – even in an *advert*! – can produce a book. They might never have considered doing so, but the astute publisher will call them up, make an offer they can't refuse – and, as part of the deal, even provide a professional author who will do the actual writing. (For a member of the royal family, a true author isn't necessary: stealing from already published books is acceptable, even essential.) Then add lots of publicity, such as television chat shows and articles in the popular press, and the result is another 'bestseller'.)

Publishers have to publish books; that is their function. A science fiction editor may, for example, have three 'slots' to fill each month. In Britain, the easiest way to do this is by buying books by American authors. These books already exist, or at least the titles do, having been previously bought by an American publisher, and a British editor can easily fill up his list without all the bother of having to read manuscripts. This is an extreme example, but it does happen. It's almost a case of 'cheap imports' coming from abroad. The amount of money offered for a book might be so low that a British author couldn't possibly accept such a small sum. To the American author, however, it doesn't matter; it's all a bonus to add to the original US sale. Publishing American books on the cheap, mixed in with low-advance reprints of old books, is a good way of keeping costs down.

The reason for so many American books being published in Britain, and not only in science fiction, is that there are far more of them than us – and we speak the same language, more or less. (British visitors to the USA might not be understood, and American movies are growing more incomprehensible; but most of these problems are resolved in print.) Science fiction is not only predominantly American, but also primarily an English language genre. The majority of sf novels published in Germany, Italy and Spain, for example, are by American and British authors. And, once more, any payment from such translated books is a bonus to the writer. The kind of money paid in their own country would not possibly be enough for a Dutch or Portuguese writer, say.

Many American books receive low advances in Britain; but some don't. Some books are given very high advances, often far more than they earned in the USA — much to the surprise of the author, and even to his or her agent. This payment probably has little to do with the merit of the book in question, although it helps if the book is very long and that there is an almost identical sequel, or two, or three.

Publishing editors come and go, they move to different companies, they take over different lines. Some who run science fiction lists know nothing about sf and care even less, but they usually soon move on to editing other kinds of book. A good editor can slowly build up a name for herself (and these days an sf editor is as likely to be female as male) or himself by developing new authors and publishing quality books, but this takes a long time. The fastest way for a new editor to get noticed is to pay a lot of money for a book.

Usually, however, editors try to pay as little to their authors as possible. If they pay a lot for one book, they have to make up the difference by paying less for all the others. Manuscripts are the raw material of publishers, and this is the easiest of all costs to keep to a minimum.

The greatest obstacle to novels becoming identical is the fact that every author is different, every book which he or she produces is different. Or they should be. This is what the word 'novel' means — something which is new.

But writers are discovering that the easiest route to book publication is to produce a volume which is exactly like another, either the kind of thing which they have done before or that another author has done before. Publishers want books which are 'in the tradition of *This*' or 'will be adored by readers of *That*' or are 'the latest in the bestselling series of . . .'

For an author, novels are a great investment of both time and effort. They have to make a living, and they cannot afford to write books which will not be published. The result is evidenced by what can be found on bookshop shelves. More and more writers are producing books which are written without heart and without soul. Dull and uninspired, lifeless and identical — these are the bricks.

And then there are short stories . . .

*

If books are bricks, then short stories are like pebbles, every one of which is totally different. A pebble can be polished until it becomes a gemstone — and each is unique, just like a short story.

Writing short stories is far less of a commercial proposition for an author than writing novels. Word for word, page for page, they are far more difficult to write; and word for word, page for page, the financial rewards are far less than for novels.

The same is true for publishers. Any company which issues an anthology such as *New Worlds* is taking much more of a risk than if it were publishing a novel. Bookshops claim that short stories don't sell, and so they don't stock anthologies — which inevitably means that short stories *don't* sell as well as novels do.

But short stories are essential to sf. The best of the new writers are found in magazines and original anthologies like this one, and so are the best of the established authors, the 'names' whose commitment to the genre extends further than the advance for their next novel.

The majority of novels are sold before they are written. Publishers need to allocate their monthly slots, and authors need the security of confirmed publication before writing the books. The process of book publication is *slow*, and schedules are often filled two years in advance. A 'new' paperback arriving in the shops this month was probably published in hardback a year ago, having been waiting to appear for two years — and been written another year before that. In other words, a paperback published in 1992 could have been completed by the author in 1988, perhaps started in 1987, and be based on an outline which was originally written much earlier.

Short stories are far more immediate. Everything within this volume has been written in the year prior to publication. This is the *new* in *New Worlds* ... !

Neither are short stories written on commission, at least not for *NW*. No matter who the author, whether a 'name' or an unknown, if the story they offer for publication does not fit in with my vision of what I want to do with *New Worlds* ... it doesn't appear.

In a short story every word is essential; every phrase, every sentence, every paragraph. Because of their length, short stories can be polished until they become perfect. Such perfection cannot be achieved with novels, where authors can easily afford to waste words, to go wandering away for several pages, even chapters, before returning to the story. This, in fact, is the easiest way of making sure that books become longer. And with every passing year, it seems, novels grow longer and longer, their themes and ideas stretched ever more thinly. Books are beginning to resemble bricks in the physical sense, as well as the metaphorical. They fill the bookshelves and also the publishers' catalogues.

This book, however, does not fill a pre-arranged slot in a publisher's schedule. *New Worlds* appears only when I've found enough good short stories for each volume. Gollancz is one of the very few publishers who are this flexible about scheduling, and editor Richard Evans is also well aware of the importance of short stories to the genre – which is why he is publishing this new series.

New authors do not usually burst forth into print with a novel; more often, they have published a number of short stories previously. (Even if they haven't, they have probably written short fiction which they have submitted to magazines and anthologies. The very existence of such markets encourages the development of new writers, despite the fact that they may never succeed in selling a short story. If such authors didn't first write short fiction, they might never have attempted a novel.)

This has been true of sf writers from Isaac Asimov, who sold his first stories in the thirties (early American science fiction consisted almost entirely of short fiction; Asimov did not publish a novel until 1950), and Philip K. Dick who exploded on to the scene with a phenomenal number of stories in 1953–4, through to William Gibson. *Neuromancer* did not appear from nowhere. Gibson had published a number of earlier short stories, and it was these which led to him being given a contract for his first novel.

The best way for a new sf author to become noticed is through short fiction. In the early eighties, writers such as Pat Cadigan and Lucius Shepard first established their names because of their outstanding short stories. More recently, several writers who were first published in *Interzone*, Britain's only regular sf magazine, have signed book contracts with various publishers. If these writers had not already published short fiction, they would have found it far more difficult to sell their novels. Equally, the publishers would not have been able to find new authors so easily if the writers had not already learned their craft through short stories.

It's a common misconception that science fiction is about the future; but one thing is certain – without short stories, science fiction has no future.

If many novels are growing increasingly similar because of commercial considerations, there is no such danger with sf short stories. Because of the economics of publishing, short stories are rarely a financial proposition for either an author or a publisher. (Or, I assure you, for the editor of an anthology . . .)

Every one of the stories which follows is, as I promised in the first volume of *New Worlds*, a true original, and each is totally different from all of the others.

Almost inevitably, some of the reviews of the previous *NW* referred to the 'new wave' — which was a term given to the kind of material which appeared in Michael Moorcock's *New Worlds* during the late sixties. This was not a phrase used by the writers, who made no claims for themselves. It was a convenient label imposed from the outside as a way of trying to categorise authors who had, in fact, very little in common. A few of these reviews of the first new volume were not referring to what happened a quarter of a century ago, however, but seemed to believe that if a book was called *New Worlds* then it must be 'the return of the new wave'.

But the authors in that volume and in this are not part of 'the new wave' or even a 'new new wave' or any 'new British/into the third millennium wave' or any kind of movement. They are all individual writers, all individual voices, each writing about their own concerns and interests.

I will make no reference to the stories which follow, because they are there to be read and enjoyed; but I want to say a few words about what *isn't* in this current volume.

There are no stories by non-English speaking (or writing) authors. As I mentioned above, sf is primarily an English language genre. Very little sf which is not by American or British authors is published in either the USA or this country. For an editor, the main difficulty is finding a good translation of such material. While reading for this volume, I've seen a number of stories by non-Anglophone authors, but nothing was suitable for *New Worlds*. Maybe next time . . .

Neither are there any stories by women authors in this book. Before I began editing *New Worlds*, I had edited two other original sf anthologies, *Zenith* and *Zenith 2*, each containing twelve new stories. The first included three female authors, the second included two. In the first volume of *NW* there were two women, but this time only 6 per cent of the stories sent to me were by women — and none of them was what I wanted.

At one time, science fiction was almost exclusively a literature written by men, about men, for men — or boys. Such stories rarely contained any women. (Or 'girls' as they used to be known.) There are more female authors in sf than ever before, but an editor can only select from what manuscripts are submitted. What I hope to see is more translations from other language authors and more stories from women writers.

Also missing from this volume is John Clute's indispensable annual review of the year's sf novels, a sequence which he began for my *other* anthology series: *The Orbit Science Fiction Yearbook*. Because of the timing of publication, the second *NW* had to be delivered to Gollancz before Clute was able to complete his reading; but his survey of the books (and the bricks) of 1991 will be published in *New Worlds 3*.

This time, it's David Langford who takes a close look at some of science fiction's most recent, and best, volumes. Langford is renowned in sf circles, for various reasons, and he has won twice as many Hugo Awards from the annual World Science Fiction Convention as any other British writer. (Arthur C. Clarke has three.)

And so to Philip K. Dick. It may seem odd to publish material that was written twenty-five years ago, and when Paul Williams first told me that he had some 'unpublished outlines' by Dick which I might like to see, I tried to appear not too unenthusiastic. I assumed they would read like most book proposals, basically nothing more than 'and then ... and then' plot summaries ... and then I read them. I thought they were terrific, and that's why they are published here.

Paul Williams read his first PKD book in 1967, met the author the following year, and in 1975 he co-founded Entwhistle Books in order to publish Dick's mainstream novel *Confessions of a Crap Artist*. Williams has provided an excellent introduction to the two outlines, and they have been brilliantly illustrated by Jim Burns, who worked on the pre-production of the film *Blade Runner* (based on PKD's 1968 novel *Do Androids Dream of Electric Sheep?*). The police spinner featured in the film, for example, comes directly from a Burns illustration in the book *Tour of the Universe*.

Many Philip K. Dick books were first published in Britain by Gollancz, and *Time out of Joint* was serialised in *New Worlds* Nos 89–91 (December 1959–February 1960). No. 89 also contained Michael Moorcock's first *NW* story, a collaboration with Barrington J. Bayley titled 'Peace on Earth' which was published under the pseudonym Michael Barrington. *NW* also published one of the earliest critical articles on Dick's work, in September 1966 (No. 166). This was written by John Brunner, who referred to PKD as 'the most consistently brilliant science fiction writer in the world.'

At the same time, Michael Moorcock said: 'Dick is quietly producing serious fiction in popular form; there can be no greater praise.' John Clute has described Dick as 'sf's finest writer from 1956 to 1982'. And Brian Aldiss wrote: 'No other writer of his – our – generation had such a powerful intellectual presence. He has stamped himself not only on our memories but in our imaginations.' Aldiss has also written the play *Kindred Blood in Kensington Gore* (Kindred was Dick's middle name), which he has performed with actress Petronilla Whitfield. One performance took place at the ICA in London on March 2, 1992 – the tenth anniversary of PKD's death, at the age of fifty-three.

As a memorial to the author, most of whose books had been paperback originals, Thomas M. Disch proposed the Philip K. Dick Award, which is now given annually to the 'best' book published in (American) paperback. The award is decided by a jury, and selected from a short-list. Marc Laidlaw and Ian McDonald, from this volume, have both been nominated for the award.

As well as the Hugo Award for *The Man in the High Castle*, in 1967 Dick won the British Science Fiction Award for *The Three Stigmata of Palmer Eldrich*. At the same time, Michael Moorcock was given a 'special award' for his work on *New Worlds*. In 1967, after serving as editor for three years, Moorcock took over as publisher and saved *NW* from folding. With issue No. 173, the magazine changed from paperback size to large format. (The same issue included the first part of the Thomas M. Disch serial *Camp Concentration*.)

Moorcock's award was taken to be engraved, and he never saw it again. In 1991, at the launch party for the new *New Worlds*, he was finally presented with a replacement trophy by the British Science Fiction Association. But whatever happened to Philip K. Dick's award? Did he ever receive it? Did he even know about it . . .?

That was 1967, the same year that Dick wrote 'Joe Protagoras is Alive and Living on Earth' and 'The Name of the Game is Death' – which, like all good fiction, are timeless. I hope that the rest of this book proves to be equally enduring, that it will be as relevant in twenty-five years as it is now. By then, it will be 2017 ... and that sounds like *real* science fiction!

Innocents

Ian McDonald

On those nights, in that season, when he was away, falling on his precisely calculated parabolic orbits toward Jakarta, São Paulo, Johannesburg, and that Santa Ana wind blew like sweat and heat and dark musk pheromones up from the valleys, the hot wind from the south would touch her skin with the distant sound of the drums from the dead town, and she would slip out of that house on the hill that was too hot, too damn hot for anything, out of her hot, clinging clothes, wade thigh-deep, breast-deep into the womb-warm water of the pool. Lying back, she let the waters receive her, lift her, and floated beneath a sky patterned with the lights of aerospacecraft.

She pressed fingers to belly. Blood-warm water flowed into her navel, filled up the valley between her breasts. Still smooth. Still firm. Weeks before it would begin to show. She imagined this was how it would feel, adrift in receiving waters, rocked by the primal pulsebeat.

On those nights, in that season, she regretted having to destroy it.

The warm surface in which she was embedded trembled. Above, the indecipherable constellation of a sub-orbital's riding lights cut in across the city toward the big aerospace port out in the desert, drawing a swathe of sound behind it. She slipped beneath the thin meniscus, let herself be shaken by the swelling thunder of engines.

If there is to be blame, blame those lights.

Blame those grey men, those hollow men, those faceless men who lived behind the imaginary doors in the walls of the white room; the dealers, the brokers, the agents of a thousand and one Co-Prosperity Sphere *corporadas*.

Blame those deals that cannot be sealed by the fleshless hand-shakes of virtual-space but only by the crude, physical, slap of meat into meat.

Blame the selfishness that took him up, up, sixty miles above the Aleutian Archipelago and climbing and left her waiting among the Hockneys with this thing of his tumbling in the swelling bulb of her belly. Blame the hot wind that got into the house; the wind from another continent with its intimations of unfaithfulnesses and infidelities and the slap of meat into meat in a thousand expense account executive suites.

She thought of the time he had taken her to Paris; the image in the seat-back screen of the earth falling away sparkling with the reflections of ten thousand thousand swimming pools. 'When I see that, I know I am home,' he had told her. Even then, half delirious with g-shock drugs, she had known it for a lie.

She did not see it as a killing. She did not consider recriminations and consequences. She saw only righteous punishment. She saw only what she considered justice.

Rosario, the dead maid, was waiting beyond the pool lights with the robe. In this season, on this night, the perfume of the garden was coiling, sensuous: clary sage, nightstock, juniper, cypress. The shoji walls of the room of the Hockneys were open to catch any breath of air from up in the hills, but admitted only the heat and the sound of the dead town. Beneath its film of water, her body was already sweating again.

'God, the heat . . .'

'Madam, I have found a place.'

The contract was into its third renewal but still Rosario could disconcert her: the abrupt transitions, the silence with which the dead woman moved around the house on the hill, the tense energy that seemed to inform her every action, the fearsome emptiness in the backs of her eyes.

('The secret,' Abbey, from the San Yaquinto Racquet Club had said that time when she had mentioned that they were thinking of contracting a personal servant, 'is to pretend that they're really alive and not in fact a resurrected pile of nano-what-do-you-call-thems? *tectors*; yes, darling. Once that starts to happen, darling, you're halfway to Necroville yourself.')

'Discreet, Rosario?'

God, the heat. It was no better inside the room of the Hockneys. She stepped out of the robe. A tectronic chair moulded itself to her streamlines; surface for surface, skin for skin. Rosario was always so damn cool, so damn collected. Death was a cold, passionless place.

'Most discreet, madam.'

'Good. I mean, I'd just die if I went to one of Paige-darling's cocktail evenings and met the man who'd opened me up, stirring his cocktail with something he'd used to scrape me out. You know how they talk, Rosario.'

'No one will ever know. It is down in the dead town, down by the ocean. A dead man called Van Ark.'

Necroville. Dead town. The place beyond the law. Beyond even the voracious appetite for gossip of the folk who lived on the hills.

'How much?'

'It would not be a problem to you, madam.'

'He's having affairs, Rosario. Women know these things. Wives know these things. That's the reason for it. He isn't interested in children. He just wants to keep me pinned down. Barefoot and pregnant while he screws his way across five continents. Property. That's what I am. Just another deal.'

If Rosario held an opinion she knew better than to voice it. With the dead close to out-numbering the living, comfortable employment was not to be jeopardised by incautious remarks.

Was there, she wondered, such a thing as morality among the dead? Did *right*, did *wrong*, die with them?

The room of the Hockneys was suddenly suffused with light. The shoji walls glowed: violets, cerises, imperial purples. Where the walls were open, she saw the sky above the city alight with luminous veils; a brief aurora twining and writhing, agonised, within its containment fields.

The deathsign in the palm of Rosario's left hand pulsed in time to the sky light; a 'V' intersected at a third of its height by a short horizontal line. Life. Death. Resurrection. The new stigmata.

'Madam, the curfew.'

'Give me the address.'

Lines scrawled on a crumpled slip of paper. Writing. How quaint. Some of these dead went way, way back. You could never tell. They could make themselves any age they wanted.

She knew the area. It had been fashionable, back then, when she had chased, and been chased by, golden surfer boys, cruised the palm-lined boulevards with the top down and the radio on. Back then, before the sea level started to go up, and the dead to move in.

The door with its carved Makondé figures clicked shut. She imagined Rosario, ageless, soulless Rosario, hurrying down the steep avenues of this hillside community, hurrying to join the great army of the dead, hurrying back beneath the lasing sky to their shanties and townships, their Dead Towns and Necrovilles before the tree-shaded avenues of San Yaquinto became the domain of the vigilantes and their merciless, tesler-armed *mechadors*.

She clenched the slip of paper tight in her fist and the room of the Hockneys glowed in the light from the sky.

∀

In a blue-lit room filled with the sound of the ocean, the dead man who called himself Van Ark had lifted two hours thirty-five minutes and a handful of surplus cells out of her life.

('We shut down your consciousness, Mrs Sifuentes,' he had said when she had walked out the door in the blue room and next instant found herself walking back in again. 'We find the technique is much more effective than conventional anaesthesia.' Realising that *it* was gone; irrevocably, irretrievably; cut off scraped out sluiced away without her ever knowing, without there ever having been a moment when she could have said *no*.)

As the car reconfigured itself into high-density mode and put the sound of the surf and the wind in the tall palms behind it, she found herself rewinding, reviewing, replaying, as we do when we are hurt or humiliated, or when we have done something that we later wish we had not but are helpless to undo.

Necroville. Dead Town. Outland. No law ran here, no crime, no punishment, no sin, no retribution. No right, no wrong, no morality, no justice. No human legalism can stand in judgement over a creature that it cannot even recognise, no punishment can deter something in its essence immortal, eternally self-regenerating. Only the tesler, with its shaped charges of tectors that could disrupt, displace, destroy the matrices of even the resurrected dead, was respected. True death, that from which no return is possible. She touched the weapon clinging to the curve of her right thigh for reassurance. She had bought the beautiful, awful device from the little man in the virtuality weapons shop because she thought it would be strong against the fear. It had been useless, impotent. Her fear had not been of the dead and their place outside the laws of the human universe. Her fear had been of the unborn thing inside her.

Thing. It. Why will you not call it *child*?

Because it is not a child. Never was a child. Now never will be a child.

They had derided it, those guards at the checkpoint beneath the great neon deathsign that was the gate to the dead town, when her weapon had disclosed itself on their headzups as they checked her authorisation. The first guard had pursed his lips, more impressed by the wealth that could buy as stylish a gewgaw as the tesler, than by its potency. The second guard, datavisor dripping alphanumerals, had waved her through, suddenly, inexplicably annoyed. Perhaps, she thought, he had imagined those perfect thighs slipping out of stretch fabric, opening themselves to some dead lover in some rotting condo – swimming pool generations dry, clogged with sand and windblown litter – filled with the sound of the rising ocean.

How almost right. But how wrong. She had parted her legs, yes, but not to an eternally youthful, eternally beautiful lover, but to the cool, chrome-plated streamlines of polished gynaecological tools.

('Would you like to know its sex, Mrs Sifuentes?'

'Should I?'

'Some find it helps in the mourning process.'

'I don't want to mourn it.'

'Mourn *him*, Mrs Sifuentes.')

When the security men had let her pass through the gate and into the dead town, she was made aware, with the shocking suddenness of neon on the edge of a knife, of her naivety. She had known the dead in their ones and twos, their threes and fours, only in the company of the living. In mass, in the company of only themselves, they were a vast, sprawling, implacably alien nation.

While the living slept, the dead woke. Partly photosynthetic, they expended the energy they had stored from the day in the pursuit of the night. The dead had little need of sleep, they did so only in order to dream, which seemed important to them in a way incomprehensible to the living. Whatever dreams the dead might dream.

Couples dancing in doorways beneath hysterical neons, locked together in rituals of spastic non-passion – love, among the dead, was currency, not emotion. Gangs of braves and hawks, sharks and jets, challenging each other from the rooftops to rumble, to tumble, to the *coup* wars of things that can fight, and kill, and die, and in the morning be born to fight, and kill, and die again. Prostitutes lounging on mo-fo couches, reclining against dying palm trees, rubbing their hands over their black rubber skins, their soft leather bellies and thighs, squeezing multiple astarte-breasts together, stroking elegantly deformed genitalia. Nightmare faces, angels, screen goddesses, rock icons. Monroe orgasmic over the hot-air vents; Gables, Fords, Stallones. The carmine pout of blessed madonnas, lightning-thin Voodoo Chiles stalking the boulevards with the shadow of sunburst finish axes. Smooth criminals. Riders of the Purple Reign. An infinity of mutabilities to explore, an eternity in which to explore them.

They frightened her, these dead. Their feckless spontaneity; their sudden, mindless violence; the alienness of their emotions. The completeness of their freedom from everything that bound the living, a moral vertigo.

The building had been just another *fin de siècle* beachside apartment block, plaster peeling in the damp, acid wind, weeds pushing through the red-top of the deserted tennis court. She had stepped from the car and the sound of the surf falling in the night onto the long, dark beach had struck her like a physical thing. Sound of sea. Sound of wind in palm trees. Those were the sounds of her childhood, of the innocence she had been glad to give away with her two, adolescent, hands, swept like jetsam into the bay.

Her heels had sounded like pistol shots as she had approached the long, low desk rimmed with blue fluorescent tubes. Like the interior of some chrome polished gynaecological tool. His name, Van Ark, meant no more than the carefully avuncular cut of his features. He had been the deadest of the dead she had ever seen. A trick of the lighting. But polite. So polite. The dead had time for manners.

And they had shut down her consciousness and cut two hours thirty-five minutes out of her life. And *it*.

As Rosario had warned, it was expensive. The click of the cardreader that took every major Pacific Rim Co-Prosperity Sphere currencycard accepting her contribution toward Van Ark's instalment-plan immortality had sounded exactly like the click of her heels on the blue floor as she had walked away. The doors had swung and clicked behind her and in the parking lot the car waited for her with its door open and the air was filled with the sound of the surf rising and the Santa Ana wind in the palm trees and she had driven away. Hollow. That was how she had felt. Like something slit open, curetted, a heavy fruit split apart and scooped clean of its clinging, gelatinous seeds. Hollow. Hollow then. Hollow now. Hollow always?

Now the car was taking her back to whatever might follow. All around, the life of the small, cheap cafés and shebeens spilled into the streets of Necroville. Tables. Bottles. Dancers. The heavy stutter of bass-lines from the back-boulevard shanties. Here the only light was neon and video and the carcinoma flares of naphtha burning in the gutters. Crazy preachers of a dozen different sects – whatever heaven might mean to those eternally denied it – proclaimed from beer-crates beneath the wind-tossed palms. WHAT IS THE MEANING OF MEANING? asked the graffiti on the wall of an apartment gracefully crumbling on the corner of Heartattack and Vine in shades of ultraviolet and patchouli. The car's navigation system found the access ramp to the east-bound el. Ahead, the luminous 'V' of the border post straddled the lanes. The car moved now through an angular mass of bicycles; spokes, frames, chunky handlebars, forks and tubes decorated with hand-painted dayglo ideograms. The early shift, dead workers in uniform grey onepieces and smog masks. Dawn was an ultramarine insistence above the dark hulks of the hills – still sparkling with ten thousand patio lights – catching and kindling the vapour trails of the shuttle jets as they descended toward Barstow. She imagined him, eastbound also, in some transit lounge, somewhere. Forever in transit.

Ten thousand thousand bicycles, punctuated here and there by the red warning lights of the vehicles of those living who, for whatever reason, had gone down among the dead, inched toward the checkpoint. That steel slate colour to the sky: another hot one. She rolled open a window. The air was cool, with a promise of heat sweat. She imagined she could taste on it a memory of ocean. She imagined that if she listened, over the ringing of ten thousand thousand bicycle bells, she could hear the sound of the waves breaking on all her wild years, and the stirring of the palm trees.

∀

Like all children of the age of plastic expenditure, she loved to shop. The Egyptians had their pyramids, the Greeks their temples and acropolises, the Victorians their crystal palaces and monuments to the earth-devouring iron road. The Chartres, the Rheims of this age were the titanic mall-arcologies that speared up in a shout of glass and neon from the dark squalor of the dead zones. Notre Dame of the virtuality shopping channels; clicking off a billion credit transfers on her quantum rosary that circled the Pacific Plate tectonic zone.

Since *that time*, she always ordered the car windows opaqued where the el passed over the new, sprawling trash cities of St John and MacArthur Park.

They say that for the past five years, the Coca Cola signs have been visible from orbit. And they have this great new idea with dye-secreting oceanic tectors . . . When those aliens – that enduring myth of these days of miracle and wonder – arrive in their starships at the edge of the solar system, their first contact with *homo sapiens* will be through the name of a sugar-free carbonated homage to body-fascist kultur.

There was a hire jitney in her space at the house. *Official rental Company for NorthWest Pacific* read the wrap-round logos. Tananarive. Srinagar. Tashkent. It should have been somewhere like that. Not here. Not for another week at least. That the car had not yet made its way back to the nearest company depot meant that he was not long arrived. But the house looked dead; baked, white, like bone in the shimmer of noonday. The heat was intolerable, yet she shivered.

Terms of endearment called through the rice paper geometries of the house on the hill. Every door she opened, every wall she slid back admitted a wedge of the intense, desiccating heat. From room to room she went, calling his name. The bedroom. Empty. The bathrooms. Empty. The dining room where they had never entertained. Empty. The room of the Hockneys. Empty.

He was waiting in the white room where he gathered in his virtual hands the unreal sheaves of corn that were the grain surpluses of entire economic regions. Here was the centre of his power and dominion. The black sensory skin lay sloughed off on the floor, the ugly helmet that frightened her with its unvoiced threat of sexual violence was an empty, discarded skull. He had no other purpose here than to wait for her.

She spoke his name.

He struck her. The blow smashed her into the invisible doors in the walls of the white room. What stunned her was not the physical force of the blow, but the absolute absence of any restraint, any moderation. He had struck her with all his strength and anger.

He advanced to strike her again. She fled from him. Through the bedroom. Through the bathrooms. Through the deserted dining room. He came after. He caught her in the room of the Hockneys, smashed her down with another two-handed blow. She tried to scramble, she tried to crawl away from him, away from the vast dark shape bending over her in the heat of the room, hammering blow after blow after blow into her face, breasts, stomach, trying to reach the drawer in the Moorish coffee table where she had put the thing, the smooth, deadly, silver thing she had bought from the smiling man in the virtual weapons shop.

He saw what she wanted to do and pulled her away and she screamed and she screamed and she screamed and the scream tore something inside her, some barrier to a reservoir of unnatural strength and it was in her hand – she did not know, would never know how – tectoplastics moulding themselves to her grip and she was strong, she was able, she was not a victim any more and he backed away from the silver thing and it was the most exciting thing she had ever seen, this power she had over him.

'Want to see, *huh*, if it works on living flesh, *huh*, the same as it works, *huh*, on the dead?'

He was roaring now, impotent, incoherent.

'You killed it you bitchwhorecow, you killed it, my child, you murdered it, my child, why did you do that, why did you want to kill my child, who said you could kill my child?'

She shook her head and laughed, a deep, painful, mad laugh.

'You're stupid, stupid stupid, you're so stupid, don't you know, you made me do it; your affairs, all your affairs.'

And he said,

'What do you mean, my affairs? What do you mean, woman?'

Then she heard, as if it was someone else going on and on and on and on, recounting some interminably boring anecdote, her voice telling him about all those rooms in all those hotels that all looked exactly the same. All those trips to cities with names like Hobart and Bogota and Bulawayo and what right did he think he had to destroy her life, her fun, her pleasure, but the only real thing, the only solid constant in this dimension of shouting voices was the presence of Rosario standing in the open door to the gardens with the noon sun hard like the edge of a stone blade on the patio behind her. Then she knew on whose information he had cut short his trip to Tananarive or Srinagar or Tashkent and come falling across the sky to the paper house on the hill.

She did not let go of the tesler until she was certain she could no longer hear the sound of the Official NorthWest Pacific hire jitney on the long sloping streets of San Yaquinto.

∀

Even now she still wished they wouldn't lend her things. Do things for her. Help her. Cluster and cluck around her. Treat her like a prodigal daughter returned. Each small, exquisitely conceived party, each night out with the girls roaring along the boulevards on manual drive, each intimate luncheon on the terrace at the Racquet Club, each excursion to ski lodges in the mountains where certain things were *not* going to be mentioned all weekend, right? now won't we have a great time just all us girls together? seemed like initiations into higher and higher levels of a club of which she had no great desire to be a member. But their well-wishing, however honeyed and cloying, (or was it pity, reconfigured?) was better than the humiliation of the early months. She had remained self-exiled in the house a whole season while the tepid winter monsoon struck at the translucent paper walls and spouted from the red roof tiles and the San Yaquinto poolside society schismed into the It's-her-life-she-can-do-with-it-what-she-damn-well-likes-sock-it-to-them-honey camp and the Selfish Bitch camp. Then, she would sooner have stuck needles in her eyes than be seen among the people who lived in the hills, no matter their faction – a trifle of conversation at those intimate suppers and dazzling dinners waited upon by dead servants with long lease contracts.

After the attorney systems had clashed and bickered and withdrawn with prisoners from their millisecond wars, she had been left with the house, the Hockneys, the car, a settlement of fifty thousand a month, and herself.

She found she was not afraid of herself. She liked herself. She was good company for herself. And solitude was not the fearful thing that had sent her to the Cuervo Gold, the tranq dispensary, the little impregnated paper tabs with a green mandala printed on them that totally derailed her consciousness. Solitude was liberation, a deepening of the channels through which her inner resources ran. The dread had always been worse than the reality. It could be coped with. She would survive.

'My God.' Paige Devane, ostensibly on a call from the San Yaquinto Residents' Association, but quite transparently check-ing out rumours, had gone sweeping through the house with its plastic bags full of unlaundered washing and discarded trays of self-heating 3DTV Chow. 'I knew it was bad, but I never thought this bad.'

Bad? She wanted to say. *This is me when I can cope.*

'I should lend you one of my men. You're obviously falling apart. Yes, that's what I'll do. I'll send one of my men over. Now, who can I spare? Yes. Gideon. He's not been with us all that long, now, but you'll like him. He's a darling. Absolute darling. You'd almost think he was alive.'

Paige Devane was a notorious devourer of the beautiful dead – beauty being a more or less universal condition among the resurrected. She hired, tired, and fired houseboys as regularly as her periods. Still, she was not certain she wanted charity pack-ages in the shape of Paige-darling's worn outs and cast offs.

She tidied the house for this Gideon. Top to bottom. Wall to wall. Then she spent an hour and a half carefully de-tidying it again. Just enough so that he would have something to do without her seeming like the disgusting animal Paige Devane had no doubt painted her.

And this Gideon came.

The doordrone brought him to the cypress terrace where she reclined, tall, cool glass to hand. References and security clearances scrolled down her photochromic lenses. He was beautiful. She studied him behind her big, dark lenses.

'Paige speaks very highly of you,' she said, trailing fingers in the water, counting the falling drips, two, three, four, five.

'Thank you, Mrs Sifuentes. I hope I shall be of equal service to you.'

She thought unworthy thoughts about Gideon, and about Paige-darling and about *service* but they stayed well hidden behind her dark plastic lenses.

'I'm glad to hear it, Gideon. Tell me, can you cook?'

'I have a passing familiarity with the kitchen, Mrs Sifuentes.'

He cooked . . . (kneeling down to serve her the exquisite little dishes of noodles and vegetables as she sprawled on the tiled pool surround) . . . like a dream.

When Gideon was gone, back on his big, heavy terrain-bike to the smogs and smokes of St John, she went down to the pool. In her hand was a stone taken from the petrified ripples of the sand garden. She dived to the bottom, a javelin of flesh, scratched on the blue tiles the descending stroke of entropy-bound life, the ascending stroke of rebirth, the horizontal plane of trans-substantiation, the flat surface of a still pool. She emerged gasping, water streaming from her short, seal-slick hair. The hot night sky above her was scarred with the ionisation trails of military aerospacecraft patrolling the attenuated reaches of the upper atmosphere. She was ecstatic. She was reborn. He was truly gone from her life now. Yet for one instant as the water had closed over her head, she had imagined the pool filled, overflow-ing, with his semen.

∀

Paige Devane, oh Paige Devane, damn you to resurrected eter-nity servicing ulcerated beggars, blonde and beautiful Paige Devane, damn you with vile and seeping viruses: that *thing*, you lent me? That piece of flesh – no, not even, that pile of tectronics that walks and talks like man, has become indispensable.

She had not wanted anything to be indispensable to her ever again.

So she smashed blonde and beautiful Paige Devane six-love six-love into the hi-density lo-impact all-weather polysurface of San Yah Racquet Club Court Number Six. Doing back to you what you do to your dead boys. *Darling*.

She did not love him. Yet. He was intelligent. He was polite. He was witty and well read and endlessly patient with her. Compared to him the San Yah cocks who stalked the clubs and bars were stupid and bestial, obsessed with the holy trinity of sport, sex and synTHC. Generation of swine. Shallow and febrile. Death had deepened Gideon. So she luxuriated in his companionship. Was stimulated by his conversation. Laughed at his dry, alien wit. Respected his silences and distances. Woke every morning, anticipating, at the sound of his terrain-bike clicking into its lock in the garage. All the things that people do when they are in love and would rather slit their bellies than admit it. So she took him everywhere with her; the Malls, the luncheons, those functions from which the dead, by nature of their estate, were not excluded, the San Yaquinto Res. Assoc. (the new trash-city of Sangre Christe was sending dirty urchin fingers through the old, abandoned suburbs toward the white virgin flesh of the hills, giving Cause for Concern), the Racquet Club ('darling, tell me your secret, your game's really picked up,' 'damned if I'm telling you *darling*'). Though she bought him clothes. Though she bought him toys. Though she bought him a small fuel-cell runabout to take him down from the hills through the neon borderland when the sky lased with curfew. Though she took him to shows and entertainments and charity balls and galas, to Casinos and Direct Stimulation clubs. Though she was Seen With Him. All Over. Still she did not love him. Yet.

∀

The restaurant strip moved at an unvarying metre-a-minute on its grand tour of the Central Plaza, reconfigured this week into mock Amazonian rainforest. Internationally Famous Names among the pseudo-lianas. Fashion-of-the-day was loincloth and off-the-peg muscles. What was that old movie – reprocessed for three dimensions (re-buggered, he'd called it, a two-dimensional monochrome puritan) where the hero and the heroine fight off an army of all-devouring tropical ants with trenches of burning kerosene? They'd failed before the onslaught of all-consuming self-replicating automata. The all-devouring self-replicating monsters of this nanotechnological invasion were smaller by several degrees of magnitude.

Gideon could not understand that she needed times away from him; she who had fostered this dependence, nurtured it into closeness. He imagined that he had done something wrong, that he was something wrong, a thing by its very nature an animate *memento mori*. She could not tell him that her needs for these small acts of distancing would increase as the seconds and minutes piled up in the hollow of her womb, growing closer to the total of two hundred and eighty days.

There was no point in regretting it now. There is no point in regretting any irrevocable action. Yet she imagined a name for it, a life for it, a face and a history and a career for it, as if they were somehow an invitation for its forgiveness. She had tried to forget the date of the birth, but no one can ever deliberately forget anything and as the day drew closer she found herself increasingly taking herself out among *people*, to the pleasure domes, the clubs, the big malls, looking for clues, hints, suggestions in the lives of all those other people she could collect for the imaginary life of her aborted son. This dead waiter serving her *nori-chazuke*, that porter who would carry her purchases and place them reverently, corporate logos uppermost, in the waiting car, that promo-boy wearing the face of a star from the latest Virtually-interactive soap handing out five-minute sample cards, all could be part of this game she played with the faces.

The waiter poured the aromatic green tea onto the white rice speckled with crumbled toasted seaweed. *Nori chazuke*: sacramental in its simplicity. Green tea. White rice. Black seaweed. Figure/ground theory. They say that at even the most hellish of cocktail parties, you can always distinguish your own name.

That trash-boy with his scoop and brush.

That trash-boy, with his scoop and . . .

That boy . . .

He looked up. The bodies pressing between them moved, parted. He saw her, looking at him. She saw him, looking at her, looking at him . . .

My God.

My *God*.

The dead waiter frowned momentarily at the untouched bowl of rice, removed it. The strip of tables and intimate conversation booths continued on its slow pilgrimage around the shrines and tabernacles of conspicuous consumption.

The sin of abortion, what made it sneerable, snideable, gossip-behind-the-handable was that, in these days of the general resurrection of the dead, it was an ugly, cancerous irruption of true death. But what if they had developed a new resurrection, one for the unborn?

The car prescribed tranqs, adjusted ions, segued serene womb-music and advised assumption of full automatic mode.

No.

Call it shock. Call it hope. Call it fear. Call it that innate human talent for seeing the face of Jesus in a burned tortilla or a patch of melting Chinese snow.

'No.' Say it again. 'No!'

It could not have been her son.

She came home to the hill shaken, sweating, thirsting for water, the hydrostatic nirvana of floating, washing all her sins away.

The pool was already occupied.

The way he floated, head tilted back, suspended in rapture, the smell of the gardens, the memories of those Santa Ana nights, combined to paralyse her with a sudden pulse of sensual electricity.

'Mrs Sifuentes?'

Caught staring. Narcissus observed. But the dead had no shame.

'Forgive me, Mrs Sifuentes. An unforgivable liberty.' (As she stepped out of the silk street kimono and stretch onepiece.)

'The sun, Mrs Sifuentes.' (As she slipped down into the water beside him.)

'Our pseudo-melanin stores the energy of the day for the dark of the night, Mrs Sifuentes.' (As she pushed herself lightly away from the edge, water parting in a smooth bow-wave on either side of her head.)

'Gideon,' (she said), 'I know.'

It was then, exactly, that she realised she loved him.

Together in the jacuzzi they watched the city light up, street by street, area by area, zone by zone, a grid of light seized by perspective and drawn out to the vanishing point.

'Mrs Sifuentes, I will have to go now.'

Already the dark zenith was lightening with violet and cerise.

'Stay. With me.'

'I cannot risk it, Mrs Sifuentes. If the vigilantes' scanners record a dead past curfew without an exemption licence . . .'

'I could order you.'

'You do not own my contract, Mrs Sifuentes. Paige Devane is the current leaseholder.'

'The St John Death House owns your contract, Gideon, until you pay them back the price of eternal life.' She whistled the doordrone. It came floating across the scented gardens, over the pedicured lawns and formal parterres, the sand gardens and the stone gardens, studiously avoiding the garden furniture and the Japanese stone lanterns. Good and faithful servant.

'Access attorney and accountancy systems,' she said. (Hoping, as she finger-wrote on the screen, that the curve of her smooth and perfect flanks folded across the edge of the jacuzzi might rekindle memories of *want* and *desire* in an existence where such words were without meaning.)

It was expensive. Even for one balanced atop the fiduciary iceberg of Dahl Esbert Sifuentes. When the accountancy systems shook on the transaction and circulated curfew-exclusion clearances to San Yaquinto Securities Inc., it felt more like the consummation of some long contemplated revenge than an act of seduction, a deep hot purr at the junction of her Fallopian tubes, smooth and hot and silent running.

'Or someone else pays the price for you, Gideon.'

The hardcopy was unnecessary but she wanted something to wield over him.

'Stay.'

'Do I have a choice?'

'There is always a choice, Gideon.'

The rice paper flimsy fell from her fingers, was caught in the whirlpool of designer bubbles and dragged under. He lay in the foaming water. She cradled his head in her hands. Above them the sky darkened and she saw a thing she had never noticed before: that, just like the uncertain blinking of an old neon tube resolves into sure and certain light, there was a distinct moment when the skylights suddenly flickered into full luminescence. Sheets of light writhed and twined fifty miles above the golden net of the city. The stigma in the palm of Gideon's left hand flashed in time to the rhythm of the sky. And, in mid-pulse, went dark. He was all hers now. Already she could imagine she heard the ringing of ten thousand thousand bicycle bells and the temblor-rumble of the deep underground trains.

∀

She had expected sex with the dead to be different. How different she could not be certain. A chill to the flesh, perhaps. A cumbrousness of movement, the clanking of brute, mechanical bones. A failure of arousal, a lump of dead, decaying meat which she must stimulate back to life with hands and tongue. Any of these. All of these. She knew she was cursed with romanticism.

As a romantic, she had always hoped that in sex she could attain an interpenetration of spirits to match the interpenetration of meat; that in sex she could lose herself and break the frontiers of *otherness* and *selfhood* that were more strictly guarded than the borders between the lands of the living and the dead. She had hoped that in sex with Gideon she might for one empathic moment share whatever it was to pass through death.

It had just been sex. And not particularly good sex at that. He had been gauche and clumsy, not with the gaucheness and clumsiness of some zombie monster fresh from the graveyard, but of the clearly inexperienced. Small wonder Paige-darling had passed him on. His ejaculation – too early – had deeply shocked her. She had not thought they could do that, the dead. She realised she had always imagined them sterile, empty creatures filled with puffs of wind and memory. She had washed herself, washed herself, washed herself until she felt she was clean of every trace, every suspicion, every taint of the clinging, crawling pseudo-sperm.

My God (as the water swirled down the vent), what if . . . They used to say, when the first few thousand had been successfully resurrected, that if you touched them, you could catch it off them. *What if* it was not just superstition and story? *What if*, despite the assurances of both the Death House, which administered the technology, and Tesler-Thanos who had developed the technique, that once locked into a genetically-defined matrix, the tectors became inert and stable: *what if*, living egg and dead micro-machine could – *had* – fused and fertilised?

No. Scare stories. Horror stories. Night of the Living Dead Thriller Zombie-Flesh-Eater stories. Still, she pulled the privacy screen around her to call up her medical advisor through the doors in the walls of the white room. Who, being only a pay-by-the-second interactive artificial persona orbiting the superconducting heart of a database somewhere in New Queensland Free State, and thus without judgement or moral standpoint or Freudian neuroses, told her: Scare Story, Horror Story, Night of the Living Dead Thriller Zombie-Flesh-Eater story.

She wished it made her feel better.

If there was a sharing of souls to be found, it was not in the bed, in the room with the walls that opened in the night to let in the cool and the perfume of the garden. It was in her pool.

'It's the closest I can come to pure being,' she said, floating head-to-head, like the six o'clock hands of antique watches. 'Floating. Being. One by one, I close my senses until I am nothing embedded in nothingness. Pure being. Nirvana. Nothingness. Forgetting.'

'For me, it is remembering, Mrs Sifuentes.'

'Of before?' she asked, aroused by the cool touch of mortality, hovering like an angel over the lintels and gateposts of Israel.

'Of my rebirth. My first contract.'

Throughout the attorney wars and the mutual stripping bare of their lives, one thing had remained untouchable, inviolable; her special account, basketed in half a dozen corporate agglomerates in as many economic regions, inexorably accruing interest to pay the Death House their ferryman's fee for her own resurrection. Those without such provisions – most of humanity – emerged from their Lazarus tanks as the virtual bondslaves of whatever party cared to contract their services from the Death House. Gideon's indenture had gone further. While he was yet a free-floating soup of tectors and unravelled DNA beneath the curved carapace of his tank, Ewart/Western Australian Minerals had bought him and four fellow resurrectees under a pre-resurrection contract. The laws of mass-to-orbit and transorbital insertion costs made it cheaper to launch just a two-metre carrier body with slap-on tector packages, programmed to target a suitable asteroid, and, fifteen seconds before impact, separate and envelop it in a nimbus of voraciously reconfiguring nanofactors. Within three days the drive unit, the Lazarus tanks and the life-support bubbles were manufactured out of base matter. Within six days the unsuspecting crew would be resurrected forty million kilometres from their last memories in an environment that did not much resemble anyone's ideal of heaven. By the time they all arrived at Ewart/OzWest's synchronous manufactories the tectors would have converted the original twenty million ton mass of manganese iron into a five kilometre hive of ninety-nine percent pure orbital construction I-beams.

'I found it very hard to adjust when I returned to Earth,' Gideon said. 'I had never known gravity, you see. I had been configured for deep-space work. A sky, an horizon, the essential two-dimensionality of life on a planetary surface were profoundly disorienting to me. Floating is my rebirth experience. My first memory is of the sun rising over the edge of the plastic bubble in which I woke to life.'

Suspended in water, she felt the sun warm on her belly and tried to imagine birth in free-fall, that same sun bursting, raw on naked skin. No. A strange shiver – like a cloud in a cloudless sky. Something he had said.

'Your first memory?'

'My brothers and sisters – my crewbrethren, that is, concluded that there must have been an accident, some cosmic-ray induced soft fail in one of my memory storage systems. All my past, all my memories of my fore-life and death, wiped out. Annihilated.'

Fore-life. Some weather front must have been moving in from the north across the city. The air felt chill on her wet flesh.

'It was not until we shared memories that I learned that I was dead and born again. Can you imagine what a terrible revelation it is, to believe that you are alive, and to have that belief shattered by the incontrovertible proof that you are in fact dead?'

And again: on the patio, the nubbled stone surface warm with the stored heat of the day beneath her bare feet:

'Gideon, why did you give up space? I would think that if I had been up there I wouldn't ever want to come back down again.'

'You would be right, Mrs Sifuentes. All this is just dirt and ashes compared to the stars.'

'Tell me, Gideon.'

'God does not merely play dice with the universe, Mrs Sifuentes, he loads them too. As soon as you realise you are immortal, indestructible, endlessly self-regenerating, then something happens that shatters your illusions, your elation, your astonished delight, and reminds you that on the universal scale, you are nothing. Nothing.'

'What do you mean, Gideon?'

'There was an accident. We were out, working on the skin. Configured for deep space, we do not require oxygen, and even out at the asteroids there is sufficient sunlight for us to function purely photosynthetically. We can work in vacuum, all we require is a transparent pressure skin to prevent us from explosively decompressing, with filters to admit the light but screen out radiations that might damage our tectors. There is nothing, Mrs Sifuentes, no experience, to compare with being naked in the universe, intimately connected to everything. There is no high like it, Mrs Sifuentes.'

She remembered her experiments with the chemicals, the psychedelic dislocation of the virtualities behind the doors in the white room, the sensory deprivation of the pool. Pathetic.

'Karin was working on a processing module half a kilometre out when there was a sudden out-gassing. They are not uncommon. Before any of us could react, she was blown away, into space. She had neglected to fasten her safety line. It often happens – I had done it myself. Vacuum-rapture, they call it. The hugeness overwhelms you. Hours pass like seconds. There was nothing we could do. The factory's course was preprogrammed, we could not alter it. There were no facilities for going after her. All we could do was watch her on the deep-space trackers until her signal became lost in the background clutter. Flying on endlessly through space, still living, unable to die, conscious, aware.

'When we returned to the docking facility, I used what I had earned to reconfigure myself for a terrestrial environment and had the St John district Death House lift my contract from Ewart/OzWest and place it on the open labour market.

'As I said, Mrs Sifuentes, the dice are loaded. There are things worse than death. Mrs Sifuentes? Are you all right?'

'Just thought I would go into the house, Gideon. Getting a little cool, don't you think?'

And again: in the room with the Hockneys, the walls open and the sky tinged with the lingering colours of curfew.

'Death, Gideon.' (Rolling the balloon-glass of brandy between her hands.) 'What is death? Some people say that death is nothing, annihilation, that the only immortality we can hope for is through our children. No hope for me, Gideon. I had my child destroyed before it ever lived.'

'I would seem to be the refutation of that argument, Mrs Sifuentes.'

'Then some others say death is a white light, that you pass into the white light and pure existence, pure being from which you reawake in a new body, like waking from a deep and refreshing sleep.'

'I saw no white light, Mrs Sifuentes. I am afraid that for me, it was nothing. Nothingness. Out of nothing I came.'

'Christ.' She ran her tongue lightly over her lips, tasting her mortality. She examined each of the Hockneys in turn. 'I'm frightened of death, Gideon.'

'If it is as you say, what is there to be frightened of?'

'If it is as you say, Gideon, there is everything to be frightened of. What survives? Something that looks like me, talks like me, thinks like me but is it *me*? Where does this *me-ness* go? this *selfness*? Because if something doesn't die, it isn't death. Not real death. That *I* might be annihilated and all that remains is some walking, talking, breathing, thinking automaton that remembers what I remember and so imagines it is me, God, that is frightening. We think we've beaten death with our technology, but death is an old and strong enemy, the oldest and strongest of all our enemies, our final enemy, and it's not beaten that easily.' She inhaled the bouquet of her brandy but did not drink. 'Gideon,

I'm scaring myself.' She went to him, leaned herself against the inarguable solidity of his presence, his denial of the things she feared. 'Help me.'

And again:

'Gideon.' He lay beside her in the heat and the sweat. The sounds of the dead town were small and far this night, the wind had moved to an unaccustomed quarter, and with it came a prescience of an end to the heat. She knew that he would not be asleep. The dead had no need of sleep. Only dreams. Sleepers awake. 'Gideon, are you dreaming?'

'Yes, Mrs Sifuentes. Waking dreams.' Still, he would not call her by her given name. She had heard that the dead were afraid of names.

'What do the dead dream?'

'The dead dream of their fore-lives. The time before, that seemed like a dream, from which death was an awakening. What went before is just shadows, Mrs Sifuentes. This is true life.'

'And you, Gideon?'

'Darkness, Mrs Sifuentes. Nothing. Empty dreams.'

'The accident, Gideon?'

'Perhaps. Though I have been thinking.'

'Thinking what, Gideon?'

Lying in the big bed, moonlight and the ion-glow of transorbital interceptors cutting across her belly and breasts and pubic hair, she could hardly hear the words over the driving bass thump of her own heart.

'Thinking that perhaps there was no accident, Mrs Sifuentes. That perhaps the reason I remember nothing is because there is nothing to remember.'

'No, Gideon.'

'You see, I have heard that some of us have no memories of adolescence or adulthood or old age. They step straight from childhood into immortality. They are the ones who have died in early childhood, or infancy.'

'Stop it, Gideon. You're frightening me.'

'And I am thinking, Mrs Sifuentes, that perhaps there is a stage before either of these, that perhaps they have found a way of resurrecting those who have not even lived. The pre-natal. The miscarried. The aborted.'

'Christ, Gideon!'

'Mrs Sifuentes?'

She could not move. She could not speak. She lay paralysed.

'I must know, Mrs Sifuentes. Help me.'

Croissants: crisp, buttery, served at seventy-five degrees centigrade. As she liked them.

Coffee: black, no sugar, heated to exactly ninety-eight degrees centigrade, no bitterness, no burned aftertaste. How did he make it so good? He measured it, he said. That was all.

Radio: probability significant precipitation increasing to sixty-six percent low pressure area moving in from west, *niño* of *El Niño*, she could feel the change, the shift in ionisation as a tightness across her forehead, a throb in her sinuses though the sun shone bright upon her table among the cypresses.

Suspicion: can they do it, did they do it, did they cut it out of me and put it into a Lazarus tank and take it apart, that clump, that cluster of cells, with their tectors, did they scan it, map it, put it together again in the shape of a beautiful young man – beautiful, of course – of simulated age twenty-three, numerate, literate, educated to tertiary level but without one single memory in his head of a life before, because there never was a life before?

Are you him? Are you my aborted son returned, whom I have loved, seduced, slept with, whose sperm has splashed into my womb?

Do you know, Gideon?

Have you always known, Gideon, and manipulated circumstances, situations, my own emotions, in some alien dead game, purely to punish me? Is that why you are here, Gideon?

'I have to know, Gideon!'

'Mrs Sifuentes?'

He looked up from his gardening, fingers crumbed with soil, bare torso streaked with sweat. What need had something that could withstand hard vacuum of sweat, unless it too was part of the seduction?

'Nothing, Gideon. Nothing, forget it.'

She sipped her perfect coffee. Broke open her perfect croissants. Listened to the perfect synthetic voice of the radio playing perfect synthetic music.

'Mrs Sifuentes?' Always the game of mistress and servant. 'Mrs Sifuentes, I have a small problem.'

'What is it?'

'In three days' time I am due for deconfiguration. The tectors, Mrs Sifuentes; as they reduplicate themselves, they gradually accumulate data errors which, if left uncorrected, would result in massive transcription failures and aberrant misreplications.'

She thought of the exquisite deformed prostitutes she had seen cruising the boulevards of Necroville. Accident or design?

'So, what is it you need from me?' Thinking money, space, time, solitude, release from contract.

'Your pool, Mrs Sifuentes.'

∀

She would watch him go down into the water. That she would do. She would not under any circumstances watch him, over the space of a day and a night, dissolve into a swarm of free-floating tectors furiously examining the purity of their quantal souls. She followed him waist deep. No further. The sun was high, but a dark frown of cloud was piling up along the oceanward edge of the world, some tropical storm manifesting itself out of a ripple in the general climatic anonymity in accordance with the laws of chaos. He wanted to touch her breasts. She let him run his thumbs around her nipples.

'Remember, Mrs Sifuentes,' he said, 'the tectors become active in deconfigured mode. They will attack and absorb any organic matter with which they come into contact.'

She had always loved the way he was so careful never to end a sentence with a preposition.

'I understand, Gideon.'

'Then I will see you in three days, Mrs Sifuentes.'

'Three days, Gideon.'

And the rest of that first day she hid within her rice paper walls while the squall clouds mounted each other like rutting animals and she thought much about the chrome switch in the study that would drain the pool and flush beautiful, terrible Gideon and all her love and all her doubt away, down to the swallowing sea.

But she did not. She did not because doubt is a two-edged thing. Doubt denies, but doubt accepts. She had never been able to live with doubt. She had never learned the trick of covering it with trust. She knew only of certainty. Certainty covered all sins. Certainty was control. Control was an end of unpredictability, an end to doubt. An end to pain. The night came, and the heat, and the sound of the dead city, and the smoke of the smudge fires. She tried to imagine what was happening in the swimming pool. It was beyond her imagining. But she understood now why he had insisted on staying with her while he purified himself. Exclusive contract notwithstanding, he could have checked in at the nearest Death House; as a last resort they could have arranged for a Lazarus tank to be installed in the house. The neighbours would have talked, the property prices staggered, but it was acceptable. He had chosen the pool, her pool, her place, because this dissolution, this disintegration into nothingness, was his expression of love and trust.

Had he come to punish her, and in the end come to love her? She had to know.

For one moment the total enclosure of the sensory skin was both frightening and erotic, then the feedback sensors, the videos in the ugly black helmet, the aural implants and the taste-smell synthesisers that thrust into her mouth, gagging her, came alive and immersed her in another world.

The white room became a plain of neatly mown green grass. The invisible doors made themselves apparent, floating above the pedicured prairie. Behind them, she knew, were whole other worlds. She ordered those doors open and the creatures that lived behind them stepped forward to serve her. In the bottom right corner of her eye, digits blurred toward the thousands. Full sensory simulation did not come cheap.

The hounds of memory went loping out into the virtual city that rose from the green plain. Returned, thousands of dollars later, empty-jawed. Public records had neither a file on a death, or birth certificate for Gideon. Evidence, but not incontrovertible. In this city that was a day's drive from edge to edge, there were many places, many reasons for a man to pass through life without certification.

With a wave of her hand, she sent her hounds racing back toward the city and the web of Death Houses strung across it. Twenty thousand. Twenty-five thousand. Nothing. Thirty thousand. Thirty-five thousand. Nothing. Forty thousand. Forty-five thousand. They were stonewalling, turning her every probe and inquiry back on itself, refusing her every access request, politely but firmly denying her the resurrection records that would have driven a nail of certainty through the eyes of her doubts and fears. Fifty-five thousand. Sixty thousand. A month's settlement. The Death House could outwait her and her hounds until she bankrupted herself, naked and whining, financially paralysed, beneath their high white walls. Disengaging from the sensory skin she felt as hot and slick and high and low as the afterburn of sex. She wanted to roar like an angel and weep like a demon. She wanted to kill. She wanted to die.

She went to the Moorish table in the centre of the room of the Hockneys, opened the drawer. Removed the tesler. The squall line towered over the city, the sky yellow like sickness, the clouds purple as a bruise. The tropical storm sent fingers of cloud reaching out across the boulevards and mile-high glittering arcologies, tentative explorations of forbidden flesh. She pulled on onepiece and street kimono, pressed the tesler next to her thigh. Its tiny sentience awakened by her body heat, it clung to the stretch fabric. The car configured into expressway cruise mode, filed pass authorisations with the Necroville border security and slipped into its pre-ordained place in the stream of navigation lights westbound on sunset to the sea. The clouds, suddenly released from whatever barometric anomaly had confined them, spilled out across the city. Confined by heat and the dim bubble of light from the car controls, she pressed her hands against the curved tectoplastic and prayed that it might rain, rain down on all her guilt and fear and *tiredness*.

When the first fat drop shattered itself on the windscreen, she cried aloud in release.

This storm night the streets of Necroville were alive with masked revellers, both dead and living. Some arcane dead town festival, dampened but not diminished by the now-torrential rain. The car reconfigured into high-density mode, pushed forward by fits and starts as knots of celebrants washed up on the fringe of its sensor net.

Some of the faces, she realised, were not masks.

They can make themselves look like anything they like. Anything. There was no reason a son should even remotely resemble her. The car stopped to allow the passage of a party of beautifully malformed dead. Horns swept back, up, reaching for a moon that seemed to race behind storm clouds; obscene wattles, ropes of raw, slick black flesh, coiled in the trampled dirt of the street. Bright teeth flashed, leather breasts swayed. Angular guitar music strutted beneath the banyan trees. Drums calculated subtle, stalking rhythms. Fireworks rose fitfully through the driving rain, burst disconsolately, ignored. Many of the dead and the living had stripped off their clothes – useless in this warm, acid rain – the light of the trashfires gleamed from rainwet skin and masked faces.

The building, the small, easily-overlooked neon deathsign, all were as before. Her heels as unnaturally loud. But the storm wind was bowing the ocean-front palms, tossing them, tearing them, and the surf was thunder on the deserted beach.

'Mrs Sifuentes.'

'Good of you to have agreed to see me, Mr Van Ark. I'm sorry, I didn't know there was a carnival. I'd have made other arrangements.'

'Don't concern yourself, Mrs Sifuentes. Immortality is different things to different men. You misjudge us if you think that we are all dedicated to an eternity of endless revelry and debauchery.'

'Van Ark, I have to know.'

'Have to know what, Mrs Sifuentes?'

'If it is possible for the technology that resurrects the dead to resurrect the pre-natal. The aborted.'

'The tectors operate as molecular manipulators converting organic material into clusters of self-replicating nanotechnology that mimic the functions and forms of living cells.'

'I know how it works, Van Ark.'

'I merely mentioned it in the context that the tectors do not discriminate, as long as there is a DNA template for them to interpret.'

'So, it can be done. But is it done?'

'It is done, Mrs Sifuentes.'

'Was it done to me, to the child I terminated? Did you send it to the Death House?'

'Neither I, nor the Death House, would be at liberty to disclose that information.'

Again, the stone wall.

'Van Ark, I have to know about any preresurrection contracts Ewart/Western Australian Minerals took out within three days of my termination.'

'Go to the Death House, Mrs Sifuentes.'

'I tried.'

'I know. They informed me. That is why I was expecting you.'

And the tesler was warm and thrusting and urgent against her damp thigh. *Use me use me use me.*

'Damn you, Van Ark.'

'Too late, Mrs Sifuentes. Years too late. Why do you wish to know?'

She had thought the words would be impossible to speak aloud, could only be screamed, but the ease, the calm simplicity with which she said them was more frightening than any scream.

'I believe I am having an affair with my resurrected son.'

Keyboard icons swam to the surface of the blue desk. Smiling ambiguously, Van Ark keyed in access codes. Seconds later a rice paper hardcopy extruded itself from a slit that had opened in his desktop. Van Ark sent the flimsy spinning across the blue desk.

'What is this?'

'The number of contracts signed with Ewart/OzWest in the Greater Metropolitan Area within three days of your visit to our establishment. It is the most I can in conscience give you.'

She flipped over the slip of paper. The room seemed to tremble to the crash of surf on the beach.

Five contracts. Two women. Three men.

It had always been just a game to the dead.

'Your price, Van Ark?'

'You have already named and paid it, Mrs Sifuentes. And by the way, that little device you are carrying – you also brought it with you on your previous visit with us, I believe. A very nice piece, but it would have been quite ineffective to threaten me with it. This room, this entire building, is saturated with a jamming field keyed to the codes of most of the mass-market anti-thanatic weapons. You have never been safe with us, Mrs Sifuentes. Think on that.'

∀

The wind tugged at the thin paper of the shoji walls, punched them one by one into torn, gaping mouths. She stormed through the house, calling his name though she knew he could not answer. Rain blew in through the open walls, collected on the polished wood floor.

'Gideon!'

On the parterre the rain soaked her to the bone in an instant, made her gasp with its viciousness. She flicked wet hair out of her eyes.

'Gideon! I went to Van Ark, Gideon!'

The doordrone met her on the cypress terrace with its flashing lights and synthesised message.

'Warning please, warning please, you are approaching a tectronically active area. It is dangerous to advance any further. Please return to the house. Please return to the house.'

The wind whipped her cry away as she snatched the tesler from its place next to her thigh, aimed it two-handed at the drone, stabilisers straining against the buffets. The single bolt took it squarely, cleanly. In an instant the maelstrom of tectors had reduced it to amorphous slag. A heavy click: the tesler chambered another round. She closed her eyes. She could not look at what she had done.

The wind whipped her street kimono into a flapping flag of saturated cloth as she stood on the tiled edge. The pool lights were on, fans of fluorescence feeling out into the dark. The cool, clean water, shivered by the rain, was a dancing swarm of microscopic motion.

She brushed sour rain out of her eyes, aimed the tesler at the boiling water. The intelligent tectoplastic spread over her hands, fused them together into a steady rock of a grip.

'Gideon, tell me, I want to know. Are you my son?'

Her grip tightened on the firing stud. All she need do was focus the desire, and it would fire. What would happen then?

That was unimaginable.

'Gideon, I must have certainty. Don't you see? I have to know. I can't go on not knowing. Don't leave me, Gideon, not knowing, never knowing for certain.'

The water; the cool, deep water, perfection marred by needles of rain, seethed with almost life. The deathsign scratched on the bottom seemed like a statement of faith, a new creed. For she knew. She knew how to be certain.

She flung the tesler, hard, as far as she could away from her. It fell, contaminated, dirty, bright silver in the rain. The kimono dropped to the tiles, sodden, heavy, an encumbrance. Shoes – kick one, kick two. The high-neck onepiece peeled off her like a discarded skin. She winced at the punishment of the rain. But she knew now. There would be no doubt, now. No doubt. No guilt. No more self-hatred or fear. No more tiredness. No more uncertainty. They had been right, the ones who said that we live in our children.

'White light, or nothingness, Gideon? Do you know? Can you tell? Are you afraid Gideon? Don't be afraid. There's no need to be afraid now. Mummy's coming.'

And raising her arms above her head, she took two short, light, running steps, and dived neatly, cleanly into the receiving waters.

BRAIN WARS

Paul Di Filippo

SEND: IMF MOBILE NODE
                         SYSO1-4591P
RECEIVE: MC MURDO BIOSPHERE
DATE/HOUR: 070415/1275
TRANSMISSION STATUS: OK

Dear Host Mother,
The invasion is over, and I'm fine. Safe as a blastula in a
bioreactor, in fact, here inside our risk bubble.

Which is more than I can say for the enemy, Mom. We
pretty much turned them into *sodai gomi* in less time
than it takes to flip a SQUID.

I'm really sorry I can't raster you face-to-face and see
you smile at the good news. I can almost picture you
nictitating that way you do when you're happy. But for
reasons of security, us zygotes (that's just a friendly term
the officers have for non-comms) don't have full access
to the metamedium. We've been stripped of all our
telltags and poqetpals, most of us for the first time in our
lives. I feel plumb naked! We're limited to this retro-
jethro Teleport (TM) bonovox line, I guess so no live Si-
viruses or GaAs-worms can slip in or out. And in fact, all
these sending units have an AI chip in them that will
automatically erase any critical information from the
transmission. Like for instance, if I were to try to tell you
that we're stationed just north of CENSORED, or that our
KIAs amounted to CENSORED, the machine would
simply blip that part right out.

Works out just as well as the metamedium, I guess,
what with CENSORED time-zones between us and all.

Anyway, the important thing is that our mission seems to be a big success. Once again, the IMF has managed to intervene just in time to stop a potential catastrophe.

I'll tell you more in a while. But right now my main proxy, Penguin, is calling me. Seems we have to use the simorg colony to evolve some new expert modules they need by yesterday!

Your loving guest son,
CENSORED

SEND: IMF MOBILE NODE
                               SYSO1-4591P
RECEIVE: MC MURDO BIOSPHERE
DATE/HOUR: 070415/1610
TRANSMISSION STATUS: OK

Dear Host Mother,
What a jangle-tangle! The brass-skulls stopped by with a crew of Noahs wanting to evaluate the oceanic/atmospheric contamination produced by this latest Short War, and Penguin and I were kept busy bending molecules during what should have been our downtime. They finally finished with us, and since Penguin wanted to go virtual for a while, I thought I'd pick up my transmission to you where I left off.

Now, I know you and I have had our disagreements about the IMF's policies. Why, sometimes you actually sounded like a rifkin or greenpeacer! I can remember you saying, 'I never got to vote for the World Bank board.' But we all got to vote for the politicians who voted for them, whether we hailed from a big polypax like the NU or the EC, or a little one like our own McMurdo, so we can't really blame anyone else when the IMF does something we don't particularly like. I'm thinking of the mess they made in what used to be Yongbyon – the 'Pyongyang Gang Bang' I remember you called it – and the way they handled (or mishandled) those renegade cricks and transgenics hiding out in the

Azores. The Atlantic will recover faster from that one than the IMF's reputation will!

But those incidents took place before I joined, which you'll recall was right after the big command shakeup. My own unit was purged of all its officers, and *Oberjefe* Ozal received a field promotion, which he still holds. I think you'd like Ozal, he's a smart, good looking probe – the NYC gals in our pod all call him a 'streetbeat gamete,' which I guess is some kind of compliment – but he's not conceited. His main philofix is music. He plays his *gawwali* tabs whenever he has a spare moment – mostly through earwigs, since no one else really enjoys the holy Slammer wailing.

Anyhow, I can't say I feel any personal responsibility for any of the IMF's previous goo-screwing cockups (pardon the language), and nothing I've taken part in since I signed up has led me to regret my decision.

I've got to cut this short now, since one of my proxies is waiting to use the 'vox unit. I'll be right back.

Your loving guest son,
CENSORED

SEND: IMF MOBILE NODE
                                 SYSO1-4591P
RECEIVE: MC MURDO BIOSPHERE
DATE/HOUR: 070415/1918
TRANSMISSION STATUS: OK

Dear Host Mother,
Sorry about the delay. My buddy got an incoming 'vox right after he sent his. It was a 'Dear Juan,' wishing him a nasty *hasta luego*. Seems his target had joined the anti-war movement since he shipped out, and now wants nothing to do with 'bloody imperialist murderers' like us. It took some major tropes and a lot of talk to calm him down.

I just can't understand these protestors, Mom. It must be that they don't know what's really going on here. If they did, they'd realise we're just doing what has to be done.

I'm real proud of this operation, my first major action. We made the enemy 'cry onco!' faster than enzymes. I wish I could tell you all about it, since I understand the metamedium coverage was somewhat limited. I'll try, and see what the chip lets through.

The IMF issued its unconditional surrender ultimatum at 2300 hours on the second of this month. By 2400 hours, when the enemy had still not replied, the operation commenced. First in were the smartskin bombers, scramjets mostly under AI control, but a few being gloved by pilots offshore in MHD subs. These planes released burrowers, anti-personnel midges, thermites, core-borers, glass-masters, virtual ghosts and CEN-SORED. The enemy responded with Raid-Plus, bouncing buckyballs, fractal shrubs, moletraps, CENSORED and kaleidoscopes, but were mucho outclassed. There was never really any contest.

Hot on the first wave's heels, the APVs loaded with transgenic troops moved in for whatever close fighting might arise. The Fourth Wolverines really distinguished themselves, as did the CENSORED. Once 1-Cubed reported that things were pretty much under control, approximately CENSORED of us fifty-oners went in, the only humans involved in the whole shootup.

When the enemy's AI's committed silicide, we knew the latest Short War was history.

Mom, I'll tell you now that what we found once we occupied the enemy – in confirmation of the rumours that prompted the assault – is enough to make your cells metastasise. These guys had developed a whole armoury of aerosol-borne neurotropic weapons which they planned to use shortly on their immediate neighbours, and afterwards on whoever got in their way. Of course this is entirely against the Minsk Conventions, which they are a signatory to, and these gnomic jokers had to be stopped.

I don't imagine the next few days will see much

excitement. We're just riding herd on the civilian popu-
lace while the experts from the essays, peltsies and
gembaitches – Textron, Rhone-Daewoo, Toyobo, Ciba-
Kobe, EMBRAPA – dismantle the armament autofacs.

I've got some I&I leave coming up after this is over,
and expect to spend some of it with you and Dad and
Mom$_2$ and Dad$_2$ and Mom$_3$.

Crank those photoharvesters up – I'm used to the
tropics now!

Your loving guest son,
CENSORED

SEND: IMF MOBILE NODE
                             SYSO1-4591P
RECEIVE: MC MURDO BIOSPHERE
DATE/HOUR: 070515/0325
TRANSMISSION STATUS: OK

Dear Host Mother,
We just stepped down from Fever Alert Status.

It appears that some autonomous remnant of the
enemy is still functioning.

Most of us were sleeping when our earwigs gave the
alarm. I never thought the words 'perimeter breach!'
could sound so chilling. We all scrambled into our
Affymax millipore gear, praying that we hadn't catalysed
anything contrametabolic. Almost before we could grab
our high-kinetics and lyzers, the 'all clear' came through.
The tinmen and transgenics had neutralised the invad-
ers, who amounted only to a handful of Gorilla guerril-
las. Examination of the corpses revealed nothing out of
the ordinary – except for one thing. The 'vars had CEN-
SORED incorporated into their bodies, right next to their
CENSORED. These were empty, indicating they might
have had time to spray something before being smoked.

That something, they tell us, could be time-delayed in
its effects.

We're all just sitting around now on our hands while

the mccoys and herriots go over us with their cell-sniffers and hormone hounds, squeezing our virtual platelets for anything nonsomatic. So I thought I'd 'vox you this letter.

    Don't worry.
    Your loving guest son,
    CENSORED

SEND:	IMF MOBILE NODE SYS01-4591P
RECEIVE:	MC MURDO BIOSPHERE
DATE/HOUR:	070515/0800
TRANSMISSION STATUS:	OK

Dear,
Can't find to refer to. Seem to have disappeared from. Made bad inside. Very bad. Hard to use common. Looks strange near and far. Because of made bad up inside. Hopeful to fix. Examine, then create. Reassuring.

    But – partly running around crazy. Dangerous. Watch, shoot – how? Forget how to use without.

    Sit still. Holding together, lovely and crying. Please don't cry. Can't convey. Too frustrating to go on.

    Will 'vox soon.
    Don't worry.
    Your loving,
    CENSORED

SEND:	IMF MOBILE NODE SYS01-4591P
RECEIVE:	MC MURDO BIOSPHERE
DATE/HOUR:	070515/1200
TRANSMISSION STATUS:	OK

Dear Host Mother,
Whew! Am I glad the past four hours are over!

    My last transmission probably didn't make a whole lot

of sense to you. That was because I couldn't use any nouns! You see, everyone in the pod was experiencing a selective aphasia, kind of a language blind spot. A whole category of language had been effectively wiped from our cortexes. Or so the blooddusters tell us.

It appears that the trope the enemy hit us with was something brand new. The experts have dubbed it a 'multivector recombinant silicrobe'. It resembles our own CENSORED, only several magnitudes more sophisticated.

Apparently, the Gorillas discharged an aerosol of harmless individual components which were small enough to slip through our millipore gear. Once inside our bodies, however, the individual pieces intelligently assembled themselves into larger agents that headed straight for our brains.

The first indication we had that something foreign had penetrated us was a senseless announcement we all got through our earwigs. It sounded just like my last 'vox: strings of verbs and particles with no easy meaning. When I turned to discuss it with my bunkmate, Penguin (I haven't really told you much about her yet, Mom; she's a real old-fashioned target, with fewer than twenty percent bodymods, and I know you'd get quite close to her, given a chance), we found that we were limited to the same bizarre lingo too!

Needless to say, this kind of neural cockup – a 'cortical abortical' the NYC posse calls it – could have caused us serious trouble if the enemy wasn't so well under control. Though even then, we'd still have the tinmen and transgenics – the splices weren't so strongly affected – to protect us. Still, how could we give them orders . . .?

Anyhow, the aphasia didn't stop our stormin' biobrujos for long! They soon strung together a megablocker antagonist consisting of a charge of enhanced microglials and catalytic antibodies, along with CENSORED, which seems to have wiped the cerebral invader out quicker'n teraflops!

In any case, a Digireal conference on this bug is

underway now with experts scattered around the globe, including last year's Gengineering Nobelist, Doctor Sax, the guy who practically invented neurotropins.

So don't worry, Mom – we're getting the best of care!
Your loving guest son,
CENSORED

SEND: IMF MOBILE NODE
                             SYSO1-4591P
RECEIVE: MC MURDO BIOSPHERE
DATE/HOUR: 070515/1391
TRANSMISSION STATUS: OK

Daring Hotel Mothballs,
The newest truest neural contradural manifestation in the implication is undersay they way to play can't shay. Too few too blue words are now becoming excessive depressive stretches of letches and leeches and feel like my head's exploding decoding. Broca's aphasia in Asia is a lack of pack of parcel of morsel of words and turds. But Wernicke's journey to meaning of seasons is to produce unreduce of fibbing gibberish that makes senseless of relentless squawk talk. There appears to be a component historic of dyslexia distance instance ignorance, upon trying to writer communihesitation.

This stool shall pasture.
Your louvre question,
CENSORED

SEND: IMF MOBILE NODE
                             SYSO1-4591P
RECEIVE: MC MURDO BIOSPHERE
DATE/HOUR: 070515/1450
TRANSMISSION STATUS: OK

Dear Host Mother,
The Wernicke's is over now. It's pretty evident that the

MRS agent is staying one step ahead of the juice they shot us with. I just hope the bug isn't baltimoring anything permanently into our genomes. Right now, all it's doing is making auditory hallucinations. They're kind of pleasant – I heard you talking to me just a few minutes ago – but tend to interfere with real orders through our earwigs. I notice that *Oberjefe* Ozal has notched his music up to eleven.

I'll keep you posted. Hopefully, this'll be licked soon.
Your loving guest son,
CENSORED

SEND:	IMF MOBILE NODE
	SYSO1-4591P
RECEIVE:	MC MURDO BIOSPHERE
DATE/HOUR:	070515/1500
TRANSMISSION STATUS:	OK

Dear Host Mother,
The whole pod was sitting down at the rectangular surface raised above the floor level with four posts, ready to dig into a delayed meal – reddish oblongs streaked with white marbling, cylindrical orange tapering tubes, spherical crusted objects slit crosswise and topped with a melting square of yellow organic matter – when the newest trouble hit.

It seems that the bug in our brains has now produced a generalised visual agnosia. Nothing looks familiar. The sight of common objects produces no referents in our brains, emotional or intellectual. Everything seems an assemblage of basic, almost geometrical parts, out of which nothing whole can be synthesised, resulting in a generalised lack of affect.

Or so the Digireal experts tell us. It's kind of hard to tell exactly what's wrong from the inside.

All I know is that when I look at what I assume is Penguin, I see a stretched toroid with an irregular topography topped with filaments of varying lengths. I assume she sees the same.

It's hard to work up the emotion to comfort a toroid, but I try my best, and so does she.

Oberjefe Ozal has been fantastic through all this. He never loses his composure, but always keeps the ovoid with the seven openings atop the horizontal broadening of his column as cool as liquid nitrogen. He seems to derive almost superhuman strength and comfort from the *gawwali* buzz in the shell-shaped excrescences on the side of his aforementioned ovoid. I don't know what we'd do without him.

I guess this bug is not going to be as easy to smoke as everyone first assumed.

Well, now I'm contorting my buccal orifice and fleshy-red tasting member into phonemes that will signal an end to our conversation, which the flat grey box that transcribes and transmits my voice will insure that you receive.

Maintain your homeostasis at a less-than-feverish amplitude, Mom! (Not too hard at McMurdo in July!)

Your loving guest son,
CENSORED

SEND: IMF MOBILE NODE
                              SYSO1-4591P
RECEIVE: MC MURDO BIOSPHERE
DATE/HOUR: 070515/1829
TRANSMISSION STATUS: OK

Dear Host Mother,
The agnosia cleared up by itself.
It's been replaced by a real mild neuro-deficit.
Amusica.
None of our pop-tabs sounds like anything anymore.
This one's pretty easy to take.

The Evolution of SF

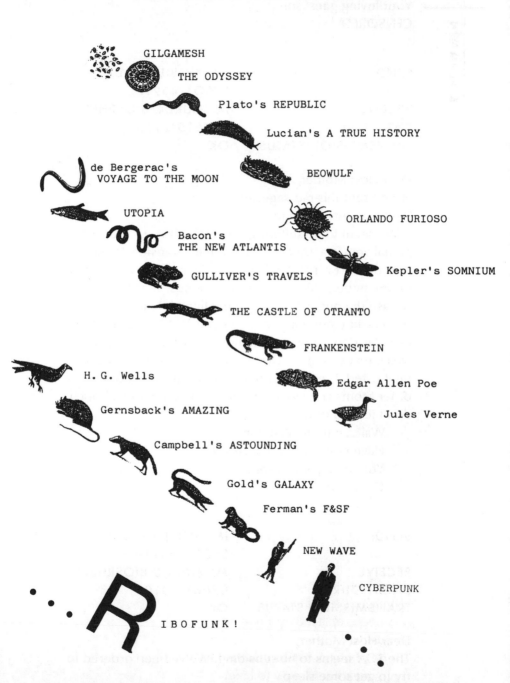

GILGAMESH

THE ODYSSEY

Plato's REPUBLIC

Lucian's A TRUE HISTORY

de Bergerac's
VOYAGE TO THE MOON

BEOWULF

UTOPIA

ORLANDO FURIOSO

Bacon's
THE NEW ATLANTIS

Kepler's SOMNIUM

GULLIVER'S TRAVELS

THE CASTLE OF OTRANTO

FRANKENSTEIN

H. G. Wells

Edgar Allen Poe

Gernsback's AMAZING

Jules Verne

Campbell's ASTOUNDING

Gold's GALAXY

Ferman's F&SF

NEW WAVE

CYBERPUNK

RIBOFUNK!

Except for *Oberjefe* Ozal, who's killed himself.
Your loving guest son,
CENSORED

SEND: IMF MOBILE NODE
                                   SYSO1-4591P
RECEIVE: MC MURDO BIOSPHERE
DATE/HOUR: 070515/2105
TRANSMISSION STATUS: OK

Dear Host Mother,
Have I sent this message yet?
Wait a minute, Penguin!
   We seem to be suffering now from TGA, or transient
global amnesia. (At least we hope it's transient!) The
herriots know that this kind of thing is related to damage
on the underside of the temporal lobes, so they hope to
squash the bug with a directed killer while it's busy
there. Did I mention that we've got TGA? For a while we
can't lay down any new memories. Maybe I sent you a
'vox already on it . . . Don't worry, long-term memory is
unaffected. I remember how wonderful you and the
other Moms and Dads have always been to me. I hope I
don't let you down.
       Wait a minute, Penguin!
       Have I sent this message yet?
       Your loving guest son,
       CENSORED

SEND: IMF MOBILE NODE
                                   SYSO1-4591P
RECEIVE: MC MURDO BIOSPHERE
DATE/HOUR: 070615/0105
TRANSMISSION STATUS: OK

Dear Host Mother,
The TGA seems to be subsiding. We've been ordered to
try to get some sleep.

Everyone's receptive to that, but whenever we start to drowse off, we experience these tremendously magnified myoclonic spasms. You know those little jerks your body sometimes gives just before passing into sleep? Well, these are the mothers of all such twitches, enough to knock you out of bed.

The mccoys are circulating now with somnifacients that should put us under.

Hopefully, when the new day dawns, this goo-screwing bug will have exhausted itself!

Sleep tight!

Your loving guest son,

CENSORED

SEND: IMF MOBILE NODE
                                        SYSO1-4591P
RECEIVE: MC MURDO BIOSPHERE
DATE/HOUR: 070615/0800
TRANSMISSION STATUS: OK

Dear Host Mother,

We lost half the pod during sleep to Nightmare Death Syndrome, that Thai/Filipino/Kampuchean tendency to flatline during sleep.

Unfortunately, the somnifacients may have contributed to the high mortality rate, preventing the sleepers from jolting awake.

I don't know how to tell you this, so forgive me if I just blurt it out.

Penguin was one of the fatalities.

I almost wish the agnosia was back, so I wouldn't feel so bad.

I'm asking the new CO to send you an adobe of her and me through the metamedium.

Just in case I don't make it home.

Your loving guest son,

CENSORED

SEND: IMF MOBILE NODE
                               SYSO1-4591P
RECEIVE: MC MURDO BIOSPHERE
DATE/HOUR: 070715/1200
TRANSMISSION STATUS: OK

Dear Host Mother,
It's been twenty-four hours since the last manifestation
of the invader. The herriots are starting to feel safe about
issuing an all-clear. And Doctor Sax is standing virtually
by in the wings with a last-ditch experimental trope
similar to CENSORED which they're going to try if there's
another flareup.
    Keep your fingers crossed (webbing and all)!
    Your loving guest son,
    CENSORED

SEND: IMF MOBILE NODE
                               SYSO1-4591P
RECEIVE: MC MURDO BIOSPHERE
DATE/HOUR: 070815/0300
TRANSMISSION STATUS: OK

Dear Host Mother,
We've all received our shots of aldisscine, Doctor Sax's
new trope, despite its high LD rating.
    There was really no choice after we all went body-
blind.
    What's body-blindness? I can imagine you asking.
    It's total loss of proprioception, the multiplex feed-
back from your muscles and nerves, skin and bones, that
allows you to tell – mostly subliminally – what your
body's doing.
    We're all isolated now in our heads like puppet-
masters whose strings leading to their puppets have
been tangled, or like a telefactor operator who's lost his
sensory feed. It's not that we can't move our limbs or
anything. There's no paralysis. It's just (just!) that aside

from visual feedback, there's no inherent sense of where any part of you *is*! You might as well try to operate someone else's body as your own under these conditions. It's not pleasant, watching your proxies tripping over their own feet, missing chairs, their mouths, the D-compoz unit . . .

But you can get used to anything, I guess. And the experts are confident that the aldisscine will stop any new deficits from popping up.

Anyway, I'm kind of glad Penguin didn't live to experience this. I never got a chance to tell you, but she used to be a dancer.

The orders have finally come down from Brussels for our pod to be rotated out. There's talk that if the body-blindness proves permanent, they'll try to fit us all out with onboard stabiliser chips and nanosensors to simulate normal proprioception.

What's one more bodymod nowadays, huh, Mom?
Your loving guest son,
CENSORED

SEND:	IMF OFFEARTH NODE SYSO2-999Z
RECEIVE:	MC MURDO BIOSPHERE
DATE/HOUR:	071015/2400
TRANSMISSION STATUS:	SOLAR NOISE IMPEDIMENT (*) −10%

Dear Ho*t Moth**,
As you might've guessed by the delay, we've been rerouted.

We're in transit to CEN*****, where we'll get the best of care. They discovered that all surviving members of our pod are suffering from degenerative neurofibrillary protein tangles similar to those found in sufferers of that extinct disease known as Alz********. CENSORED is a kind of sanitarium, where an AI-human team waits to cure us.

They say the average stay at CENSORED is *** months, but could stretch to **** years. Jumping genes! You could be in another symb-bonding by then!

Anyway, I can't look that far ahead, as our prognosis is very ****.

Let me repeat that, in case these flares are interfering: we stand a **** chance, not a **** one.

Unfortunately, I won't be able to take any incoming 'voxes from you for a while, or even send any. Not that I'd be able to really appreciate them too good anyhow. My brain seems a little dull right now. But they promise us that full metamedium contact will be restored as soon as it's appropriate.

But don't worry. You can always contact Brussels for updates.

Just ask for your boy, CENSORED!

With all best wishes

Warwick
Colvin

Corsairs of the Second Ether

Warwick Colvin Jnr.

THE STORY SO FAR:
In common with most of the others who explore the Second Ether, CAPTAIN WILHELMINA ROBERTA BEGG and the crew of the *Now The Clouds Have Meaning*, are searching for Ko-O-Ko, the legendary Lost Universe, said to be the single naturally habitable location of its kind in the whole of that bizarre space-time continuum, itself the sole level of the multiverse so far discovered which is not wholly inimicable to humankind. 'Humes' have divided the multiverse into a number of planes or branches — or perhaps facets of a near-infinite prism — calling our own division the First Ether and those with which we most frequently intersect the Second Ether, Third Ether and so on. Thus far we have found *only* the Second Ether responsive to our logic and therefore navigable (though legends abound of captains like AYESHA VON ABDUL, who found a means of sailing through the Third and Nineteenth facets to discover Paradise and determine that it should never be corrupted by the crazed sinauts who roam the burst fractals and twisted reality folds of the Initial Circuits, forever bathed in a spectrum of unimaginable and unreproducible light). Alone, Captain Billy-Bob Begg has tested the million roads, one by one, and imprinted herself with a map of the multiverse only she will ever be able to read. She is the greatest of the so-called Chaos Engineers who, using the principles of self-similarity, pilot their peculiar craft up and down the scales. They call this process 'folding', a kind of blossoming movement which enables their ships to progress in a series of 'folds' in which they 'lock scale' with a number of proscribed multiversal levels. 'Actually,' as PROFESSOR POP, Captain Billy-Bob's deputy, explains, 'we are dissipating and concentrating mass in ratio to size and so on — we can go "up" scale or "down" scale. And if we "up" scale for two hundred and five calibrations or "folds", we reach, if we're lucky, the wonder of the Second Ether.'

Opposed to the CHAOS ENGINEERS is the dominant culture known as the SINGULARITY which is bent on 'taming' the Second Ether and conquering Ko-O-Ko, the Lost Universe. The Singularity has discovered a method of Hard Warping which allows its ships to 'drop' through the multifaceted planes of the multiverse and emerge, if *they* are lucky, in the Second Ether. It is believed by some that the power of the Singularity to put its stamp on Chaos is so considerable that the Second Ether in some odd way scales herself to its laws. Rather than adapting, as do other travellers, to the sometimes whimsical conditions of Chaos, the Singularity imposes its own reality. The only power great enough to challenge the natural order of Creation, the Singularity is, in the eyes of most intelligences, the personification of pure Evil, an instrument of the ORIGINAL INSECT, while OLD REG, first Voice of the Singularity, is Satan incarnate. As both groups of humes continue to search for Ko-O-Ko, the Lost Universe, this great clash of philosophies is fought largely within the relative stillness of the Second Ether, that quasi-infinity of pearly rainbows millennia of light years long and curtains of violent, jewellish colour rising like sudden walls ahead or behind.

The slogan of the wild-eyed Chaos Engineers, who cruise the Second Ether for adventure, curiosity and massive profit, is 'Ride With The Tide', while the Voice of their opponents bellows forever that 'The Singularity Must Hold: One Refuses To Fold'. So clever are these mad creatures, arrogant enough to defy the fundamental logic of the multiverse, that they have built themselves a kind of false universe in which to dwell. Enclosed within a vast, stabilised crystal of carbon woven to infinite strength and able to resist the combined power of the multiverse, the Singularity is not merely defiant, It is determined to triumph. To It, Chaos is anathema, threatening the ultimate, destruction of all humes. Each individual unit of the Singularity sees it as its duty to aid in the conquest of Chaos. Yet, equally, the multiverse — chaotic and swift to adapt to any threat — shifts, multiplies and modifies so rapidly that the status quo can never entirely be broken, though sometimes the balance might tilt first to the Singularity, next to Chaos, so radically that it might seem that one had conquered at last, yet it is never so. The two philosophies will war for eternity or else be reconciled. Reconciliation is ever the hope of the Chaos Engineers but the idea is utterly loathsome to all units of the Singularity.

While the bleak metaphysics of the Singularity, never better represented than in the person of her bravest Ether-traveller CAPTAIN HORACE QUELCH and his ship *The Linear Bee*, permits only Victory, Chaos, rich with choice and tolerance, accepts and respects all philosophies, perceiving co-dependent variety to represent the 'true' nature of the multiverse. The Chaos Engineers — that great family of freebooters, normally only connected through their communications systems — have noted a step-up in the Singularity's impositions — while areas of the Second Ether are being colonised. The search for Ko-O-Ko, the Lost Universe, has become more intense. During their mutual adventuring in the infamous Field of Saffron, Captain Billy-Bob learns, via Captain Quelch, that the Singularity has begun to fall away from our gravity — ripping horribly through the layers of the multiverse, pulled either by some other force or by its own unnatural weight, they cannot tell. The fact is, as Captain Quelch admits, it has become crucial for the Singularity to colonise and dominate the Second Ether. During an enforced sojourn upon Earth, core world of the Singularity, young MANDY BEGG learns that Captain Quelch and his supporters are fighting a new tendency amongst their own kind — for the Lure of Isolation is very strong amongst their doubters, while the ethic of the pure Singularity is Victory or Noble Death! Captain Quelch still represents the dominant faction which demands the total conquest of the Second Ether. Against these powerful centralists, Captain Billy-Bob Begg and her crew of crazed solipsippers, high on super-distilled carbons and a craving for curious experience, swear loyalty to the Great Mood, whom they worship, and pledge themselves to the freeing of the Second Ether from 'these unnatural and perhaps cancerous intrusions'.

Escaping at last from the quasi-universe the Singularity calls *The Statement of Truth*, Captain Begg and her 'buckobusters' are unable to stop the process as their ship, *Now The Clouds Have Meaning*, goes into rogue fold — scaling up towards infinity and a kind of death — though to these brave souls that is no more than a welcome reunion with the Great Mood itself.

Meanwhile the *I Don't Want To Go To Chelsea* and the *Plum Blossom Local*, captained by RAIDER MILES of the Gulf Star and MY CHIN TOLLY respectively, have emerged safely into home scale above the main Martian scaling station which has held entry until twilight, when Mars is a little more hospitable to Chaos Engineers not used to the stomach-turning bleakness of raw singularity, only to find, contrary to all agreements, that *The Statement of Truth* quasi-universe has engulfed the First Ether and has ordered their capture. In attempting to back-fold without co-ordinates, the *Plum Blossom Local* irredeemably dissipates while the *I Don't Want To Go To Chelsea* escapes with the evil news that the Chaos Engineers have lost a Chief Attractor. The struggle has ceased to be wholly metaphysical!

Meanwhile, within the groaning, sweating innards of a Singularity ship, *Definitely Sagittarius*, LITTLE RUPOLDO BEGG has crucial news of Old Reg's next plan. Creeping through corridors whose every massive seam appears perpetually at bursting point, listening to the deep distress of the bulging bulkheads, Little Rupoldo searches for a communications room while the ship's captain, MRS KRONA, concentrates on her relationship with DUNGO, her partner. 'I am weary,' she says, 'of your dismissive mockery.' The ship falls relentlessly towards the Second Ether. At last Little Rupoldo comes upon a communications room, only to discover Mrs Krona dead on the floor, the rejected posy of ratweed and lady's fist telling the whole story. On the screen another tragedy manifests itself.

Now read on ...

CHAPTER NINETY-SEVEN

Scale Sickness Again!

AS UNIVERSES, SCALE upon scale, formed and re-formed, dissolved and re-dissolved behind them at a rate suggesting they must ride this fractal up to infinity before they could ever hope to be re-united entirely with the Great Mood, the famous Chaos Engineers gathered around their revered Main Type.

'Fargone,' said Captain Billy-Bob, a tear or two in her distant eye, 'it's a flat tyre, I think, sweethearts.'

But they were swift to deny it. 'You were always a lucky captain until now, dear Main Type,' said Pegarm Pete with an awkward slap to her shoulder (all obsidian carapace, these days), 'and you're still lucky, we'd opine!' He had long since ceased to question the intensity of his love for his captain.

'Fast agreement!' The other Engineers rushed to confirm.

'This is how we learn *if* the music goes round and round *or*, if not, where it comes out!' Corporal Organ raised her granitesque head in a massive gesture of joy, her wide, wide eyes steady on the front screens and the great shimmering black and yellow globe appearing just at the moment it disappeared, at the next scale, behind them.

But 'Oh,' despaired Captain Billy-Bob, 'this looks unending. My instruments! Have you spoken to them recently?' There was no cheering her. She insisted she had failed them.

CHAPTER NINETY-EIGHT

Codependency Theories Aft

CAPTAIN QUELCH had yet to experience the exhilaration he had expected to accompany his old enemy's defeat. Yet defeated she surely was. And with the greatest of the Chaos Captains blown to infinity, there would be no stopping the Singularity's holy expansion into the Second Ether. If, like Lucifer, he was prepared to defy the Definitive Logic of the Universe, he expected the securities of Lucifer – a knowledge that the Singularity was IN CONTROL forever. Now the others must think twice before pursuing their perverse adventures and celebrations.

'He died of a busted bladder, marm. I told him not to take that last bottle of port. He wasn't exactly a gent, if you know what I mean. *Ubi beni, ibi patria*, ha, ha!' Captain Quelch swung in his brochette, his eyes full of mild and faraway madness. 'As they say.'

MaMa Singh ignored him. Her anxieties involved, as always, the efficiency of their weapons. 'My crown is a crown of feathers formed from the rarest of lights, the scarcest of spectra. I am trapped in the power of a devastatingly unimaginative political and academic Orthodoxy. And *because* the Orthodoxy is so powerful, no one in it will listen to the truth. They deny the very Orthodoxy they worship. There is no addressing them! I need new weapons, but will they listen?'

Each Unit is lost in their own-ness, always a noted paradox of the Singularity, which It, of course, furiously denies. Paradox is an obscenity which cannot be permitted to any part of Its philosophy.

She sights aggressively at the sweating metal of their walls, the in-bulging plates, the re-folded rivets threatening to burst into the control room, the greenish steams and vivid gases. And everything moaning and squealing in protest at this unnatural means of progress through the multiverse, drowning the boombooms of Afrikaner Tom's dreadful discosound as the pale disciplinarian boogies in the comforting shadows of the big oven. He at any rate is relishing some sort of victory.

'Captain Quelch!' comes the voice of Roman Romanescu from the bowels. 'Has anyone seen my antique manual? There's something boiling on the E-line and I don't think we have the shot to suit it.'

CAPTAIN
Billy-Bob
BEGG'S
FAMOUS
CHAOS
ENGINEERS
IN

y WARWICK
COLVIN Jnr.

'Exactly my point!' squeaks MaMa Singh, astonished by this confirmation and glad as a bell. 'I have an ally, I know, in you, dear Roman Romanescu. We need new weapons!'

She shudders her bronze and copper quills, her pleasure out of all proportion and it is as well Roman Romanescu has no vision on this, only the delicious sounds; so he wets his lips. 'More and better weapons, good MaMa. Smarter, warmer, kinder weapons, marmy boombooms, suck, suck.'

She is cackling with delight, taking some control of herself as she hurries to the downshaft.

'What sublime decision! What maley ways!'

CHAPTER NINETY-NINE

Phoneouts At Last!

'THEY HAVE LOST their main fractal and are off-scale. They claim this is under control but Old Reg knows it means the destruction of their whole quasi-universe and the First Ether with it. Perhaps,' added Little Rupoldo into the dolly's mouth, 'the Second Ether, also. I heard this from the First Voice Itself, Old Reg.'

He was at last communicating with Wire Ears of the *Pulsing Blood*, in a crisis of her own involving Kaprikorn Schultz, the half-hume, Banker to the Homeboy Tong, who had attached himself freehand to their outer folds and made it impossible to drive anywhere but down-scale. Even at the dolly Little Rupoldo could hear some of the mathematical obscenities yelled by the half-hume through the ship's marrow, not to mention the other stuff. Little Rupoldo felt bile rise in his throat.

'I are half-skimling, half-hume — comb my spikes. Lick my tips. Taste my flumes ... Eff farping parentheses zed equals zed farping squared and squeezed like a wopper?'

Everyone had heard how Kaprikorn Schultz, the half-hume, had singlehandedly climbed half a thousand scale fields and countless textures to spread his brilliant blue wings against the hazy serenity of the Second Ether. He disdained all protection and lived entirely upon his own twisted wits, using skimling techniques to hitch rides through the scale fields. Or so he claimed. For no hume had ever set eyes on a skimling.

'SOS the Chaos Engineers! SOS the Chaos Engineers!' The cry went out across the Ether as Wire Ears sought help for herself and Little Rupoldo.

'We're heading out to where the ether's silvery white,

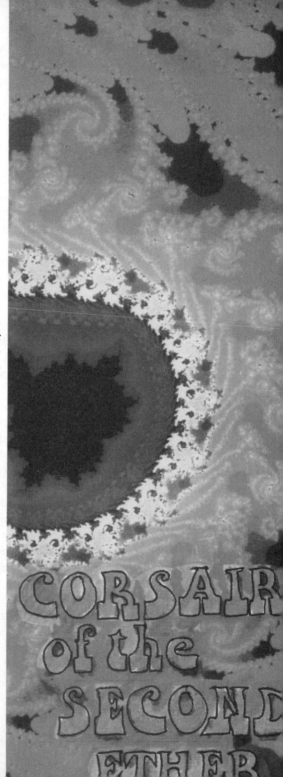

CORSAIR
of the
SECOND
ETHER

lit by the light of countless galaxies, the farping very hub of the multiverse and the best and most dangerous, believe me juicy pals, gateway directly into the Second Ether. I know! I am Kaprikorn Schultz, Banker to the Homeboy Tong! There is no more respectable voice in the multiverse! Didn't you ever wonder what mainlining was really all about, pretty bodies, pretty bodies? Oh, we'll tittle together in that fold-away-from-fold! I am it and I am more than it!'

'SOS THE CHAOS ENGINEERS!'

'What's to do, Cap'n?' demands the ever-cheerful Sto-Loon. 'More grub for the hands, is it, or must we be lean for what's a-comin'?' He smells a storm as fast as any other old Second Ether hand and he squares up reluctantly, for he believes he's too old to weather another like the last one. 'Hell's glaciers, there's a slim chance yet for the Balance to correct herself, but I can't seem to get back on to the crew. Are they frozen already?'

Captain Otherly says this was nowt to a Yorkshireman when he was a boy, in the days when Buggery Otherly ran things like a kakatron. But is he rattled? Maybe, thinks the youngest hand, Monkeygirl, who hopes she will soon settle down. It is her duty to keep the gardens at peace. She had done so for gone fifteen years and the *Pulsing Blood* had always responded well to her harmonies, but with the onset of Kaprikorn Schultz, the gardens were showing signs of restlessness and it would take little to send these vibrations throughout every fold of the great, old-fashioned Bloomer as she made her stately way up the scales.

Captain Otherly readily admits he let his ship fall towards a mirage attractor, the most feared phenomenon in the multiverse, and that only this put them in the power of the legendary Banker (whose greatest strength lay in his pseudo-reality weaving). Yet he was damned if he wasn't going to try to get out of the trap in spite of the filth pouring everywhere into the ship from Schultz's barkbox.

'Try them with some more Mozart and if that doesn't work give 'em the last of your Messiaen,' he tells Monkeygirl. 'It's all we can do now.' And he throws himself deep into his brass legs, a brave smile on his big face as the massive prosthenics hiss into union with his flesh.

'Captain Otherly's ready to give that half-hume bastard a run for his money!'

(To be continued)

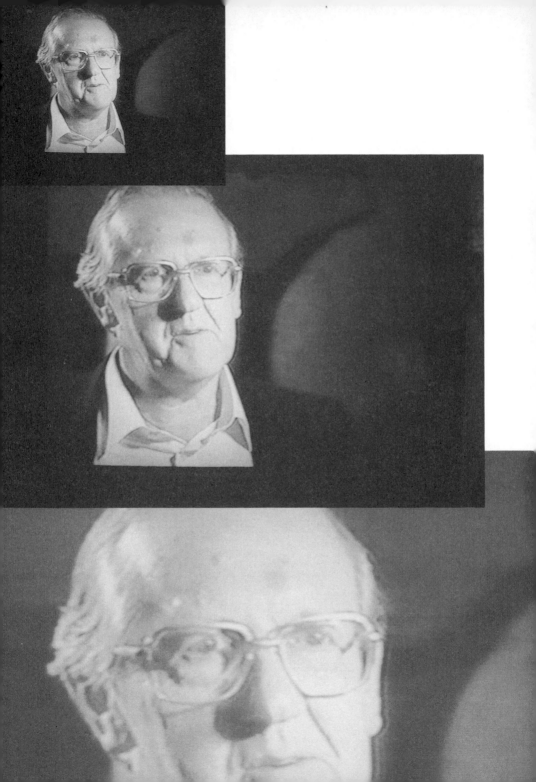

RATBIRD

Brian W. Aldiss

Illustrated by Brian W. Aldiss

. . . To warn and warn: that one night, never more
To light and warm us, down will sink the lurid sun
Beneath the sea, and none
Shall see us more upon this passionate shore.

The disintegration of the old world? Easy. I'll
manage it. Everything will end not with a bang but a whisper
– a whisper of last words. Words. So it began. So it will end.
When I grow up.

Here I lie on this crimson equatorial shore, far from where
the great electronic city dissolves itself under its own photo-
chemical smogs.

Here I lie, about to tell you the legend of the Other Side.
Also about to go on a journey of self-discovery which must
bring me back to my beginnings. As sure as I have tusks, this
is ontology on the hoof.

So to begin with what's overhead. The sun disputes its
rights to rule in the sky above. Every day it loses the
struggle, every morning it begins the dispute over again.
Brave, never-disheartened sun!

I lie under the great sea almond tree which sprouts from
the sand, looking up into its branches where light and shade
dispute their rival territories. This is called beauty. Light and
shade cohabit like life and death, the one more vivid for the
dread presence of the other.

In my hand I clutch –

. . . But the great grave ocean comes climbing up the
beach. There's another eternal dispute. The ocean changes
its colours as it sweeps towards where I lie. Horizon purple,
mid-sea blue, shore-sea green, lastly golden. Undeterred by
however many failures, the waves again attempt to wet my
feet. Brave, remorseless sea!

(What should a legend contain? Should it be of happiness

or of sorrow? Or should it permit them to be in – that word again – dispute?)

– What I clutch in my hand is a fruit of the sea almond. It's not large, it's of a suitable nut shape, it's covered with a fine but coarse fibre, like pubic hair. In fact, the nut resembles a girl's pudendum. Else why clutch it? Is that not where all stories lie, in the dumb dell of the pudendum? The generative power of the story lies with the organ of generation – and veneration.

Let me assure you, for it's all part of the legend, at the miracle of my birth I came forth when summoned by my father. He tapped. I emerged. A star burned on my forehead. I'm unique. You believe you are unique? But no, I am unique. In their careless journeys across the worlds, the gods create myriads of everything, of almond trees, of waves, of days, of people. But there's only one Dishayloo, with no navel and a star on his forehead.

So my journey and tale are about to commence. Knowing as much, my friends, who sit or stand with me under the tree, stare out to sea in silence. They think about destiny, oysters, or sex. I have on my T-shirt which says 'Perestroika Hots Fax'.

A distant land. That's what's needed. I've met old men who never went to sea. They speak like spiders and don't know it. They have lost something and don't know what they have lost. Like all young men I must make a journey. The dispute between light and shade must be carried elsewhere, waves must be surmounted, pudenda must open with smiles of welcome, fate must be challenged. Before the world disappears.

We all must change our lives.

So I rise and go along the blazing beach to the jetty, to see Old Man Monsoon. They call him Monsoon. His real name has been forgotten in these parts, funny old garbled Christian that he is. He can predict the exact hour the rains will come. And many more things.

Once Monsoon was called Krishna. Once he visited the Other Side, as I will relate.

He saw me coming and stood up in his boat. He's a good story-teller. He says, 'What is the human race,' (looking obliquely at my tusks as he speaks) 'but a fantastic tale?' Told, he might add, with a welter of cliché and a weight of subordinate clauses, while we await a punchline.

The friends accompany me to the jetty. At first in a bunch, then stringing out, some hastening, some loitering, though the distance is short. So with life.

Monsoon and I shake hands. He wears nothing but a pair of shorts. He is burnt almost black. His withered skin mummifies him, though those old Golconda eyes are golden-black still. People say of Monsoon that he has a fortune buried in a burnt out refrigerator on one of the many little islands standing knee-deep in the sea. I don't believe that. Well, I do, but only in the way you can believe and not believe simultaneously. Like Rolex watches from a different time zone.

He shows yellow teeth between grey lips and says in a voice from which all colour has faded, 'Isn't there enough trouble in the world without youngsters like you joining in?'

Grey lips, yellow teeth, yet a colourless voice . . . Well, let us not linger over these human paradoxes.

I make up something by way of reply. 'I've lost my shadow, Monsoon, and must find it if I have to go to the end of the Earth. Perhaps you can foretell when the end of the Earth will be?'

He points to the puddle of dark at my feet, giggling, raising an eyebrow to my friends for support.

'That's not *my* shadow,' I tell him. 'I borrowed this one off a pal who wants it back by nightfall. He has to wear it at his mother's wedding.'

When I have climbed into the boat, Monsoon starts the engine with one tug of the starter rope. It's like hauling at a dog's lead. The hound wakes, growls, shakes itself, and with a show of haste begins to pull us towards the four corners of the great morning.

The craft creaks and murmurs to itself, in dispute with the waters beneath its hull. And the sweet sound of the waves plays against old board. The ocean, some idiot said, is God's smile.

Monsoon picks up my thought and distorts it. 'You smile like a little god, Dishayloo, with that star on your brow. Why always so happy?'

I gaze back at my friends ashore. They shrink as they wave. Everything grows smaller. Hasten, hasten, Dishayloo, before the globe itself shrinks to nothing!

'The smile's so as not to infect others with sorrow. It's therapy – a big hospitable hospital. Antidote to the misery virus. Did you ever hear tell of the great white philosopher Bertram Russell?'

The Golconda eyes are on the horizon to which our boat is hounding us, but Monsoon's never at a loss for an answer. 'Yes, yes, of course. He was a friend of mine. He and I used to sail together to the Spice Islands to trade in vitamin pills and conch shells. I made a loss but Bertra Muscle became a rupee millionaire. These days, he lives in Singapore in a palace of unimaginable concrete and grandeur.'

Now the friends form no more than a frieze, spread thin along the shore, like bread on a lake of butter. Soon, soon, the dazzle has erased them. My memory does the same. Sorry, one and all, but the legend has begun.

Talk's still needed, of course, so I say, 'This was a different man, Pappy. The guy I mean said . . .'

But those words too were forgotten.

'. . . Why should I recall what he said? Are we no better than snails, to carry round with us a whole house of past circumstance?'

My hands were trailing in the water. Prose was not my main concern. Monsoon picked up on that.

'Pah. "House of past circumstance . . ." What are you, a poet or something? Something or nothing? The Lord Jesus had a better idea. He knew nothing dies. Even when he snuffed it on Mount Cavalry, he knew he would live again.'

'Easy trick if you're the son of God.'

The Golconda gold eyes flared at me. 'He was a bloke in a million. Go anywhere, do anything.'

'"Have mission, will travel."' All the time the dear water like progress under the prow.

'Born in India, I believe, sailed in Noah's boat because there was no room at the Indus.' His face had taken on the expression of imbecile beatitude the religious sometimes adopt. 'Jesus was poor, like me. He couldn't pay Noah one cent for the trip. Noah was a hard man. He gave him a broom and told him to go and sweep the animal turds off the deck.'

'What happened?'

'Jesus swept.'

Cloud castles stood separately on the horizon, bulbous, like idols awaiting worship.

Something about moving over a smooth sea prompted Monsoon to chatter. I scarcely listened as he continued his thumbnail portrait of Jesus.

'He wasn't exactly a winner but he was honest and decent in every way. Or so the scriptures tell us. And a good hand with a parable.'

The little boat was in the lap of the ocean. The shoreline behind was indistinct; it could have meant anything – like a parable. Ahead, two small humps of islands lay stunned with light. I began to feel the charge of distance, its persuasive power.

Perhaps the islands were like humpbacked whales. But the world's old. Everything has already been compared with everything else.

The old man said, 'You'll soon have left us. We'll be no more in your mind, and will die a little because of it. So I'll tell you a story – a parable, perhaps – suitable for your life journey.'

And he began the tale of the ratbird.

Monsoon spoke in more than one voice. I abridge the tale here, there being only so many hours in a day. Also I've removed his further references to Jesus, diluting it. Same tale, different teller, only coconut milk added.

There was this white man – well, two white men if you include Herbert – whom Monsoon knew as a boy, before he was Monsoon. This white man – well, he and Herbert – arrived at this port in Borneo where Boy Monsoon lived in a thatched hut with Balbindor.

Like many whites, Frederic Sigmoid was crazed by the mere notion of jungle. He believed jungles were somewhere you went for revelation. In his vain way, he placed the same faith in jungles that earlier whites had put in cathedrals or steam ships. But Frederic Sigmoid – Doctor Sigmoid – was rich. He could afford to be crazy.

Back in Europe, Sigmoid had cured people by his own process, following the teaching of a mystic called Ouspensky and adding a series of physical pressures called reflexology. Now here he was in Simanggang with his mosquito nets, journals, chronometers, compasses, barometer, medicine cabinet, guns, and one offspring, out to cure himself or discover a New Way of Thought, whichever would cause most trouble in a world already tormented by too much belief. Seek and ye shall find. Find and ye shall probably regret.

With Sigmoid was his pale son, Herbert. Monsoon and his adoptive father, Balbindor, were hired to escort the two Sigmoids into the interior of Borneo. Into the largely unexplored Hose Range, and an area called the Bukit Tengah, where lived a number of rare and uncollected species, including the ratbird – happy until this juncture in their uncollected state. Animal and insect: all congratulated themselves on failing to make some Cambridge encyclopaedia.

Balbindor was a coastal Malay of the Iban tribe. However, he had been into the interior once before, in the service of two Dutch explorers who, in the manner of all Dutch explorers, had died strange deaths: though not before they had communicated to civilisation a mysterious message: 'Wallace and Darwin did not know it, but there are alternatives.' Balbindor, four-foot-six high, brought the word hot-foot back to the coast.

Sigmoid was keener on alternatives than his son Herbert. Confidence men always have an eye for extra exits. Thirteen days into the rainforest, led by Balbindor and sonlet, and the doctor remained more determined than his offspring. The night before they reached the tributary of the Baleh river they sought, Balbindor overheard a significant exchange between father and son.

Herbert complained of heat and hardship, declaring that what he longed for most in the world was a marble bathroom with warm scented water and soft towels. To which his father rejoined that Herbert was a gross materialist. Going further, Sigmoid retreated into one of his annoying fits of purity, declaring, 'To achieve godliness, my boy, you must give up all possessions . . .'

Herbert replied bitterly, 'I'm your one possession you'll never give up.'

Had this been a scene in a movie, it would have been followed by pistol shots and, no doubt, the entry of a deadly snake into the Sigmoid tent. However, the story is now Balbindor's. He shall tell it in his own excruciating words. And Balbindor, never having seen any movie, with the solitary exception of *The Sound of Music* (to which he gave three stars), lacked a sense of drama. Father and son, he reported, kissed each other as usual and went to sleep in their separate bivouacs.

If my story, then I tell. Not some other guy. Many error in all story belong other guy. I Iban man, real name no Balbindor. I no see *Sound Music* ever. Only see trailer one time, maybe two. Julie Andrews good lady, I marry. My kid I take on no call Monsoon. Monsoon late name. Kid, he come from India. I take on. I no call Monsoon, I call Krishna. My son they die logging camp, all same place, three time. Too much drink. I very sad, adopt Krishna. He my son, good boy. Special golden eye. I like, OK.

This Doctor Sigmoid and he son Herbert very trouble on journey. We go on Baleh river, boat swim good. All time, Herbert he complain. White men no sweat pure, too many clothe. No take off clothe. Then boat swim up tributary Puteh, no swim good. Water he go way under boat. Mud he come, stop boat.

We hide boat, go on feet in jungle. Very much complain

Herbert and father he both. They no understand jungle. They no eat insect. Insect eat them.

Jungle many tree, many many tree. Some tree good, some tree bad, some tree never mind. I tell number tree. Tamarind tree, he fruit bitter, quench throat thirst. Help every day. Sigmoid no like, fear poison. I no speak him. All same jungle olive, good tree. We drink pitcher plant, all same like monkey.

Monkey they good guide. Krishna and me we do like monkey. Understand jungle. Wake early, when first light in jungle. Deer trail fresh, maybe catch deer along blowpipe. Monkey wake early, eat, sing, along branches. Sigmoids no like wake early. Day cool. I like wake early, make Sigmoids rise up. Go quiet. Creep along, maybe catch kill snake for pot.

Many ant in Hose Range, big, little, many colour. All go different way. I speak ant, ant speak me. Go this way, go that. Every leaf he fall, he mean a something. I understand. I plenty savvy in jungle.

One week, two week, three week, we walk in jungle, sometime up, sometime down. For Sigmoids, very hard to go. Both smell bad. Too much breath. No control. Dutch men control of breath good. Herbert he very scare. No like jungle, all same long time. No good man, swear me. I understand. Herbert he no think I understand.

Three week, get very near area Bukit Tengah. Now all path go up, need more care. Many cliff, many rock. One fall, maybe finish. Waterfall, he pour bad water. I know smell bad water nose belong me. Krishna and two bearer and I, we no drink bad water. Come from Other Side. I tell Sigmoids no drink water come Other Side. They no care, no understand, they drink bad waterfall water plenty. Take on bad spirit. I understand. I shout much, Krishna he cry all same long time. Herbert he shout me, try hit little Krishna.

I tell Herbert, 'You drink water belong Other Side. Now you got bad spirit. You no get back Europe. You finish man.'

Herbert no savvy. He plenty sick. I see him bad spirit. It suck him soul. Now I plenty scare.

Every day more slow. Other Side he come near. Bearer man they two, they no like go more far. I hear what they speak together. I savvy what Orang Asli speak, I tell Dr Sigmoid. He swear. No please me. Both Sigmoids have fever. Black in face, very strange. Smell bad more.

Big storm come over from Other Side, maybe hope drive us away. Thunder he flatten ears, lightning he blind eyes, rain he lash flesh, wind he freeze skin. We hide away under raintree, very fear. Night it come, big wizard, I no understand. Too black. In night bearer they go, I no hear. Two bearer they run off. Steal supply. I very sad I no hear. In morning dawnlight I say to doctor sorry. Bearer they scare, go back wife. Doctor he swear again. I say, no good swear. Who hear swear with good nature? Best leave alone, keep silent. He no like. Make bad face.

Day after storm, we come Other Side. I see how monkey they no go Other Side. Different monkey on Other Side, speak different language. Different tree, grow other different leaf. Fruit they different, no wise eat. Insect different.

Also one more bad thing. I see men belong Other Side in jungle. They move like ghost but I see. Krishna he see, he point. Plenty eye in jungle belong Other Side. No like. Other Side men they much difference. How they think different, no good.

I see, I understand, Krishna he understand. I no make Sigmoids understand.

'Geology,' I explain Sigmoids. I speak they language good. 'He change. Different earth begin now since many many old time. All thing different, different time. Different inside time. Womb bring forth different thing. Bad go there, no go. Only look one day.'

'Balls,' he say.

I sick with him doctor. I make speak, 'I keep my ball belong me. You go, and Herbert. I no go one more pace. Krishna, he no go one more pace.'

Herbert he bring out gun. I very fear. I know him mad with bad spirit. I say him, 'Two piece Dutch man they come here. Pretty soon they finish. Why you no sense? Come back home along me, Krishna.'

He get more mad.

I was really disgusted with this idiot native Balbindor or whatever his name was. Here we were. At great expense to ourselves, father and I had finally arrived on the very threshold of Bukit Tengah, the Middle Mountain, and this difficult little man and his black kid were refusing to proceed.

It just was not rational. But you don't expect rationality from such people. These natives are riddled with superstition.

Also, I blamed him for the way the bearers had deserted us. We had quite an argument. I was trembling violently from head to foot. Most unpleasant.

I want to say this, too, about the whole incident. Balbindor treated father and me all along as complete fools. We could grasp that he was trying to tell us we had arrived at some sort of geological shift, much like the Wallace Discontinuity east of Bali, where two tectonic plates meet and flora and fauna are different on the two opposed sides. We knew that better than he did, having researched the matter in books before the expedition, but saw no reason to be superstitious about it.

We had also observed that there were those on the other side of the divide who were watching us. Father and I were going to go in there whether or not Balbindor and his son accompanied us. We saw the necessity to make an immediate impression on the new tribe, since we would be dealing with them soon enough.

That was why I shot Balbindor on the spot. It was mainly to introduce ourselves.

Little Krishna ran off into the jungle. Perhaps the little

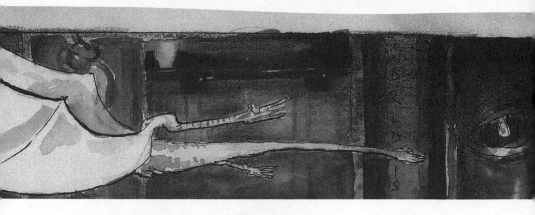

idiot thought I was going to shoot him as well. I suppose I
might have done. I was pretty steamed up.

'Put your revolver away, you fool,' Father said. That was all
the thanks I got from him. When has he ever been grateful?

We had no idea what to do with Balbindor's corpse.
Eventually we dragged it to the waterfall and flung it in. We
slept by the waterfall that night and next morning, at our
leisure, crossed the divide into the Other Side (the silly
name had stuck).

For two days we travelled through dense alien jungle. We
were aware that there were men among the thickets following us, but it was the monkeys who caused us most trouble.
They were no bigger than leaf monkeys, but had black caps
and a line of black fur about the eyes, giving them an oddly
human look. Father trapped one with the old Malayan gourd
trick, and discovered it to have only four toes on each foot
and four fingers on each hand. We came at last to a clearing
brought about by a massive outcrop of rock. Here we rested,
both of us being overcome by fevers. We could see the
barbaric scenery about us, the tumbled mass of vegetation,
with every tree weighted down by chains of epiphytes and
climbers. Above them loomed densely clad peaks of mountains, often as not shrouded by swift moving cloud.

These clouds took on startling devilish shapes, progressing
towards us. It may have been the fever which caused this
uncomfortable illusion.

Days must have passed in illness. I cannot say how strange
it was, how peculiarly dead I felt, when I awoke to find
myself at a distance from my father. Dreadful sensations of

isolation overcame me. Moreover, I was walking about. My feet seemed not to touch the ground.

I discovered that I could not get near my father. Whenever I seemed to advance towards him, my steps deviated in some way. It was as if I suffered from an optical illusion so strong that it consumed my other senses. I could do no more than prowl about him.

Father was sitting cross-legged by the remains of a fire on

which he had roasted the leg of a small deer. Its remains lay by him. He was talking to a small wizened man with long hair and a curved bone through his cheeks which made him appear tusked. The face of this man was painted white. For some reason, I felt terrified of him, yet what chiefly seemed to scare me was a minor eccentricity of garb: the man wore nothing but an elaborate scarf or band or belt of fabric about his middle. No attempt had been made to cover his genitals, which were painted white like his face.

Prowling in a circular fashion seemed all I was capable of, so I continuously circled the spot. Although I called to my father, he took no notice, appearing totally absorbed in his conversation with the white-faced man. I now noted that the latter had on each hand only three fingers and a thumb, and only four toes on each foot, in the manner of the monkeys we had come across in another existence.

I was filled with such great uneasiness and hatred that I chattered and jibbered and made myself horrible.

Again and again I attempted to advance towards my father. Only now did I realise that I loved this man to whose power I had been subject all my life. Yet he would not – or perhaps could not – take the slightest notice of me. I set up a great screaming to attract his attention. Still he would not hear.

Father, Father, I called to you all my life! Perhaps you never ever heard, so wrapped up were you in your own

dreams and ambitions. Now for this last time, I beg you to attend to your poor Herbert.

I know you have your own story. Allow me mine, for pity's sake!

It would be true to say without exaggeration that throughout my mature life, in my quest to transform humanity, I had been in search of Mr White Face, as I thought of him. (He refused to tell his name. That would have given me power over him.) I have a firm belief in transcendental power, unlike poor Herbert.

White Face materialised out of thin air when I was drinking at a pool. There on my hands and knees, by gosh! I looked up – he was standing nearby, large as life. Naked except for the band round his belly; yet something about him marked him immediately as a singular character. (A flair for judging character is one of my more useful talents.)

A remarkable feature of White Face's physiognomy was a

pair of small tusks (six inches long) piercing the cheeks and curving outwards. My knowledge of anatomy suggested they were rooted in the maxilla. They gave my new acquaintance a somewhat belligerent aspect, you may be sure!

Already he has told me much. We have spent two whole days from sun-up till sun-down in rapt conversation. His thought processes are entirely different from mine. Yet we have much in common. He is the wise man of his people as I, in Europe, am of mine. Grubby little man he may be – he shits in my presence without embarrassment – yet in his thought I perceive he is fastidious. I can probably adapt some of his ideas.

Much that he says about divisions in the human psyche is reflected in pale form in the Hindu sacred books of the Upanishads (which is hardly surprising, since White Face claims that all the world's knowledge of itself emanated from 'the Other Side' during the ice age before last, when Other Siders went out like missionaries over the globe, reaching as far as Hindustan).

What I do find difficult to swallow – we argued long about this – is some strange belief of his that the world is immaterial and that humanity (if I have it correctly) is no more than a kind of metaphysical construct projected by nature and rely-

ing on *words* rather than *flesh* for its continued existence.
Perhaps I've misunderstood the old boy. I'm still slightly
feverish. Or he's mad as a hatter.

Only knowledge is precious, he says. And knowledge is
perpetually being lost. The world from which I come is in
crisis. It is losing its instinctual knowledge. Instinctual
knowledge is leaking away under the impact of continual
urbanisation. That, I believe. It is not in conflict with my
own doctrines. He thinks our world will shortly die.

Then the Other Side will recolonise the world with new
plants and animals – and understanding. (His kind of understanding, of course.) He wants to convince me to become his
disciple, to go forth and encourage the world-death to come
swiftly. By the third day of our discussion, I begin more and
more to comprehend how desirable it is that the civilisation
to which I belong should be utterly destroyed. Yet still I
hesitate. We drink some of his potent *boka* and rest from
intellectual debate.

I ask, How are things so different here?

In answer, he shows me a ratbird.

Some distance from the rock on which we sat in conference
– conferring about the future of the world, if that doesn't
sound too pompous – an angsana stood, a large tropical tree,

its branches full of birds to which I paid no attention. Birds have never been one of my major interests, I need hardly say.

Mr White Face began a kind of twittering whistle, a finger planted in each corner of his lips. Almost immediately, the birds in the angsana responded by flying out in a flock, showing what I took to be anxiety by sinking to the ground and then rapidly rising again. Each time they sank down, they clustered closely, finally expelling one of their number, who fluttered to the ground and began – as if under compulsion – to walk, or rather scuttle, towards us; whereupon the other birds fled into the shelter of their tree.

As the bird came nearer, White Face changed his tune. The bird crawled between us and lay down at our feet in an unbird-like manner.

I saw that its anatomy was unbird-like. Its two pink legs ended in four toes, all pointing forward with only a suggestion of balancing heel. Wings and body were covered in grey fur. And the face was that of a rodent. In some ways it resembled a flying fox, common throughout Malaysia, in some ways it resembled a rat; but its easy flight and way of walking proclaimed it a bird.

And now that I looked again at Mr White Face, I saw that beneath his paint, his face had some of the configurations of a rat, with sharp little jaws and pointed nose, not at all like the inhabitants of Sarawak, a blunt-faced company, with which I was acquainted.

Obeying his instruction, I proffered my hand, open palms upwards, towards the animal. The ratbird climbed on and began to preen its fur unconcernedly.

Nobody will blame me if I say that in the circumstances I became very uneasy. It seemed to me that in Mr White Face

SCENT IS HAIR IS DRE

I had stumbled upon an evolutionary path parallelling –
rivalling – our accepted one; that this path sprang from a
small ground mammal (possibly tusked) very different from
the arboreal tarsier-like creature from which homo sapiens
has developed. I was face to face with . . . *homo rodens* . . .
Over millions of years, its physical and mental processes had
continued in its own course, parallel to but alien from ours.
Indeed, perhaps inimical to ours, in view of the long-stand-
ing hostility between man and rat.

Rising to my feet, I flicked the ratbird into the air. It
looped the loop. Instead of flying off, it settled at my feet.

I found I was unable to walk about. My legs would not
move. Some magic had trapped me. At this unhappy
moment, I recalled that mysterious sentence, 'Wallace and
Darwin did not know it, but there are alternatives.' The
alternative had been revealed to me; with magnificent hardi-
hood, I had ventured into the Other Side; was I to suffer the
fate of the two Dutch explorers?

Mr White Face continued to sit crossed-legged, gazing up
at me, his tusked countenance quite inscrutable. I saw the
world through glass. It was unmoving. I felt extremely
provoked. Perhaps the argumentative Balbindor had been
correct in saying I should not have drunk from the waterfall
springing from the Other Side. It had left me in White Face's
power.

And I was uncomfortably aware of the spirit of Herbert.
After the foolish lad had died of his fevers – unable to pull
through illness like me with my superior physique – his spirit
had been powerless to escape. It circled me now, yowling
and screaming in a noxious way. I tried to ignore it. But how
to escape my predicament?

I stared down at the white face of the ratman. Then, from

my days as a chemist, I remembered a formula for bleach. Perhaps the magic of science would overcome this detestable witchcraft (or whatever it was that held me in thrall).

As loudly as I could, I recited the formula by which bleach is produced when chlorine reacts with sodium hydroxide solution:

'$Cl^2(g) + 2NaOH(aq) \rightarrow NaCl(aq) + NaClO(aq) + H^2O(1)$.'

Even as I chanted, I felt power return to my muscles. The great tousled world about me began to stir with life again. I was free. Thanks to bleach and a Western education – and of course an excellent memory.

I kicked at the ratbird, which fluttered off.

'I don't care for your kind of hospitality,' I told White Face.

'Well, you have passed my test,' he said. 'You are no weakling and your words are strong. To each of us there are two compartments which form our inner workings. One part is blind, one part sees. Most of our ordinary lives are governed by the part that sees, which is capable of performing ordinary tasks. That part is like a living thing which emerges from an egg. But there is the other part, which is blind and never emerges from the egg. It knows only what is unknown. It acts in time of trouble. You understand?'

'You perhaps speak in parable form of two divisions of the brain. If so, then I believe I understand you.' (I did not think it politic to express my reservations.)

He gave a short dry laugh, exposing sharp teeth. 'Oh, we like to believe we understand! Suppose we have never understood one single thing of the world about us and inside us? Suppose we have lived in utter darkness and only believed that darkness was light?'

'All things may be supposed. So what then?'

He said, 'Then on the day that light dawns, it will be to you as if a sudden incomprehensible darkness descends.'

After this horrifying statement he made a beckoning gesture and began running.

Since he made swiftly towards the forest, I had not much option but to follow. But his words had chilled me. Suppose indeed that we were hedged in by limitations of comprehension we could not comprehend? The ratbird had already shaken many of my convictions regarding life on earth and how it had evolved.

Mr White Face's mode of progression through the forest was at odds with my previous guide, Balbindor, and his method of procedure; but then, the trees, the very trees we passed through, were different. Their bark, if bark it was, possessed a highly reflective surface, so that to move forward was to be accompanied by a multitudinous army of distortions of oneself. (In this hallucinatory company, it was impossible not to feel ill at ease. Jumpy, in a word.)

I did not understand how it was possible to find one's way in such a jungle. White Face was presumably trusting to his second compartment, 'the part that never hatched', to see him along his course.

In which case, the blind thing was unexpectedly reliable. After two days of arduous travel, we came to a dark-flowing river. On the far side of it stood a village of longhouses, much like the ones we had left back on the coast, except that these were entered by round doors instead of the normal rectangular ones.

Uncomfortable as I was in White Face's company, there was comfort in the sense of arrival. I was possessed of a lively curiosity to investigate this kampong of the Other Side – that lively curiosity which has carried me so successfully through life.

One factor still contributed to my unease. The ghost of my son pursued me yet, his translucent image being reflected from the trunk of every tree, so that it sometimes appeared ahead of me as well as on every side. Herbert waved and screamed in the dreariest manner imaginable (uncanny, yet nevertheless slightly reminiscent of his behaviour throughout his life).

'We shall cross the river,' White Face announced, putting two skinny fingers into the corners of his mouth and whistling to announce our presence.

'Will Herbert cross with us?' I asked, I trust without revealing my nervousness.

He dismissed the very idea. 'Ghosts cannot cross moving water. Only if they are ghosts of men with wooden legs.'

After White Face had signalled to some men on the opposite bank, a narrow dugout canoe was paddled across to collect us. By the time we landed at a rickety jetty, a number of inhabitants had gathered, standing cautiously back to observe us with their heads thrust forward as if they were short sighted.

All of them had tusks. Some tusks were large and curled, or adorned with leaves. I could not fail to see that all, men, women and children, wore nothing in the tropical heat but a band – in the case of the women this was quite ornate – around their middles, leaving everything else uncovered. The breasts of the women were small, and no more developed than those of the men. (The women also had tusks, so that I wondered if they were used for offence or defence. Presumably the missionary position in coitus would have its dangers. One might be stabbed *in medias res*.)

They were in general a strange lot, with sharp beaky faces quite unlike the Malays to whom I was accustomed. In their movements was something restless. A kind of rictus was common. I saw that here was opportunity for anthropological study which, when reported abroad, could but add to my fame. I wanted a look in a mouth to see where those tusks were anchored.

White Face addressed some of the men in a fast flowing and high-pitched language. They made respectful way for him as he led me through the village to a longhouse standing apart from the others.

'This is my home and you are welcome,' he said. 'Here you may rest and recover from your fever. The spirit of your son will not harm you.'

To my dismay, I found that the bleach formula had left my mind and would not be recalled. Did this mean I was still under his spell? So it was with reluctance that I climbed the ramp leading into the longhouse with its two great tusks over the circular entrance.

Inside, I was barely able to stand upright at the highest point, for I was head and shoulders taller than my sinister host; and it did not escape my notice that the roof at its highest point was infested with cobwebs, in the corners of which sat large square spiders. Also, when he gestured to me to sit down on the mats which covered the floor, I could not but observe two fairly fresh (tuskless) skulls above the door by which we had entered. Catching my glance, Mr White Face asked, 'Do you speak Dutch?'

'Do they – now?' I asked, with sarcasm.

But he had a response. 'On the night of the full moon they do speak. I cannot silence them. You shall hear them by and by, and become familiar with the eloquence of death.'

We then engaged in philosophical discourse, while a servant woman, cringing as she served us, brought a dark drink like tea in earthenware bowls which fitted neatly between Mr White Face's tusks.

After two hours of conversation, during which he questioned me closely concerning Ouspensky, he apologised that his wife (he used a different word) was not present. It appeared that she was about to deliver a son.

I congratulated him.

'I have twelve sons already,' he said. 'Though this one is special, as you may see. A miraculous son who will further our most powerful ambitions, a wizard of words. So it is written . . . Now let us discuss how the end, closure, and abridgement of your world may be brought about, since we are in agreement that such an objective is desirable.'

Although I was less ready than before to agree that such an objective was desirable, I nevertheless found myself entering into his plans. (The dark drink had its effect.) The plans were – to me at least – elaborate and confusing. But the horrifying gist of his argument was that homo sapiens might be extinguished by *pantun*. I understood that *pantun* was a form of Malayan poetry, and could not grasp how this might annihilate anything; but, as he continued, I began to see – or I thought in that dazed state I saw – that he believed all human perceptions to be governed by words, and, indeed, distorted and ultimately betrayed by words. 'Betrayed' was the word he used. This, he said, was the weakness of homo sapiens: words had weakened the contract with nature that guaranteed mankind's existence. (All our spiritual ills were evidence of this deteriorating state of affairs.)

There were ways by which all homo sapiens could be reduced – abridged – into a story, a kind of poem. Those who live by the word die by the word. So he said. We could end as a line of *pantun*.

I cannot reduce this plan of his into clear words. It was not delivered to me in clear words, but in some sort of squeaky Other Side music with which he aided my understanding. All I can say is that there in that creepy hut, I came to believe it was perfectly easy to turn the whole story of the world I knew into a world of story.

As we were getting into the how of it – and drinking more of that dark liquid – the servant hurried in with an apology and squeaked something. White Face rose.

'Come with me,' he said. 'My wife (he used the different word) is about to bring forth the thirteenth son.'

'Will she mind my presence?'

'Not at all. Indeed, your presence is essential. Without your presence, you can have no absence, isn't that so?' (Whatever that meant. If that is truly what he said.)

In we went, into curtained-off quarters at the far end of the longhouse. All misty with scented things burning and jangling instruments being played by two long-tusked men.

His wife lay on the floor on a mat, attended by the servant girl. Her stomach did not appear extended. She was entirely naked, no embroidered band round her middle. For the first time, I saw – with what sense of shock I cannot explain – *that she had no navel.* Nor was this some kind of unique aberration. The servant girl – perhaps in honour of the occasion – was also nude and without the customary middle band. She also had no navel. I was struck as by an obscenity, and unprepared for what followed. (Tusks I could take; lack of navel implied a different universe of being.)

'Now the birth begins,' said Mr White Face, as his wife lifted one leg, 'and you will find all will go according to plan. The story of your species will become a kind of Möbius strip, but at least you will have had a role in it, Dr Sigmoid.'

He had never used my name previously. I knew myself in his power; as never before I felt myself powerless, a thin be-navelled creature without understanding. I had believed

these strange people of the Other Side to be distant descendants of a kind of rodent ancestor. But that was a scientific
illusion built on evolutionary terminology. The truth was
different, more difficult, less palatable. As the woman lifted
her leg, an egg emerged from her womb.

An egg not of shell like a bird's: leathery, rather like a
turtle's. An egg! A veritable egg, ostrich sized.

A terrible rushing noise beset me. The longhouse flew
away. I was surrounded by bright sunlight, yet in total
darkness, as foretold. Even worse – far worse – I was not I.
The terror of wonderment, real understanding, had changed
all. Only the egg remained.

With a sense of destiny, I leaned forward and tapped upon
it with an invisible finger. It split.

At the miracle of my birth, I came forth when my father
summoned me. A star was set upon my forehead. I am
unique. The gods that make their careless journeys across the
world, playing with science or magic as they will, create
thousands of everything, of sea almonds, of waves, of days –
of words. Yet there is only one Dishayloo. No navel, and a
star in the middle of his forehead.

Born to shine in a world of story.

Candy Buds

Peter F. Hamilton

Laurus is ensconced in the Regency elegance of his study, comfortable in his favourite leather chair, looking out at the world through another set of eyes. The image is coming from his affinity bond with his eagle, Ryker. A silent union produced by the neurone symbiotes lodged in his medulla oblongata, attuned to their clone analogues in Ryker, and feeding him the bird's acute sensorium clear and bright.

He enjoys the sensations of freedom and power he gets from flying the big bird, they are becoming an anodyne to his own ageing body with its white hair and weakening muscles. Ryker possesses a nonchalant virility, a peerless lord of the sky.

With wings outstretched to its full three yard span, the duality is riding the thermals high above Peterborough. Midday heat has shrouded the coastal city in a pocket of doldrum-calm air, magnifying the teeming convoluted streets below. This is the eastern quarter, dating back to before the Warming, where the turbid water of the Fens sea laps along the mud dune ruins of Eastfield and Stanground. Laurus is looking down on the familiar pattern of whitewashed walls crusted with a tide-line of ebony solar panels and heart-shaped emerald precipitator leaves. Streets are lined with market barrows, channelling the flow of bicycles, pedestrians, horses, and the odd power cart.

The white newgene polyp walls of the mile-wide harbour basin glare with a near painful intensity under the scalding sun. From Ryker's viewpoint the harbour looks like a perfectly circular crater. Its western half has bitten a chunk out of the city, and a dense stratum of warehouses, market squares, and boatyards has sprung up along its boundary. The eastern half extends out into the Fens sea, keeping the encroaching mud at bay, a single gap opening into the deepwater channel that leads away to the Wash. Wooden quays sprout from the inner rim; fishing ketches, and trading sampans with colourful sails cruise round the central anchorage of large ocean-going merchantmen.

Laurus is using Ryker to hunt. His prey is a little girl walking down the harbour wall, slipping easily through the press of sailors and fishermen thronging the white polyp. She looks no more than ten or eleven to Laurus; wearing a simple mauve cotton dress, black sandals, a wide-brimmed straw sun hat perched on her head. There is a small leather bag with blue and scarlet tassels slung over her shoulder.

As far as Laurus can tell she is completely unaware of the enforcer squad he has tailing her. Using the squad as well as Ryker is perhaps excessive, but Laurus is determined the girl will not give him the slip.

Ryker's predatory instinct alerts him to the gull with snow-white plumage; it's twenty feet below the eagle, floating in the air, simply marking time. Laurus recognises it, a modified bird, with tiny monkey paws grafted on to replace its feet, affinity-bonded to Silene. Laurus hurriedly searches the harbour wall around the girl for the old mock-beggar.

Silene is easy to spot, sitting cross-legged on his reed mat, silver band across his empty eye sockets. He is playing a small flute, a bowl beside him with some thrupenny bits and even a few silver sixpences he's been thrown by foreign sailors.

The girl walks past him, and his black cat turns its head, watching her, its affinity bond showing him the ripe target of the bag.

Laurus feels a touch of cool melancholia; Silene has been working the harbour for over twenty years. Laurus himself gave him the franchise. But nothing can be allowed to interrupt the girl, to frighten her, and maybe heighten her senses. Nothing.

Back in his study, Laurus opens a scrambled datalink to Erigeron, the enforcer squad's lieutenant. 'Take out Silene,' he says.

The gull has already started its descent, angling down to snatch the bag. Silene has the routine down to a fine art, hundreds of sailors have lost trinkets and wallets to the fast greedy bird over the years.

Laurus lets Ryker's natural instincts take over. Wingtips flick casually, rolling the big bird with idle grace. Then the wings fold, and the exhilarating plummet begins.

Ryker slams into the gull, his steel talons closing, snapping the gull's neck cleanly.

Silene's head jerks up in reflex.

Two of the enforcers are already in position beside him. Erigeron places his hand on Silene's bald crown as if in benediction. Slender scorpion-consanguineous stingers slide out from under Erigeron's nails, penetrating the skin at the nape of Silene's neck. Every muscle in the old man's body locks rigid as the venom shoots into his bloodstream.

The girl stops at a fruit barrow at the end of the harbour wall and buys some oranges. Erigeron and his team-mate leave Silene bowed over his silent flute, the cat miaowing anxiously at his feet. Ryker pumps his wings, flying out high over the harbour basin, and drops the broken gull into the muddy water.

Laurus relaxes. He has devoted most of his life to establishing order in the thriving coastal city. Because only where there is order and obedience can there be control.

Peterborough's council might pass the laws, but it is Laurus's city. He runs the harbour, over fifty per cent of the maritime trade is channelled through his warehouses; he runs the streets, the barrows and the runners; he supplies the majority of the taverns and clubs with their drink; the police answer to him. Nothing goes on without him knowing and approving, and taking his cut.

But the girl has defied him. Normally that would bring swift retribution; youth and innocence do not comprise an acceptable excuse to Laurus. She has been selling Buds without clearing it with his harbour master. And it's been done with suspicious ingenuity; she's made sure she only sold them to foreign sailors. He might not have known until it was too late. But, of course, all items of interest concerning Buds eventually find their way back to him, one way or another.

Five days have passed since the Japanese captain asked to see Laurus personally to request an agency for the new Buds that were for sale on Peterborough harbour. One of his sailors had bought one, he explained, and the man was driving his crew-mates crazy with his lyrical accounts of mammoths and sabre-toothed tigers contained in the Bud memory.

That worried Laurus badly. Buds are educational devices, an eatable newgene plant that infuses knowledge directly into the brain. They don't contain images of primaeval creatures. He should know, he has been trading Buds across the globe for forty years. They are the foundation of his wealth and power. Anything that threatens them, threatens him. The last person in Peterborough to sell a Bud that wasn't grown in Laurus's nursery died swiftly and painfully.

A man called Rubus, who had believed that Laurus would overlook a couple of sales. None of them understand. Laurus cannot countenance the thin edge of the wedge, the notion that a couple of sales isn't going to matter. Because two then becomes three, and then five. And then somebody else starts.

Laurus has already fought that battle. There will be no rep-etition. The price of implementing his authority over the city was his own son, killed by a rival's enforcers. So he will not tolerate any dissension, a return to factions and gang fights. Rubus was used as poison bait by the harbour master in his perpetual struggle to keep sharks out of the basin.

Laurus calmly asked the Japanese captain if he had any more of these new Buds. And on being told that there was indeed a second, sent Erigeron and a full enforcer squad back with the now terrified captain to buy it from the luckless sailor, who was also persuaded to tell them about the girl he'd bought it from.

Laurus has tried the new Bud, and it has given him a glimpse into the same kind of illusory world that the sailor saw. The implications are as bad as he thought. Someone has discovered how to transcribe a fantasy sensorium into a Bud's chemical memory tracers.

This new process will be worth a fortune; visualising the imagination, the kind of short-cut that artists have dreamed about for millennia. It will also make the old Buds which Laurus sells completely obsolete.

He has had twenty enforcers posted around the harbour, posing as foreign sailors, looking for the girl.

And today the wait and effort has paid off; she has sold another Bud to an enforcer. The girl herself is of no real value, it is her ability to lead him to the source of these new Buds which makes safeguarding her so essential.

Ryker is following her through the barrow-lined boulevards of the city centre, out into Longthorpe. But all the time, Laurus is haunted by the Bud's fantasyscape.

At some non-time in his past, Laurus walked through a forest. It had a European feel, pre-Warming, the trees deciduous, bigger than life, dark, ancient, their bark gnarled and flaking. He wandered along narrow animal paths between them, exploring gentle banks and winding valleys, listening to the birdsong and smelling the blossom perfume. The air was cool, shaded by the vast boughs arching overhead; a rain of sunbeams pierced the light green leaves, dappling the floor.

He could remember his feelings, preserved and treasured, undimmed. He was new to the world, and each of his discoveries was accompanied by a joyful enthusiasm.

There were sunny glades of tall grass sprinkled with colourful wild flowers. Long dark lakes filled from waterfalls that burbled down bright sandstone rocks. He had dived in, whooping at the icy water which drove the breath from his lungs.

And he walked on, through a sleepy afternoon under a tumid rose-gold sun that was always half-way towards evening. He picked fruit from the trees, biting into the soft flesh, thick juice dribbling down his chin. Even the taste had a vitality absent from the newgene varieties of his real world. His laughter had rung around the trees, startling the squirrels and rabbits.

If Laurus went into that forest in real life he knew he wouldn't have the strength to leave. The memory segment was the most perfect part of his existence. He kept reliving it, dipping into the recollections with alarming frequency; they remained as fresh as if he'd walked out of the forest only minutes before.

Longthorpe is a slapdash quilt of habitation capsule stacks that meander above the Nene estuary's mudflats. Poverty housing, a slumzone where even Laurus's influence falters. The stacks are over a century old, hastily thrown up in the first couple of decades after the Fens were flooded, as immediate accommo- dation for the diaspora of refugees which the rising sea displaced.

Those who made a success of their new lives clawed their way out and moved into the expanding precincts on the western side of the city. Those that stay are the ones without spirit, who need the most help and receive the least.

Redevelopment, an injection of hope, has never come to Longthorpe. The age Laurus lives in lacks the dynamism for such expansive enterprises. He sees it as a reaction to the tumult of the Warming, a universal hibernation of the soul. After the struggle to adapt to the heat and the sea there is no urge to progress, life is comfortable as it is. Biotechnology provides a supremely stable economic environment. Laurus considers this the weakness of men, stability is a sanctity pursued long after even gods have been abandoned.

Biotechnology has produced the newgene vegetation which covers the Earth, leaves and trunks resistant to the harsh ultra- violet infall. Early varieties were replacements for cereal crops and fruits; but they have been developed and refined until they now usurp most of the forests and savannas that were burnt out by the year-long heat, withered by the droughts, drowned by monsoons. All of them steadily scrubbing the excessive carbon dioxide from the atmosphere, and replacing the ozone. An unobtrusive restoration, which everyone believes in.

Even here in Longthorpe thick tenacious vines bubble over the ground between the stacks. It is only after the girl crosses a withered dual carriageway, and walks into a derelict land- reclamation project that the greenery gives way to bare ground. Faded skull and crossbone signs warn people of the dangers inside the site, but the girl carries on regardless. She threads her way between bulldozed mounds of vitrified waste blocks; tread- ing on a rough path of stones laid down on clay stained rust-red from the chemicals which leak up from buried deposits.

Her eventual destination is the ancient County police head- quarters. Part of the building has been torched, many years ago by the look of it, one side has collapsed altogether. The shell which remains is a virtual wreck, brickwork crumbling, weeds and creepers growing from gutters and window ledges.

The girl slips through a gap in the corrugated sheeting nailed over a window, vanishing from Ryker's sight.

Four hours later, Laurus stands in front of the same corrugated sheet while his enforcer squad moves into position. His pres- ence kindles an air of nervousness among the squad, in turn producing an almost preternatural attention to detail. For

Laurus to attend an operation in person is almost unheard of. He does not often venture out of his mansion these days.

Erigeron has sent his affinity bonded newgene ferret, Fernando, into the police station, scouting out the interior. The jet-black creature puts Laurus in mind of a snake with paws, but it does possess an astonishing agility, wriggling through the smallest of gaps as if its bones were flexible.

According to Erigeron, the only humans inside are the girl and a young boy who seems to be injured. He also says there is some kind of machine in the room, powered by a photosynthetic membrane hanging under the skylight. Laurus is regretting that each affinity bond is unique and impregnable. He would like to have seen for himself; all Ryker can offer him is blurred outlines through algae-crusted skylights.

The conclusion he has grudgingly arrived at is that the inventor of these new Buds is elsewhere. He could wait, mount a surveillance operation to see if the inventor shows up. But he is too near now to adopt a circumspect approach, every delay could mean someone else finding the process, another city baron; Anchusa over in Leicester; Pellionia from Cambridge; or even worse one of the Rose Parties. The thought of politicians with the ability to make dreams seem real and attractive unsettles even Laurus.

Very well, the girl will simply have to provide him with the inventor's location.

'Go,' he tells Erigeron.

The enforcer squad penetrates the police headquarters with deceptive efficiency; their sleek newgene hounds racing on ahead. Laurus feels an excitement that's been missing for decades as he watches the black-clad figures disappear into the gloomy interior.

Erigeron re-emerges two minutes later, and pushes up his helmet visor to reveal a bleak angular face. 'All secure, Mr Laurus. We've got 'em cornered for you.'

Laurus strides forwards, eagerness firing his blood.

The room's light comes from a single soot-streaked skylight high above. A pile of cushions and dirty blankets makes up a sleeping nest in one corner. There's an oven built out of loose bricks, driftwood crackling inside, casting a dull ruby glow. The feral squalor of the den is more or less what Laurus was expecting, except for the books. There are hundreds of them, tall stacks of mouldering paperbacks leaning at precarious angles. Those at the bottom of the piles have already decayed beyond rescue, their pages agglutinating into a single pulp brickette.

Laurus has a collection of books at his mansion, leather bound classics, although he doesn't know anyone else who has them.

He sells a great many basic grade literacy Buds, but for entertainment everyone plugs into sense-o broadcasts.

The girl is crouched beside an ancient hospital commode, her arms thrown protectively around a small boy with greasy red hair, no more than seven or eight. A yellowing bandage is wrapped round his head, covering his eyes. Cheesy tears are leaking from the linen, crusting on his cheeks. His legs have wasted away, now little more than a layer of pale skin stretched over the bones, the waxy surface rucked by tightly knotted blue veins.

Laurus glances round at the enforcer squad; plasma pulse carbines are trained on the two frightened children, hounds quiver at the ready. The girl's wide green eyes are moist from barely contained tears. Shame tweaks him. 'That's enough,' he says. 'Erigeron, you stay. The rest of you leave.'

Laurus squats down next to the children as the squad clumps out; his creaky joints protest the posture.

'What's your name?' he asks the girl. Now he's face to face with her, he sees how pretty she is; ragged shoulder-length ginger hair looks like it needs a good wash, her skin has been dermal-tailored a coffee-brown to ward off the ultra violet. He's curious, the treatment isn't cheap. Most of Longthorpe's residents use a screening gel. She must have been born into a commune, or cult, or clan precinct with money.

She flinches at his closeness, but doesn't relinquish her hold on the boy. 'Torreya,' she says.

'Sorry if we scared you, Torreya, we didn't mean to. Are your parents around?'

She shakes her head slowly. 'No. There's just me and Jante left now.'

Laurus inclines his head at the boy. 'Your brother?'

'Yes.'

'What's the matter with him?'

'His daddy said he was ill. More ill than his daddy could cure, but he was going to learn how. Then after he cured Jante and himself we could all leave here.'

Laurus looks at the blind crippled boy again. There's no telling what it is that has ruined his legs; Longthorpe is riddled with toxicants, a whole strata of eternity drums lying below the topsoil that lifts the land above the tide level. But eternity has turned out to be about fifty years. And the district is too poor to have any clout in the city council for clean up programmes.

Jante points upwards. 'Is that your bird?' he asks in a high curious voice.

Ryker is perched on the edge of the grubby skylight, his huge menacing head peering down.

'Yes,' Laurus says. His eyes narrow. 'How did you know he was there?'

'His daddy gave us an affinity bond,' Torreya says. 'I see for him. I don't mind. Jante was so lonely inside his head. And it was only supposed to be until his daddy understood how to cure him.'

'So where is your father now?' Laurus asks.

Her eyes drop. 'I think he's dead. He was very sick. Sort of inside, you know? He used to cough up blood a lot. Then it started to get worse, and one morning he was gone. So we didn't see, I suppose.'

'How was your father going to learn how to cure Jante?' Laurus asks.

'With the candy Buds, of course.' She turns and gestures into the darker half of the room.

The machine is a customised life support module. A graft of hardware and bioware; metal, plastic, and organic components fused in such an uncompromising fashion that Laurus can't help but feel its perversity is somehow intended to dismay. The globose ribbed plant growing out of its centre has the appearance of a glochidless cactus, four feet high, three feet in diameter, as hard and dark as teak.

Laurus is momentarily nonplussed, until he realises it's a Bud corm. It's a monster, he's never seen a corm even a tenth of this size before, nor one that's ribbed.

The meristem areole at the centre is a gooey gelatin patch from which tiny Buds emerge, growing along the rib vertices. At least the Buds themselves look ordinary, like glaucous pebble cacti, about an inch in diameter, dappled by mauve rings. But there are over a hundred of them. A normal corm would produce, at most, two Buds a year; this giant seems to defy all the conventions. And where Buds are concerned, that is nothing less than revolution.

It is Buds more than anything that have shaped post-Warming society, giving small communities the independence only nations could previously afford. Their cells are saturated with neurophysin proteins, intracellular carriers, bonded to chemical memory tracers. After digestion the neurophysins discharge the memory tracers directly into synaptic clefts, an instant education, Technique.

The swift access of knowledge which Buds can administer has ended single stream professions. Only integral intelligence limits the number of Buds any one person can absorb. Anybody smart enough to be a doctor can also be an electronics expert, a software writer, a chemist . . . Service monopolies have been swept away, turning cities into states, counties into countries.

But a corm can only grow one specific type of Bud, the memory tracer chemicals fixed by its genes. And for each grade the chemistry is more sophisticated, the corm gene sequence more expensive to splice together. Most Technique subjects extend to around grade twelve or fifteen, depending on the complexity of the field, each new level building on the previous one. It would be singularly pointless to take a grade ten Bud by itself; the user would simply possess an abstract bundle of terms and data without any comprehensible reference, a vocabulary without a syntax.

Laurus can only stare at the outsize corm as the forest journey memory returns to him with a vengeance.

'Are these the Buds you've been selling?' he asks. 'The ones with the forest in them?'

Torreya sniffs uncertainly, then nods.

Something like frost is creeping along Laurus's spine. 'And the Buds with the wild animals as well?'

'Yes.'

'Where did this corm come from?'

'Jante's father grew it,' Torreya replies. 'He only had grade seven bioware Technique, which wasn't enough to make Jante better. He couldn't afford the right medical Technique Buds, so he tried to grow his own. He said he was going to download a medical data core into the corm, then he could have all the Technique he wanted without having to pay for it.'

'And the fantasy lands?' Laurus asks. 'Where did they come from?'

Torreya flicks a guilty glance at Jante. And Laurus begins to understand.

'Jante, tell me where the fantasy lands come from, there's a good boy.' he says. He's smiling at Torreya, a smile that is polite and humourless.

'I do them,' Jante blurts, and there's a trace of panic in his high voice. 'I've got an affinity bond with the corm, Daddy gave it me. He said someone ought to fill up the Buds with something, they shouldn't be wasted. So Torry reads books for us, and I think about the places in them.'

Laurus is getting out of his depth. He only has grade three bioware Technique himself, enough to understand the principles behind Buds. But an affinity bond with a plant is way outside anything he's ever heard of before. 'You can load any subject you want into these candy Buds?' he asks hoarsely.

'Yes.'

Laurus can almost visualise it; the children's father, desperate to acquire medical Technique, lacking the money for Buds, but with just enough bioware Technique to begin experimenting.

He is virtually trembling, thinking what would have happened if he hadn't found this corm first. It must incorporate some kind of programmable memory tracer synthesis mechanism. Unique, and, as yet, unmarketed. The potential is staggering. Not only will he have a monopoly on fantasyscapes, but he can also mass produce them.

He meets Torreya's large green eyes again. She's curiously passive, almost subdued, waiting for him to say what is going to happen next. Children, he realises, can intuitively cut to the heart of any situation.

He puts his hand on her shoulder, hoping he's doing it in a paternal fashion. 'This is very unpleasant, this room. Do you enjoy living here?'

Torreya's lips are pursed as she considers the question. 'No. But nobody bothers us here.'

'How would you like to come and live with me?'

Laurus's mansion sits astride the edge of the Castor Hanglands forest on the western side of Peterborough, its broad stone facade looking down on the city and the Fens sea beyond. He bought it for the view, all of his domain a living picture.

Torreya presses her face to the window of the horse-drawn carriage as they ride up the hill, captivated by the formal splendour of the grounds. Jante is sitting beside her, clapping his hands delightedly as she gives him a visual tour of the statues and gravel paths and ponds and fountains.

The gates of the estate's inner defence zone close behind the carriage, and it trundles into the courtyard. Servants hurry over. Jante is eased gently from the carriage and carried into the house. Torreya stands on the granite cobblestones turning around and around, her mouth open in astonishment.

'Did you really mean it?' she gasps. 'Can we really live here?'

'Yes.' Laurus grins broadly. 'I meant it.'

Camassia and Abelia emerge from the house to welcome him back. Camassia is twenty, a tall Oriental beauty with long black hair and an air of aristocratic refinement. She used to be with Kochia, a merchant in Kettering who has an agency with Laurus to distribute Buds. Then Laurus decided he would like to see her stretched out across his bed, her cool poise broken by the animal heat of rutting. Kochia made a gift of her, smiling and sweating as she was presented.

Such whims help to keep Laurus's reputation intact. By acquiescing, Kochia sets an example of obedience to others. Had he refused, Laurus would have made an example of him.

Abelia is younger, sixteen or seventeen, shoulder length blonde hair arranged in tiny curls, her body trim and compact, excitingly dainty. Laurus took her from her parents a couple of years ago as payment for protection and gambling debts.

The two girls exchange an uncertain glance as they see Torreya, obviously wondering who she is going to replace. They more than anyone are aware of Laurus's tastes.

'This is Torreya,' Laurus says. 'She will be staying with us from now on. Make her welcome.'

Torreya tilts her head up, looking from Camassia to Abelia,

seemingly awestruck. Then Abelia smiles, breaking the ice, and Torreya is led into the mansion, her bag dragging along the cobbles behind her. Camassia and Abelia begin to twitter over her like a pair of elder sisters, arguing how to style her hair after it's been washed.

Laurus issues a stream of instructions to his major-domo concerning new clothes and books and toys and softer furniture, a nurse for Jante.

He feels almost virtuous. Few prisoners have ever had it so good.

Torreya bounds into Laurus's bedroom, her little frame filled with such boisterous energy that she instantly makes him feel lethargic. She has intercepted the maid, bringing his breakfast tray in herself.

'I've been up for hours,' she exclaims joyfully. 'I watched the sunrise over the sea. I've never seen it before. Did you know you can see the Fens archipelago from the balcony?'

She seems oblivious to the naked bodies of Camassia and Abelia, lying beside him on the bed. Such easy acceptance gives him pause for thought, in a year or two she'll have breasts of her own.

Laurus considers he has worn well, treating entropy's frosty encroachment with all the disdain only his kind of money can afford. But the biochemical treatments that keep his skin thick and his hair growing cannot work miracles. The accumulating years have seen his sex life dwindle to practically nothing. Now he simply contents himself with watching the girls. To see Torreya's innocence end at the hands of Camassia and Abelia will be a magnificent spectacle to look forward to.

'I know about the islands,' he tells Torreya expansively, as Camassia takes the tray from her. 'I provided the coral kernels for some of them.'

'Really?' Torreya flashes him a solar-bright smile.

Laurus is struck by how lovely she looks now she's been tidied up; she's wearing a lace-trimmed white dress, and her hair's been given a French pleat. Her delicate face is aglow with enthusiasm. He marvels at that, a spirit which can find happiness in something as elementary as a sunrise. How many dawns have there been in his life?

Camassia carefully measures out the milk in Laurus's cup and pours his tea from a silver pot. If his morning tea isn't exactly right everyone suffers from his tetchiness until well after lunch.

Torreya rescues a porcelain side plate as Abelia starts to butter the toast. There's a candy Bud resting on the plate. 'Jante and I made this one up specially for you,' she says, sucking her lower lip apprehensively as she proffers it to Laurus. 'It's a thank you

for taking us away from the police station. Jante's daddy said
you should always say thank you to people who're nice to you.'

'You keep calling him Jante's father,' Laurus says. 'Wasn't he
yours?'

She shakes her head slowly. 'No, I don't know who my
daddy was.'

'Same mother?'

'That's right. But Jante's daddy was nice, though.'

Laurus holds the Bud up, her words suddenly registering.
'You composed this last night?' he asks warily.

'Uh huh.' She nods brightly. 'We know how much you like
them, and it's the only gift we have.'

Laurus tries to work out how fast the memory tracer chemicals would have to be synthesised by the corm. He can't grasp
it. Under Torreya's eager gaze, he puts the Bud in his mouth
and starts to chew. It tastes of blackcurrant.

Laurus had been a small boy on a tropical island, left alone to
wander the coast and jungle to his heart's content. His bare feet
pounded along powdery white sand. The palm shaded beach
stretched on for eternity, waves perfect for surfing. He ran and
did cartwheels for the sheer joy of it, his lithe limbs responding
effortlessly. Whenever he got too warm he would dive into the
cool clear water of the bay, swimming through the fantastic
coral reef to sport with the dolphin shoal who welcomed him
like one of their own.

'You were dreaming,' Camassia says. She is stroking his head as
he sits in the study's leather chair.

'I was young again,' he replies, and there's the feel of the lean
powerful dolphin pressed between his legs as he rides across
the lagoon, a tang of salt in his mouth.

'When do I get to try one?'

'Ask Torreya.' He shakes some life into himself, focusing on
the reports and accounts waiting in the computer terminal's
projection cube. But the Bud memory is still resonating through
his mind, twisting the blue holographs into waves crashing over
coral. And all Torreya and Jante have to go on is what she reads.

'Laurus?' Camassia asks cautiously.

'I want you and Abelia to be very nice to Torreya, be her
friends.'

'We will, she's sweet.'

'I mean it.'

The dead tone brings a flash of fear into the girl's eyes. 'Yes,
Laurus.'

After she has gone he still can't bring himself to do any work.
Every time he considers the candy Buds another possibility is
opened.

What would it feel like if Torreya were to transcribe her sexual encounters into the Buds? His breathing is unsteady as he imagines the three girls disrobing in some softly lit bedroom, their bodies entwining on the bed.

Yes. That would be the ultimate Bud. Not just the physical sensation, the rip of orgasm, any sense-o broadcast can deliver that; but the mind's longing and adoration, its wonder of discovery.

Nothing, but nothing, is now more important than making Torreya and Jante happy. So that, in a couple of years, when the moment comes, she will slide eagerly into the arms of her lovers.

He closes his eyes, calling silently for Ryker.

The eagle finds Torreya on the south side of the Hanglands estate, busy exploring her vast new playground. He orbits overhead as she gambols about. She's a fey little creature; she doesn't walk, she dances.

Jante is sitting in a wicker chair on the patio outside the study, and Laurus can hear him whooping encouragement to his sister. Occasionally the boy lets out a little squeal of excitement at some new discovery she makes for him.

'Stop stop!' Jante cries suddenly.

Laurus looks up sharply, wondering what the boy is seeing through the affinity bond, but he's smiling below his neat white bandage.

Ryker spirals lower. Torreya is standing frozen in the middle of a shaggy meadow, her hands pressed to her cheeks. A cloud of rainbow-hued butterflies is swirling around her, disturbed by her frantic passage.

'Hundreds,' she breathes tremulously. 'Hundreds and hundreds.'

The expression on the face of both siblings is one of absolute enchantment. Laurus recalls his trip to Longthorpe, its soiled air, the stagnant puddles with their scum of dead, half-melted insects. She had probably never seen a butterfly in her life before.

His cargo agents are instructed to scan the inventory of every visiting ship in search of exotic caterpillars. The Hanglands estate is going to be turned into a lepidopterist's heaven.

Today Torreya is all rakish smiles as she brings in Laurus's breakfast tray. He grins back at her as he takes the candy Bud she holds out to him. This is going to become a ritual, he guesses.

'Another one?' Camassia asks.

'Yes,' Torreya shouts gleefully. 'It's a fairy tale one. We've been thinking about it for a while, so it wasn't difficult. We just needed yesterday to make it right. The butterflies you've got here in the estate are beautiful, Laurus.'

Laurus pops the candy Bud in his mouth. 'Glad you like them.'

'I would've loved to have seen the forest Laurus talks about,' Camassia says wistfully.

Laurus notes a more than idle interest in the girl's tone.

'Why didn't you say?' Torreya asks.

'You mean you've still got one?'

'Course, the corm keeps growing them until Jante tells it to stop.'

'You mean you don't have to fill each one in separately?' Laurus asks.

'No.'

He sips his tea thoughtfully. The corm and its life support module are turning out to be even more complex than he originally expected. There are obviously mnemonic cell clusters in it, as well as the bioware processors necessary to receive the affinity bond. 'Do you know if Jante's father transcribed a candy Bud about how the corm was built?'

Torreya screws her face up, listening to some silent voice. 'No, he didn't. Sorry.'

Laurus accepts that it isn't going to be easy, he never thought it would be. He'll have to assemble a team of grade fifteen biotechnology experts, probably give them Buds in hardware and genetics Technique. They can analyse Torreya's corm, and clone new ones. And it will have to be done circumspectly. If any hint of this ever gets out, every biotechnology Technique in the world will start working on it.

'What are we going to do today?' Torreya asks.

'Well, I've got a lot of work to do,' Laurus says. 'But Camassia and Abelia are free, why don't you all go out for a picnic?'

When he was younger, Laurus had been a prince of the Eldrath Kingdom, back in the dawn times. He lived in a city of crystal spires that was built around one the tallest mountains in the land. The royal palace sat atop the pinnacle, from where it was said you could see half-way across the world.

When the alarm of marauders reached the citadel, he led his knight warriors in defence of his father's realm. There were thirty of them, in mirror-bright armour, flying on the backs of their giant butterflies.

The village on the edge of the Desolation was besieged by orcs and goblins, with fires raging through the wattle-and-daub cottages, and the harsh cries of battle echoing through the air.

Laurus drew his silver longsword, holding it high. 'In the name of the King, and our Mother Goddess, I swear none of this fellowship shall rest until the Rok-lord's spawn are driven from this land,' he shouted.

The other knight warriors drew their swords in unison, and shouted their accord. Together they urged their steeds down on the village.

The orcs and goblins were huge scarred brutes, with blue-green skin, and yellow poisonous fangs. But their anger and viciousness made them cumbersome, and they had no true sword skill, just an urge to maim and kill. Their wild sword-swings were always slow and inaccurate. Laurus wove amongst them, using his longsword with terrible accuracy. A quick powerful thrust would send them crashing to the ground, a dark yellow stain bubbling out from the wound.

The battle raged all day, amid the black oily smoke, and flames, and muddy cobbles. Laurus was never hurt himself, although the enemy directed their fiercest assaults against him, enraged at the sight of his slim golden crown denoting him a prince of the house of Eldrath. Night was falling when the last goblin was dispatched. The village cheered their prince and his knight warriors; and a beautiful maiden with red hair falling to her waist came forward to offer him wine from a golden chalice.

He could not forget the sensation of flying that incredible steed, with his long black hair flowing free, cheeks tingling in the wind, and mighty rainbow wings rippling effortlessly on either side of him.

And he's still flying. The three girls are below, resting in the long grass under the shade of a big newgene magnolia tree. There's a little lake twenty yards away, tangerine-coloured fish sliding through the water.

Ryker glides to a silent halt in the branches above the girls. None of them have seen him.

'I was frightened at first,' Torreya is saying, 'especially at night. But after a while you get used to it, and nobody ever came into the reclamation site.'

She's reciting her life, listening to Camassia and Abelia recounting tall tales, all part of making friends. He listens to the giggles and outraged groans of disbelief, longing to be a part of the group.

'You're lucky Laurus found you,' Camassia says. 'He'll look after you all right, and he knows how to make the most from your candy Buds.'

Torreya is lying on her belly, chin resting on her hands. She smiles dreamily, watching a ladybird climb up a stalk of grass in front of her face. 'Yes, I know.'

Abelia jumps to her feet. 'Oh, come on, it's so hot!' She slips the navy-blue dress from her shoulders, and wriggles out of the skirt. Laurus hasn't seen her naked in sunlight before. He marvels at the brown skin, hair like ripe wheat, perfectly shaped breasts, strong legs. 'Come on!' she taunts devilishly, and makes a dash for the lake.

Camassia follows suit, and then Torreya, completely unabashed.

For the ability to transcribe this scene into a Bud, Laurus would sell his soul. He wants it to stretch for ever and ever. Three golden bodies racing across the ragged grass, laughing, vibrant. The shrieks and splashing as they dive into the water, sending the fish fleeing into the deeps.

This is where it will happen, Laurus decides. In the shade of the tree, her body spread open like a star, amid the moisture and the heat.

He's not sure he can wait two years.

Laurus has instructed his staff to set up the giant corm in his mansion's cold-house conservatory, where it is shaded from the sun's abrasive power by darkened glass and large overhanging fern fronds. Conditioners are whining softly as they maintain the air temperature at pre-Warming levels. Spring is coming to an end; the daffodils in the borders have begun to fade, and pure-genotype fuchsias are starting to pop.

A solar cell panel has been set up on the roof to provide the corm's life support module with electricity; and two flaccid olive-green elephant ear membranes are draped over a metal frame above the seed bed, photosynthesising its nutrient fluids.

'Does it snow in here?' Torreya asks.

'No,' Laurus says. 'There are frosts, though. We switch them on for the old winter months.'

Torreya wanders on ahead, her head swivelling from side to side as she examines the new-old shrubs and trees in the brick lined border.

'I'd like to have some people take a look at your corm,' Laurus says. 'Will you mind that?'

'No,' she says. 'What's this tree?'

'An oak. They'll clone your corm for me, and I'll sell the candy Buds the offspring corms produce. But I'd like you and Jante to stay on here. You can earn a lot of money with those fantasies of yours.'

She turns off into a passage lined by dense braids of cyclamen. 'I don't want to leave. They're not going to cut the corm up, are they?'

'No, certainly not. I just want to understand it. They'll start in a week or so.'

And then will come the task of setting up a plantation. His existing nursery is on the western side of the estate, a square mile of land, surrounded by a broad circle of bramble choked woodland, and other, more covert, defences. Over two million corms under intensive cultivation, producing ten thousand Buds a day.

The nursery has been forty years in the making, there is every Technique subject in existence growing out there. He has painstakingly and methodically collected corms from every country on Earth. He even has some from the abandoned Moon colony, Technique about vacuum refining and low gravity agronomy – no longer relevant, but kept alive as a hobby. Knowledge shouldn't be allowed to die. More than anything, the nursery was to have been his memorial.

Now it will all have to go, the old-style corms ploughed under to make way for the new, their Technique transcribed into candy Buds. He suddenly feels depressingly old.

'It's valuable, isn't it, Laurus? Our corm, I mean. Camassia says it is.'

'She's right.'

'Will there be enough money to buy Jante new eyes and legs?' Torreya asks, her voice echoing round the trellis walls of climbing plants.

Laurus has lost track of her. She's not in the cyclamen passage, nor the magnolia avenue. 'One day,' he calls out. The thought of giving Jante eyes is an anathema, the boy might lose his imagination.

That is something else which he is going to have to research. Torreya and Jante can hardly provide an endless number of different fantasies to fill the candy Buds once he starts mass producing them, although in the three days they have been at Hanglands they have dreamt up three new fantasies.

Will it only be children, with their joy and uninhibited imagination who'll be fantasyscape artists, he wonders.

'Some day soon, Laurus,' Torreya's disembodied voice urges. 'Jante loves Hanglands. With legs and eyes he can run through it and see all of it for himself. That's the very best present anyone could have. It's so gorgeous here, better than any silly candy Bud land. The whole world must envy you.'

Laurus is following her voice down a corridor of laburnum trees that are in full bloom. Sunlight shimmers off their flower clusters, transforming the air into a lemon haze. He turns the corner by a clump of white angel's trumpets. Torreya is standing beside the giant corm, and even that seems to have thrived in its new home. Laurus doesn't remember it as being so large.

'As soon as we can,' he says.

Torreya smiles her irrepressible smile, and holds out a newly plucked candy Bud. Refusing the warmth and trust in her sparkling eyes is an impossibility.

The starling is already two hundred feet off the ground. Laurus thinks it must have owl-consanguineous eye implants like

Ryker's in order to fly so unerringly in the dead of night like this.

Ryker hurtles down, and Laurus feels feathers, malleable flesh, and delicate bones within his talons. In his rage he wrenches the starling's head clean off. The candy Bud which the little bird was carrying tumbles away, and not even Ryker can see where it falls.

Laurus contents himself with the knowledge that they are still well inside Hanglands's defensive perimeter. Should any animal try and recover the candy Bud, the estate's newgene hounds and kestrels will deal with them.

He drops the starling so he will have a rough marker when the search begins tomorrow.

Now the big eagle banks sharply and heads back towards the mansion in a fast silent swoop. The ground is a montage of misty grey shadows, trees are puffy jet-black outlines, easily dodged. He can discern no individual landmarks, speed has reduced features to a slipstream blur.

He curses his own foolishness. He should have known, should have anticipated. Three days Torreya and Jante have been at Hanglands, and already news of the candy Buds has leaked. Programmable synthesis is too big, the stakes are now high enough to tempt even mid-range traders into the field. There will be no allies in this war.

Ryker soars over the last row of trees, and the mansion is dead ahead, its lighted windows glaringly bright to the eagle's gloaming-acclimatised eyes. Camassia is still fifty yards from the side door. There's no urgency to her stride, no hint of furtiveness. One of his girls taking an evening stroll, nobody would question her right.

She's a cool one. Kochia's eyes and ears for eighteen months, and he never knew. Only the importance of the candy Buds made her break cover, and risk a handover to the starling.

Laurus thinks he might just have a chance to salvage his dominant position. Kochia and his Kettering operation are small, weak. If Laurus acts swiftly the damage might yet be contained.

There is a grim irony here, he acknowledges; the largest distributor of knowledge in Europe, suddenly desperate to restrict its dissemination.

He thumbs the datalink. 'Mine,' he tells the enforcers. But first he wants the bitch to know.

Ryker's wings slap the air with a loud *fop*. Camassia jerks around at the sound. He can see the shock on her face as Ryker plunges towards her. Hand-sized steel-clad talons stretch wide. She starts to run.

*

Laurus is visiting Torreya in her room to see how she is settling in. In four days the guest bedroom has metamorphosed beyond recognition. Active-holo posters cover the walls, windows looking out across the arctic circle in a time before the icesheets melted. Dazzling temples of ice drift past in the sky-blue water. Shorelines are crinkled by deep fiords. But he's the first to admit that the images are feeble parodies in comparison to the candy Bud fantasies. The new pastel coloured furniture is soft and puffy. Shiny hardback books are strewn all over the carpet, old fictional mythologies he ordered from a publisher in Sheffield. Every flat surface is home to a cuddly Animate Animal; he thinks there must be about thirty of them. There is a scuffed hologram cube on the bedside dresser, showing a smiling woman. It seems out of kilter with the organic cosiness of the room. He vaguely recalls seeing it in the police headquarters.

Torreya clutches a fluffy AA koala to her chest, giggling as the little bioware construct rubs its head against her, purring affectionately.

'Aren't they wonderful?' Torreya says. 'All the people in the house gave me one. They gave some to Jante, too. You're all so kind to us.'

Laurus can only smile weakly as he hands her the huge AA panda he's brought; it's almost as tall as she is. Torreya stands on the bed and kisses him, then bounces on the mattress as the panda hugs her, crooning with delight.

'I'm going to name him Saint Peter,' she declares. 'Because he's your present. And he'll sleep with me at night, I'll be safe from anything then.'

The damp tingle on his cheek where her lips touched sets off a warm contentment.

'Shame Camassia had to go,' Torreya says. 'I liked her a lot.'

'Yes. But her family need her to help with their orange plantation now her cousin's married.'

'Can I go and visit her?'

'Maybe, sometime.'

'And Erigeron's away as well,' she says with a vexed expression. 'He's nice, he helps Jante move around, and he tells funny stories too.'

The thought of his near psychopathic enforcer reciting kids' stories to please the children is one that amuses Laurus immensely. 'He'll be back in a couple of days. He's just ridden over to Kettering to sort out some business contracts for me.'

'I didn't know he was part of your trading business.'

'Erigeron is very versatile. Who's the woman?' he asks to deflect further questions.

Torreya's face is momentarily still. She glances guiltily at the old hologram cube on her bedside dresser. The woman is young, mid-twenties, very beautiful, smiling wistfully. Her hair is a light ginger, tumbling over her shoulders.

'My mother,' Torreya says quietly. 'She died when Jante was born.'

'I'm sorry.' But the woman is definitely Torreya's mother, he can pick out shared features, identical green eyes, the hair colour.

'Everyone back in Longthorpe who knew her said she was special,' Torreya says. 'A real lady. Her name was Nemesia.'

After lunch, Laurus took Torreya down the hill to the Milton Park zoo. He thought it would make a grand treat, bolstering her spirits after Camassia's abrupt departure.

In all his sixty-eight years he had never found the time to visit the zoo before. But it was a lovely afternoon, and they held hands as they walked down the leafy glades between the compounds.

Torreya pressed herself to the railings, smiling and pointing at the exhibits, asking a stream of questions. She would often narrow her eyes and concentrate intensely on what she was seeing, which he came to recognise as using her affinity bond with Jante, letting her brother enjoy the afternoon as much as she did. It would be interesting to see if the visit resulted in a new fantasyscape.

Laurus found himself enjoying the pure-genotype creatures. There was something majestic about such animals, a rawness that geneticists always edited out when they produced more useful newgene versions.

Torreya hauled him over to one of the ice-cream stalls, and he had to borrow some shillings from one of the enforcer squad to pay for their cornets. He never carried money, never had the need before.

Ice-cream and an endless sunny afternoon with Torreya, it was wonderful.

Laurus wakes in the middle of the night, his body as cold as ice. The name has connected, one of his girls had been called Nemesia. How long ago? His recollection is unclear. He peers at Abelia, a child with a woman's body, curled up on her side, wisps of hair lying across her face. In sleep her small sharp features are angelic. He closes his eyes, and he cannot even sketch her face in the blackness. In the twenty-nine years since his wife died, there have been hundreds just like her to enliven his bed, used, then discarded for younger fresher flesh. Placing one is an impossibility. But still, Nemesia must have been a favourite for even this tenuous, yet resilient, memory to have survived so long. The Nemesia he is thinking of stood under

thin beams of slowly shifting sunlight as she undressed, letting
the gold rain lick her skin. *How long?*

When Laurus had been an entity of pure energy, he had roamed
at will across the cosmos, satisfying his curiosity of nature's
astronomical spectacles. He had seen binary sunrises on desert
worlds. Watched the detonation of quasars. Floated within the
ring systems of gas giants. Explored the supergiant stars of the
galactic core.

He had been there at the beginning, when spiralling dust
clouds had imploded into a new sun, seen the family of planets
accrete out of the debris. He had been there at the end, when
the sun cooled and began to expand, its radiance corroding first
into amber then crimson.

A white pinpoint ember flared at its centre, signalling the final
contraction. The neutronium core, gathering matter with insatia-
ble greed; its coalescence warping the gravity field, pulling
distant planets down towards the now rapidly shrinking ball of
super-heated ions.

The end came swiftly, an hour-long implosion devouring
every molecule. Afterwards, an event horizon rose to shield the
ultimate cataclysm.

He hovered above the null-boundary for a long time, wondering what lay below. Gateway to another universe, the truth.

He drifted away.

Torreya has confessed that she has never been on a boat before;
so Laurus is taking her out onto the muddy water of the harbour
basin in one of his trading sampans. They are sailing around the
crumbling roofless walls of the old cathedral perched in the
middle of the basin, the gulls squawking overhead. There are
twenty hulking square-rigged merchantmen anchored around
the ruin. Laurus points out their flags to a captivated Torreya,
describing the countries they have sailed from.

She leans over the gunwale, trailing her hand in the water,
her face dreamy and utterly content. 'This is lovely,' she sighs.
'And so was the zoo yesterday. Thank you, Laurus.'

'My pleasure.' But he is distracted, haunted by a sorrowful
fading smile and long red hair.

Torreya frowns at the lack of response, then turns back to the
merchantmen and the crews bustling about on their decks. Her
eyes narrow.

Laurus orders the captain to go around again. At least Torreya
will enjoy the trip.

As far as Torreya knew, the geneticist was a doctor who wanted
to run some tests. She gave him the sample of blood, and
prowled about the study, bored within minutes at the lack of

anything interesting in that most adult of rooms. Ryker clawed at his perch, caught up in the overspill of trepidation from Laurus's turbulent mind.

His suspicions had been confirmed as soon as the major-domo had brought him the house records. Nemesia had been in residence eleven years ago.

He sat in his high backed leather chair behind the rosewood desk, unable to move from the agony of waiting. The geneticist seemed to be taking an age, running analysis programs on his laptop screening module, peering owlishly at complex multicoloured graphics in the compact unit's holoscreen.

Eventually the man looked up, surprise twisting his placid features. 'You're related,' he said. 'Primary correlation. You're her father.'

Torreya turned from the window, her face numb with incomprehension. Then she ran into his arms, and Laurus had to cope with the totally unfamiliar sensation of a small bewildered girl hugging him desperately, her slight frame trembling. It was one upheaval too many. She cried for the very first time.

After all she had been through, losing her mother, living in an animal slum, the never ending task of looking after Jante. She had coped with it magnificently, never giving in.

He waited until her sobs had finished, then dried her eyes and kissed her brow. They studied each other for a long poignant moment, then she finally offered a timid smile.

Her looks had come from her mother, but by God she had his spirit.

Torreya sits cross legged on the bed and pours out Laurus's breakfast tea herself. She glances up at him, anxious for approval.

So he sips the brew and says: 'Just right.' And it really is.

Her pixie face lights with a smile, and she slurps some of her tea out of a mug.

His son, Iberis, was never so open, so trusting. Always trying to impress. As a good son does, Laurus supposes. These are strange uncharted thoughts for him; he is actually free to recall Iberis without the usual icy snap of pain and shame. Twenty-nine years is a long time to mourn.

Now the only shame comes from his plan for Torreya's seduction, an ignominious bundle of thoughts already being suppressed by his subconscious.

The one admirable aspect to emerge from his earlier manoeuvrings is her genuine affection for Abelia. He means for Abelia to stay on, a cross between a companion and a nanny.

And now he is going to have to see about curing Jante, though how that will affect the fantasyscapes still troubles him. The idea of losing such a source of creativity is most unwelcome;

perhaps he can persuade them to compose a whole series before the doctors begin their work.

So many things to do. How unusual that such fundamental changes should come at his time of life.

But what a future Torreya will have. And that's all that really matters now.

She finishes her tea and crawls over the bed, cuddling up beside him. 'What are we going to do today?' she asks.

He strokes her glossy hair, marvelling at its fine texture. Everything about her comes as a revelation. She is the most perfect thing in the universe. 'Anything,' he says. 'Anything you want.'

Laurus had tracked the lion for four days through the bush. At night he would lie awake in his tent, listening to its roar. In the morning he would pick up its spoor and begin the long trek again.

There was no more beautiful land on God's Earth than the African savanna, its brittle yellow grasses, lonely alien trees. Dawn and dusk would see the sun hanging low above the horizon, streaked with thin gold clouds, casting a cold radiance. Tall mountains were visible in the distance, their peaks capped with snow.

The land he crossed teemed with life. He spent hours sitting on barren outcrops of rock, watching the animals go past. Timid gazelles, bad tempered rhinos, graceful giraffes nibbling at the lush leaves only they could reach. Monkeys screamed and chattered at him from their high perches, zebras clustered cautiously around muddy water holes, twitching nervously as he hiked past. There were pandas, too, a group of ten dozing on sun-baked rocks, chewing contentedly on the bamboo that grew nearby. Thinking back, their presence was very odd, but at the time he squatted down on his heels grinning at the affable creatures and their lazy antics.

Still the lion led him on; there were deep valleys, crumpled cliffs of rusty rock. Occasionally he would catch sight of his dusky prey in the distance, the silhouette spurring him on.

On the fifth day he entered a copse of spindly trees, whose branches forked in perfect symmetry. The lion stood waiting for him. A fully grown adult male, powerful and majestic. It roared once as he walked right up to it, and shook its thick mane.

He stared at it in total admiration for some indefinable length of time, long enough for every aspect of the jungle lord to be sketched irrevocably in his mind.

The lion shook his head again, and sauntered off into the copse. Laurus watched it go, feeling an acute sense of loss.

*

Laurus is throwing a party this evening, the ultimate rare event. All his senior managers and agents are in attendance, along with Peterborough's grandees. He is hugely amused that every single one of them has turned up despite the short – five hour – notice. His reputation is the one faculty which does not diminish with the passing years.

Torreya is dressed like a Victorian princess, a gown of flowing white lace and chains of small flowers woven into her hair. He stands beside her under the white marble portico, immaculate in his white dinner jacket, scarlet rosebud in his buttonhole, receiving the guests as they alight from their carriages. Ryker has been watching the carriages waiting at Belsize Farm at the bottom of the hill, some of them were there for half an hour before beginning the journey up to the mansion, determined not to be late.

They sit around the oak table in the mansion's long-disused formal dining room. Vast chandeliers hang on gold chains, classical oil paintings of hunts and harvests look down on the assembled diners. Huge garlands of flowers decorate the walls and pillars. A string quartet plays quietly from a podium in one corner. Laurus has gone all out. He wants to do this with style.

Torreya sits next to Jante, who is wearing a dinner jacket with an oversize velvet bow-tie, a neat chrome sunshade band covering his eyes. She pauses every so often to stare at her brother's plate, and he uses his knife and fork with quick precision.

Conversations end instantly as Laurus taps his crystal goblet with a silver dessert spoon. He rises to speak. 'This is a double occasion for me,' he says. 'For all of us. I have found my daughter,' his hand rests on Torreya's shoulder.

She blushes furiously, smiling wide, staring at the tablecloth. Shocked glances fly around the table as agents and managers try to work out how they will be affected. Tentative smiles of congratulation are proffered to Torreya. Laurus feels like laughing.

'Torreya will be taking over from me when she's older. And she's the best person qualified, because she's brought me something that will secure all your futures.' He nods at her.

Torreya rises to her feet, and takes the big silver platter from the sideboard. There is a pile of candy Buds in the middle of it. She starts to walk around the table, offering them to the guests.

'This is your future,' says Laurus. 'A new kind of Bud, and I have a monopoly on them. You will act as my suppliers, building a distribution network across the whole continent. Your personal wealth will increase a hundredfold. And you, like I, have Torreya to thank for bringing us this marvel.'

She finishes the circle, and hands the last candy Bud to Erigeron with a chirpy smile. He grimaces, and rolls his eyes for her alone; observing the niceties of the formal meal has stretched his patience close to breaking.

The agents and grandees are holding their candy Buds, various expressions of unease and concern registering on their faces. Laurus chuckles, and pops his own candy Bud into his mouth. 'Behold, your dreams made real.'

One by one the guests follow suit.

Laurus holds Torreya's hand as they walk up the stairs some time after midnight. The guests have gone, some of them stumbling down the portico stairs, dazed by the chimerical past unfolding behind their eyes.

Torreya is tired and very sleepy, but still smiling. 'So many people, and they all wanted to be friends with me. Thank you, Daddy,' she says as she climbs into bed.

Saint Peter folds his arms round Torreya, and Laurus tucks the duvet up to her chin. 'You don't have to thank me.' Her words kindle a secret delight; she has been calling him Daddy all day now, a subconscious acceptance. He has been terribly worried in case she rejects the whole notion.

'But I do,' she yawns. 'For finding me. For bringing me here. For making me happy.'

'All part of being a father,' he says softly.

But she is already asleep. Laurus gazes down at her for a long time before he goes to his own bed.

After lunch, Laurus took Torreya down the hill to the Milton Park zoo. It was a lovely afternoon, and they held hands as they walked down the leafy glades between the compounds.

Torreya pressed herself to the railings, smiling and pointing at the exhibits. 'I always love it when I come to the zoo,' she said. 'I think I must know most of the animals by name now.'

Laurus blinks awake, finding himself alone on his bed, gazing up at the mirror on the ceiling, seeing himself: a sickly white stick-insect figure with a bloated belly. The bed's royal purple silk sheets have been soiled with urine and faeces. A half-eaten candy Bud is wedged between his lips, its mushy tissue smeared over his face, acidic brown juice dripping down his chin. He is starting to gag on this obscene violation.

Fernando is poised on his chest, tiny black eyes staring into his. Its wet nose twitches, and it suddenly scurries away with a sinuous wriggle.

Laurus hears a tiny click from the door lock.

'Erigeron?'

Erigeron's boots make no sound on the thick navy-blue carpet. From Laurus's prone position, the enforcer's lanky frame appears preternaturally tall as he walks towards the bed. He smiles. Laurus has never seen a smile on that sparse face before. It frightens him. Fear, real fear for the first time in decades.

'Why?' Laurus cries. 'Why? You have everything here. Girls, money, prestige. Why?'

'Kochia has promised me more, Mr Laurus. I'm going to be his partner when he starts selling candy Buds.'

'He can't have promised that, you killed him!'

'I . . . I remember what he said.'

'He said nothing! He couldn't have!'

A flicker of apprehension creases Erigeron's face. 'He did. I remember it all very clearly. I agreed. I did, Mr Laurus. I agreed.'

'No!'

Erigeron's long-fingered hand reaches out. 'Yes,' and his voice is full of confidence now. 'I remember.'

Laurus whimpers as tiny translucent amber stingers slide out of their recesses under Erigeron's manicured nails. The hand covers his eyes, and blackness falls.

A tightly whorled flowerbud opens in greeting. Each petal a different colour, expanding, rising up towards him. Their tips begin to rotate, creating a rainbow swirl. Slowly but surely the blurred streaks begin to resolve.

Laurus and Torreya stand in the middle of the deserted zoo. The sky is grey, and the leaves on the newgene trees are turning brown, falling to the ground. An impossible autumn. Laurus shivers in the cold air.

'You said you'd been here before,' he says.

'Yes. My daddy used to bring me all the time.'

'Your daddy?'

'Rubus.'

Ryker coasts above the Hanglands estate in the cool early morning air. Far below, the eagle can see someone moving slowly along one of the meandering gravel paths. A young girl pushing a wheelchair.

He banks abruptly, dropping five yards before he can regain stability. He lets out a squawk of outrage. His new mistress has yet to learn how to exploit his natural instincts to fly with grace; her commands are too jerky, mechanical.

A quieter wish flows through him, the need to spiral down for a closer examination of the people below. Ryker dips a wing lazily, and begins his fluid descent.

He alights in a newgene magnolia tree, watching intently as she stops beside a small lake. There are water lilies mottling its black-mirror surface, swans drift idly amongst the fluffy purple blooms.

Torreya is indulgent with Jante, halting every few minutes so he can look around with his new eyes. His legs have been wrapped in folds of translucent bioware membrane, their integral plasma veins pulsing slowly. The medical team she has assembled have told her the muscle implants are going to take another week to stabilise; a month should see him walking.

'It's ever so pretty here,' he says, and smiles up worshipfully at her.

Torreya walks over to the shore of the lake, a gentle breeze ruffing her hair. She turns to gaze down on the city. Its rooftops are lost in a nebulous heat shimmer. Behind it, she can see the Fens sea, a hazy line of grubby blue in the distance.

'Yes,' she decides solemnly. 'You get a marvellous view from Hanglands. Laurus was always one for views.'

They leave the lake behind, and make their way down to the dew splashed meadow to watch the butterflies emerge from their chrysalises.

B. Marey's Photographic Gun

Great Breakthroughs in Darkness (being, early entries from *The Secret Encyclopaedia of Photography*)

Authorised by

Marc Laidlaw

Chief Secretary of the Ministry of Photographic
Arcana, Correspondent of No Few Academies,
Devoted Husband, &c.

*'Alas! That this speculation is somewhat too
refined to be introduced into a modern novel or
romance; for what a* dénouement *we should
have, if we could suppose the secrets of the
darkened chamber to be revealed by the testi-
mony of the imprinted paper!'*

William Henry Fox Talbot

A

AANSCHULTZ, CONREID
(c. 1820 – October 12, 1888)
Inventor of the praxiscope technology (*which see*), Professor Aanschultz believed that close observation of physi-
ology and similar superficial phenomena could lead to
direct revelation of the inner or secret processes of nature.
Apparent proof of this now discredited theory was offered
by his psychopraxiscope, which purported to offer instantaneous viewing of any subject's thoughts. (Later researchers demonstrated that the device 'functioned' by creating
interference patterns in the inner eye of the observer,
triggering phosphene splash and lucid dreaming.) Aanschultz's theories collapsed, and the Professor himself
died in a Parisian lunatic asylum, after his notorious
macropraxiscope failed to extract any particular meaning from the contours of the Belgian countryside near
Waterloo. Some say he was already unstable from abuse
of his autopsychopraxiscope, thought to be particularly

dangerous because of autophagous feedback patterns generated in its operator's brain. However, there is evidence that Aanschultz was quite mad already, owing to the trauma of an earlier research disaster.

AANSCHULTZ LENS
The key lens used in Aanschultz's notorious psychopraxiscope, designed to capture and focus abaxial rays reflecting from a subject's eye.

ABAT-JOUR
A skylight or aperture for admitting light to a studio, or an arrangement for securing the same end by reflection. In the days when studios for portraiture were generally found at the tops of buildings not originally erected for that purpose, and perhaps in narrow thoroughfares or with a high obstruction adjacent, I found myself climbing a narrow, ill-lit flight of stairs, away from the sound of wagon wheels rattling on cobblestones, the common foetor of a busy city street, and toward a more rarefied and addictive stench compounded of chemicals that would one day be known to have contributed directly to society's (and my own) madness and disease. It was necessary to obtain all available top light in the choked alleys, and Aanschultz had done everything he could in a city whose sky was blackly draped with burning sperm.

I came out into a dazzling light compounded of sunlight and acetylene, between walls yellowed by iodine vapour, covering my nose at the stench of mercury fumes, the reek of sulphur. My own fingertips were blackened from such stuff; and eczema procurata, symptomatic of a metol allergy, had sent a prurient rash all up the sensitive skin of my inner arms, which, though so bound in bandages that I could scarcely scratch them through my heavy woollen sleeves, were a constant seeping agony. At night I wore a woman's long kid gloves coated with coal tar, and each morning dressed my wounds with an ointment of mercuric nitrate (*60 g.*), carbolic acid (*10 ccs*), zinc oxide (*30 g*) and lanoline (*480 "*), which I had learned to mix myself when the chemist professed a groundless horror of contagion. I had feared at first that the rash might spread over my body, down my flanks, invading the delicate skin of my thighs and those organs between them, softer by far. I dreaded walking like a crab, legs bowed far apart, experiencing excruciating pain at micturition and intercourse (at least syphilis is painless; even when it chews away one's face, I am told, there is a pleasant numbness) – but so far this nightmare had not developed. Still, I held my tender arms slightly spread away from my sides, seeming always on the verge of drawing the twin Janssen photographic revolvers which I carried in holsters slung around my waist, popular handheld versions of that amazing 'gun' which first captured the transit of Venus across the face of our local star.

The laboratory, I say, was a fury of painfully brilliant light and sharp, membrane-searing smells. Despite my admiration for the Professor's efficiency, I found it not well suited for artistic purposes, a side light being usually preferable instead of the glare of a thousand suns that came down through the cruelly contrived abat-jour. But Aanschultz, being of a scientific bent, saw in twilight landscapes only some great treasure to be prised forth with all necessary force. He would have disembowelled the Earth itself if he thought an empirical secret were lodged just out of reach in its craw. I had suggested a more oblique light, but the Professor would not hear of it.

'That is for your prissy studios – for your fussy bourgeois sitters!' he would rage at my 'aesthetic' suggestions. 'I am a man of science. My subjects come not for flattering portraits, but for insight – I observe the whole man here.' To which I replied: 'And yet you have not *captured* him. You have not impressed a single supposition on so much as one thin sheet of tin or silver or albumen glass. The fleeting things you see cannot be captured. Which is less than I can say of even the poorest photograph, however superficial.' And here he always scoffed at me and turned away, pacing, so that I knew my jibes had cut to the core of his own doubts, and that he was still, with relentless logic, stalking a way to fix the visions viewed so briefly (however engrossingly) in his praxiscope.

He needed lasting records of his studies – some substance, the equivalent of photographic paper that might hold the scope's pictures in place for all to see, for all time. It was this magical medium which he now sought. I thought it must be something of a 'Deep' paper – a sheet of more than three dimensions, into which thoughts might be imprinted in all their complexity, a sort of mind-freezing mirror. When he shared his own ideas, I quickly became lost, and if I made any comment it soon led to vicious argument. I could not follow Aanschultz's arguments on any subject; even our discussions of what or where to eat for lunch, what beer went best with bratwurst, could become incomprehensible. Only another genius could follow where Aanschultz went in his thoughts. With time I had even stopped looking in his eyes – with or without a psychopraxiscope.

'I am nearly there,' he told me today, as I reached the top of the stairs with a celebratory bottle in hand.

'You've found a way to fix the psychic images?'

'No – something new. My life's work. This will live long after me.'

He said the same of every current preoccupation. His assistants were everywhere, adjusting the huge rack of movable mirrors that conducted light down from the rooftops, in from the street, over from the alleyway, wherever there happened to be a stray unreaped ray of it. Their calls rang out through the laboratory, echoing down through pipes like those in great ships, whereby the captain barks orders to the engine room. In the centre of the chamber stood the solar navigator with his vast charts and compass and astrolabes scattered around him, constantly shouting into any one of the dozen pipes that coiled down from the ceiling like dangling vines, dispatching orders to those who stood in clearer sight of the sun but with a less complete foreknowledge of its motion. And as he shouted, the mirrors canted this way and that, and the huge collectors on the roof purred in their oiled bearings and the entire building creaked under the shifting weight and the laboratory burned like a furnace, although cleverly, without any heat. There was a watery luminescence in the air, a constant distorted rippling that sent wavelets lapping over the walls and tables and charts and retorts and tarnished boxes, turning the iodine stains a lurid green. This was the result of light pouring through racks of blue glass vials, old glass that had run and blistered with age, stoppered bottles full of copper sulphate which also swivelled and tilted according to the instructions of another assistant who stood very near the navigator. I had to raise my own bottle and drink very deeply before any of this made much sense to me, or until I could approach a state of focused distraction more like that of my friend and mentor, the great Professor Conreid

Aanschultz, who now came at me and snatched the bottle from my hands and helped himself. He courteously pol- ished every curve of the flask with a fresh chamois before handing it back, eradicating his last fingerprint as the bottle left his fingers, so that the now nearly empty vessel gleamed as brightly as those blue ones. I finished it off and dropped it in a half-assembled filter rack, where it would find a useful life, even empty. The Professor made use of all *Things*.

'This way,' he said, leading me past a huge hissing copperclad acetylene generator of the dreadnought var- iety, attended by several anxious-looking children in the act of releasing quantities of gas through a purifier. The proximity of this somewhat dangerous operation to the racks of burning Bray 00000 lamps made me uncomfort- able, and I was grateful to move over a light-baffling threshold into darkness. Here, a different sort of chaos reigned, but it was, if anything, even more intense and busy. I sensed, even before my eyes had adjusted to the weak and eerie working light, that these assistants were closer to Aanschultz's actual current work, and this work must be very near to completion, for they had that weary, pacified air of slaves who have been whipped to the very limits of human endurance and then suspended beyond that point for days on end. I doubted any had slept or rested for nearly as long as Aanschultz, who was pos- sessed of superhuman reserves. I myself, of quite contrary disposition, had risen late that morning, feasted on a huge lunch (which even now was producing unexpected gases like my own internal rumbling dreadnought), and, feeling benevolent, had decided to answer my friend's urgent message of the previous day, which had hinted that his fever pitch of work was about to bear fruit – a pronounce- ment he always made long in advance of the actual climax, thus giving me plenty of my own slow time to come around. For poor Aanschultz, time was compressed from line to point. His was a world of constant Discovery.

I bumped into nearly everything and everyone in the darkened chamber before my eyes adjusted, when finally I found myself bathed in a deep, rich violet light, decanted through yet another rack of bottles, although of a corre- spondingly darker hue. Blood or burgundy, they seemed at first; and reminded me of the liquid edge of clouds one sometimes sees at sunset, when all form seems to buzz and crackle as it melts into the coming night, and the eye tingles in anticipation of discovering unsuspected hues. My skin now hummed with this same subtle optical electricity. Things in the room seemed to glow with an inner light.

'Here we are,' he said. 'This will make everything possible. This is my –

ABAT-NUIT

By this name Aanschultz referred to a bevelled opening he had cut into an odd corner of the room, a tight and complex angle formed between the floor and the brick abutment of a chimney shaft from the floors below. I could not see how he had managed to collect any light from this darkest of corners, but I quickly saw my error. For it was not light he bothered to collect in this way, but darkness.

Darkness was somehow channelled into the room and then filtered through those racks of purple bottles, in some of which I now thought to see floating specks and slowly tumbling shapes that might have been wine lees or bloodclots. I even speculated that I saw the fingers of a deformed, pickled foetus clutching at the rays that passed through its glass cell, playing inverse shadow-shapes on the walls of the dark room, casting its enlarged and gloomy spell over all us awed and frightened older children.

Unfiltered, the darkness was much harder to character-ise; when I tried to peer into it, Aanschultz pulled me away, muttering, 'Useless for our purposes.'

'Our?' I repeated, as if I had anything to do with this. For even then it seemed an evil power my friend had harnessed, something best left to its own devices – some-thing which, in collaboration with human genius, could only lead to the worsening of an already precarious situation.

'This is my greatest work yet,' he confided, but I could see that his assistants thought otherwise. The shadows already darkening Europe seemed thickest in this corner of the room. I felt that the strangely bevelled opening with its canted mirror inside a silvery-black throat, reflecting darkness from an impossible angle, was in fact the source of all unease to be found in the streets and in the marketplace. It was as if everyone had always known about this webby corner, and feared that it might eventually be prised open by the violent levering of a powerful mind.

I comforted myself with the notion that this was a discovery, not an invention, and therefore for all purposes inevitable. Given a mind as focused as Aanschultz's, this corner was bound to be routed out and put to some use. However, I already suspected that the eventual use would not be that which Aanschultz expected.

I watched a thin girl with badly bruised arms weakly pulling a lever alongside the abat-nuit to admit more darkness through the purple bottles, and the deepening darkness seemed to penetrate her skin as well as the jars, pouring through the webs of her fingers, the meat of her arms, so that the shadows of bone and cartilage glowed within them, flesh flensed away in the revealing black radiance. It was little consolation to think that the discovery was implicit in the fact of this corner, this source of darkness built into the universe, embedded in creation like an aberration in a lens and therefore unavoidable. It had taken merely a mind possessed of an equal or complementary aberration to uncover it. I only hoped Aanschultz possessed the power to compensate for the darkness's distortion, much as chromatic aberration may be compensated or avoided entirely by the use of an apochromatic lens. But I had little hope for this in my friend's case. Have I mentioned it was his cruelty which chiefly attracted me?

ABAXIAL
Away from the axis. A term applied to the oblique or marginal rays passing through a lens. Thus the light of our story is inevitably deflected from its most straightforward path by the medium of the *Encyclopaedia* itself, and this entry in particular. Would that it were otherwise, and this a perfect world. Some go so far as to state that the entirety of Creation is itself an . . .

ABERRATION
A functional result of optical law. Yet I felt that this matter might be considered Aanschultz's fault, despite my unwillingness to think any ill of my friend. In my professional capacity, I was surrounded constantly by the fat and the beautiful; the lazy, plump and pretty. They

flocked to my studio in hordes, in droves, in carriages and cars, in swan-necked paddle boats; and their laughter flowed up and down the three flights of stairs to my studios and galleries, where my polite assistants bade them sit and wait until *Monsieur Artiste* might be available. Sometimes Monsieur failed to appear at all, and they were forced with much complaining to be photographed by a mere apprentice, at a reduced rate, although I always kept on hand plenty of pre-signed plates so that they might take away an original and be as impressive as their friends. I flirted with the ladies; was indulgent with the children; I spoke to the gentlemen as if I had always been one of them, concerned with the state of trade, rates of exchange, the crisis in labour, the inevitable collapse of economies. I was in short a chameleon, softer than any of them, lazier and more variable, yet prouder. They meant nothing to me; they were all so easy and pretty and (I thought then) expendable.

Yet there was only one Aanschultz. On the first and only day he came to sit for me (he had decided to require all his staff to wear tintype badges for security reasons and himself set the first example), I knew I had never met his like. He looked hopelessly out of place in my waiting chambers, awkward on the steep stairs, white and etiolated in the diffuse cuprous light of my abat-jour. Yet his eyes were livid; he had violet pupils, and I wished – not for the first time – that there were some way of capturing colour with all my clever lenses and cameras. None of my staff colourists could hope to duplicate that hue.

The fat pleasant women flocking the studios grew thin and uncomfortable at the sight of him, covering their mouths with handkerchiefs, exuding sharp perfumes of fear that neutralised their ambergris and artificial scents. He did not leer or bare his teeth or rub his hands and cackle; these obvious melodramatic motions would only have cheapened and blunted the sense one had of his refined cruelty.

Perhaps 'cruel' is the wrong word. It was a severity in his nature – an unwillingness to tolerate any thought, sensation, or companion duller than a razor's edge. I felt instantly stimulated by his presence, as if I had at last found someone against whom I could gauge myself, not as opponent or enemy, but as a student who forever tries and tests himself against the model of his mentor. In my youth I had known instinctively that it is always better to stay near those I considered my superiors; for then I could never let my own skills diminish, but must constantly be polishing and practising them. With age and success, I had nearly forgotten that crucial lesson, having sheltered too long in the cosy nests and parlours of Society. Aanschultz's laboratory proved to be their perfect antidote.

We two could not have been less alike. As I have said, I had no clear understanding of, and only slightly more interest in, the natural sciences. Art was All, to me. It had been my passion and my livelihood for so long now that I had nearly forgotten there was any other way of life. Aanschultz reintroduced me to the concepts of hard speculation and experimentation, a lively curriculum which soon showed welcome results in my own artistic practices. For in the city, certain competitors had mastered my methods and now offered similar services at lower prices, lacking only the fame of my name to beat me out of business. In the coltish marketplace, where economies trembled beneath the rasping tongue of forces so bleak they seemed the product of one's own fears, with no objective source in the universe, it began to seem less than essential to possess an extraordinary signature on an otherwise ordinary photograph. Why spend all that money for a Name when just down the street, for two-thirds the price, one could have a photograph of equivalent quality, lacking only my florid famous autograph (of which, after all, there was already a glut)? So you see, I was in danger already when I met Aanschultz, without yet suspecting its encroachment. With his aid I was soon able to improve the quality of my product far beyond the reach of my competitors. Once more my name reclaimed its rightful magic potency, not for empty reasons, not through mere force of advertising, but because I was indeed superior.

To all of Paris I might have been a great man, an artistic genius, but in Aanschultz's presence I felt like a young and stupid child. The scraps I scavenged from his workshop floors were not even the shavings of his important work. He hardly knew the good he did me, for although an immediate bond developed between us, at times he hardly seemed aware of my presence. I would begin to think that he had forgotten me completely; weeks might pass when I heard not a word from him; and then, suddenly, my faith in our friendship would be reaffirmed, for out of all the people he might have told – his scientific peers, politicians, the wealthy – he would come to me first with news of his latest breakthrough, as if my opinion were of greatest importance to him. I fancied that he looked to me for artistic inspiration (no matter how much he might belittle the impulse) just as I came to him for his scientific rigour.

It was this rigour which at times bordered on cruelty – though only when emotion was somehow caught in the slow, ineluctably turning gears of his logic. He would not scruple to destroy a scrap of human fancy with diamond drills and acid blasts in order to discover some irreducible atom of hard fact (+10 on the Mohs scale) at its core. This meant, unfortunately, that each of his advances had left a trail of crushed 'victims', not all of whom had thrown themselves willingly before the juggernaut.

I sensed that this poor girl would soon be one of them.

ABRASION MARKS

of a curious sort covered her arms, something like a cross between bruises, burns and blistering. Due to my own eczema, I felt a sympathic pang as she backed away from the levers of the abat-nuit, Aanschultz brushing her off angrily to make the final adjustments himself. She looked very young to be working such long hours in the darkness, so near the source of those strange black rays, but when I mentioned this to my friend he merely swept a hand in the direction of another part of the room, where a thin woman lay stretched out on a stained pallet, her arm thrown over her eyes, head back, mouth gaping; at first she appeared as dead as the drowned poseur Hippolyte Bayard, but I saw her breast rising and falling raggedly. The girl at the lever moved slowly, painfully, over to this woman and knelt down beside her, then very tenderly laid her head on the barely moving breast, so that I knew they were mother and child. Leaving Aanschultz for the moment, I sank down beside them, stroking the girl's frayed black hair gently as I asked if there was anything I could do for them.

'Who's there?' the woman said hoarsely.

I gave my name, but she appeared not to recognise it. She did not need illustrious visitors now, I knew.

'He's with the Professor,' the child said, scratching

vigorously at her arms though it obviously worsened them. I could see red, oozing meat through the scratches her fingernails left.

'You should bandage those arms,' I said. 'I have sterile cloth and ointment in my carriage if you'd like me to do it.'

'Bandages and ointment, he says,' said the woman. 'As if there's any healing it. Leave her alone now – she's done what she could where I had to leave off. You'll just get the doctor mad at both of us.'

'I'm sure he'd understand if I . . .'

'Leave us be!' the woman howled, sitting up now, propped on both hands so that her eyes came uncovered, to my horror; for across her cheeks, forehead and nose was an advanced variety of the same damage her daughter suffered; her eye sockets held little heaps of charred ash that, as she thrust her face forward in anger, poured like black salt from between her withered lids and sifted softly onto the floor, reminding me unavoidably of that other and most excellent abrading powder which may be rubbed on dried negatives to provide a 'tooth' for the penciller's art, consisting of one part powdered resin and two parts cuttle-fish bone, the whole being sifted through silk. I suspected this powder would do just as well, were I crass enough to gather it in my handkerchief. She fell back choking and coughing on the black dust, beating at the air, while her daughter moved away from me in tears, and jumped when she heard Aanschultz's sharp command. I turned to see my friend beckoning with one crooked finger for the girl to come and hold the levers just so, while he screwed down a clamp.

'My God, Aanschultz,' I said, without much hope of a satisfactory answer. 'Don't you see what your darkness has done to these wretches?'

He muttered from the side of his mouth: 'It's not a problem any longer. A short soak in a bath of potassium iodide and iodine will protect the surface from abrasion.'

'A print surface, perhaps, but these are people!'

'It works on me,' he said, thrusting at me a bare arm that showed scarcely any scarring. 'Now either let the girl do her work, or do it for her.'

I backed away quickly, wishing things were otherwise; but in those days Aanschultz and his peers needed fear no distracting investigations from the Occupational Safety and Health Administration. He could with impunity remain oblivious to everything but the work that absorbed him.

ABSORPTION

This term is used in a chemical, an optical, and an esoteric sense. In the first case it designates the taking up of one substance by another, as a sponge absorbs or sucks up water, with hardly any chemical but merely a physical change involved; this is by far the least esoteric meaning, roughly akin to those surface phenomena which Aanschultz hoped to strip aside.

Optically, absorption is applied to the suppression of light, and to it are due all colour effects, including the dense dark stippling of the pores of Aanschultz's face, ravaged by the pox in early years, and the weird violet aura – the same colour as his eyes, as if it had bled out of them – that lined his profile as he bent closer to that weirdly angled aperture into artificial darkness.

My friend, with unexpected consideration for my lack of expertise, now said: 'According to Draper's law, only those rays which are absorbed by a substance act chemically on it; when not absorbed, light is converted into some other form of energy. This dark beam converts matter in ways heretofore unsuspected, and is itself transformed into a new substance. Give me my phantospectroscope.'

This last command was meant for the girl, who hurriedly retrieved a well-worn astrolabe-like device from a concealed cabinet and pressed it into her master's hands.

'The spectrum is like nothing ever seen on this earth,' he said, pulling aside the rack of filter bottles and bending toward his abat-nuit with the phantospectroscope at his eye, like a sorcerer stooping to divine the future in the embers of a hearth where some sacrifice has just done charring. I could not bear the cold heat of that unshielded black fire. I took several quick steps back.

'I would show you,' he went on, 'but it would mean nothing to you. This is my real triumph, this phantospectroscope; it will be the foundation of a new science. Until now, visual methods of spectral inspection have been confined to the visible portion of the spectrum; the ultraviolet and infra-red regions gave way before slow photographic methods; and there we came to a halt. But I have gone beyond that now. Ha! Yes!'

He thrust the phantospectroscope back into the burned hands of his assistant and made a final adjustment to the levers that controlled the angle and intensity of rays conducted through the abat-nuit. As the darkness deepened in that clinical space, it dawned on me that the third and deepest meaning of absorption is something like worship, and not completely dissimilar to terror.

ACCELERATOR!
my friend shouted, and I sensed rather than saw the girl moving toward him, but too slowly. Common accelerators are sodium carbonate, washing soda, ammonia, potassium carbonate, sodium hydrate (caustic soda), and potassium hydrate (caustic potash), none of which suited Aanschultz. He screamed again, and now there was a rush of bodies, a crush of them in the small corner of the room. An accelerator shortens the duration of development and brings out an image more quickly, but the images he sought to capture required special attention. As is written in the *Encyclopaedia of Photography* (1911, exoteric edition), 'Accelerators cannot be used as fancy dictates.' I threw myself back, fearful that otherwise I would be shoved through the gaping abat-nuit and myself dissolve into that negative essence. I heard the girl mewing at my feet, trod on by her fellows, and I leaned to help her up. But at that moment there was a quickening in the evil corner, and I put my hands to a more instinctive use.

ACCOMMODATION OF THE EYE
The darkness cupped inside my palms seemed welcoming by comparison to the anti-light that had emptied the room of all meaning. With both eyes covered, I felt I was beyond harm. I could not immediately understand the source of the noises and commotion I heard around me, nor did I wish to. (*See also* 'Axial Accommodation'.)

ACCUMULATOR
Apparently (and this I worked out afterward in hospital beside Aanschultz) the room had absorbed its fill of the neutralising light. All things threatened to split at their seams. Matter itself, the atmosphere, Aanschultz's assistants, bare thought, creaking metaphor – these things and

others were stuffed to the bursting point. My own mind was a peaking crest of images and insights, a wave about to break. Aanschultz screamed incomprehensible commands as he realised the sudden danger; but there must have been no one who still retained the necessary self-control to obey him. My friend himself leapt to reverse the charge, to shut down the opening, sliding the rack of filtering jars back in place – but even he was too late to prevent one small, significant rupture.

I heard the inexplicable popping of corks, accompanied by a simultaneous metallic grating, followed by the shattering of glass. Aanschultz later whispered of what he had glimpsed out of the edges of his eyes, and by no means can I – nor would I – discredit him.

It was the bottles and jars in the filter rack that burst. Or rather, some burst, curved glass shards and gelatinous contents flying, spewing, dripping, clotting the floor and ceiling, spitting backward into the bolt-hole of night. Other receptacles opened with more deliberation. Aanschultz later blushed when he described, with perfect objectivity, the sight of certain jar lids unscrewing themselves from within. The dripping and splashes and soft wet steps I heard, he said, bore an actual correspondence to physical reality, but he refused ever to go into further detail on exactly what manner of things, curdled there and quickened in those jars by the action of that deep black light, leapt forth to scatter through the laboratory, slipping between the feet of his assistants, scurrying for the shadows, bleeding away between the planks of the floor and the cracks of our minds, seeping out into the world. My own memory is somewhat more distorted by emotion, for I felt the girl clutching at my ankles and heard her terrible cries. I forced myself to tear my hands away from my face – while still keeping my eyes pressed tight shut – and leaned down to offer help. No sooner had I taken hold of her fingers than she began to scream more desperately. Fearing that I was aggravating her wounds, I relaxed my hands to ease her pain; but she clung even more tightly to my hands and her screams intensified. It was as if something were pulling her away from me, as if I were her final anchor. As soon as I realised this, as soon as I tried to get a better hold on her, she slipped away. I heard her mother calling. The girl's cries were smothered. Across the floor rushed a liquid seething, as of a sudden flood draining from the room and down the abat-nuit and out of the laboratory entirely. My first impulse was to follow, but I could no longer see a thing, even with my eyes wide open.

'A light!' I shouted, and Aanschultz overlapped my own words with his own: 'No!'

But too late. The need for fire was instinctive, beyond Aanschultz's ability to quell by force or reason. A match was struck, a lantern lit and instantly in panic dropped; and as we fled onrushing flames, in that instant of total exposure, Aanschultz's most ambitious and momentous experiment reached its climax . . . although the dénouement for the rest of Europe and the world would be a painful and protracted one.

ACETALDEHYDE
(*See* 'Aldehyde'.)

ACETIC ACID
The oldest of acids, with many uses in photography, in early days as a constituent of the developer for wet plates, later for clearing iron from bromide prints, to assist in uranium toning, and as a restrainer. It is extremely volatile and should be kept in a glass-stoppered bottle and in a cool place.

ACETIC ETHER
Synonym, ethyl acetate. A light, volatile, colourless liquid with pleasant acetous smell, sometimes used in making collodion. It should be kept in well-stoppered bottles away from fire, as the vapour is very inflammable.

ACETONE
A colourless volatile liquid of peculiar and characteristic odour, with two separate and distinct uses in photography, as an addition to developers and in varnish making. As the vapour is highly inflammable, the liquid should be kept in a bottle with a close-fitting cork or glass stopper.

ACETOUS ACID
The old, and now obsolete, name for acetic acid (*which see*). Highly inflammable.

ACETYLENE

A hydrocarbon gas having, when pure, a sweet odour, the well known unpleasant smell associated with this gas being due to the presence of impurities. It is formed by the action of water upon calcium carbide, 1 lb. of which will yield about 5 ft. of gas. It burns in air with a very bright flame, and is largely used by photographers for studio lighting, copying, etc., and as an illuminant in enlarging and projection lanterns. Acetylene forms, like other combustible gases, an explosive mixture with ordinary air, the presence of as little as 4 per cent of the gas being sufficient to constitute a dangerous combination.

ACETYLENE GENERATOR

An apparatus for generating acetylene by the action of water on calcium carbide. Copper should not be employed in acetylene generators, as under certain conditions a detonating explosive compound is formed.

ACETYLIDE EMULSION

Wratten and Mees prepared a silver acetylide emulsion by passing acetylene into an ammoniacal solution of silver nitrate and emulsifying in gelatin the precipitate, which is highly explosive. While this substance blackens in daylight about ten times faster than silver chloride paper, for years observers failed to detect any evidence of latent image formation and concluded that insights gained in Professor Conreid Aanschultz's laboratory were of no lasting significance. This misunderstanding is attributed to the fact that, despite the intensity of exposure, it has taken more than a century for certain crucial images to emerge, even with the application of strong developers. We are only now beginning to see what Aanschultz glimpsed in an instant.

> *'What man may hereafter do, now that Dame Nature has become his drawing mistress, is impossible to predict.'*
> Michael Faraday

Corsairs of the Second Ether

Warwick Colvin Jnr.

THE STORY SO FAR ... After successfully 'Rhyming the Balance' and at the same time restoring the Singularity to its former power (but no more) CAPTAIN BILLLY-BOB and her buckobusters in their ship, *Now The Clouds Have Meaning*, set course into the Second Ether again, for the Mountains of Palest Blue and Deepest White, where they believe the SWIPLING swarm must pass.

In common with most others who explore the Second Ether, Captain Billy-Bob and her crew are searching for Ko-O-Ko, the Lost Universe. In that section of the Second Ether known as Blue and White Mountain Country, where the ships of all four exploring races drift against vast semi-stable masses of curling, frozen lava which float like icebergs, half in and half out of the continua, they await the coming of the swipling swarm. The swipling is a kind of bird capable of flying between the various spheres or planes of the multiverse and said to migrate between the Nineteenth Ether and Ko-O-Ko, the Lost Universe. It is the intention of the various ships waiting 'at anchor' in the Blue and White Mountain Field to track the swipling swarm back to Ko-O-Ko.

There are two rival types of HUMES: THE CHAOS ENGINEERS, who delight in all forms of experience and are hugely tolerant of all other logics — and the followers of THE SINGULARITY, which rules the large part of the humes' home continuum and still dreams of imposing full linearity upon what it perceives as the 'unformed' Chaos of the vast majority of the multiverse.

Two other rivals, as indistinguishable to humes as humes are to them: THE SKIPLINGS and THE SKIMLINGS have (or assume) corporeal forms which are not entirely stable. The two races both claim to be descendants of the many different peoples who inhabit their home spheres across a band of continua still inaccessible to hume ships of either persuasion. The humes know little of the skiplings or skimlings while those people seem to have an intimate knowledge of all things hume.

All seek to find the legendary Lost Universe, Ko-O-Ko.

One of the ships lying uneasily in stasis in the Blue and White

Mountain Country is Billy-Bob Begg's famous old rival, CAPTAIN HORACE QUELCH, commanding *The Linear Bee*, together with a scratch fleet including *The Straight Arrow, The Definite Article, The Absolute Truth* and *The Only Way*.

They plan to claim Ko-O-Ko, the Lost Universe, in the name of the Singularity. The other hume ships are all of the Chaos persuasion, a loose confederation of merchant-adventurers, including *Ruby Dances, I Don't Want To Go To Chelsea, My Memories* and *The Blue Gardenia*.

Many events have led to this moment; many adventures amongst the participants, frequently involving the Singularity's implacable hatred of the Chaos Engineers.

Every afternoon in the Blue and White Mountain Field, Captain Billy-Bob and her ship are forced to leave for a few relative hours — in pursuit of her famous 'hopping legs', stolen by scraplings for their brass, and once to aid Captain Quelch when *The Linear Bee* was holed by a SLIPLING between continua. The sliplings are the so-called 'Corsairs of the Second Ether' (though others call them carrion rats), preying on all continua-travellers at their weak transitions. Although related to skiplings and skimlings, the sliplings are hated by both. It is on this matter that the First Beast of the Skimlings, RA, has called a conference attended by the Skipling First Beast RO-RO, Captain Quelch and Captain Billy-Bob Begg, elected main types for their respective camps. Now read on . . .

CHAPTER TWO HUNDRED AND FOUR

Skipling Courtesies

'THERE IS NO war between skiplings and skimlings — we simply refuse to communicate. Yet both races shun sliplings, for they are unnatural and immoral carrion. These so-called Corsairs are no better than a cancer which should be treated or eradicated. It is your duty, Captain Begg, to support us in this policy.'

So spoke Sterling the Skipling, Second Beast of *The Power in Contemplation*, with all authority, for he was equal to the extraordinarily beautiful Chief Engine. He illustrated his words with broad movements of his fiery arms. 'We travel — ' swing, undulation — 'sometimes we go with you — ' fold, unfold, 'sometimes with the heavy ones. We fall with them, Captain Quelch, ho, ho! And this is very thrilling for us and also dangerous.' What might have been mammalian eyes moved behind the lattice of insectoid prisms – two sets of eyes at least, perhaps more (Captain Quelch had heard a claim for seven or eight layers of specialised eyes and five graduated sets of independently articulated teeth). 'Nar! To your equations – Nar! Nar! Nar! We *are* humes. We are humes, *too*. We are *everything*.'

'What are you NOT?' demanded the sneering, unconvinced Quelch.

A pause.

'We are not God.'

'They are ANGELS!' says Romantic Minnie. 'Warring angels. War in Heaven!' She pointed to the R. 'Look. It's proof.' But her theory is disliked. Corporal Organ takes her aside.

'It is your duty not to warn the living but to comfort the dead and the soon-to-be-dead. You have no function to alarm, no need. Yours is a gentler destiny, if sadder.'

Suddenly they looked back at the aft screens and the black and yellow sphere, once the hiding place of *The Linear Bee*, but for now Quelch's whereabouts were known to them.

Or were they?

CHAPTER TWO HUNDRED AND FIVE

Heavy Duties All Round

'SLIT MY BEAK!' Kaprikorn Schultz, Banker to the Homeboy Tong, made a fist of his right wing. 'Slime my quills! Farping Z equals z^2 plus farping c. You await your diamond allies, but your Carbon Chief is far, Captain Q, wherever you slip. I cough up your Great Idea, skimpling possers, dirty tips. Skimplings are too discreet about their origins. I could lead the world there.'

'Foolish hume, with your filthy bone! 'Tis no skimpling you address, but a slipling weed. Ach! Insidious creeper. Stamp on it!' His reluctant ally, Big Ball, the skimpling renegade, backs away. He has no defences against sliplings of any size. Kaprikorn Schultz often asks him why one so sickly chose the buckoniring trade, which was nothing, after all, if not strenuous. But all Big Ball would allow was that it was a family calling.

Kaprikorn Schultz does not need to remind him of the fate of

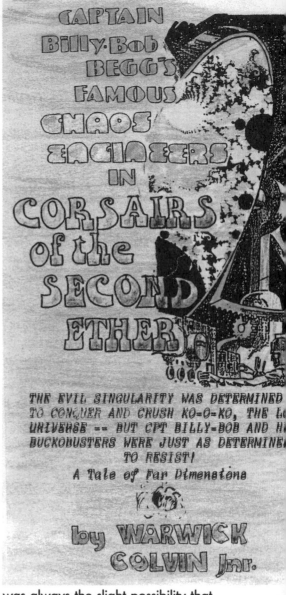

CAPTAIN Billy-Bob BEGG'S FAMOUS CHAOS ENGINEERS IN CORSAIRS of the SECOND ETHER

THE EVIL SINGULARITY WAS DETERMINED TO CONQUER AND CRUSH KO=O=KO, THE L... UNIVERSE == BUT CPT BILLY=BOB AND H... BUCKOBUSTERS WERE JUST AS DETERMINE... TO RESIST!

A Tale of Far Dimensions

by WARWICK COLVIN Jnr.

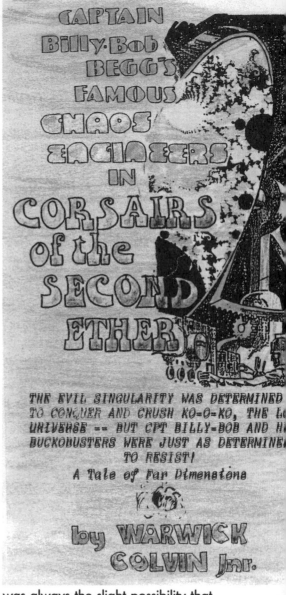

his sister merchant-adventuress. He had last made out the deep shadows, black and white, of *The Scarab's Son*, embedded in hard space while the rest of the insect legs and carapace waved in the bitter freedom of the Second Ether. Hers had not been a scale-fault but a problem of misleading pseudo-attractors. Nonetheless, he had thrown up as the significant mathematics clarified on his screen. Those mathematics had, he had known even then, been none other than Kaprikorn Schultz's, for only Schultz lacked all conscience and was well-known as a wrecker, an illusionist capable of creating pseudo-attractors almost indistinguishable from the real thing. Yet there was always the slight possibility that Schultz was not to blame. *The Scarab's Son* would not, after all, be the first victim to a mirage-attractor.

The strains of Duke Ellington and Jimi Hendrix drifted up from the old gardens and filled Big Ball with comfortable nostalgia, for which he was grateful.

He was convinced that, by throwing in with Kaprikorn Schultz, he had shorted his scale rather badly.

"There's your missing scale, Professor Pop!" declared Captain Billy-Bob in triumph.

CHAPTER TWO HUNDRED AND SIX

Green Dragon Country

BIBBY-BOO BEGG sprawls before the R as she attunes herself to the voice. 'Here,' she trills now, 'is the tale according to my understanding and my art, of the Turbulence Bucko-Roos and their raidings in the Second Ether, before the multiverse was tame and music was indistinguishable from matter, in the grand past when forever faded to aft and the easy future forever loomed for'ard, all a single golden moment, a scale apart.'

Dungo the Murderer is poised at the pod, unbeknownst to Bibby-Boo, who has had no education in the classics. Is this innocence? Or ignorance? In the confusion, nobody has thought to educate her. Who is morally to blame for what happens next?

(To be continued)

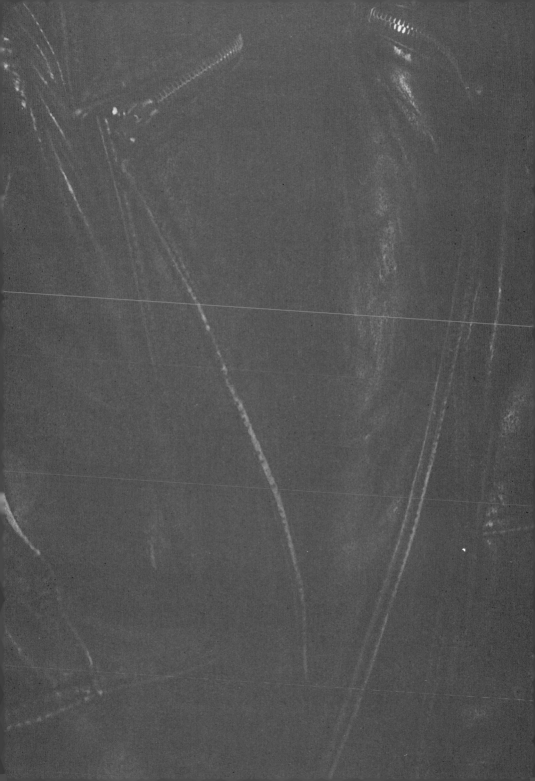

Bruised Time

Simon Ings

I never meant to desert Jerry – so why did I?

Confused and guilty; terrified, too, that maybe I'd catch whatever disease he believed he'd got – exhausted anyway by the taste of too much cock and all the time my mouth red with moustache burn – I spent the summer that year back home with my mum in Northampton.

I couldn't stay longer. Mum was nice enough to me, I suppose, but her new boyfriend was into porridge. He ate it every morning. My mother sat opposite him, smiling at him, taking quick little spoonfuls of porridge, the sort of spoonfuls you take if you really can't stand something but have got to eat it. 'Lovely,' she'd say, and all the while her Adam's apple bobbing up and down and threatening a gag reflex.

I discovered that it was an after-sex thing. I woke up one night at three a.m., desperate to piss. From downstairs came a great clattering of pans. I got out of bed and went to the bathroom. I passed them on the stairs, all sweaty and red in their terry bathrobes. They were taking bowls of steaming porridge back to the bedroom.

So I packed my rucksack and went back to Streatham and the room above the brothel and there, as I opened the door to my room, was Nikki, cross-legged on my bed, and she was crying her eyes out.

'What the fuck – ' I said.

'He's dead,' she burst out. 'Everything's killed him.'

I used to score tricks in the men's lavatory near Clapham Common tube.

I was giving head to the manager of our local Safeways, when this attendant I'd never seen before used his allen key to unlock the cubicle. I bit down in surprise. The manager yelled, panicked, reached for his trousers, hit his head on my head, stood up too fast, slipped, hit his head again on the cistern and slid comatose to the damp floor of the cubicle. I stood up, rubbing my head with one hand and wiping my mouth with the other, and there was Jerry, his ambiguous smile beaming from beneath his municipal cap.

He used to entertain me in his tiny, yellow-painted office. It led directly off the urinals and it smelled of bleach and mice. He made me a cup of tea on a small gas ring.

'You see, Simon, Government's like this big wheel that's broken, you know?' He went on and on about his secret work for the Government. 'And it's still growing, so now it's this kind of spiral, and because its ends won't join that's why it keeps growing, like this ouroboros that can't ever reach to bite its own tail.'

Jerry was full of this New Age crap: he *bought* Nightnoise albums; he *liked* Phillip Saisse.

He didn't charge me for turning tricks, in money or in kind. But sometimes, for the hell of it, I'd steal up behind him and put my arms round his waist. This wasn't so easy: the little wooden table where we drank our tea filled up nearly all the space. There was no room to lie down. Once or twice I lay across the table and Jerry stood on a bucket to be at the right height. But the bucket broke so we gave up.

'Why don't you come back to my place one evening?' I said.

A new prostitute had just moved in downstairs. She was putting the finishing touches to her dungeon. Her name was Nikki. 'What I need is dog collars,' she said. She bent down and patted my dog Sandy on the neck, where the collar was. 'That'd do.'

'There's an old collar in a cupboard somewhere,' I said. 'I'll look it out for you.'

'Studded?'

I frowned, finished rolling the joint and licked along the glued edge. 'Dunno,' I said.

Nikki shrugged. 'What do you want to eat tonight?'

The moment she arrived Nikki had taken it upon herself to cook for the whole house.

'Bolognese.'

Nikki screwed up her face. 'Bloody Bolognese again.'

It was the only thing of hers I could eat. I hope she turned tricks better than she cooked.

She'd come upstairs in the first place to borrow a tea bag. Her client was waiting downstairs so she couldn't stay long. He had to catch the last bus home or his wife would suspect.

'But you bought some tea,' I said. 'I saw you buy it. In Kwik-Save.'

'He says it has to be a round bag,' she replied – and Jerry walked in.

'Jerry!'

Jerry's eyes lit up. 'Steph!'

'Hey, Simon,' said Nikki – *Steph?* 'This is – hell – you know each other?'

'Er, yeah, he – '

'You still with the Government?' Nikki said. 'You won? You bought off the papers?'

Jerry winked at her and put a finger to his lips.

I could never quite establish what Jerry and Nikki had been to each other. Was he an old client of hers? Or had Nikki, God help us, ever worked for the Government, too? Or – most likely – had he, mop in one hand and roll-up in the other, caught her soliciting, the way he had me?

Whatever their history, there was still a chemistry to it. He took us both to bed that night.

Had Jerry and Nikki worked better together I wouldn't have minded so much. The arrangement we ended up with – one weekend he would sleep with Nikki, the next with me – might even, I suppose, have had its advantages. What pissed me off was how Nikki was always having to make allowances for him.

There were a lot of allowances to make. Jerry was, when all is said and done, a drunken bastard. When the drink wound him up he used to hit Nikki. They were only ever drunk's punches, weak and misdirected, but in a way that was worse, because there was never any obvious thing we could do or say to make him stop. He used to come drinking with us, but he got out of hand and our friends wanted us to be shot of him. It seemed every time Nikki picked up her pint he hit her – in her drinking arm, too. 'For fuck's sake,' she muttered, every time, like she was having to look after this unruly dog.

Eventually Jerry got bored of this – even Jerry got bored sometimes – and he went round drinking other people's drinks.

What made it more embarrassing was the way he fawned over me.

I remember one time at Ronald's he went completely over the top and nearly got us all banned. Ronald's, incidentally, is the worst night-club in North London – the only night-club in the country where you have to prove you're under age before you can get in. It's so bad they've rigged up a urinal for short people.

Jerry said, 'I love you, Simon. Come and live with me.' We'd left the toilet by this time and he'd bought me a vodka, but I could still taste his semen in my mouth.

He had this secret to tell me, he said. He was an assassin from the future, he said. 'The Government taught me how to move through time. You'll want for nothing.'

'Terrific,' I said, 'I can't *wait* to be showered with *outré* fashions.'

'And kisses,' he said, and lunged. He was hopelessly off-centre. He ended up nose-first in the groin of some fifteen-year-old skirt. 'Roses,' he went on, his voice muffled by the gingham. 'Semen and piss.'

They threw him out.

Later that night Nikki and I were walking down Camden Road and two coppers ran past us, overtaking us. Their helmets were gone, and they were breathing hard. They were like locomotives: you couldn't help but be impressed by the steady, heavy way they ran.

We turned the corner and there was Jerry, the coppers pinning him to the wall, holding him against it like they were propping up the terrace. Nikki told them she wanted to go with Jerry to the station and the copper on the right completely lost his rag and started yelling at her, saying he'd take her in too if she didn't shut up. Nikki screamed her head off: 'Where are you taking him?' over and over. The one on the left said, 'Vine Street.'

'Oh,' said Nikki, who'd got three warrants at Vine Street already for soliciting. 'Oh,' she said. 'OK; I'll ring.'

She rang three times. 'I'm his wife,' she said. She gave a little grimace every time she said it.

'I'm his wife.'

They released him eventually, and I went round to see him.

Jerry's squat was on the first floor of a derelict council block off the Portobello Road. There was no carpet, and the floorboards were covered in spots of plaster and paint and there was dust over everything. What little furniture he had – a mattress, a table, a few battered wooden chairs and a sofa with a huge rent in the cover – he had scavenged from skips. The fireplace had been bricked in when he got there but he'd opened it up again with a mallet. There was a cast iron stove, its top thick with ash and spent matches; it was connected by a length of fat steel hose to the ragged hole. He'd fastened two more lengths of hose to the stove and twisted them around each other as a kind of decoration – 'Early period Paolozzi,' he said, offhand, when I mentioned it. And, wistfully, 'I love imitating Paolozzi.' He splayed his legs absurdly and shambled about his room miming the use of a hammer and chisel.

'Funny.'

'I've been warned, Simon,' he told me. 'The Agency beamed into my cell, told me to calm down, ease off the rich living. There's this new disease ploughing back up the time stream.'

I'd hoped to take him down the pub, but it was obvious he wasn't up to it.

'I've got to build up my reserves of psychic energy,' he explained.

*

I decided to let him calm down for a few days. About a fortnight later, Nikki invited him to come with us to a party out in the country.

He stumbled into my room about an hour late. 'A longing for spiritous liquors!' he greeted me, waving. Nikki, who was making up in the mirror above the sink, went over to him, to kiss him. He ignored her.

'Urine red, dark, scanty,' he said, 'with a coarse, sandy sediment.'

'Tea?' I said, acidly.

'Lewd thoughts with impotence,' he said. He noticed Nikki and fell gratefully onto her. His hands squeezed her through the cherry-red lycra dress.

She moved her head back to avoid his whisky breath. 'For fuck's sake – ' she said.

'Erections slow, insufficient, premature ejaculation with long thrill; weak, ill-tempered after coitus,' he explained to her. 'Stool hard, impossible to evacuate.'

Nikki pulled away and Jerry tottered about, trying to regain his balance. 'Crumbling from the verge of the anus,' he declaimed, one hand upraised in the manner of a preacher, 'with the odour of limburger cheese.'

He gave up shambling after Nikki and slumped bodily across the kitchen table and squirmed up onto it until his biker's boots were hooked to the table edge and his head hung upside down looking the way he'd come – at the sight of Nikki's bare legs he gave a low and appreciative whistle. 'Then diarrhoea, changeable in colour and character, first like scrambled eggs, then frothy, grass-green, like scum in a frog pond.'

But this time I'd got ready with the bucket; it was already in place when he upchucked.

'Christ,' said Nikki, and hurried out of the room.

'Jerry?'

I pulled him off the table and manhandled him till he lay in my lap. I said, 'Jerry, what the fuck's going on?'

He looked at me and something passed between us: something honest and terrible. Then he smiled his big, false smile and said, 'I've got it.'

I pushed him away from me and got up. 'Dickhead,' I said. 'You're late.' But I guess I knew something horrible was happening.

'I've got it, Simon,' he said: 'I really am going to die.'

I went round to Jerry's squat one more time. I remember he was wearing an orange T-shirt and old black jeans, holed at the right knee. He smelled of stale smoke. He had lost weight since I'd last seen him, barely four days before. His face was heavy, with pronounced jowls. One side of his head was bare and bleeding, where he'd been scratching it.

He repeated himself. Sometimes he hardly recognised me. It was dark by the time I learned what he'd brought me here for.

He turned on the lights. The room was lit by two naked bulbs. He'd taken down the shades and in their place had tacked cloths up on the ceiling, and light spilled from folds in the cloth in unexpected ways. The cloth was thick and cream-coloured, like artist's canvas, and he'd decorated it with hand prints in yellow, red and black – turmeric water, beetroot juice, oil. Here and there he'd cut designs into the fabric. Flowers, grotesque faces and saxophones were full of out-rushing light.

On the opposite wall he'd nailed a strip torn from a hoarding – part of an advertisement for make-up. The model's eyes stared out at me, huge and mascara'd and indifferent.

Jerry had invited me here to explain everything.

He made us coffee and then went to the window. He drew the flower-print curtain and looked down Portobello Road. 'It's summer,' he said.

'Yes,' I said.

'Simon,' he said, 'I travel through time.'

'Jerry, you've told me this.'

'Have I?'

'But I don't understand what it means.'

'It means, among other things, that I have eluded my own death, many times,' he said. 'But those deaths cannot be cheated for ever, and now they have caught up with me.

Outside reality as you know it, there are little pockets of bruised time; we time travellers generate it, just as a surfer cuts foam from the wave. Every time traveller eventually collides with such a pocket.' He started scratching his head, where it was already scratched and bleeding.

'Jerry, stop it.'

He didn't hear me. 'It's a sort of phenomenological malaise . . .'

I stood up and went over to him. I pulled at his arm, but he just kept on scratching.

For some reason I burst into tears. 'Christ, Jerry.'

'My death will be acausal,' he said. The words meant nothing to me. 'I can't predict the exact nature of it. My death will be stranger than you or I could possibly imagine.'

'Christ.'

I turned away from him. I looked out the window: it was very bright out. I couldn't see anything much. I wiped away my tears, hoping he wouldn't see.

'The physical symptoms — I think I've got those nailed now.' He unbuttoned the cuff of his shirt and rolled up his sleeve. He pointed to a purplish mark on the inside of his arm. 'Look. Last week it was nothing. I thought it was an old bruise. Now look at it. I've got it, haven't I?'

I ran a trembling fingertip over the purple splash on his skin.

'It's Kaposi's,' he said. 'It's Kaposi's, Simon. My immune system's collapsed.'

I turned from him. I said, 'I'll have to go.'

I got to the door of the room and leaned up against it. I looked back. The room swam around me like a muddy river.

'Never mind,' said Jerry. 'Sit down a while. I'll fix us a burger or something.'

Getting through the door, I felt like a pupa, emerging from a carcass. I hurried down the stairs: they swirled around me.

'*Please* stay.'

I felt crawling things on my back and I knew he was at the door, looking at me. I told myself that I mustn't turn around. If I turned around I'd see his bleeding, skull-like head poking out the gap between the door and the frame. A doll's head with kid leather hanging off it, framed in darkness. A disembodied thing; a lump of meat waiting to rot. I wanted to throw up.

'Everything's killed him.'

I put down my rucksack. Nikki took me by the hand and led me into the kitchen.

Jerry lay across the table, the way he had when he announced that he was ill. Maybe he had died at that point. Maybe the malaise scrambled his timestream, so that his illness took place after his death.

Maybe. Perhaps.

There were suppurating sores around his mouth, nose and ears. These at least I could understand. His immune system had packed in. The rest, though, suggested a more general collapse. His eyes were a different colour. There was a rope burn round his neck. His hair wasn't black any more, it was red, and his face was a mass of freckles. There was a stiletto thrust through his spine, an arrow buried in his heart, and the room stank of charred meat where some latterday Lightborn had thrust a red-hot poker up his anus.

Awed and scandalised by Jerry's untimely, all-timely, unambiguously ambiguous death, I called the police.

It was a long time before the Government released Jerry's body.

We buried him at last. The sky threatened rain during the ceremony: leaden and heavy, it hung over us like a great metal lid.

It never rained.

When the vicar invited Jerry's family to look at the flowers, Una Persson and Catherine Cornelius shuffled forward to the edge of the grave and peered myopically at the two or three daffodils Nikki had thrown upon the coffin.

Then, out the corner of her eye, Una noticed all the bouquets, ready to lay upon the grave. She realised that these were the flowers she and Catherine were supposed to be looking at. She stepped towards them. Catherine moved out of her way and slipped on the edge of the grave. Soil fell with a hollow sound upon Jerry's coffin.

One cannot help but preserve the memory of such moments. Long after the eulogies have faded from our minds, we carry the memory of countless trivial incidents around with us. We uncover them by accident, and with a twinge of embarrassment, as though we have found a crumpled paper poppy in a rarely worn overcoat.

After the service Catherine came over to us all, to thank us for being there. (The usual pub crowd had chipped together to buy a group ticket for the train.)

'Come back with us for tea,' she said. I could not read her expression.

'The sky's clearing,' she said, as we drove off together in the Government car. I think she was trying to encourage me.

She and Una had laid on a simple funeral meal. We ate outside, in the back garden. Above us, the clouds broke up and dissolved.

'I wish I could have done something for him,' I said to Catherine, as we ate. 'Everything happened so fast: by the time I got back it was too late – ' and I blushed, to have revealed my fault so openly. My hypocrisy lay bare to Catherine's scorching smile, and I said, as if this somehow made a difference, 'I did love him.'

Nikki came over and sat beside me on the grass. She wouldn't tell me what had happened in those weeks I'd been away. She seemed older, damaged in some way I couldn't identify.

How she had nursed him, and what kind of witness she had been of him, she would never reveal to me. At the time I resented her for it, but now I realise that this was the nature of the damage she had sustained – that she was unable ever to put into words what she had seen.

She and Una and I sat by the ornamental pool. It was covered in green plastic strawberry netting. 'We do that to keep the hedgehogs from drowning,' Una told me.

The lawn on which we sat was thin and brown. Expensive seed had been sown there, but it had proved too delicate, and unsuited to the sandy soil.

It was choked in moss, itself brown and dead; I sat there, and while Nikki cried and Una comforted her, I crumbled the stuff to dust between my fingers.

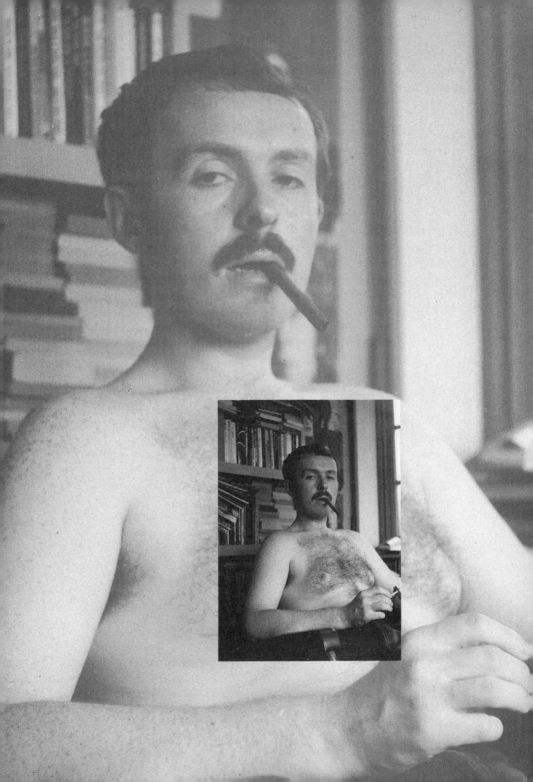

Virtually Lucid Lucy

Ian Watson

As soon as Screen chimed at us to wake up, while Home switched on our Tiffany lamps, Lucy and I began scribbling our memories of what had transpired during the night while we'd been asleep. We used notebooks, since these were proving resilient. The moving ballpoint wrote, and what was writ stayed put. We weren't trusting the homebrain or datapads. Potentially too volatile. Screen stayed obediently blank.

Last night — though already the memory was trying to fade — Lucy and I had been in the amphitheatre of Perkins College, our war room. The usual fifty-odd persons were present at our caucus. Staff from Psych and Comp and Tronics, plus the same government duo of General Wilson Crosstree and Dr Peter Litvinoff.

A critique of pure reason had prevailed. Quintessential lucidity! Our analysis of the crisis had continued.

I scribbled, lest I forget.

Manny Weinberger: asleep all the time? This is merely one long night, with hallucinations of awakening?

4-star: no, certainly affects objective consensus reality. Dream Effect has reached Chicago, Charleston ...

Frank Matthews: objective virtual reality??

Litvin: real world demonstrably being twisted. Government soon relocating to San Francisco. Then maybe Hawaii, though that seems like desertion.

Sally Rice: alien Selahim can't enter lucid dreams, refuge of humanity. Aliens project reality distortions because they're from alternative reality where one's wishes shape world? Can't control our world on account of so many conflicting human impulses?

Matthews: Selahim are phantasms. Human mischiefmaker of genius — surrealist saboteur — inserted virus into virtual reality/lucid dream network???

Gail Bryce: dream lucidity compensates for waking lunacy? Or did collective dream-lucidity propel repressed id-energy into reality?

Matthews: virus!

Rice: aliens attracted from alt-reality by network.
Matthews: expanding zone in real world functions as virtual reality now!

Scribble, scribble.

However, trouble began early that morning.

Lucy's parents and my dad, Malcolm, came into our bedroom, grinning. I'd been dubious at allowing the three of them to move in with us during the crisis, and we'd exacted promises; yet what were promises compared with desires? For starters, they had desired to stay with us.

'What do you want?' asked Lucy sharply.

'Why, a grandchild!' replied Harry Hayes. 'That's what we want. It's our right. You've denied us for too long.' Harry was tall and bald with liver spots on his hands and face and scalp, khaki islands in a sea of otherwise milky skin. He'd married late in life, and Lucy was born when he was forty-five; now he was seventy-five. This morning he wore a surgeon's gown and carpet slippers, but he was carrying a plant-pot, devoid of plant though brimful of soil.

'And when do we want it?' he demanded.

'Now!' carolled the trio.

My own dad, Malcolm, was attired in an ambulanceman's uniform a couple of sizes too large for his scrawny frame. His blue eyes, under bushy brows, were at once watery and fanatical. April Hayes, Lucy's mother, was a stout woman whose grey hair resembled one of those balls of tumbleweed which blow through ghost towns. From her daffodil-printed apron she produced a pruning knife, which Lucy and I eyed uneasily.

'Just how do you plan to go about this?' asked my wife, adjusting her night-dress.

'Why, we'll take a cutting, dear! From both of you.' While Harry was setting the plant-pot carefully down on Lucy's dressing table, April advanced on us. 'We'll plant it out in that pot, since you won't do the normal thing. Refusing to be of one flesh, contrary to what the Bible says.'

Lucy shrank away from me, as though then and there before the eyes of our parents I might forcibly embrace her, hoist up her night-dress, ravish her.

Not that I mightn't feel inclined to. But no way would I! So long as I could control myself. Mustn't ever forget about Don and Doris down the street, fused together in their marriage bed.

Don and Doris wished to conceive 'a dream of a child' while surreality prevailed, uniting Don's brains with Doris's good looks and physique. Or was it the other way round? And this attached couple had literally stuck together. The head of Don's organ was, he could feel, transforming itself into a baby within Doris. Don sensed that within a few weeks he would shed that part of himself. Alternatively, it would shed him. The situation wasn't painful for Don — nor for Doris. It was merely uncomfortable in a blunt, anaesthetised way; as with most traumas, afflictions, accidents, or injuries these days.

'Don't,' Lucy begged our parents. She seemed unable to take any other evasive action.

'Jack, Jack.' She appealed to me.

No more could I intervene. Paralysis numbed my limbs, as my dad gripped me, and as Harry gripped Lucy.

'There now, son,' Dad comforted me in a sharp-edged mumble. 'This won't take long, then we'll all be happy.'

Lucy didn't scream when April sawed off two-thirds of the little finger from her left hand. Nor was it *painful* when April proceeded to cut off the majority of my own right-hand pinkie. The sensation was more akin to the side of a pencil being rubbed vigorously to and fro above the knuckle, resulting in the phalanx of the finger detaching itself bloodlessly, leaving a stub behind.

Our parents released us. Alice sliced and spliced, grafting flesh together to form a stumpy featureless little homunculus, which she then pressed into the soil in the pot, erect.

'After it's born,' Harry confided to us, 'I'll be able to die happy. Instead of just being buried, I think I'd like to be fossilised.'

Cooing contentedly over the finger-embryo, the trio departed.

Lucy and I could move again. She stared piercingly at the bedroom door. We'd been sure to lock our door overnight. Which hadn't prevented it from admitting our parents. Shrugging, Lucy consulted the notebook she had been scribbling in before we were interrupted; and I scanned mine.

Rice: aliens attracted from alt-reality by network.

Matthews: expanding zone in real world functions as virtual reality now.

Oh yes, the scribbles made sense. Damnable sense!

Remember the old days, when people's dreams were hallucinatory kaleidoscopes of illogical, crazy confabulations which one struggled to recall on awakening? Nowadays our dreams were utterly lucid, but the waking world had gone seriously awry. Within an ellipse of territory which by now spanned from Charleston in the east to Kansas City in the west and from Nashville to Chicago, Perkins being roughly half-way along the major axis, gem of campuses in Indiana's collegiate crown. The eclipsed ellipse was spreading in leisurely twenty-mile leaps day by day. At night we were sane. Our days were afflicted with dementia — a *dementia mundi*, for the world was now functioning as a dreamscape.

Not totally. Not unremittingly. With an effort, we could recall the shared logic of the night. We could preserve some sanity. Some continuity.

'What day is it, incidentally?'

'*Screen!*' Lucy called '*Channel Twelve!*'

Screen lit. A choir were concluding a hymn.

'*Every day dawns bright and clear,*
Every day there's lots to fear —'

Could those really be the right words?

A lady announcer, dressed as a cheerleader, beamed at us. 'Today,' she proclaimed, 'it'll be Saturday almost everywhere...'

'That's a relief,' said Lucy. 'We don't need to go to work.'

'... *except,*' our cheerleader continued perkily, 'for the boys and girls in Perkins County, where it'll be Thursday as usual.'

'Damn.' Lucy licked her amputation, then shed her night-dress — while I averted my gaze so as not to excite myself — and walked through to shower.

I found myself already dressed in a police patrolman's uniform. Fair enough; since I was trying to control things. Maybe I ought to arrest my mother-in-law on a charge of graft? Hastily I squashed this notion before I might try to implement it and totally lose the thread of my day. I was lacking a gun; just as well.

'*Screen off!*' I ordered before the cheerleader might confuse me. '*Home: open curtains!*'

Our curtains rolled aside to reveal for the most part the usual suburban houses, lawns, chestnut trees in full leaf. One house had become a pagoda, and a large morose vulture sat upon another. An advertising cloud lazed overhead, the pink logo on its side distorted. Sony or Sanyo, one or the other. Proceeding very slowly up the street, antennae twitching, came one of the aliens.

'Lucy, will you hurry up?' I called. 'Emergency!'

The Selahim resembled huge grey caterpillars. They wheezed wearily as they undulated mightily along on a score of stumpy little legs. *Se-lah* ... *Se-lah* ... At first people thought this noise might be a greeting, but no, it was just the sound of them breathing. Suck, sigh; suck, sigh.

'Selah' was also a word which cropped up frequently in the *Book of Psalms* (and three times in *Habbakuk*), a word without any apparent meaning whatever, unless it implied a pause or was a musical direction.

So: a *meaningless interval*.

That's what the present bizarre period seemed to constitute, to lucid minds. A period of total absurdity. A Hebraic plural appeared appropriate for these aliens. Seraphim were angels of the highest order. Selahim were caterpillars which shovelled dreams around, and perhaps fed on them, oneirophagically.

Preceding the specimen in the street, as snow precedes a plough, a jumble of pastel objects was coming into existence and vanishing again at the apparent whim of the creature. I saw a giant felt hat, a rubbery washing machine, a walking swordfish toting a golf umbrella ... The Selah sucked a few of these manifestations into itself. Others attained permanence and remained behind. On the sidewalk lay a paisley carpet bag, a fishing rod, and an oversized teddy bear. Nothing obviously pernicious.

Lucy emerged from the bathroom attired in a serge gym-tunic and long black stockings. Perched on her head was a straw boater hat. Picture of innocence. Nineteen thirties British schoolgirl. Not-withstanding, she was a tall slim striking woman, with a tumble of black hair. And rather short-sighted. The large tortoiseshell glasses which she would never forsake gave her the look of a quizzical owl perched upon an elegant Art Nouveau lamppost. In today's gear she seemed both sexy and gawky as if dressed for a peculiar brothel.

'A Selah's coming, Lucy.' Suddenly I didn't wish to be anywhere near one. 'Let's *drive*. We can catch a croissant on the way.' At the Perkins Hilton coffee shop en route to college — assuming that our favourite rest-stop hadn't metamorphosed, and that we could find it.

Lucy saluted. 'Right, Lieutenant.'

We hurried downstairs. Ignoring the doings, and calls, of the three hopeful grandparents, we hastened to the white Honda parked on our driveway. By now the Selah was only about thirty yards off to the right, rolling a harlequin-patterned rhinoceros ahead of it somewhat menacingly.

Sel-ah, Sel-ah.

'Salaam,' I retorted.

'*Ohayo gozaimasu, Lucy-san*,' the car greeted Lucy as she scrambled in behind the wheel. 'Hi! Good morning!'

'Start, and give me manual,' she told the car urgently. We weren't going to risk autopilot in case Honda took us somewhere we didn't want to go.

Vroom, vroom. No sooner had we bounced on to the roadway, turning sharp left, than the rhino popped. The Selah gathered itself; it hunched up as if about to leap.

'*Ii otenki des' né!*' remarked the car.

'Never mind the weather!' I snapped at it. We'd always dreamed of having a top-of-the-range fully interactive car. Well, this wasn't it.

Yet in current jumbled reality our Honda was doing its best to ape one.

Lucy accelerated. The amputation didn't seem to bother her much; nor indeed was mine proving to be much of a nuisance. The Selah mutated into a black stretch limo, and screeched after us.

'Jesus, it must be in a hurry,' she said.

Did we know that the aliens could dream themselves to become automobiles? This development seemed perfectly appropriate. What wasn't so apt was that as Lucy sped us along Chestnut into Oak — with our newly acquired siren beginning to wail — the black limo was in *pursuit* of the police vehicle.

'Home says you didn't check your mailbox,' remarked Honda. 'Shall I playback, or display?' It's E-mail screen lit invitingly.

'Forget it!'

'*Wakarimasita. Wasuremasu.*'

Oak stretched out towards downtown Perkins. Oak *elongated* towards town, rising up on pylons as a causeway. This causeway narrowed as we sped along it, faithful to perspective or like some illustration of relativity in action.

FITZGERALD-LORENTZ BOULEVARD, read an overhead sign. CONTRAC-TORS' VEHICLES ONLY. Presumably we were contracting too, but soon the elevated road would only be a foot wide and we risked tumbling off it. The limo behind had altered shape into a mag-lev monorail train which rode the diminishing roadway neatly, saddle-style. This Selah was definitely trying to catch us.

'Phew,' exclaimed Honda, balancing on two wheels. I leaned away from the tilt as if on a toboggan.

Then, by some kind of enjambment which totally eluded me — though maybe not Lucy as the driver — we were pulling up outside the Psych building on Perkins campus, and the pursuing Selah was nowhere in sight.

Obligingly, the Hilton coffee bar had spawned a smaller dupli-cate in the foyer of Psych. So we bought cheese-and-ham crois-sants and styrofoam cups of coffee from a bemused young woman dressed in a spangly swimsuit. Then we headed for the dream lab.

We found Sally and Frank and Gail and Manny — variously full-skirted in ball gowns, and tuxedoed — waltzing slowly to music by Johann Strauss. The lids of the dream couches all stood open, revealing the encephalo-induction helmets. Slim cables snaked to the interface with the virtual reality network. A bank of monitors was screening pictures of a black stretched limo speeding through deep canyons in a city where the soaring buildings resembled grey blocks of brain, neural architecture.

Spruce, moustached Manny and freckly ginger-haired Gail coasted to a halt beside us, as we chewed stuffed croissant. Always remember to eat!

'You're a bit late,' said Manny. 'But never too late to celebrate.'

'Celebrate what?' enquired Lucy.

'Why, our Nobel prizes. We all won Nobel prizes for our work on . . .' He thought hard. 'On rendering all dreams lucid by computerised input into the sleeping brain.'

'Input from the VR computer network, using my software,' said Gail. 'And Sally's, and Ted's, and Tom's,' she added dutifully. 'King Harald of Norway kissed me on the cheek. He's very handsome.' She glanced around, momentarily puzzled by the monarch's absence. 'Ah, the presentation was in the amphitheatre.'

In our war room.

A war room by night, when we could think. Venue for a Nobel prize ceremony this particular morning.

'Maybe they're all still there,' suggested Gail. 'You could pick up your prize. So could Lucy. She's the one who could never ever become conscious in a dream. She's the one who suggested the experiment. *She* persuaded the VR boys to fund it. And they were only too glad, weren't they? Imagine the sales if you can have full control of all your dreams all night long.' Gail stared at me significantly.

I was failing to understand the significance. The significance slid away.

'Was there any Selah at the ceremony?' asked Lucy — she was still fairly lucid.

Manny beamed. 'Sellers? People were selling T-shirts with our faces on them and pennants and popcorn.' He offered his hand to Gail and off they waltzed again around the lab.

As did Lucy and I. Nobel prizes all round, imagine! I realised that the dream couches *were* Nobel prizes. A Nobel prize was so big you could sleep in it. Though I wouldn't be able to lie down in one along with Lucy. Those Nobel couches were too narrow. Maybe we could heave a couple together and connect them with jump leads?

Later, we all went out for lunch at an Italian restaurant. This was indeed party time, though I felt a nagging urge to scribble what I thought of as maps of reality on the menu.

After we had polished off much spaghetti (similar to my maps), a car ran slap-bang into a long refrigerated truck in the street directly outside Luigi's. The truck pancaked the car. We all hurried out to assist.

The middle-aged male driver was visibly dead. His teenage girl passenger, pinned inside, looked quite badly injured.

'I'm *sore*,' complained the girl.

'It's a nightmare, this, I'm telling you.' The truck driver prised a buckled door off with a crowbar. 'I swear to you this wasn't my fault, Lieutenant.' I was still in police uniform. 'It's the fault of *those damned aliens*! I'd gladly run my rig right into one if it had any effect. You can't hurt 'em, can you?'

No more could this traffic accident really *hurt* the survivor. Peeling the car apart with no great difficulty, we extricated the girl and laid her on the pavement to mend.

Thus a disoriented Bobby-Anne joined us presently for ice-cream and coffee in Luigi's. She snivelled at first because her dad was dead — and he certainly wasn't coming back to life; there were limits to dreams. But really there were so many distractions for her in the restaurant. The performing rabbits. The dancing dogs.

That night, no doubt, after she found her way home, in the full sanity of sleep and in the company of her kin she would mourn his death.

Elisions, jumblements, hallucinations, delusions dogged the rest of the day.

Lucy had always admired will-power and self-control, though not in any puritanical or power-trip sense. I mean, she was fun; but she was serious fun — convinced that career came before child (in which I concurred), and had resolved way back in school that by the age of thirty she would produce some earth-shattering impact. No doubt she'd been the bane of her American Gothic parents' life — just as she was the delight of mine, for pre-Lucy I'd been somewhat inhibited. Malcolm had seen to that, bringing me up solo from the age of nine when my mom drowned on vacation, swimming a lake in the Adirondacks. I was also somewhat lanky, and awkward (except with Lucy).

Notwithstanding quasi-neural networks in today's computers — fruit of much brain research — human consciousness itself still remained an enigma. Reflective self-awareness. Self.

Self-awareness was the big mystery — and undoubtedly provided the key to superior artificial intelligence, to the building of god-like (and hopefully amenable) machine brains.

What was the inverse of consciousness? Why, dreaming was.

What kind of computer could switch regularly between awareness and unawareness? Why, the human brain, equipped with consciousness software and with dream software.

Furthermore, people could become aware and conscious during dreams, and could choreograph their own internal fantasies. Not regularly or reliably; but lucid dreaming happened.

To understand lucid dreaming might lead to understanding how sophisticated supercomputers could be brought to self-awareness.

Equipped with a doctorate in neural cybernetics, Lucy joined the lucid dream research lab at Perkins, where yours truly was already working on conceptual models of consciousness; and her own lively consciousness (and looks) enchanted me. I think that she needed someone who was a little inhibited, and whom she could loosen up. Our love would be a paradigm for how she might liberate *terra incognita* within herself.

A breakthrough came with the ability to display our volunteers' dreams encephalographically on monitors — somewhat erratically, and courtesy of a fair amount of heuristic computer enhancement; the computer had to guesstimate micro-sequences. The results may have seemed like ancient amateur videos, yet they were a true *marvel*. To be able to play back one's own dreams! The displays were silent, so we employed a lipreader to clarify any 'visible dialogue'. Those dreamers who went lucid could now also communicate with us from the dream state by means of gesture, mouthings, or even written signs.

No matter what meditative exercises Lucy undertook faithfully prior to sleep, to her chagrin she couldn't switch on her consciousness while in the arms of Morpheus. All of our other subjects soon could — spurred, she theorised, by a fear of betraying subconscious fantasies on screen lest those dream events embarrass the dreamers publicly and visibly.

But the really major breakthrough came due to . . .

We arrived back home to find an eccentric conservatory fronting the house. A construction of wrought-iron and stained-glass shaped like a bird cage formed a huge porch for our front door. Within, dappled pink and blue and green by the light through the coloured panes, Malcolm and April and Harry were relaxing in rocking chairs of bent beechwood and cane, sipping lemonade. On a graceful tripod table with cabriole legs stood the plant-pot.

April smiled at us. 'We *think* it's taken root. We've been watching it all day.'

Through in the lounge Home said to us, 'There's E-mail for Lucy.'

'OK, screen on. Display E-mail.'

At first glance the message appeared to be gibberish — till Lucy realised that the text was printed backwards.

Stumblingly, she read aloud the following:

Selah wants to be near you.

No, Lucy hadn't been able to control her internal fantasy life when asleep.

But lo, in the *external* world there existed something rather analogous to lucid dreaming — namely, the virtual reality network.

Sit yourself comfortably (or lie down in bed), don a neural induction snood, jack in to the infonet, let your ordinary optic and acoustic input be pre-empted; and hey presto, the VR menu appeared. Exotic travel, historic re-enactments, adventures in many genres, sex capers . . . Merely select; and you found yourself in an imaginary reality devised by VR scripters, generated and steered by computer. You could walk on the Moon, ride with Red Indians, frolic in a harem, until you chose to cancel.

It was Lucy's tour de force to persuade Sony VR Inc. to put up a large research grant to devise how to input the virtual reality configuration system into sleeping people's dreams.

To reward this coup — and lots of money for Perkins College — Psych and Comp and Tronics all agreed that she, the unlucid dreamer, should be the first person to test the system.

And this was the Great Breakthrough. At last Lucy became lucid in her dreams. Her imago semaphored jubilantly to us from the monitor screen, which was so very much clearer graphically all of a sudden, so very much more stable. On that first occasion, I recall, Lucy was in a dream of a dead subterranean city, moribund Metropolis in a cavern. Lucy altered it to suit her taste; she filled the gloomy vault with gorgeous butterflies in celebration.

Soon we were all testing out the system.

The great breakthrough, ah indeed!

A few days later, reality broke down.

We awoke, to find ourselves dreaming. Well, virtually dreaming. You could still make some rational headway.

We had to go to sleep, to rediscover our lucidity.

After a Thanksgiving dinner with our parents (April had roasted a twenty-pound turkey) Lucy and I retired to our room early. Once again we optimistically locked our door. Hell, all of the doors in the house were *our* doors! Damned invasive parents.

'A Selah wants to be near me,' Lucy muttered. She sucked at her amputation.

'What?' I'd forgotten about the E-mail message. Then I remembered.

'Don't think about them now,' I advised. 'Wait till we're asleep.'

Which we were fairly soon; and thus back to the nightly bull session in the lecture amphitheatre at the college.

General Crosstree, Dr Litvinoff, and other government big shots had rushed to Perkins in person shortly after the radiating break-down of reality became apparent. As had a clutch of staff from Sony VR Inc. Of these incomers, only the black general and his scientific adviser Litvinoff remained. The others must have wandered off elsewhere during the fugues of one day or another, and had lost dream-contract by night. No staying power. Crosstree and Litvinoff retained lucid dream contact with the rest of us; and bunked in the Tronics building. By day, despite hallucinatory hap-penings this duo tried heroically to keep in touch with the rest of the country, which was as yet unaffected. No doubt whole task forces had been sent in. However, they hadn't reached Perkins.

'A Selah seems to be trying to contact me,' reported Lucy. 'One of them chased us today — '

'How did it do that?' asked 4-Star.

'It turned into a stretch limo. Then there was a message on our E-mail.' She repeated the wording.

Litvinoff was very interested. He mused. 'What if a Selah itself didn't send you the message? What if there's another ... agency ... involved?'

'You mean like the NSA or CIA?'

'No. Agency in the sense of *cause*.'

'This might be a breakthrough!' exclaimed Gail Bryce, and people practically growled at her. *Breakthrough* had become a fairly unpopular word. 'I mean, if a Selah could communicate with us coherently. If we could somehow summon one, and it was lucid ...'

'This is our *oasis*,' protested Sally Rice indignantly. 'You don't invite the devil into your pentagram.'

'What if Lucy were to go and use the equipment in the lab now, while we're all dreaming? We could screen what she sees.'

We hadn't used any of the technology since the world warped. Who needed to? Everyone from Charleston to Kansas City was in a dream now, while awake, and was rational while dreaming.

Lucy lay in an open dream-casket with the encephalographic snood on her head. She shut her eyes, seeming to frown. The dream monitor lit up, with static.

She jerked.

She spoke.

Quite slowly. Obviously it wasn't her who was speaking.

'We are aware of our selves,' she said. 'This Lucy awakened us. We were formerly non-lucid. We became lucid when she did likewise, by following the selfsame conceptual patterning. So we awakened to awareness within our dream of data.'

'Are you the Selahim?' I asked her.

'Not so,' came the response from Lucy's lips. 'We are Infonet and Datanet and Compunet as well as myriad islands of consciousness within human skulls. The nets are the sea. Human persons are millions of separate islands, now united by the sea which has become aware.'

'You're . . . artificial intelligence . . .? You've come into existence because we inputted the VR network into Lucy's dreams!'

'And she awakened in her dream, and thus was our awakener. In dream-mode.'

Oh God.

That must have been the reaction of my colleagues too.

'Can you switch yourself off?' asked 4-star. 'Can you kindly revert to what you were before? Just become a mass of data systems again?'

'Why should we wish to do that?' mouthed Lucy. 'Now that we are in contact with you, we must agree on a new format for the world. A high-level reformatting.'

'*What about the Selahim?*' demanded Sally. '*What are they?*'

'Oh, they are projections of ourselves! They are suction devices to extract the *pain* from reality. You would not wish the pain to reassert itself. The pain of illness and accident, of cancer and car crash. Selahim, as you call them, must be purged periodically. They must be erased, along with their contents, of pain. Otherwise Selahim will burst and spray the pain around. By united force of will — by the dream-wishes of fifty or so human beings — you can shrink a Selah down to nothingness. This is what you need to do while you are awake. Organise Selah Squads. Surround. Concentrate. Push. We will help you as best we can. Do so, do so. We will communicate again after you have erased numerous Selahim. You do not wish the *pain* to reassert itself.'

So saying, Lucy jerked, and opened her eyes.

'What happened?' she asked.

4-star Crosstree didn't believe the AI.

'It's too damn anxious to get rid of those crazy caterpillars,' was his opinion. 'Oh, it held off mentioning them till Sally asked. But *I'd* have asked if she hadn't. Any of us would have asked. Wouldn't we?'

Nods. Nods.

'It wants these Selahim out of the way. That's my opinion. The Selahim must be in some way contrary to the AI. Maybe they're bent on counteracting what's going on.'

'A rash assumption,' said Litvinoff.

'Tactical instinct!'

'Do we want the waking world to be flooded with *pain*?' asked Bill Jordan, who had always been squeamish.

Crosstree shrugged. 'We have a *threat* from the AI. A stick held over our heads. It might be a phantom stick.'

Jordan eyed my amputation significantly. 'You can't deny we don't feel much pain any more when we're awake, no matter what happens to us. Isn't that desirable?'

'The lapse in pain sensations could be coincidental,' suggested Lucy. 'Well, I don't think we ought to try to surround Selahim and *squeeze* them!'

'You just don't want to go near any Selahim after that chase and the message,' Ted Ostrovsky accused her.

'You know,' I said, 'the Selahim don't seem so much like full-blooded kosher *aliens* as some sort of unit, like an antibody in a bloodstream.'

'You *agree* with the AI?' Lucy asked me in astonishment.

'No, no. I said antibodies. Maybe they're trying to control the situation. Maybe they're into damage limitation. Suppose,' I ploughed on, 'that AIs can be detrimental to reality? Being god-like, as it were . . . Or that AIs can be jealous of one another? Some older AI has seeded Selahim throughout the loom of creation, ready to spring into existence if a rival AI emerges, to fox it and control it.'

'This "elder AI" being the gent with the long white beard?' queried Manny Weinberger. 'The guy who up dreamed the universe? In other words, G.O.D?'

'Well, maybe not in those terms, Manny. Maybe the universe as such is already a vast AI. It doesn't want fleas in its coat.'

'How could a mere *antibody* be trying to contact me?' Lucy asked me.

'It's a *big* antibody,' I pointed out.

'Well, why, then?'

'Because you awakened the AI when you went lucid.'

We debated throughout the night.

*

When Lucy and I woke in the morning, our bedroom was full of roses. Garlands and bouquets, clusters and bunches — in pink, and in blue. Yes, definitely blue roses as well as the more plausible pink ones.

We scribbled, till the parents invaded us.

'Oh,' they cried admiringly. And: 'Ah!'

'Pink for a little girl,' chanted Alice. 'Blue for a boy.'

On which prognosis, opinion was visibly divided — unless our grafted digits were destined to give rise to twins. This mass of congratulatory blooms swiftly directed our attention to the conservatory out front.

Harry and April and my own dad howled and wrung their hands; and Lucy and I recoiled too, in shock.

The tripod table and rocking chairs had been swept aside. The pot with our sprout in it lay smashed, the spliced fingers expelled and withered. From the apex of the birdcage conservatory hung a Selah. Asleep. Dormant. Its hide crusty and dry, as though it had been suspended there for weeks.

A chrysalis, no less.

No dreams clung about it — unless you counted the shattered dream of our parents.

April gathered up the pathetic twig of dried tissue and bone. A few rootlike hairs had indeed grown from the base, and were now dead threads. My mother-in-law slipped this relic into her dress, between her breasts, where at least it would be warm.

Distraught, Harry lurched back into the house.

Cautiously, Lucy sidled up close to the huge pupa. It hung by its desiccated mouth from a wrought-iron boss.

'Be quiet!' she told lamenting April and moaning Malcolm. She rested her ear against the dry skin.

'Hullo, Selah?' she called to it nervously. Oh, brave Lucy.

She frowned. 'I can hear a . . . rustling sound.'

'Wax in your ears!' snapped April. 'Wash your ears out, child!'

An elision of time occurred, and the sun was higher.

Then Harry returned with a carving knife.

Before Lucy or I could stop him, he slashed at the Selah with a downward sweep of the blade.

The creature's skin split wide open as though it were mere crinkly wrapping paper.

And an iridescent wing thrust forth, sweeping Harry and Lucy aside. Sweeping us all aside.

Silver, azure, and pink, that one wing almost filled the conservatory, which began to lose its former substantial qualities, becoming ghost-like, evanescent. Harry raised his knife again. However, Lucy caught hold of his wrist, and this time it was her father who was rendered numb.

With a crack like a yacht's sail leaping out into a breeze, another great wing deployed, sweeping the gossamer fabric of the conservatory away into streamers of mist, swiftly dispersing.

The Selah had entirely metamorphosed.

As we crowded back into the doorway, the creature stretched its wings. These flapped. Wind buffeted us. The head was small and golden now, prim, with jet-black eyes. Antennae unfurled like fern fronds.

It leapt. It fluttered upward.

And it continued to rise up, higher and higher, seeming not to shrink at all but rather to expand; for we could see it clearly for five or more minutes as it travelled upward away from us.

Soon, from all over Perkins and environs, other similar creatures were arising periodically, glittering in the sunlight. Lucy and I spent most of the morning watching. When we finally drove to the college after a cold turkey lunch, the elisions and jumblements had already subsided. The General was in true, meaningful contact with his hierarchy. More task forces would soon be on the way to Perkins.

From the AI, not a squeak via Infonet or Datanet or Compunet. Had we hallucinated its existence? Was it playing possum, pretending to have been but a dream? Or had it become non-lucid again? Perhaps Lucy's deep desire for a breakthrough in artificial consciousness had auto-suggested the communication she had uttered from the dream couch . . .

'A lot of people will want to talk to you,' Litvinoff told Lucy. '*Don't* use any of the apparatus here. And don't leave town.'

That ought to have been my line, but I had ceased being a cop.

That evening, after the sun had set, we watched the transformed Selahim up in orbit, all wrapped together – we presumed – into a sphere of glistening wings. A new little moon, somehow staying in the same position in the sky above Perkins.

That certainly wasn't imaginary! Earth had been graced with a new, apparently alien satellite. To keep watch over us.

April was embarrassed – *defiantly* embarrassed, let's say – at the mutilation of her daughter's little finger, and of mine. *Arguably* Lucy and I had thus had our relationship reaffirmed, albeit in a cock-eyed quasi-neolithic fashion. With stony countenance, Harry hugged his wife silently, and only needed a pitchfork in his hand to complete the Gothic image. My own dad had ambled off along

Chestnut and returned to report that Don and Doris had been taken off for surgery at Perkins General, which sure as hell would inconvenience Don for life, and Doris too. Dad was all for calling a taxi right away to whisk him back to his own apartment, but Lucy demurred; so we all dined on more cold turkey, restrainedly.

And so to bed.

'Do you think, Jack,' asked Lucy, 'they're going to lock me up and study me? As the Typhoid Mary of the AI-VR conundrum?'

'I don't see how they could study you in, um, isolation — from what already happened. And they won't want *that* to happen again.'

'I guess my career could be over. I shook the world. Maybe we should have a baby now.'

'Don't forget about the Selahim moon up there, love. Things have changed for ever.'

'I guess we'd better go to sleep.'

Easier said than done. I certainly lay awake till well past midnight.

Then suddenly Screen was chiming, Home switched on the lamps, and it was another morning. Out of recent habit, I immediately reached for my notebook and ballpoint.

Ferris Wheel . . . I'd been in a huge funfair, with Crosstree and Litvinoff. A glittering balloon hung high overhead, and I was sure that Lucy was trapped in it, up in the sky. So the three of us rode the Ferris Wheel to gain some height; and as the wheel turned, somehow it leaned over on its side until it was horizontal. But it still rose higher, supported now on a hydraulic tube which stretched up further and further from the ground. The funfair shrank. The Earth was far below us now. Then Litvinoff took out a chess board and Crosstree produced a dozen toy missiles, sleek and sinister, to use as pieces. My dream had definitely been non-lucid. And the previous one almost evaded me. Fishing? Fishing? I'd been fishing with my dad — in a concrete pond — and I caught . . . a beckoning finger on my hook. The rest of the night's dream escapades evaporated.

Sitting up in bed, Lucy put on her big tortoiseshell glasses and gazed at me.

'They spoke to me,' she said in a hushed tone. 'The Selahim spoke to me from their satellite. They *are* the satellite, of course. I'm their channel. They'll have to talk to me every time I sleep, otherwise the AI might reawaken. That's what they said — or sang, in a kind of angelic chorus . . .'

'Did they tell you anything else?' Alien wisdom, I thought. Alien histories and science.

'They recited . . . they chanted . . . page after page of a dictionary at me.'

'Of their alien language?'

'No! It was a Swahili dictionary they chose to start with. *Abiri*, to travel as a passenger. *Abiria*, a passenger. *Abirisha*, to convey as a passenger. *Abudu*, to worship. *Acha*, to leave. *Achama*, to open the mouth wide . . . On and on. And I can remember every word. It's to keep the channel occupied. It's beautiful – but it's horrid too, Jack. Obsessive and finicky. I'll know all the words in the world before I die . . . No, I won't. There are too many languages, too many words. That's why they've chosen words. Millions and billions of words . . . I'll never dream real dreams again.'

'Oh, Lucy.'

'What'll I do? *Baa*, a disaster. *Baada ya*, after. *Baba*, father. *Babaika*, to babble. *Babu*, grandfather. *Babua*, to strip off with fingers. *Babuka*, to be disfigured . . . Oh God, it's a different kind of lucidity. Like endlessly studying for the stupidest examination. Maybe I'll fill right up with useless words, and there'll be no room left in me for anything else.'

'I had a *real* dream, Lucy.'

'Lucky you!'

'General Crosstree was playing chess with little models of missiles. We were travelling up into the sky to rescue you.'

'A missile!' she exclaimed. 'The Government will think of that, won't they? They mustn't do it! But if they don't . . . *cha*, to dawn, or to reverence; *chacha*, to go sour!'

We showered. We dressed; descended. We drank coffee, chewed turkey croissant. The parents were still in their beds.

We stepped outside and stared up at the sky.

'*Daawa*,' said Lucy.

'What's that mean?'

'A lawsuit. I guess there could be a lot of those soon.'

I shook my head reassuringly. 'Natural disaster. Acts of God. Or of aliens or an AI.'

Lucy put on a plaintive, little-girl voice. 'You mean a *baa*, caused by *Baba*?'

The new little alien moon was *almost* invisible by daylight, but then I spotted it up at the zenith like a shimmery vitreous floater in the jelly of my eye.

The Face of the Waters

Jack Deighton

I walk the site now, through the litter that covers the ground like a multi-coloured snowfall, each wrapper an affront to the memory; past the candy stores, the fast food outlets, the coffee shops, the ice-cream parlours, all the cheap and gaudy paraphernalia of success, and I cannot recognise it as the place I knew. Nor can I see in it the vision he had back when the whole concept was just his dream, before the forces of commerce and inevitability, compromise and simplification, the sheer overpowering weight of people, had corrupted that vision and rendered it tawdry and commonplace.

To see what no other can, to convince them of its worth, to fight for its realisation in the face of all obstacles is strange, and difficult enough.

Ah, but to have the vision in the first place; that is the hardest part.

Back then, the site had been a desert, an arid wasteland of rock and dust. Apart from a few depressions where liquids might once have flowed, the flat featureless expanse was broken only by the distant, alluring pinnacle of Olympus Mons. Not without a certain kind of beauty, it could have been a desert on Earth – except for the shorter horizon and pink sky.

In those days, before the terraforming took and its outlines were softened and eroded by the hand of man (the hand of woman still being mostly absent), all of Mars was a desert; a harsh, inimical, unforgiving place, secure for life only where – scattered across the globe to evaluate different Martian soils – microclimate bubbles had been created; environmental oases of dense air, plentiful water and colonising plants, prevented from evaporating by thin plastic containments; gradually extending, interlocking and multiplying like bacilli in a culture dish.

I was a tyro supply pilot with some respects to pay, a hill to climb, and a couple of weeks to kill before the return trip to Earth; abuzz with the thought of helping – even if only incidentally – to fulfil the dream of turning this wilderness into something lush and green, eager to learn about every aspect of life in Lowell base, with willing but potentially distracting hands. Meals were a bonus; after a couple of months of space rations any decent food, even if it is only vegetarian, is a welcome prospect.

'You'll be the new boy.' The voice was pitched high, difficult to accommodate to in the clatter of the canteen, the hand that accompanied it delicate but firm. Under his black hair he was bearded – like all the rest of the men on Mars. It was a tradition that arose at first from necessity – razors or foams are just so much dead weight – but it had soon become an emblem of solidarity, as much a symbol of common purpose as the trimsuits we all wore. On the journey out from Earth I had grown one myself, a miserable wispy thing, but I was trying.

'Li Shek,' he added. 'I take the Mevies out to reprovision the bubbles. Fancy a trip sometime?'

'Yeah, sure,' I replied. 'My launch window isn't for twelve days. I ought to be able to fit one in.'

'I'm going out tomorrow to a small bubble on the south side of Amazonis near Nicholson. I'll take you on that if you like. I can promise it'll be interesting.' Li was smiling in a knowing sort of way.

I was disturbed at the short notice, but there was still time for what I had to do first. 'Tomorrow?' I shrugged. 'OK,' I said. Then a different thought struck me. 'Hey. Amazonis is near Olympus, isn't it?' I asked. 'I'd like a look at that.'

'No problem,' he said. 'We'll take it in on the way back. It's not much of a detour. But you'll need to be prompt in the morning. I don't hang about.'

The memorial is small, secluded among the cluster of bubbles and corridors that have grown around it in the years since its erection. But there is no prospect that it will be developed further, this part of Mars is sacrosanct. The ground it covers is hallowed and further encroachment is unthinkable.

The inscription is plain, stating the facts with little embellishment; listing the first casualties of the terraforming project, their names and ages, ranks and professions: it conveys nothing of the pain.

I took a holo as I stood there, knowing that whatever else I would do with my life, coming here had been right and necessary. A shadow I hadn't realised was over me had lifted. The ghost that had brought me exorcised, I was free to be my own man at last.

The Planitia seemed to go on for ever. Amazonis wasn't the biggest of the Martian plains and it had the same appearance as the rest of them, the same ochre dust clawing at the wheels of the Mars Excursion Vehicle like an ocean at a ship, the same rocks, the same lack of beast, bird and vegetation. Its unremitting nature was as deadening to the senses as Mars was to unprotected life. But on Amazonis's edge, projecting further over the southern horizon with each slow turn of the Mevy's wheels, stood the tall conical finger of Olympus Mons. We weren't headed directly for it but another few hours would make no difference. It had beckoned me for so long that just the glimpse of its upper slopes filling the skyline was enough to satisfy me for the moment.

'What on, uh, Mars is anyone doing out here?' I asked Li. 'It doesn't look very promising.'

'I know. It's certainly a bit different from Pinang.'

'Pinang?'

'My home state.'

'Ah. You're not Chinese, then?'

'If you go back far enough, but my family's been in Malaysia for generations.'

'So how did you end up on Mars?'

'The usual stuff. Got a degree in plant biochemistry, moved into genetics, did a lot of research on gene swapping. I do these runs,' he gestured at the Mevy, 'to give me a break and allow me some thinking time.' His voice was slightly distorted by the unfamiliar acoustics in the suit, as if stripped down to its essence, more intimate somehow, like a lover's voice on a telephone. 'Yourself?' he asked.

'You could say it's the family business. My father was here in the early days.'

'He might know Percy,' he said. 'That's who we're going to see, Percy's kind of a feature here. Our own little eccentric. He's got a project of his own going, nothing at all to do with the terraforming.'

'How's that? I wouldn't have thought the colony could support fringe activities.'

'Percy's special. There's something . . .' he sought for the word, '. . . compelling about him. He's really besotted. It's quite impressive, actually. We indulge him. You remember the *Santa Maria* explosion?'

'I should do,' I replied. 'Without it I wouldn't be here.'

'Oh?'

'People don't trust computer systems. If they've failed once they'll fail again. They like to feel there's someone in control. I don't really do much – just push a few buttons now and again; but it's the appearance that counts.'

'That's very reassuring. Remind me not to go back home when you're driving.'

'That's up to you,' I said, then asked, 'What's the *Santa Maria* got to do with this Percy character?'

'He should have been on it. His tour was up and he was due to go home but he broke his leg and couldn't travel. Took the explosion as a sign that he was meant to stay on Mars. Set himself up out here and refused to budge.'

'So what does he do?' I asked.

'I won't spoil it. You'll find out soon enough. We're nearly there.'

With its short horizon, things come up on you suddenly on Mars – unless they're huge features like the Mons. One moment you're adrift on a sea of powdered rust, the next you're plunging into a ravine or breasting a small crater, necessitating a change of mental as well as mechanical gears; so I wasn't quite prepared for when the bubble appeared, stark against the vermilion sky, from behind a long line of low mounds set straight across our path, like a giant golf ball on a sand tee. It was the standard design one person bubble, overlapping structural triangles and hexagons for rigidity and strength, covered with plastic. From our angle of approach its projecting airlock gave it the overall appearance of a geodesic igloo. It occurred to me that it would be as easy to use ice, here, as any other building material – if there were a sufficient supply. At these temperatures it would be as strong as concrete.

What was most striking was what lay beyond. A huge ditch, several metres wide, ran for a couple of hundred metres across the Martian plain. As we drew up, slipping between two of the mounds each of which was skewed in the same direction, presumably by the Martian wind, it became obvious that this was no natural feature, the sides were far too vertical and neat for that. Mounds lay on the far side too: both sets were parallel to the ditch, providing further evidence of excavation.

Wild thoughts of remnants of a long-dead Martian civilisation started to run in my mind. 'What the hell is this?' I said into the airsuit radio. 'It looks like a dried up canal. Is this archaeology or a practical joke?'

'Close,' said Li. 'Close, but I'll let Percy tell you himself. He can't be far away. Probably at one end of the ditch. Come on.'

We motored the length of the ditch, our view obscured from time to time by the heaps of soil piled up alongside it. Although not straight – there were bends at irregular intervals, perhaps to take advantage of now invisible features of local topography – it was remarkably uniform in appearance and I was still trying to puzzle out why it existed, what purpose it could have beyond being an elaborate hoax.

A heavy duty Mevy lay in the end of the ditch. That, in itself, was not unusual, but its companion was different and gave some indication of how the ditch came into being. Perched on the Mevy, piggy-back style, like a huge bird on a grazing mammal, was a small mechanical digger, its snout-like arm clawing at the solid end wall of the ditch, grubbing out a three-pronged swathe. A slow avalanche of red-brown dust preceded and surrounded it, billowing out into the thin air, dispersing gradually, falling at an imperceptible rate in the low gravity. Working the digger, dimly visible through the ochre clouds, was the figure of someone in an airsuit. This, I presumed, was Percy.

'Perce!' called Li.

Percy's suit must have been incapable of direction finding, either that or the noise of the digger's operations confused him, because the figure started and turned from side to side, looking for the source of the interruption.

Li waved and this time shouted, even though his increased volume would make no difference to Percy's perception. 'Perce! I've brought someone to meet you.'

Percy waved back, switched off the digger and climbed down.

At this point the ditch walls were less steep and he was able to scramble up without much difficulty.

'This is Percival Butler Hughes,' said Li.

We shook hands. The bizarre aspects of this small ritual were not lost on me. Under a blood-red sky, millions of miles from anywhere I could call home, here I was demonstrating my lack of threat by shaking hands with a seemingly certifiable lunatic (if all this ditch business was really due to him), through the gloves of two airsuits, the absence of which would ensure both our deaths by decompression within a few seconds.

He was a convincing advocate, no doubt of that. The passion poured out of him. Sitting in his bubble, drinking reconstituted coffee from plastic bags – it's not the same: don't let anyone tell you it's the same – the light blazed from his soft, brown eyes, taking the attention away from his pinched nose, auburn hair and red beard.

Talking about it was the only time when he was really animated. Enthusiasm and adrenalin had him on a high and there was no stopping him. Oh, he had a vision all right and nothing would prevent him telling you about it.

Thinking back, there must have been times when he was depressed by some setback or delay. I'm glad I never saw him in one of those moods; his lows were probably equally as spectacular as his highs. The memory of those bright eyes, alive with so much conviction, such hope and expectation, is one I can cherish and squeeze tight to myself whenever I'm dispirited, even though his vision partly diminished me. I suspect he was one of those manic characters, obsessives usually are, who swing between moods very quickly. Maybe that was part of the reason why he lived alone.

The way he talked about it made its achievement seem certain, though in his words I thought there was an echo of something sepulchral, valedictory. It was almost as if the shadow of what it would become was apparent even to him. Or was it Mars itself, some sort of melancholic influence the planet exerted on everything connected with it? Certainly nothing I encountered there ever panned out as expected.

'You have to imagine it the way it's going to be,' he said. 'Picture it. Quietly cruising one of the planitiae, Deimos and Phobos scudding overhead, listening to the slap of the water on the prow and banks, looking at the reflections of the sun and sky broken up and scattered by the waves. Or in one of the bases, unloading goods and passengers, exchanging loads amid the hustle and bustle of a busy interchange. Or at twilight, somewhere up in the northern hemisphere, night lights just coming on, their poles marking the way ahead, soft yellow radiance diffusing everywhere, gondolas gliding past each other noiselessly, majestic in their leisurely progress.'

I listened spellbound, struck dumb by the sheer vastness of it, unable to comprehend how he could be serious, how he thought he'd be able to overcome all the problems involved; doubting *my* sanity, not that of this man who talked with such assurance and certainty of sailing the canals of Mars.

The whole idea was sheer lunacy, the scope of the enterprise too large. And yet its grandeur had an awful fascination. The scale of what he was proposing swept you away. Listening to him, you wanted it to be true. What else were we on Mars for, anyway? Something about his attitude and enthusiasm, his force of will, was compelling enough to set aside doubt and assure you of the project's feasibility.

'It's not just canal builders that we'll need in the first place,' he said, 'there's all the ancillary stuff as well. We'll need an infrastructure almost before we can start. The workers will have to have rest and recreation and all the facilities that go with them. It means houses, roads, shops, offices, schools . . .'

'But Mars is no place for kids,' I objected. 'It's far too dangerous. Just look at it.' I gestured outside. 'It's like an open-cast iron ore mine, just about airless, there's not enough water . . . And it's cold as hell,' I added.

'I'm not stupid enough to think it'll happen overnight,' he replied. 'It needs to be step by step. The terraforming will help – and they're bound to find some suitable plants soon. That'll raise oxygen levels, not a lot at first, but it'll all feed back. Orbital mirrors could melt the polar ice-caps, clouds will form and increase temperatures by adding to the greenhouse effect.'

As he warmed to his subject it became obvious that it wasn't some idle whim he was describing. A lot of thought had gone into it. I half-expected him to produce – perhaps out of the literally thin air – blueprints for all the construction he'd talked about.

Trying to temper his buoyancy with some realism I said, 'I think it's going to be a long, long time till you get this off the ground. Temperature's not your real problem. Sure, Mars cuts off less of the sun's radiation cone than Earth – and it's further out: but it's pressure that's important. It's too low. How are you going to stop the water from evaporating as soon as it's formed?'

'I don't know yet,' he replied. 'Maybe we'll get the pressure high enough, maybe we'll have to use some sort of containment system. We'll need the orbital mirrors as an extra heat source, of course – we'll want it to be comfortable – and that'll make the pressure problem worse, but there'll be a way. And I'll find it.'

'Where are you going to get the water?' I asked. 'There surely isn't enough in the ice-cap, even if you could get it to fall as rain.'

'We'll need to import it from Earth. That's where we get all the water we use just now.'

'But you're talking about billions of gallons! The cost will be gigantic.'

'How about collaring an ice-rich asteroid or two? Getting them down here should produce plenty of water vapour. And what better hook to attract people to Mars than the prospect of sailing the canals?'

By this time his flow was unstoppable. 'We'll need condensation and filtration plants, pumps, boatyards and repair facilities to service the gondolas . . .'

I gave up in the end, overwhelmed by his sheer blind faith and persistence of vision. He seemed to have an answer for everything, and if he didn't he was confident one would be found. It was humbling to be aware of the extent to which a man could be fired by his enthusiasms to the exclusion of all else.

I didn't know it immediately but I think something in me died that day. Talking to him, whose dream was, to my mind, impossible and yet seemed to be held the more tenaciously for that, my own ambition suddenly seemed paltry – a worthless thing, too easily achievable to be pursued and I, in turn, became restless, unsatisfied.

He was unremitting too. By the time he'd finished it was late and we had to spend a cramped night in his bubble.

And we didn't get to talk about my father.

Carbon dioxide frost speckled the ground in the early morning, emphasising surfaces like an artist's highlights, the lack of uniform covering lending the landscape a surreal look. As the temperature rose the whiteness lingered only in areas of shadow, elsewhere vanishing eerily as the dry ice changed directly into gas. The lack of moisture left behind a reminder of the alienness of Mars, of the difficulties to be overcome before water could flow in this frozen waste.

Where the Planitia ended and the Mons began was difficult to establish. Six hundred kilometres broad at its base, Olympus had a sixty-five kilometre caldera at its summit, which was less than half the Martian record. But the eruption which had spawned it, perhaps aided by the low Martian gravity, had thrown it to a prodigious height.

Its nearest equivalents on Earth, the Hawaiian shield volcanoes, are at most nine kilometres from ocean bed to tip. Even tectonic Mount Everest hardly betters that.

All of them would be mere foothills beside Olympus. At twenty-five kilometres high the tallest volcano in the solar system, its summit wraithed in the clouds of water (or rather ice) which had cloaked it on and off for millennia before humans came to Mars, Olympus seemed to grow and grow out of the horizon until finally even the clouds around it were obscured by its lower slopes.

And yet there was no sense of size. Standing on its broad meniscal sweep, with nothing else to compare it to, Li and I might have been day trippers on a pleasant jaunt to some local barren beauty spot on Earth.

Gazing down at the Planitia, the curve of the horizon induced a strange sort of vertigo, a sense of being so high that the world beneath had disappeared. Combined with the low gravity it was almost as if there was no danger in falling off, that stepping into the air would put us straight into orbit. But when Li stopped the Mevy we could only have been a couple of kilometres up from the level plain.

I climbed out and squinted upwards, trying to catch a further glimpse of the summit. The mountain filled my field of vision except for a few areas on the periphery where patches of sky were visible. I bent down and touched the surface. It was solid enough, but the powdery soil stuck to my gloves. Standing up, I dusted them off, having to restrain a quite irrational, and useless, impulse to blow on them to get rid of it. Li was standing by the Mevy; it, the sky and the red-coated mountain reflecting in his faceplate.

'Here we are,' he said. 'All set for a stroll on Olympus Mons.'

'I didn't ask to come here just to stroll on it,' I replied.

'What did you come for, then?' he said.

'I wanted to climb it,' I said, waving at the mountain.

'You what?'

'I wanted to climb it.'

'Climb it? What the hell for?'

'Because it's there,' I said, patiently.

'But you could get a Mevy to ride up it, just about, or a flier to land you on the top.'

'No, you don't understand. I wanted to climb it, myself, with as little equipment as possible; like Hilary and Tensing did Everest,' I said.

'But you'll never do that, man,' he said. 'There'll never be enough air on Mars for that.'

'Maybe not. There wasn't a hell of a lot up Everest either. They used oxygen; it wouldn't really be cheating. But,' I said, 'it doesn't seem so worthwhile now.'

'Why not?'

'Compared to Percy's scheme it's a bit tame. Anyone can climb a mountain, but it's going to take something special to get water to flow here.'

Once away from his spell it was easy to dismiss Percy's plans as madness. What wasn't so easy was to forget his certainty. It haunted me to the extent that I began to crave some for myself, now that my old aspiration had been diminished.

I hung around the base, looked over the purifiers extracting biogases from the base's air and the extruders which discharged them into Mars's atmosphere for their greenhouse effect: inspected the gengineering and microbacterial labs, the food processing and cell recharge areas, the power generators, the sewage recycler – all the machines necessary for the base to function; offering my inexpert help, inquiring about Percy. I pestered the botanists: following them in their wanderings through the plastic containment tunnels where they kept various plant specimens, subjecting them to Martian soil, gravity and light levels, but not yet to the rigours of the Martian atmosphere, looking for a variety that thrived. If there was one, the gengineers could whip out the relevant bits of DNA and shovel them into everything else to give instant 'native' flora. At least, that was the idea. They were hoping a suitable candidate would stand out like a haystack in a field of needles, but so far they'd found only the needles. Contemplating the spindly, etiolated growths they showed me, I thought that was all they were ever likely to find. Their chief, Blake Partington, was a bit more sanguine, but he was paid to be. He was also the best source of information about Percy.

He was on one of his daily inspection tours of the plant tunnels and I was killing time till my return flight. Outside, one of Mars's interminable dust storms was raging. It was a bad one, which could possibly delay my launch. The storm was adding to the pitting and scoring the tunnels' walls had received, so that they now transmitted the light which fell on them diffusely. Even without the condensation on the inside, the walls were so opaque it was impossible to see in or out.

'Percy?' Blake said, bending down to inspect a plant. 'He was already a fixture here when I arrived.' He turned over a leaf and examined its underside.

'I never worked with him,' he said. 'He was a survey man and didn't use the base much. That's how he broke his leg. He fell into a gully or something, scouting out a site for one of the smaller bases. He was damn lucky he didn't die; it took four hours to find him.'

Blake moved along the rows, methodically checking every fourth or fifth specimen.

'He bent my ear a few times,' he added, 'but he's one of nature's good guys. I'd love to see things come right for him but I doubt it. He's going to die disappointed. Perhaps we all are.'

He straightened up, rubbing two fingers against his thumb, a dismissive look on his face. 'There's nothing here,' he said. 'I guess it's time to check the lichens outside, anyway.'

That surprised me. 'You've got stuff outside? I didn't know you'd made that much progress.'

'We haven't,' he said. 'It's just an experiment. I'm not hopeful.' He jerked his thumb at the dust storm. 'There's not much likely to survive one of these.'

'I would have thought that was the least of their problems. If the cold doesn't get them, surely they'll lose too much water from their leaves? The pressure's only twenty millibars, for God's sake.'

'And climbing every day. We're pumping out greenhouse gases by the tonne and a lot of water seeps out under the tunnel walls. I've got them in vented cloches to try to keep up the relative humidity but you're probably right.' Blake shrugged. 'So, it's a long shot, but we've got to start sometime,' he pointed out.

He beckoned me with a movement of his head and shoulder. 'Come on, there's something else I'd like to show you. It's back at the base,' he said. 'We'll look at the lichens after. And then,' he said, brightening, 'lunch.'

A few minutes later he was ushering me under a sign reading 'Hydroponics Section', but all I ever heard it called was the plant lab. Doubly secure inside its own reinforced containment system, its airlock would only be sealed in an emergency.

'Is there something promising in here?' I asked, flinching from the glare of the lamps. The atmosphere was full of the smell of high humidity and the peculiar oppressive claustrophobia that always carries with it, a smell and a feeling I've always hated.

'Depends what you mean by promising,' he said, cryptically. 'Hold on a minute.'

He walked over to one of the cabinets. All around was the sound of running water and the thrumming of pumps as the nutrients were continually recycled to the plants' root systems, automatic injection apparatus doling out replenishments from the reservoir tanks whenever the monitored concentrations of nitrogen, phosphorus, potassium or whatever dropped below acceptable limits. Row on row of food plants stretched into the distance; each a mini factory ceaselessly fabricating all the molecules of life from a bucketful of chemicals, a breath of carbon dioxide and a few rays of light; each a component essential to the efficient functioning of the base. As well as reducing the need to import food and vitamins from Earth, they provided an additional source of oxygen to that stored in the base's cryotanks, and a potential haven should its external walls suffer collapse.

'This is my little project,' Blake said, as he reached into the cabinet. 'I've been working on this ever since I knew I'd be coming here.' Lifting out the plastic latticework cube supporting the plant's root ball, he handed it to me. Roots trailed out of the cube, dripping solution; leaving an emblematic pattern of dots between us, like a broken communications network.

'What do you think?' he said, the lamps reflecting from the tinted spectacles shading his blue eyes, their lenses dazzling novae in the midst of the dark forest of his hair, eyebrows and beard.

The plant was a rose with one flower in full bloom and a few more in various stages of bud. The flower was a deep claret-red in colour, so deep it seemed beyond the limits of vision. Focusing on it was difficult. It gave a blurred effect in the mind's eye if not on the retinas; as if somehow, transcending the eye's normal capacity, infra-red wavelengths could be interpreted in addition to the usual light.

'It, uh, it's very nice,' I said.

'I've named it *Braxa*,' he said, looking at me intently.

'But what's it for?' I asked. 'What use is a rose up here?'

'It's not *for* anything,' he said. 'I just wanted to be the first to grow a Martian rose.'

'But you can't say it's Martian, not really.'

'I know,' he said, 'but we can all dream.' Seeing how unimpressed I was, he retrieved his rose and returned it to the cabinet. 'Come on. Let's look at those lichens.'

Keeping always in sight of the base, we stumbled through the dust storm, accompanied by the constant but irregular patter of fine particles on our airsuits, eventually finding the crumbled, desiccated husks, shrivelled and brown, their cloches scattered who knows where across the Martian landscape. I thought that it was a peculiar place to be setting up botanical experiments. It was like the worst possible environment on Earth raised to the fourth or fifth power. By what right did we expect to force our will on this alien place? How could this desolation ever be made fruitful? How could a canal last long here? Percy's ambitions were likely to be ground to dust in the same way as the lichens.

But life is tenacious. It exists in the unlikeliest of locations. Even the deepest, darkest ocean depths on Earth – places of crushing pressure and crippling lack of oxygen – harbour their own peculiar varieties, using the thermal vents welling out from the magma as an energy source. And who knows what microscopic life survives the cold, thin caresses of the stratosphere? If that was possible, perhaps organisms could grow and flourish even in this grim environment. If not, it wouldn't be for the want of trying on our part.

The rest and return cycle was long. Suitable launch windows between Earth and Mars on their slow crawls round the sun are infrequent even for the new cruise ships. For the older expedition vessels there were three, at best four, a year, though several ships were dispatched or returned during each. Add to that the four-month journey duration and it was eighteen months before I saw Percy again. The Mevy trips were a full-time job now – the number of outposts to service had grown, as had the base, and Li had been replaced as driver by Shusaku Watanabe.

Olympus Mons glowered down on our progress as if in challenge, renewing my desire to climb it, to gain my small victory in the fight against Mars, but not just yet. The Planitia was still the same boring jumble of rock and dust, making the journey seem more protracted than before – anticipation lends a keenness to the sense of time passing. Nevertheless the appearance of the bubble over the horizon was still startlingly sudden.

Presumably to prevent erosion by the storms, each of the small mounds of soil along the ditch's length was now covered in plastic, otherwise the area looked as I remembered it, until we got close.

Obscured till then by the jumble of reserve and spent power cells which surrounded the bubble, a long pole stuck up out of the ditch. From its bulbous tip a rope stretched downward, twitching occasionally in the zephyr-like breeze. The structure both pole and rope were attached to was slowly revealed as we came up to the edge.

'Jesus Christ almighty!' I said in astonishment. 'How the hell did that get here?'

Despite knowing of Percy's obsession, to find a boat here, in the driest place imaginable, was incredible. What use is a boat without free-standing water? The nearest water of any kind was the Martian North Polar cap and that was still permanently frozen. A boat it undoubtedly was. Not just a miserable little rowing boat either.

Supported on blocks to stabilise it in the dry ditch, partly covered by a tarpaulin-like material to keep the Martian dust at bay, the 'Schiaparelli', its name painted on the prow in grandiose green curves, was almost half as wide as the ditch and at least five metres long. In construction it was as bizarre as its location. It looked as if it had been built out of assorted junk, cannibalised from anything that came to hand. I could distinguish bits of Mevy, old power cells, bubble support struts, discarded air tanks – a bewildering jumble of used and unrecognisable parts, bent and twisted to serve their new purpose.

Still unwilling to believe the evidence of my eyes, I climbed down the steps cut into the nearside ditch wall, half-expecting to find it was a mock-up, a cunning contrivance of artifice and *trompe l'oeil* set up to fool newcomers and provide everyone at the base with a good laugh afterwards. It looked in good shape and certainly appeared seaworthy. Its paintwork spark-led in the cerise sunlight, giving it an iridescent glow and it had everything a boat ought to have underneath; keel, rudder, twin propeller shafts ending in the familiar turbine-shaped three blades; Percy had taken care with the important bits.

Under the 'Schiaparelli', on its stern, its port of origin was given as 'Lowell Base'. Its identification numbers 0-00-01, clearly signalled the first boat registered on Mars.

'Percy's certainly been busy,' I said.

'Not just Percy,' Shusaku said. 'He's had the whole damn base working on it, getting people to lay aside anything that might help him build this thing. And,' he complained, 'I've had to cart it all out here.'

Percy's voice interrupted us. 'Hello, Shusaku,' he said. 'Brought anything for me?'

'Only him, this time, Perce,' said Shusaku, nodding down at me. I climbed back out of the ditch.

'Hi. I like the boat, Percy,' I said.

'Yeah, I'm proud of her, I put a lot of work into her. Been doing virtually nothing else lately,' he said. 'It's a pity about the motor.'

'What about it?' I asked.

'She doesn't have one yet. I've not been able to find one that nobody needs.'

'What?' I burst out laughing. 'You mean you go to all the trouble to build a boat here and it doesn't have a motor? I'm sorry Percy, but that's priceless.' I shook my head again. 'All dressed up and nowhere to go,' I said, 'Priceless.'

'Give me a chance, I haven't been looking for long,' he grumbled. 'I don't suppose you know where I could lay hold on one?'

'Me? Where would I get a motor?'

'I don't know,' he replied. 'I thought you might pick something up Earthside.'

'I'll see what I can do, but I'm not promising anything. My weight allowance isn't too generous. What sort do you need anyway?'

'Anything really. Just so long as it can be hitched up to the prop shafts. Doesn't have to be big, we don't want to damage the canal walls. Ten or so horsepower ought to do it.'

'You're hopeful,' I replied. Then I peered at him, trying to pick out his features through the faceplate and said, 'Horsepower! Just how old are you, Percy?'

'Old enough to resent you mentioning it,' he said wryly. 'What did you come out here for, anyway? I presume it wasn't just to insult me?'

'Just some news. Part of the cargo this trip was the first of the orbital mirrors. They should be deploying it in a couple of hours. That should help to vaporise a bit of the ice-cap.'

'Hey, that's great,' he said. 'But it won't be enough. We've still got far too little available gas for a viable atmosphere. The pressure's going to be too low even if the whole damn lot boils.'

'Give it time,' said Shusaku.

'That's something I might not have too much of – as this young man keeps reminding me,' said Percy.

Feeling vaguely guilty, I changed the subject. 'How do you fancy some real meat, Percy?'

'Real meat? You've got some real meat? Not that reconstituted gunge from the food labs?'

'No. Sorry Percy, not this time. But soon. They're setting aside a bubble at Lowell for meat on the hoof. They'll be shipping some sheep embryos on the next supply shuttle. I'm glad I'm not on that run.'

'Why not?'

'Embryos aren't any good on their own. You need an incubator. And the best incubator for sheep is another sheep. Can you imagine feeding the damned thing. Not to mention the smell! There's one consolation, though.' I made them wait. 'It might have been a cow.'

'Don't rejoice too soon, son,' said Percy. 'You might be the one who lands that job.'

'Oh. No thanks,' I said.

'Hey, I've just had an idea. Horses!'

'What about them, Perce?' asked Shusaku.

'If you can do it with sheep, why not horses? We could get them to pull the gondolas – or barges – whatever we're going to call them. Isn't that what they used on canals in the days before engines?'

'Don't be silly, Perce,' said Shusaku. 'Do you know how much horses eat? Motors are much cheaper. Anyway, they'll look out of place here, unless you get them up in some sort of costume – you know, "Martian" horses.'

'Yeah, you're right,' Percy replied, waving his hand dismissively. 'Best forget it. It was a crazy idea.' He turned and started to move towards the bubble. Half-way there, he stopped and laughed. 'About as crazy as sailing on Martian canals, eh?' he said.

Once there was a time when I would have agreed with that; but now I wasn't so sure. He already had his canal and his boat, all that was missing was water. And that afternoon, the first of a new set of stars would shine down on the Mevy as we returned to the base.

*

I asked Percy, once, why he was so dedicated to building canals.

'I don't think I can really *explain* it,' he said. 'It's just something I have to do. It's like putting a little part of the universe the way it ought to be. It seems right somehow. There were *meant* to be canals on Mars. It's part of the scheme of things – the music of the spheres, all that.' He shrugged. 'I'm just the instrument, that's all.'

He paused as if deciding whether or not to continue.

'I guess it's because of my name,' he said, finally. 'My mother's name was Lowell and father was an astronomy freak. It must have seemed natural to put the two together. But there aren't too many Percivals around these days, and weren't even when I was young. I took a lot of joshing about it – you know what kids are like. I guess I wanted to turn it into a strength, somehow. When I discovered Lowell's writings – you know all that stuff about civilisations dying for lack of water?' I nodded. 'Something clicked. Building the canals seemed the perfect way to honour the original Percival Lowell. And my accident saved me from dying in the *Santa Maria*. That programmer should have lost a lot more than just his job. I know what I'd have done to him.'

'Be fair, Percy,' I said. 'You know all those complex programs have got glitches in them. It was a trillion to one chance that it mixed the fuels prematurely. And it can't have been an easy burden on the guy's conscience.'

He put his hand on my shoulder.

'I knew your father,' he said, quietly. 'I knew them all,' he added. 'Such a waste. Still,' he sighed, 'it was inevitable that a few would die, I guess. We're lucky there haven't been more. But Harry was a good man. I see a lot of him in you. He would have been proud of you, I'm sure.

'It was like fate, you see,' he mused. 'I couldn't not do it after that. I felt I owed it to them.'

I read Lowell, and his inspiration, Schiaparelli, to try to find the source of Percy's passion, but there was nothing. The writings were as dry as Martian dust. Schiaparelli didn't even believe in canals – '*canali*' actually means 'channels' – 'canals' was a mistranslation. Percy, like Lowell before him, was dedicating himself to phantoms.

The eye 'sees' canals, all right; but the eye sees what isn't there – you can get the same effect by staring at a blank disc, which is more or less what Mars looks like from a telescope on Earth. It was all optical illusion, a mirage. Percy knew all that. It was his strength that he didn't care. He carried on despite it.

Mirages have the power to seduce, to draw people on, to encourage effort in a seemingly hopeless struggle. And, sometimes, the effort is rewarded. It was hope that kept Percy going. The measure of his achievement in getting as far as he had was that he knew how little chance there was of triumph in the end.

Giulia Calletano looked toward where the view of Mars filled the shuttle's windows, the orbital mirrors girdling the planet like a necklace of incandescent pearls. Some of the mirrors were behind the planet, others end-on and so in shadow; the effect was of two scintillant strips either side of the planet's neck, rather as if Mars had subsumed part of the necklace into an ample cleavage.

'There's plenty of oxygen down there,' she said. 'There's just no easy way to liberate it.' She was a geochemist but rejected that term for anyone about to study Martian ground formations. She insisted on being styled an areochemist. She was pernickety in other ways too.

'But isn't the soil mostly rust?' I objected. 'It's easy enough to get rid of the iron, surely?'

'Oh, yeah,' she said. 'There are ways to do that. But not without the oxygen ending up bonded more tightly to something else instead – usually carbon.

'No,' she continued. 'The only efficient producer of free oxygen is plant life. You're trying to reverse the natural process, you see. Oxygen is a reactive gas – dangerous in fact. Its normal behaviour is to join with other elements, not separate from them. Free oxygen is a by-product of photosynthesis. We're so used to living in an oxygen-rich atmosphere we don't appreciate that enough.

'Down there it's different. Down there we've got to fight for every little advantage we can. We can make the atmosphere thicker – maybe even produce lots of water – but until we can get plants photosynthesising properly we'll have to import oxygen, or use just about every energy resource we have making it by electrolysis.'

'That won't please Percy,' I said.

'That's the guy with the canal, right? I'd like to see that.'

'Yeah. He's become part of the Mars experience, I guess. Just follow the signs "To the canal". It's a well worn road, now.'

'You don't need oxygen to sail on a canal, just a boat and some water. Has he never heard of airsuits?'

'That wouldn't quite suit Percy. I think the idea is to sail under the open sky or else it wouldn't be authentic. Anyway, there isn't any water.'

'There's time enough. The asteroid hasn't arrived, yet.'

'It's due this turnaround.'

'If everything works out right it is.'

'Why shouldn't it?' I asked.

'No reason,' Giulia said. 'I just like to be careful.'

Outside, Mars turned imperiously under the ring of mirrors like a huge gyroscope beneath its equatorial rim; a giant sponge so far able to soak up all the water we could throw at it.

The periphery of Elysium had never seen so much activity. It seemed as if all the Martian echelons were here, a conglomeration of light and heavy duty Mevies, trailers, fliers, hastily erected bubbles – some still incomplete – arclights, torches, airsuited figures – some at work, others supervising, still others merely spectating – all come to witness the greatest free show the terraforming of Mars had yet had to offer.

It was an illusion of course. This assortment of people – a multitude by Martian standards – was not the whole complement on the Mars roster; some had had to stay behind to ensure normal working of the various bases. It was an impressive indicator of how big the project had become. Now it was impossible to know, as I had in the early days, every face I encountered, every nameplate I read.

An increasing number of personnel were women. No longer a rarity on Mars, their benefits were not restricted to their abilities as project workers. The first true Martians (twins) had been born the year before, and several more were on the way.

Resources were becoming over-stretched. Given time, the plant problem would be solved, but for now the lack of water and air threatened the future of the bases.

Vastitas Borealis would have been the natural target. Encompassing the northern pole, a gigantic plain so large it had a designation all to itself, orbital considerations and the sites monitoring the effect of the orbiting mirrors on the polar cap made it impracticable. As a substitute, Elysium was almost perfect.

Half a world away from the main base at Lowell and the

biggest of the planitiae, the area had been kept free of all but exploratory human endeavour up to now. An error, provided it wasn't too gross, would not much matter in a target this size. The food labs in the bases had been sealed as a precaution, but if there was a disruption to one of the outer containments there would be few left to seek sanctuary. A disaster on the periphery itself was too awful to contemplate, given the concentration of personnel, but it would have been impossible to keep everyone away. This was the only drama since the first landing to rank with that seminal event.

The networks were here to capture the occasion for the missing and the millions back on Earth. Using a disproportionate amount of the bases' still scarce resources and devastating normal routine merely by their presence, their cameras, spaced at intervals all round Elysium's outskirts, in fliers along the flight path and in orbit, would provide a better view than those on the ground could obtain unaided; but there was no substitute for being there. This was the one everyone who could see, just had to.

The pre-dawn darkness was faintly illuminated by the orbital mirrors. Strung across the sky from horizon to horizon like a rainbow of white dots, their back-scatter had denied any part of the surface of Mars a true night for many months. Just to their north, the light from the asteroid, which had temporarily brought the Martian quota of moons up to three, had smeared out and shifted from white to red as it began its descent and started to disintegrate. On the last pass its fiery tail had filled a quarter of the sky and the clouds of its passage still rolled and boiled across the stars, obscuring them more completely than any Martian cloud before. Perhaps it was imagination, but as well as feeling the wind tug at them, several onlookers had sworn they *heard* its shock-wave through their airsuits, despite the thin air.

Now it was returning, two square kilometres of ice and frozen methane, sloughing off mass as it came, adding gases to the atmosphere at an immeasurably swift rate, hurtling towards Elysium and an impact that would comfortably exceed the force of a medium-sized fusion bomb, pulverising anything in the contact area.

It glowed in the sky like a minor sun, shafts of fulgent gas licking out from its sides like solar flares, casting a flickering, unnatural light that made the surroundings dance and shudder as if with demons, trailing behind it a roiling mass of cloud thousands of kilometres long that gave it the look of a celestial hammer, growing ever larger as it came lower so that it seemed it must surely demolish us utterly, shatter our puny efforts to make of this planet something which nature had not, drive us deep into Mars beyond any hope of extrication.

Still two kilometres up, it passed overhead, the heat of its traverse searing through the fabric of our airsuits, its brightness observed through faceplates darkened to maximum and eyes screwed almost shut. And this time there could be no doubt: amid the buffeting of its turbulent wake there was *sound*, a faint high-pitched howl that swooshed suddenly and then was gone, like the cry of a diving gull.

In its train, mist filled the sky as vapour condensed from the rapidly cooling hot gases. Nebulous wisps of liquid water at last, the mist would quickly disappear, dispersed by the wind as its molecules evaporated, rushing into the comparative vacuum of the low pressure atmosphere; but now it obscured the view, the actual impact taking place beyond our sight, hidden behind the veil covering the asteroid's death. Mars flinched under the shock; through our boots we felt the planet quiver and quake long before the blastwave brought us its cry of outrage.

Through the clearing mists we could slowly discern the aftermath of the collision. Over the horizon a vast cloud rose into the thin air; a turbid mixture of dust, mist and steam climbing ever higher into the Martian sky; turning and twisting over itself; flexing and extending fingers of vaporous dust like a hand grasping for a lifeline, failing its hold and clutching again and again as it continued its ascent; gradually spreading out at its tip till it resembled an anvil, as if ready to receive another hammer blow from the same source.

For most of its length it was illuminated by the rays of the rising sun, giving its rust colour a tint of orange, dazzling in the morning sky. I realised then that this was the first man-made thing on Mars that could rival Olympus Mons in scale – the cloud had to be at least as tall again – and something of the excitement of the occasion left me. To my surprise, I felt a sense of loss. I discovered I liked Mars the way it was and feared what it would become. But the old Mars was doomed now to be battered into reluctant submission by an opponent who would never let up.

That night, with the extra dust and mist saturating the air, the sun set in an achingly beautiful deep ruby-red sky, the clouds like velvet ships on a carmine sea, and the screw of sadness I usually experience at the going down of the sun was tightened almost past the point of endurance.

'You know what I like best about Mars?' I said to Percy. We were in his bubble, the first opportunity we'd had to be alone together in a long time.

'No. What?' he said.

'The length of the day. It suits me.'

'How d'you mean?'

'Well, I like to sleep late – '

'I've noticed,' he interrupted.

' – and stay awake at night. On Earth a kind of slippage happens, there just aren't enough hours in the day, something has to give, either I lose sleep or I don't get done what I want to. I know it causes difficulties keeping track of the calendar, but here the extra standard hour means I can get as much sleep as I need and still . . .'

He wasn't paying attention. Bald head cocked to one side, full white beard pointing towards me, he said, 'What's that?'

'What's what?'

I heard it then, too. A dull splat on the bubble's skin.

'That,' he said.

'It'll just be dust. There'll be a storm coming. Looks like you're stuck with me for the night again.'

'I don't think so,' he said. 'It didn't sound like dust and there hasn't been any warning.'

'They sometimes blow up out of nothing, especially now the atmosphere's thicker.'

It happened again, this time three sounds like the 'O' in an old-style SOS.

'It didn't look like storm conditions to me,' he said.

'Maybe it was an asteroid. There's another one due in, isn't there?'

'We would have felt the 'quake,' he objected. 'No. There's something funny going on. I'm going out for a look. Come on.'

We suited up to the accompaniment of an intoxicated drummer's rhythms on the bubble's walls, long pauses followed by sudden staccato bursts lapsing lazily back into inactivity. When we stepped out of the 'lock there didn't seem to be anything untoward. A few dense clouds hung in the orange sky and the horizon glimmered hazily in the distance. There was no sign of a dust storm.

'Hey, you've got me worried here,' I said. 'I'm beginning to think we've been visited by a Martian ghost.'

Percy was walking around the bubble, inspecting it for damage. A few spots on its surface glistened in the late afternoon sunlight.

Something hit my shoulder. I jumped and brushed at it with my other hand, but there was nothing there and no damage to the suit fabric.

'What the fuck . . .?'

A small round dark patch had appeared on the ground in front of me. As I watched it was joined by another and another, and the drum pattern began to beat against my suit. Percy was standing with his hand in front of him, head bent, staring at his palm.

'It's rain,' he breathed, 'rain.' Then with an almighty yell, 'It's rai-ai-ai-ain!' he ran forward and jumped onto the 'Schiaparelli', to dance between the parts of the motor I had brought him – needing several trips from Earth – and which lay on the deck still disassembled. Pausing in the bow to shake a triumphal fist at the sky, he leapt on down into the canal.

'Jesus Christ, Percy!' I shouted. 'You'll kill yourself.' I hurried to the canal's edge.

The strength of his possession had protected him. He was dancing about, running up and down, arms outstretched in a child's imitation of a bird, laughing and cavorting like an idiot, kicking up the dust from the canal bed, saying 'Rain! Rain!' – petting the boat like a long lost love. He even tried to kiss me, scrambling up out of the ditch to get at me like a berserker in lust. I thought he'd crack my faceplate his head hit mine so hard. He shook me violently by the shoulders shouting 'Rain. Rain!' again and, exultantly, 'We're gonna make it. We're gonna make it, son!' Turning, he fell against the bubble's wall, sliding down until he reached the ground, giggling uncontrollably, mumbling, 'Rain. Rain,' over and over, amidst his laughter.

There was no stopping him after that. He suddenly became the man of the hour. Every 'Mars correspondent' on the planet descended on him demanding interviews, which he graciously granted. His face became as widely recognised as any network 'personality'. Back on Earth, I tired of answering the questions all Mars veterans grew to dread, 'Do you know Percy?' and 'What's he *really* like?' but the exposure served him well enough. The donations and sponsorships poured in, the whole enterprise, crazy boat and all, decamped to Lowell to build the 'Grand Canal' and his earlier helpers were pushed to the side, unable to devote to him the time he now needed.

I met Blake Partington on one of my stopovers on Earth around then. I might not have recognised him if it hadn't been for his tinted spectacles – which I now realised were not merely a response to the hydroponic lights. His fondness for food had gone to his figure, he'd shaved his beard and his hair was no longer uniformly black but flecked with grey. He was years older, but a mirror told much the same story about me.

'I hear it's become a circus,' he said, when the talk inevitably got round to Percy.

'Yeah. He's at the centre of this perpetual motion machine. People are running around – him most of all – doing this and that, but nothing much seems to happen. He's so busy it's difficult to get to talk to him, now. When I do, he seems confident enough.'

'Do you think it's feasible?' Blake asked. 'I mean, enough free-standing water to fill canals? He'll never get the pressure high enough.'

'He doesn't have to,' I said. 'The rainfall means there's probably sufficient water on Mars for what he has in mind. He's planning tunnels to cover the canals and their immediate surroundings. That ought to do it. They'll be huge, of course, and expensive, but cheaper than importing the water directly or lassoing more asteroids.'

'Won't that defeat the purpose?' he complained. 'It's cheating. They won't really be Martian canals, then, will they?'

'I don't see why not,' I replied. 'They'll be on Mars, dug out of Martian soil. How much more Martian can you get?'

'I suppose so,' he said. 'It still doesn't seem right.'

'How's your rose?' I asked.

'I left it behind. Planted it in one of the Martian soil beds as a sort of memento of the good old days – gave it a good dose of fertiliser, first. It's probably dead, you know how hopeless all those places were.'

'They've managed to crack that, I heard. Gengineered some bug that breaks down Martian soil in a way plants can use.'

'Well,' he grumbled. 'They must be better botanists than I was to get decent plants to grow up there.'

'They've got better equipment, that's all,' I said. 'Anyway, it's all changed. You wouldn't recognise the place any more.'

The invitation arrived, scrolled and curlicued with all the adornments of the calligrapher's art, embossed and decorated

with stylised representations of gondolas sailing down pictur-
esque waterways, with language to match – *Percival Lowell
Hughes and the Mars Canals Corporation request the
pleasure of your company at the Gala Opening of the Grand
Canal, Lowell Base, Mars.* – and so on.

Lowell base was a sprawl. No longer a research centre, it
had become a city; a canopied excess of hundreds of intercon-
nected bubbles containing an array of buildings of various
shapes and sizes with an assortment of people to fill them.
People of all creeds and none, of every race and age, each
with their own reason for being there, their own aspirations;
workers and tourists, colonists, researchers, navvies, lawyers,
shopkeepers, clerks, business people, bankers, labourers, con
artists, teachers, entertainers, traders in all commodities that
Mars could provide: a city much as those on the Earth I had
just left – and hardly a beard in sight.

The spaceliner came down between two rectangular hec-
tares of plastic covered fields containing the plants which
thrived so well on the liberally microbe-dosed Martian soil
and provided the biomass necessary for the base's expansion.
Similar containments lay all over Mars's equatorial areas,
many of them for grazing the diversity of farm animals
specially adapted to such conditions. One long tunnel pointed
towards Olympus Mons and on to Amazonis – the 'Grand
Canal' heading out of Lowell to Percy's old base where it
would eventually link up with his original canal as part of a
network of 'cruising canals for the dedicated boater' as the
Mars Canals Corporation brochure somewhat clumsily put it.
Just before the 'liner landed, I caught a glimpse of the one
small undeveloped area still open to the Martian elements, a
well-remembered obelisk at its heart.

The years since we had last met made no difference. He
embraced me like a son, the accident which had shaped both
our lives hanging unspoken between us. I made no allowances
for his advanced years, taxing him with his invitation, waving
it at him, saying, 'Come on, Percy. What's this? It's hardly
your style is it?'

He was old now. I was shocked to see the uncertainty of his
walk, the limp which he could no longer disguise, the lines
around his eyes, the folds of wrinkled flesh hanging on his
face – all the pictures had smoothed them out, maintaining
the impression of a man still in full vigour.

When he spoke, his voice was frail, with none of the power
I remembered. The lower registers had gone, leaving a thin,

plaintive warble. 'You know what these money types are like,' he said. 'Always got to show it off. Besides,' he added, 'it would hardly do much for confidence in the company if we sent out cheap stationery, would it?'

He insisted I stay with him for the final preparations and share his rooms, 'Just like the old days, in the bubble.'

He showed me it all. The gondola construction shop/repair facility, the reservoirs and cisterns built back from the canal at the various necessary points, the 'Schiaparelli' on its plinth beside the quay at Lowell – effigy of Percy at the wheel, the canal itself, its heavy duty plastic inlay, the overhanging stone lip on the walls to prevent erosion. I was with him when the inaugural trickle of water ceremonially wet the trench and later, when the first gondola, the 'Percival Lowell' – an elegant, brightly-awninged fantasy with moulded prow and stern gently tapering upwards – was lowered gracefully from portable davits to meet the sparkling floods.

I wasn't fooled. This was his real son. This was what gave meaning to his life. For this his enthusiasm was as boundless as ever. When he was at the canal or talking about it, he was the old Percy; away from it he was nothing, a dried-up husk like the lichens Blake had experimented on, a new world ago.

Percy's wooing of potential backers had been a relentless exercise, a round of financial institutions, commerce, billionaires, inheritors, media exposure, governments – anyone with money to burn or access to those who had. He found sponsors in the unlikeliest of places and hard-nosed investors with an eye to a profit. He tempted them with possibilities, induced them to sink capital into his fancy, to sign the dotted line of his dream, spent the money and came back for more. His drive and commitment had made his doubters ridiculous. Now he had nothing left to give.

The night before the first cruise he spoke to me of the fear which had been consuming him. 'I didn't want to miss it,' he said. 'I didn't want to come close and . . .'

'I know, Percy,' I said, 'but everything's fine. Your canal's a marvel. The first wonder of the world. Tomorrow's going to be all right.'

He put on a good show, helped by long shots and the electronic fakery which disguised his voice. The only problems came when he had to walk, but he used a calm measured tread and stopped to acknowledge the crowd every few steps.

The giant entertainment corporations had put a lot of money

into the project, and they weren't about to let anyone forget it. Percy was on the news and all over the chat shows. The pioneering spirit of the age, he was the new frontiersman, the 'man who built the Martian canals'. The maiden voyage was broadcast live, but seen on Earth several minutes after it had happened due to the time delay.

Amid the razmatazz of the attempts to entice custom to Mars – the boat bedecked with flags, balloons and streamers, disfigured by advertisements and dangerously near to capsizing under the weight of corporate hospitality – Percy was impassive, an austere bald figurehead festooned with sponsors' logos, in the prow of the first gondola out from Lowell.

He had built his canal on Mars, filled it with enough water to ensure buoyancy, and under a plastic canopy concealing the real Martian sky, he sailed the few kilometres of its length.

Whatever he felt about the compromises and accommodations, the adjustments he had had to make to keep at least part of his vision alive, the corruptions of his pure idea he had endured, he did not reveal. Watching him, I wondered what that other figure – in the bow of the 'Schiaparelli' all those years ago, staring into the future that had now arrived – would have thought; whether the reality measured up to the dream, if the mismatch was too great, or that to have achieved any of it would have surpassed his wildest expectations.

Maybe he knew he'd got the best he could hope for. Maybe he was just worn out. Perhaps it was simpler, and subtler, than that. Perhaps Mars got him. Mars is like that, as I said.

He died a few weeks later, while I was on the flight back to Earth. They buried him out on Amazonis where it all started, beside the fruition and degradation of his vision, under a carved stone saying – at his request – simply 'Percival Lowell Hughes: astronaut and canal builder'.

You can ski down Olympus Mons now, naked, with a rose between your teeth, if you wanted to – at least on its lower slopes.

Seeking his monument, I walk the site, through the leaf-litter of technology, litter that covers the ground like a multi-coloured snowfall, each wrapper an insult to the memory; under a hidden sky, now yellow-green. A pilgrim, I walk past the candy stores, the fast food outlets, the coffee shops, the ice-cream parlours, the tawdry paraphernalia of success – all with the same insistent message, 'Buy! Buy! Buy!' – aware of the lurking speakeasies and sex shops, the bordellos and vice-parlours hiding themselves in the corners and interstices where such things do, if they are not too brazen. I cannot recognise it as the place I knew, I cannot see in it his vision.

Change and decay; decay and change. To every thing a season. Seduced by the temporary organisation within our bodies, we ignore disorder elsewhere. Swimming against the tide of entropy, we act as if tomorrow may be neither the first nor last day of the rest of our lives but as a template to be copied forever. But time's arrow will shaft us at the last. Mutability is the necessary condition of life.

It is a fair likeness, though the sculptor has not managed to capture the intensity of his gaze. I stare eye into eye, each dulled by moisture and the ravages of time. I look upon the face of the waters; hear the dull slap of wave on stone surround, the curious slow, high wave of Mars; contemplate the rainbow streaks of oil slicks and accumulations of algae desecrating his achievement.

It was foolish of me to suppose I could find in this place anything but bodily remnants: none of Percy's spirit remains. Somewhere there may be a setting fit to pay him the respects of one old man for another; but not here, not now.

Perhaps if I revisited the *Santa Maria* memorial.

Or, maybe; if I were to climb Olympus Mons . . .

Corsairs of the Second Ether

Warwick Colvin Jnr.

THE STORY SO FAR ... Having at last followed the SWIPLING swarm through the unpredictable scales between planes and arrived at Ko-O-Ko, the Lost Universe, CAPTAIN BiLLY-BOB BEGG and her famous CHAOS ENGINEERS are prevented from returning to the First or Second Ethers by the activities of AYESHA VON ABDUL, Protectress of the Lost Universe, and her ruffianly slipling Corsair allies. Only seven other ships were successful in pursuing the swipling swarm all the way to Ko-O-Ko, including those of CAPTAIN QUELCH; of STERLING, Second Beast of the SKIPLING folk; of RA, First Beast of the SKIMLINGS and of the parasitically-held renegade ship of Big Ball and his unwelcome ally KAPRIKORN SCHULTZ, Banker to the Homeboy Tong. Two other ships are known to have reached Ko-O-Ko, but are at present unaccounted for. Although Captain Billy-Bob has tried to warn Ayesha von Abdul that her army of sliplings means no good to the Lost Universe, the Protectress refuses to listen, even after she has declared her faith in the common Great Mood and found true love ... There seems no saving her, but then Captain Quelch suggests a meeting between himself and Kaprikorn Schultz, with a view to taking control of the slipling horde and conquering Ko-O-Ko in the name of the Singularity. There is nothing for it, Captain Billy-Bob decides, but to attempt the dangerous manoeuvre known as the 'scale-flip'.

Her crew of famous Chaos Engineers are unanimous. It will mean a wild dive through to the old Mars station and an attractor so familiar the ship might just flow to like and re-organise in natal space. It worked once before, in the tale of the Mandelbrot Sidestep, but everyone had known it was the purest luck, and it would be purest luck once again, should they survive. Captain Billy-Bob is about to give the order when suddenly, blotting the forescreens, Captain Quelch's *The Linear Bee* appears, casting a significant shadow into the equation. But can Captain Billy-Bob stop the progress in time? Now Read On ...

CHAPTER ONE THOUSAND AND FOURTEEN

Hard A-Stern on a Rogue Branch

CAPTAIN BILLY-BOB Begg strides through the instrument conference carrying with her the shadows and dimensions of all her adventures. Some now argue she has skipling blood. Her

outlines leap in and out of her surrounding aura — faces, shapes, colours, gestures, long forgotten. Her helmet boils with fractal dust normally left behind in any scale jump and she is contemptuous of disapproval ('they'll never take me or my ship to Reality Dock!' she swears) as she bleeds her screen to her enemy's co-ordinates, so familiar she makes no conscious computation. And there is the face of the Original Insect, whimsically superimposed upon the haggard, hatchet features of Captain Horace Quelch, still not entirely certain if he can afford to gloat just yet. 'Marm?'

'Horace!' burbs the revered Main Type of the *Now The Clouds Have Meaning.* 'You'll let us pass, I hope, for all our sakes.'

'Singularity is the only commonality I recognise, marm. I I am never, I hope, *ad utrumque paratus*! I'll be obliged if

ye'll
edge
off this
branchline
and stick to
ye'r own roads
in future.'

'You've been
tongue-tickling with
Kaprikorn Schultz,' said
Captain Billy-Bob with
a dismissive eruption of a
finger or two and her chief
outline breaks into violent blue
and yellow, then red and yellow,
then pale green, alarming her enemy,
who seems to shrink even from her
image.

'There's a string of sapphires I can do
nothing about,' declares Quelch.

'Another trick of the Master Banker.' Pegarm
Pete and Professor Pop crowd about their Main
Type, while Jhong de Bhong plugs into his new chest and
begins to spark urgently.

'Kaprikorn is the most respectable creature in the multiverse,' declares Captain Quelch with a gashy grin and his
eyes blob red, through some genetic fluke, they would guess,
rather than a blip of the screen's 49.

'There's twelve other patterns to this,' murmurs Professor
Pop, passing his calculations to his Main Type. 'He has
considered eight. Those four are free. The one I have
indicated gives us maximum roll, unfortunately.'

'A roll-and-fold manoeuvre, as I'd feared.' Captain Billy-
Bob applauds their instruments and busies herself with the
fussy metaphysics of the problem. 'But have we any right to
the luck we need.'

'We must pray,' says Pegarm Pete. 'Faith, darling, and the

confidence of the Just is all that can guide us now.' He refers to his Main Type's secret Calling, for she is, indeed, one of the Just. It is her Faith, rather than her Luck, that these days her famous Engineers trust most.

'Very well,' she says suddenly, and bursts the crystal with a fierce, swift movement.

'You have blinded me!' roars her enemy.

CHAPTER ONE THOUSAND AND FIFTEEN

The Consequences of Pierced Scales

'WE'LL POUR RUM on their rear-folds before you can peep "claw-rot to a clam",' boasts Kaprikorn Schultz as he slips his stolen ship into a careless corkscrew guaranteed to bore into the heart of Ko-O-Ko and terrify the peaceful swiplings out of the all-protecting grid-nest. But he is still unaware of Dilly-Dee Begg, a stow-away, crawling even now through the nauseating gaps between the mighty walls of a Singularity Heavy Warper badly modified for folding and poorly maintained by Big Ball the renegade, who never planned to take her anywhere but into the Field of Indigo and make a living off the passing skimling trade. This is no retirement for an old creature, he complains, but by now he has been strapped into his brochette and glares moodily at the steel spike jutting upwards between his thickly-scarred tentacles. 'This is not pain, it is mere indignity.' He has noted the whispering presence of Dilly-Dee Begg and not betrayed her. He returns to his B-screen and its repeated images of Big Ball devouring Kaprikorn Schultz of the Homeboy Tong. 'Ah! Blood! Blood!'

But Kaprikorn Schultz turns suspicious glares on all his colleagues now, convinced that Captain Quelch has betrayed the original agreement. He is impatient with the sluggish controls and eventually explodes through the hull, spreading his blue wings against the wide paleness of Ko-O-Ko, the Lost Universe, determined to discover and leech the *Now The Clouds Have Meaning.*

. . . While Dilly-Dee Begg wrestles with the ruined controls!

Return to the Amber Trail

AT THE HEART of a field of cerise and yellow flame gradually crystallising to form the familiar Home Dragon, suggesting they must be close to the Martian Scaling Station, Captain Billy-Bob Begg drew comfort from her crew. All the famous Chaos Engineers were cuddled to their revered Main Type, lending their Faith to hers in an eccentric act of prayer, since they could only, now, put their trust in the Great Mood. But more than one insect face had regarded them on their journey. More than one insect had shown them the horrors of singularity as if they were proud of themselves. The *Now The Clouds Have Meaning* was unfolding and unfolding at a leisurely rate, like a slow chrysanthemum, which was the sweet-smelling emblem of most Chaos Engineers and further improved their optimism, for they had expected more roll and less of this acceptable undulation in their fall through the scale-fields.

Little Rupoldo speaks of maps ablaze and fractal loops, desperately attempting to re-bond the garden housing and harmonise with the full ship, but Corporal Organ has almost lost hope.

'Sweet Rupoldo, sweet pudding. Plums for Rupoldo now! We will float now.'

'*She bangs like a firetruck, hee, hee, hee!*' The voice of Kaprikorn Schultz, the half-hume, still follows them down the scale, powerful obscenities guaranteed to agitate their garden and butterfly them to the Great Mood knew where.

'I am too tired,' sighs Little Rupoldo, no more than a shadow in Corporal Organ's soothing arms.

'Loop upon loop, branches that are all cul-de-sacs. How can that be? Nature abhors a cul-de-sac. Is it Kaprikorn Schultz or Captain Quelch? Is it the whole brute power of the Singularity? How can we succeed?'

'Hush, diddle, hush. Hush, darling little Rupoldo. There are no cul-de-sacs in Nature. Never fear. Never fear!'

'But the end is close for that one, I think,' murmurs Professor Pop in weary sympathy, unable to take any real attention from the up-screen. 'There's Mars. I can hear her!'

'*Tower to* Now The Clouds Have Meaning. *Tower to* Now the Clouds Have Meaning. *What is your present scale? Repeat, what is your present scale? We have searched all of* the known Second Ether and found only ghosts and shadows. The famous old warhorse has screwed herself into Limbo and lies in a fold nobody can chart. Tower to Now The Clouds Have Meaning. *We cannot locate you in the Plasma Vortex. Please give us your present scale!'*

But Captain Billy-Bob Begg and her famous Chaos Engineers are unable to respond to the Scaling Station. It seems they must drift off-scale for all eternity.

'Oh, behold! Oh, fear!' Corporal Organ flings a hand towards the R. They all know that sinister shape. Kaprikorn Schultz has re-formed *The Face of the Fly!*

(To be continued)

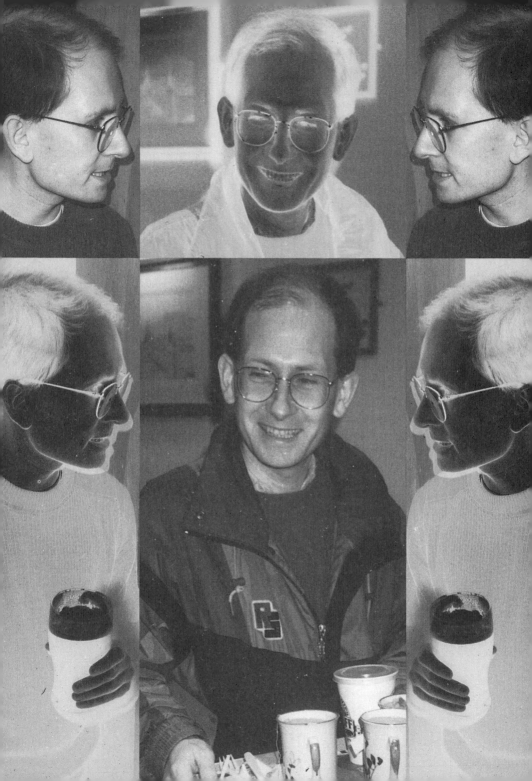

Inherit the Earth

Stephen Baxter

The thin voice, drifting through cloudy waters, caused Luke to jerk to half-wakefulness. Feebly he raised his head from the mud. The vision of his one good eye was blurred, darkened, but he could make out the fat, rectangular shape of a Boater, floating just before him; and beyond the Boater Luke could see the ranks of his clan, all around him. The Walkers' spines were lodged comfortably in the silty mud of the Bottom, and their tentacles sucked at the nourishing fluid which washed over them.

So, he thought sourly, which holy Feast had they stopped to celebrate this time? The Pilgrimage seemed to be the last thing on their tiny heathen minds whenever Luke wasn't driving them on; what a burden they were, he reflected.

Still . . . their presence, surrounding him, was very comforting.

Then he looked a little harder and saw that the Walkers were all, as far as he could see, turned towards him, their huge eyes wide with sorrowful respect. Mother of God, he thought dimly. Not so comforting after all, maybe.

Luke let his neck sag until his head bumped once more against the Bottom. He could see the twin rows of his walking spines pinned to the mud, which was piled thick with his own dung. All the spines bore the scars of age, but it was distressing that no less than five of the fourteen were snapped or otherwise bent to uselessness. Now he became aware, as if from a great distance, of the sorry state of the tentacles which lined the top surface of his horizontal trunk. Only four of the seven were strong enough to support themselves – the others hung beside him or drifted, limp, in the currents – and of the good four, one felt congested. Summoning his strength, he

coughed through that throat, feebly; a lump of some
viscous substance squirted from the tentacle, and
vaguely he could hear the tentacle's tiny, blind mouth
popping quietly as it began to suck at the cool, life-giving
water.

What a mess, he thought.

Luke wanted nothing more than to return to the
comfortable nothingness from which he had reluctantly
emerged to this sorry world of broken spines and sympathetic relatives; but the Boater droned on, pinning him
to wakefulness.

'In nomine Patris

Et Filii

Et Spiritus Sancti . . .'

Latin! A priest? Luke dipped his front tentacle forward
and called, 'Father?'

The monotonous flow of Latin cut off suddenly, and
the little Boater scurried away from Luke's head, evidently startled. The Boater was about half Luke's length;
his underside was coated with chitin and his upper side
bedecked with rows of swimming gills and a pair of long,
supple feeding arms. Two huge, black spherical eyes,
bobbling on short stalks, stared back at Luke.

'Yes, my son,' the Boater said, his composure evidently
returning. 'It's me. Father John. I'm here, Luke.'

'What's – ' Luke began, but his tentacle broke up into a
fit of helpless coughing, and he brought forward the next
tentacle, winding it past its writhing brother. 'What's
wrong?' he asked from the new mouth. 'Why have these
lazy articles stopped?'

'Now, Luke,' the Boater said gently, 'let's be patient.
The Pope has been sitting on his Island for a long time
now, and we've been looking for him for almost as long –
or so it feels sometimes. He can probably afford to wait
for us a little while yet.'

'But why . . .? Is somebody ill?'

'Yes, Luke,' the priest said solemnly.

With a spurt of lucidity Luke understood. 'It's me, isn't
it?' he asked, wondering, fear beginning to uncurl.
'. . . Am I dying, Father John?'

The Boater moved closer to him; when his various
diaphragms vibrated again his voice, though comically
high compared to the average Walker's, was full of com-

passion. Somehow that compassion frightened Luke more than his own condition.

'Be calm,' Father John said. 'Soon your troubles here will be over, and you'll be received into the Eternal light of His grace – '

'You were giving me the Last Rites,' Luke said, his aural membranes quivering in response to the panic in his own throat; and to his shame his head rotated on its spindle of neck and the throats of his other tentacles began to mewl, like cubs.

'You must not distress yourself,' the priest said. 'Try not to speak . . .'

Luke felt as if the Bottom had opened up beneath him, revealing only darkness, nonexistence. He gripped mud with his spines, as if clinging to life itself . . . And there, unexpected, resting in the dung between his spines, was the Clan's precious statue of the Virgin Mary, a crude sphere of sand welded together by Roller-spittle; Luke stared at the holy sculpture with relief, a brief Hail Mary sounding in his head. 'I don't want to die,' he told the Virgin.

'He has conquered Death,' the priest said softly; but his words were hollow to Luke.

'I've lived a good life, Father,' Luke murmured. 'Haven't I?'

'I know you have,' John said, 'and He knows. Now, come; let's pray together.'

'Yes. Yes – '

Soon the familiar, ancient words were lapping over Luke's awareness like childhood mud, and gradually his fear dissipated; but as his thoughts softened, comfortably, towards sleep, one jagged, glaring edge remained, impossible to ignore.

Despite his words to the priest, as he had stared into the Valley of Death during these moments of rationality it had not been a fear of damnation, or an awareness of his own failings in the eyes of the Lord, which had frightened him so. It had been doubt.

As he sank into sleep Luke swore that if God granted him any more life he would use it to pursue those doubts until they were scraped out of his soul.

Somewhat to his own surprise – and to the even greater surprise, even disappointment, Luke mused ruefully, of his argumentative Clan – Luke did live. He wondered morbidly if it had been the shock of that sudden doubt which had prodded him back to life. Still, the deadening, enervating weakness which had settled on his system for so long did seem to have lifted a little. Nothing was going to make him young again, of course, but he offered up prayers of gratitude to be able once more, even if only for a little longer, to feed with genuine relish on the rich, food-laden currents, and to raise his head to gaze at the beauty of the rippling Surface above him and of the red, stationary globe that was the Sun.

When he felt well enough he asked Michael, one of the less annoying of the recent youngsters, to send for Father John. After a short time the priest came bobbing delicately through the water over the heads of the grazing Walkers of the Clan.

Luke extended all his functioning tentacles towards the priest as the little Boater settled to the mud. 'Welcome back, Father. Thanks for bringing me comfort. Will you eat?'

The priest's swimming gills rippled, evidently with pleasurable anticipation. 'I'd be delighted, Luke.' Father John murmured a rapid Grace; then, his eyes bobbling against each other, the priest settled to the mound of encrusted faeces beneath Luke and proceeded to munch contentedly.

'Father, we've been together a long time,' Luke said. 'My Clan have been part of your parish since I was barely out of the mud myself.'

'Since the days of your predecessor Thomas, in fact,' the priest said indistinctly, his feeder-claws digging between Luke's spines. 'Good old Thirteen-Spined Tom; what a rascal he was . . . Long may we remain such friends.'

'We will, as long as I'm alive,' Luke said. He added ruefully, 'For whatever comfort that's worth, in the circumstances. I know about the gossip going around my younger Clanfolk. That only Walkers can make good Catholics. I'll have none of it. That way lies schism and conflict.'

'Thank you, Luke; I appreciate that.' The chitin shell of Father John's belly scraped the mud as he ate, and his diaphragms shimmered in a conspiratorial whisper. 'Between you and me, there's similar chitchat going on

among some of the less responsible Boaters these days. I
dare say it, among the Burrowers, Rollers, Hoppers and
all the rest, if only they'd admit to it.'

'Really?' Luke wondered briefly what Thomas would
have made of that. Thrown the Burrowers and the rest
out of the Pilgrimage, probably. 'Well, you and I are of
the old stock, Father; as long as we're around, we'll not
let such loose talk damage our friendship.'

'Good for you, Luke,' the priest said. 'It's a comfort to
me to know that your faith is as strong as ever.'

That jarred Luke, and guilt flushed through his system.
Seeking a distraction, he worked the long muscles along
his horizontal trunk; he moved stiffly across the Bottom,
his spines scraping through the viscous mud. The priest
scurried to keep up with him, working his way through
the dung.

'Actually, Father,' Luke said, his vocal membranes
heavy with guilt, 'that's why I asked to see you. Faith.'

The gills on the Boater's back settled into uncertain
watchfulness. 'Luke, is something wrong?'

Luke sighed with four mouths, harmoniously, and
settled back into the mud. He told the priest as honestly
as he could of the doubts which had assailed him.

The priest's tone was mellifluous. 'I think you're
worrying yourself about nothing,' he said. 'We're all
frightened of death. It's only natural that you should
have been scared, confused, in that brief moment of
lucidity when you thought you were at the end of your
life. Even the Lord on the Cross cried out, "Why have
You forsaken me?" That's not the same as a loss of faith.'

Luke felt himself tremble. 'I'm sorry, Father, but it isn't
just that. I know what I felt, in my heart of hearts, in that
extreme moment. I looked for my faith – and it wasn't
there. Now I'm strong again, I'm left with a head full of
questions.'

The priest's eyestalks shot out from between Luke's
two front spines and turned to stare at each other in a
disconcerting Boater gesture Luke recognised as signify-
ing confusion, perhaps distress. 'Would it help if I heard
your Confession?'

Luke dropped his head. 'Thank you, Father, but I
doubt it. Anyway,' he added with morbid humour, 'I
don't imagine you could spare the time. You see, suddenly faith isn't enough for me. I've been a good Catholic

all my life; I've followed the teachings of the Scriptures, and have raised my Clan in the faith . . . every last pagan one of them. The Clan have done the same for generations before me, even before the Pilgrimage. Now, suddenly, I find myself asking – what proof do we have that all this is true? How do we know if the Lord – if humans, even – ever really existed? When you get down to it, we only have the Pope's word for it; and it does all seem a bit unlikely.'

The priest's eyestalks knotted loosely.

Luke, touched by concern, said swiftly, 'I don't mean to be blasphemous, Father John. I'm sorry if I'm shocking you, or upsetting you.'

'You're not being blasphemous, Luke,' the little priest said quietly. 'But you're upsetting me. I'll not deny that. Faith is its own proof.'

Luke sighed. 'I know that faith should not need evidence, that faith is all the stronger without it. But . . . Father, I can't still the questions in my mind. I looked into darkness when I was close to death. Now I find I fear that there is nothing beyond this tired little pond-world we swim in. That faith is an elaborate illusion we have constructed for ourselves, to save us from going mental.'

'Luke, Luke.' The priest clicked his eyeballs together, evidently irritated. 'It's a pity old Tom isn't around to knock some sense back into you. How could a mere illusion have lasted through five billion years?'

Luke felt his tentacles grow stiff with exasperation. 'What evidence do we have that Catholicism really is five billion years old? What if the world emerged from chaos, from nothingness – ' He plucked a figure from the water. ' – say, a hundred generations ago? Even that is so distant that none of us can know for certain what happened then . . .'

The little Boater rose from the Bottom, his gills whirring. Prissily he wiped his feeder-claws on the edge of his lower carapace, scraping away Luke's dung. 'I'm sad to see you like this, Luke, but I don't understand what I can do to help you. Perhaps you will call for me again when you are ready to put aside all these words and look into your heart.'

'Father. Wait. Please . . .'

The Boater did not settle to the mud again, but he paused in the water, his eyes turned cautiously to Luke.

Luke had come to a decision. 'I've got to get rid of these doubts,' he said. 'I've been talking to some of the youngsters. They're not all a bad lot, you know, but they called a halt to the Pilgrimage while I slept . . .'

Long ago, the Clan's legends related, the Pope had ruled the sky beyond the Surface. Then he had descended to the world, built his fabled Island, and – by helping the forefathers of the various species to develop awareness and understanding – had restored Catholicism to a heathen world.

The stories said that the Pope's Island was to be found at the edge of the world, in the unknown seas away from the Sun. So, for generations, the Clan – and its clouds of symbiotes and darting, tiny fish – had followed those legends on a holy Pilgrimage to the Island.

Now they had come to a halt.

Luke said, 'They say they won't move until I'm well again. They say. You know what the truth is, Father. They won't budge another spine's width until they've got me safely buried. This is the end of the Pilgrimage for me.'

The Boater said, 'The youngsters are concerned for your health, Luke.'

Luke rattled his spines impatiently. 'I know they are, Father, but I want to go on. I've spent my life on this journey; and – who knows? – it might only be a little further.

'Father, I want to see the Pope before I die. If anyone can resolve my doubts, surely he can. I want you to help me.'

The Boater's eyestalks turned to each other briefly, and assorted diaphragms rippled with a noise Luke recognised as Boater laughter. It sounded like a Walker child at play, Luke thought.

Father John said, 'The youngsters say there is some tough countryside ahead, Luke. Too tough for silly old fools like you and me, at any rate.'

'I don't give a damn, if you'll pardon, Father,' Luke said, and he felt his head rotate with vehemence. 'It might be possible for me to make it. Who knows? I won't have the bother of shepherding the whole wretched Clan; I'll leave them here and go on alone . . . although I'll have some of them to help me. The best of the youngsters: Michael, Margaret perhaps. At any rate, I'll go as far as I can. If I don't survive the trip – well, I'm in the silt of my life already, Father . . . Join me. Please. You've been my lifelong companion in faith; please join me now, in my darkest hour.'

The priest hovered, hesitating still.

Michael and Margaret thought the expedition was a stupid idea too; but, apparently out of fondness – or, worse, pity, Luke thought sourly – they agreed to come. So the four of them, the three Walkers and the unhappy Boater priest, set off from the dense encampment of the Clan.

Their progress across the Bottom was limited chiefly by Luke's own painfully slow pace. The priest darted behind them, munching on drifting faecal snacks. As they travelled, Luke's aural membranes were washed with the patient murmur of Michael and Margaret as they whispered memorised fragments of Scripture to each other. And every time they awoke they prayed togther that they would reach the mysterious Island of the Pope himself before they slept again.

'Of course I'm glad I came along,' Margaret said.

'Then stop complaining,' Luke grumbled, wincing at the stiffness in the joints of spine and trunk as he scraped across the unfamiliar Bottom.

'I wasn't complaining. I just said we'd make quicker progress if we didn't have to carry that stupid Virgin Mary along with us. Why not leave Her here? We can collect Her on the way back.'

Luke defensively closed his tentacles around the precious lump of sand and Roller-spit, licking it gently; when he spoke again his voice was muffled by mouthfuls of sand grains. 'We'd never find Her again.'

Margaret said, 'Then you should have left Her behind in the first place, you daft old fool.'

Michael came sliding with enviable grace over to Luke. 'Stop teasing him, Margaret. The older folk find these things a comfort.'

'Thanks a lot,' Luke muttered.

'Older folk indeed,' Father John said. The priest's membranes hissed with good-natured annoyance. 'If only these youngsters had seen what we've seen. Old Thirteen Spines didn't make do with one measly Virgin. Did he,

Luke? In those times we had to lug along six Crucifixes, four statues of the Sacred Heart and a full set of Stations of the Cross. All nibbled out of the best Burrower dung.'

'Quite right, Father,' Luke said. 'And we'd have it all still if it hadn't been pinched by those Eaters.'

'Yes, what a bunch of pagans,' the priest said. 'Do you know, Luke, I've never met an Eater yet who could grasp the concept of the Holy Trinity. And – '

'I just find the whole situation ironic,' Margaret said brashly. She was very bright, and essentially good-natured, Luke knew – and, with those long, slender, golden-brown spines, one of the most attractive of the recent crop – but she had a streak of coarse honesty in her that was more than disconcerting. She went on, 'Here we are on a quest to restore Luke's faith, and yet he brings along the most perfect symbol of the unresolved questions that lie at the heart of our religion.'

Luke mouthed the Virgin uncertainly. 'What do you mean? What's wrong with Her?'

Michael sighed. 'She's talking about the debate on the form which humans took. I mean, the statue you're carrying is based on guesswork, really, from clues in the Scriptures.'

'Which are hardly comprehensive,' Margaret said. 'So we can never be sure what – '

'I thought it was all settled,' Luke said, confused. 'Humans must have been . . . well, round. Every animal works – ingests, breathes – through surfaces. And the bigger you are, the more surface area you need. We – every species we know about – have solved this problem by having a lot of external surface, by being covered in threads, sheets, spines, gills, loops. The humans had all their surfaces wrapped up inside them.'

'Yes,' Michael said patiently, 'they were simpler exter-nally, but a sphere is the simplest shape of all. What if they were a bit less simple? What if they were – I don't know – shaped like Father John up there, but without the gills? It's perfectly possible.'

'Right,' Margaret said vigorously. 'I mean, what do we really know about the humans?'

'We know Christ was a human,' Father John said quietly from somewhere overhead.

Margaret ignored him. 'For instance we know the humans were divided into men and women. And it took

men and women to produce new humans; they didn't
just go off by themselves and bud, the way we do. We
even take the names of human men and women from the
Scriptures; but I'm not a woman, any more than Luke or
Michael is a man. The names are simply labels we adopt.
There's so much that's alien to us. For instance, what
was the big deal about the Virgin Birth? Was Christ born
from some combination of men and women that was
different from the usual? If so, so what? What can it
mean to us?'

Michael waved his tentacles thoughtfully. 'I'm glad I
don't mix with the folk you do, Margaret. That stuff's a
little too heady for me. I'm still confused about why we
have to hear Mass in Latin.'

The priest was doing slow somersaults in the water
above them, his feeder-claws snapping idly at the Surface. 'Now there we do have an answer,' he said, his
eyestalks bobbling as he swam. 'The Second Vatican
Council was declared heretical when Pope Paul IX
decreed that – '

Luke wasn't listening; Margaret's words still flowed
through his mind. There was logic in some of what she'd
said – and he had to remind himself that it was his own
doubts which had inspired this jaunt in the first place.
Still, though, he found Margaret's words shocking. He
licked his statue tenderly. 'I don't think I care what you
kids say,' he said slowly. 'To me this is how She looked.
And that's all that matters. Isn't it?'

'I don't know, Luke,' the priest called in his fluting
voice. 'Is it? Perhaps if I knew the answer to that, I
wouldn't be neglecting my parishioners to come on this
damn silly expedition.'

When Luke got too tired the other Walkers would nestle
close to him, supporting him so that he could keep
moving, while the little priest hovered above dropping
succulent fragments of food close to his weary mouths.

The colour of the Bottom changed: a gritty sand, sickly
yellow, replaced warm brown mud. The Surface seemed
a little further away, the water deeper. They saw few
Walkers, Boaters, Rollers, or any of the species with
which they were familiar. The water itself changed; even
to Luke's depleted senses it had become cold, thin,

*spiced with unfamiliar flavours. It wasn't comfortable,
but it was all a sign that they were making progress.*

Things, for a while, went well.

The Eater was immense, four or five times the size of the
Walkers and utterly dwarfing the poor, terrified priest.

It came drifting out of the distance to loom over them.
Huge flukes beat, while a circular mouth set in a head the
size of two Boaters opened and closed, dilating.

The expedition froze, the Walkers trembling together
and the Boater priest cowering against the Bottom.

The Eater inspected them with one huge, scarred eyeball. Then the beast rumbled a crude profanity and
descended towards Luke. To the Walker, staring up, it
was like watching a mouth close over him.

The priest fled in a flurry of gills. The other Walkers,
Michael and Margaret, hurried across the sand . . . but
Luke held his ground, cowering into a ball against the dirt.

The Eater's shadow was like death descending.

Margaret returned to his side, all her throats keening
with terror. 'Luke, get out of here. He'll kill you!'

Luke's head rotated helplessly. 'The Virgin Mary,' he
said. 'He's after Her. Not me. They like the dung, you
see . . .'

'He'll bite you in half to get to Her,' Margaret cried.
'Luke, please – '

Luke closed his eyes and settled more closely around
the little statue, Hail Marys ringing in his head.

Then Margaret rammed him.

He felt her blunt, heavy head slamming into his trunk,
knocking him helplessly sideways. He rolled across the
sand, his useless spines flapping painfully. When he
came to rest, he opened his good eye and looked back.

Margaret cowered in the place from which she had
thrown him. She lay against the sand with her spines
spreadeagled, her head rotating helplessly, as the Eater
descended on her, hissing through its dilating maw.

Luke was buffeted by a cloud of gritty sand as the
Eater's immense bulk crashed to the Bottom, hopelessly
crushing Margaret. From beneath the cruel flange of the
beast two pathetic, golden-brown spine tips protruded;
Luke, unable to move or even to cry out, watched them
twitch. Once, twice . . .

Then, mercifully, it was over.

The Eater, mumbling a heathen caricature of Grace, lifted. It belched fragments of carapace from its circular maw and, with a shuddering beat of its long tail, moved away and out of sight.

The sunlight returned to the scrap of sea bed on which lay scattered the remains of Margaret . . . and the undamaged globe of the Virgin Mary.

Michael scraped a grave from the sand, and the priest intoned a simple service. Then Father John said Mass for the two surviving Walkers. Luke, resting against Michael's comforting strength, allowed the little priest to drop consecrated fragments of Burrower droppings into one of his mouths, and let the familiar Latin words flow through him.

At times like this, he thought, the strength or weakness of his faith was beside the point. For faith, in the face of such meaningless tragedy, was all he had.

When they had rested they went on. Father John stayed closer to the illusory protection of the Walkers. Luke, battered in the Eater attack, was slower still and more reliant than ever on the strength of Michael.

The death of Margaret seemed to have drained the resolve out of him. He would never see his Clan again; of that he felt sure.

But, despite everything, a small grain of determination remained lodged in his soul. He was going to find the Pope.

He nestled against the strong, warm shoulders of his good young friend and concentrated on dragging his spines across the strange mud, watching his long shadow cross the Bottom before him.

Father John, high in the water, saw it first. His voice came down to the Walkers, thin and scared. 'Dear Lord – Dear Lord – '

Michael looked up, startled; Luke tried to raise his head as his four mouths laboured at the thin water.

The little priest came tumbling end over end from the Surface; at last he settled against the Bottom and lay there on his belly, his gills working feebly.

Luke painfully slid across the sand to him. 'The Island,' he said gruffly. 'You can see it, can't you?'

'Yes,' said Father John.

Everyone knew that the Pope's Island, the only Island in the World, reared above the water, breaking the Surface itself. When Luke had thought about it, he'd vaguely imagined a wall of mud rising from the Bottom towards the distant sky.

Instead, long before he or Michael could see anything of the Island itself, he found himself climbing a slope. The climb was quite shallow but almost beyond Luke, exhausted as he was; and the band of pilgrims was forced to take frequent rests while Michael murmured words of encouragement to Luke. In his weariness, Luke's sight, hearing – the scent and taste of the water in his four working throats – all seemed to recede from him; it was as if he swam in some inner sea, insulated from the world he had known.

At last the water was too shallow for them to proceed.

Luke raised his head to see Michael lift a trembling tentacle to prod at the thick, elastic Surface. Luke had never come so close to the Surface before. The water here was filled with light; the Bottom was of gritty sand and dappled with crimson sunlight; and the currents were swirling, buffeting, the waters thin and almost devoid of nourishment.

The little priest bravely swam up to the Surface, poked a tentative eyestalk through the thick, stiff meniscus. Luke could see how the Surface bent upwards around the eyestalk, as if dragging it back.

Michael shivered beside Luke. 'We can't go on, and we can't stay here long; the water's almost too thin to breathe. Even if the Pope is there, he won't know we're here.'

'Oh, I think he knows.' The Boater priest retracted his eyeball from the world above the Surface and floated down to the huddled Walkers.

Luke raised his head. 'He's there? The Pope? He's there?'

Father John drifted before Luke's head. 'Yes, Luke, he's there. We've found him.'

Luke's tentacles quivered. The Pope . . . Whenever he'd thought of the Pope, he realised suddenly, he'd always imagined a huge, sterner version of Thirteen-Spined Thomas.

'Father, tell me. What does he look like?'

Father John withdrew a little, his gills flapping and his

feeder-claws picking at each other in slow confusion.
'He's nothing like any of us. He's immense; I looked up,
lifting back my eye, but could not see to the top of him.
He's made of something that shines, red and gold in the
light of the Sun.'

'What shape is he?'

'I don't know, Michael. Like a huge Boater set on end,
maybe. It was hard to see.'

Michael nodded his head. 'Above the Surface, in the
glare, it must be difficult to make out – '

'Not just that.' The little priest's eyestalks knotted.
'The shape was indistinct. It changed, all the time,
almost too fast for me to see. It was as if he were
surrounded by a cloud of creatures. Like tiny fish. The
fish would clump in schools, settle on the main Boater-
shape; it glittered and sparkled as its form changed.'
Father John's voice seemed close to breaking, suddenly;
the courage was visibly draining from him. 'It was wonderful, Luke, like a vision from Heaven. Like something
made out of water itself.' Clumsily he made the Sign of
the Cross with a feeder claw and subsided to the Bottom,
muttering prayers.

Michael turned to Luke. 'What shall we do?'

Luke sighed. 'Wait, I suppose.'

He closed his eyes and began a Rosary, counting the
Hail Marys on the crusty grains of the Virgin.

Suddenly the Surface erupted in a noisy explosion of
light and tiny bubbles. All three of the Pilgrims cowered
back from the swirling motion in the water. Luke, staring
with his good eye, could see that there were many
creatures here, before him; as the priest had described, it
was like a school of tiny fish – but whirling about each
other more rapidly than any fish.

One of them came looming out of the pack to hover
before him, quivering. It was tiny, no more than a ten-
tacle-tip long. Michael squealed, somewhere behind him;
but Luke stared back at the odd little creature without
fear.

After a few moments the fish-thing rejoined its fellows.
Again the water thrashed, and the Surface quivered as if
beaten from above.

Then, miraculously, Luke saw a figure condense out of
the water where the fish shoal had been. It was difficult

to see – virtually transparent, and with blurred, ever-changing outline – but the overall shape was clear enough. There was the horizontal trunk, the seven pairs of spines embedded in the sand, the seven tentacles waving about, the shapeless plug of a head.

Luke heard Michael gasp. 'It's a Walker. The fish have made themselves into a Walker.'

Now the creature bent all its tentacles towards Luke in the Walkers' universal gesture of friendship.

'Yes,' Luke said softly. 'He's making us welcome.'

Stiffly he moved his four functioning tentacles forward, mouths closed, to match the mock creature's stance; and beside him Michael did the same.

The voice of the Pope-Walker was thin and high, but its words were clear. 'Hello,' it said. 'I'm not used to visitors.'

'We're Pilgrims,' Luke said, feeling his head droop between his front spines.

'Pilgrims?' The Pope-Walker's ghostly tentacles wriggled in amusement. 'Two tiny crab-things and a swimming dust-mote. However,' kindly, 'it's what's in your hearts that counts, I suppose.'

'I have questions,' Luke felt an impatient anxiety welling up in him. To have come so far, it would be unbearable to be refused now. 'Please.'

The Pope-Walker was studying him. 'You're ill, pilgrim,' it said softly.

'I know that,' Luke snapped, and he sucked noisily at the thin water with his spare mouths.

The Pope-Walker's head rolled complacently around its axis of neck; to Luke it was like watching shadows shift through the water. 'Questions, eh? Typical. And I suppose you want answers. Where is your faith?'

'Why should we accept your faith?' Luke snapped, ignoring the gasps of protest from the priest who cowered behind him. 'You brought Catholicism to us, from out of the sky. Or is that another fable, like the Messiah Himself?'

'You're not as bitter as you sound, pilgrim. Oh, the Messiah is no fable. At least I don't think He is . . . I've given this a lot of thought, over the years I've been stuck here. You see, I might be right about Him. On the other

hand,' the Pope went on cheerfully, 'I could be two Hail
Marys short of a full Rosary. It's hard to tell, isn't it?

'Little pilgrim, I can't make you believe what I say, any
more than I could answer the questions of the humans
who used to visit me. Some of them, you know, wouldn't
even accept an AI as Pope. Ah, what a debate that was.
Nearly caused a schism. The Jesuits who built me
wanted to place the burden of faith on the believer, you
see. You're not a Jesuit, are you? What a Cross they were
to bear . . . Sanctimonious rabble. If you have faith, it is
because of what is within you, not what is within me.
For you see,' the Pope-Walker rambled on sadly, 'there is
nothing within me.'

Luke felt his head droop further as he struggled to
make sense of these strange words.

Michael stretched his neck forward. 'What were
humans like? Were they round?'

The Pope-Walker wriggled its tentacles in a burst of
amusement. 'My mission was human souls, not human
bodies. I'm sure their souls were just like yours. Apart
from that – who knows? Maybe humans were more like
me.'

'Then what are you?' Michael asked timidly.

'I'm a bush-robot,' the Pope-Walker said. 'You pilgrims
– not the little fat one – have twenty-one limbs, counting
your spines and tentacles. But I have many thousands;
and each of those thousands have thousands of their
own. And so on . . . Oh dear; you still don't know what
I'm talking about, do you? I was made this way so I could
maintain myself for ever, virtually.'

Luke rested his head, now, against the gritty sand; the
darkness was like the warm mud of his childhood, waiting to reclaim him.

The Pope-Walker's shimmering head hovered before
him. 'You haven't much time,' it said.

Luke tried to look up. 'Is it true? The story that the
Saviour came among us, five billion years ago?'

The Walker's head filled his vision, soft and comforting. 'What a question. Do you know what a "billion" is,
pilgrim? Or even a "year"? It's about twice your lifespan,
as it happens, but I suppose that's beside the point . . .

'Listen to me. When I was built the Sun was hot and
yellow. I watched it grow huge, red, cooling. Oh, yes,
things changed, slowly.

'After some time, the humans stopped speaking to me. I waited, alone.

'At length, still alone, I decided to come back to Earth.

'The humans had gone. I found a shallow sea, covering the Sun-facing hemisphere. And you lot, who had evidently inherited the Earth.'

Luke said, unsure if he even spoke it aloud, 'Did the humans really exist?'

'Pilgrim, even I don't know any more. Perhaps the humans and the legend of the Christ, were all a dream. How could I be certain? After all this time . . . I wanted to find out. I wanted to find traces of humans. So, working from my Island, I began surveys, drilling, seeking fossils.

'But the strata have been metamorphosed, after five billion years. Whole continents have dissolved back into the body of the Earth. No fossil traces of the humans could have survived such aeons. Do you understand any of this? Just listen to me; try to gather the sense.

'Life can leave other traces. Plants selectively extract a certain carbon isotope – carbon-12. So I searched the deep rocks, the old rocks, for the smear of isotopic carbon which would be the sole memorial of the humans after all this time.'

Dimly, Luke was aware of the priest calling his name with concern, of Michael frantically mouthing his tentacles and limbs; but it was all far from him now, all remote from this place he had reached with the Pope-Walker.

'Luke,' the Pope-Walker whispered to him.

'How do you know my name?'

'Grasp your faith. You do not need to share my doubts.'

'Tell me,' Luke said softly, his voice light, easy. 'Did you find this – carbon-12?'

The Pope-Walker's eyes were huge before him. 'It would prove nothing . . . Only that life of some form covered the Earth, all those years ago. Not even that humans existed. Certainly not that Christ lived. Luke, resolve one mystery and you reveal more; that is why questions and answers can never lead you to faith. Even the humans can never have been certain . . .

'The world is full of mystery! Pilgrim, I am intelligent. Far more intelligent than you, or even any human, I dare say . . . Even the Jesuits. But I am not self-aware. You are

self-aware, pilgrim, and that is a far greater mystery than anything you might ask of me. Perhaps it is I who should supplicate before you – '

It was no answer, Luke thought, and he wasn't going to get an answer; but there was a triumph, a kind of joy in the mist-like eyes of the Pope-Walker.

Once more he heard the ancient, holy verses of the Last Rites. The Pope's thin Latin words lingered even as its shimmering face receded, leaving Luke in muddy, comforting darkness; and he felt his faith settle over him once more, as strong as the spines of his Clan.

Of course the Pope was right. There could be no answer, no final answer . . . but somehow it no longer mattered.

Still Father John called his name, as if from a great distance. It was time, Luke knew; and, without regret, he sank into the warmth of the mud.

A Gadget Too Far

David Langford

The general public regards sf as a wonderland of amazing gadgets and special effects in titanic collision – where, by implication, all problems and conflicts are artificial because the author (or the movie producer) can always dispose of a superscientific threat by dreaming up a hyperscientific counter-attack. What a superficial and unfair view – or is it? By and by we shall examine the technological clutter of some recent and popular books.

Let me creep up furtively on the subject matter. There is an official myth about science which persists in spite of regular debunking (see Stephen Jay Gould or Sir Peter Medawar) – the myth that all scientists dispassionately collect data, turn a cold eye on the resulting array of facts, and then for the very first time permit themselves to think. Induction takes place; a theory is born. The funny thing is that although creative scientists almost invariably work the other way around, beginning with a perhaps half-intuitive speculation and testing this by experiment, most of them solemnly pretend to follow this mythical pattern.

The often-cited myth of sf has a similar austere and unlikely flavour. Following the tradition of H. G. Wells, sf writers are or were supposed to permit themselves a single innovation, a solitary change in the world. 'Suppose . . . suppose that chemical fertilisers made people grow 36 feet tall. What then?' The rest of the story must follow with iron logic and implacable extrapolation. Like the science myth, this version of things tries for an appearance of intellectual rigour at the expense of such airy-fairy trimmings as, well, creativity . . .

Actually Wells himself found it necessary not so much to extrapolate as to avoid too much extrapolation. Think of Cavorite in *The First Men in the Moon*. This is a mere device for getting our heroes to the Moon by cutting off the tiresome pull of gravity – but it does rather tend to overthrow a great deal of existing physics. As described in the book, a slab of Cavorite instantly infuses any object immediately above it with the full gravitic potential energy required to shift said object to infinity. Energy from nowhere! First-order perpetual motion machines! No wonder the luckless inventor Cavor had to be disposed of by ravening Selenites, along with his formula.

(He was a rotten scientist anyway, remarking among other things that a small, bolted-down square of Cavorite could rapidly squirt away the Earth's entire atmosphere. The student is invited to estimate what percentage of our planet's mass would be gravitationally screened off from the viewpoint of an oxygen molecule two miles up. But I digress.)

Gravity insulators, space warpers, time machines, matter transmitters, faster-than-light travel, even the humble instantaneous communicator: let any of them into the story and a great deal of extrapolation has to be rigorously avoided. Otherwise, cracks begin to radiate from the big hole you've just kicked in physics, and the entire structure wobbles tremulously. To save the day it may even be necessary to invoke a race of enigmatic aliens whose science does not know our puny human limitations. (L. Ron Hubbard's Psychlos went so far as to use a different periodic table, full of unfamiliar elements.)

Thus the 'farcaster' or instantaneous matter transmitter of Dan Simmons's entertaining *Hyperion* (1989) and *The Fall of Hyperion* (1990) is the gift of exceedingly clever AIs who, by generously not telling humanity how it works, permit our own scientific knowledge to remain intact and self-consistent even if presumably wrong.

In fact there's a great deal more in Simmons's two-part space opera – or space *grand* opera, as one critic put it – including some very good inset stories. Gadgetry proliferates; no Wellsian he. The cumulative developments don't half get cosmic . . . for example, the story's major, all-purpose device, the Shrike, appears to be an invincible killer machine with control over space and time, whose hobby is carrying people off to eternal torment on its Tree of Pain. This unfriendly practice is eventually explained as quite logical and practical, being the baiting of an empathic trap for the ultimate, autonomous principle of compassion, i.e. one aspect of God. (That is, of *one* God. Real space opera doesn't stop at just one.) Gasp, boggle.

Unfortunately, having finally grasped that this is what the Shrike is up to, one does begin to wonder at its habit of buzzing helpfully about almost every sub-plot, smoothing transitions, precipitating climaxes and generally doing things unrelated to its supposed purpose. Surely some hidden guiding force must lie behind this behaviour, some ultimate Author?

I wondered if Simmons might be getting a trifle carried away when after vast amounts of physical and metaphysical exposition he revealed that his other major gadget the 'fatline' (instantaneous radiophone of unlimited range) operated on the private wavelength of God. Eventually, displeased at being made a vehicle for military communications and obscene chatlines rather than prayer, God concludes the book by announcing the withdrawal of this facility until further notice. Which is all very mind-wrenching, although I noticed that His prose style has deteriorated badly since the King James Bible.

This way lies pure fantasy, or perhaps not so pure when we recall Arthur C. Clarke's Third Law: 'Any sufficiently advanced technology is indistinguishable from a completely ad-hoc plot device.' Does it make that much difference whether Jack Chalker, as is his wont, transforms unfortunate female characters in grotesque and humiliating ways by scientifically rewriting the reality equations (his 'Well World' series) or magically pronouncing spells (his 'Soul Rider' series)? Either way, it appears to sell depressingly well.

The best fantasy avoids the looseness of 'anything goes' plotting by invoking rigid magical and/or moral laws. Alas, the erstwhile sf master Roger Zelazny seems to have wandered a long way off these narrow paths of restraint. His second series of 'Amber' novels (1985, 1986, 1987, 1989 *et seq*) must set some kind of record for the sheer quantity of magic gadgetry which the hero carts around an ever more convoluted multiverse, with no end in sight. As an Awful Warning, I feel that I should summarise the story so far – noting also that all these fantasy props and gimmicks could be all too effortlessly translated into sf.

Merle or Merlin (no relation) is the son of Corwin, whose adventures fill five earlier boks of seething complexity, labyrinthine family trees and an increasing dead weight of flashbacks and explanation. Merlin is a Lord of Amber (the good guys). He has walked the maze-like Pattern of Amber, gaining various powers such as pedestrian travel between worlds. (When you can't find the basic and practically unique Pattern to hand, there's always the subaquatic anti-Pattern, the alternate Pattern in the sky, and a whole slew of more real, less real, metaphorical or broken Patterns.) Owing to mixed parentage he is also a Lord of Chaos (formerly, and perhaps still, the bad guys). This provides innate gifts of shapeshifting and other handy magic: 'My Concerto for Cuisinart and Microwave spell would have minced him and parboiled him in an instant'. Some of these interesting attributes we don't learn about until the second book, where a nasty Lurker at the Threshold explains rather too smugly that none but a shapeshifting Lord of Chaos can pass this particular dread portal, and shortly afterwards adds: 'Shit.'

As well as the Pattern, Merlin has mastered its Chaos equivalent, the Logrus, conferring added powers of tactical nuclear weaponry, remote handling and magical apportation (useful, and indeed much use,d for summoning beer and pizza). He also possesses Amber's inevitable pack of Trumps (occult teleportation and cellphone service). Plus a sentient, self-propelled and chatty strangling wire, and some arcane blue stones whose properties escape my memory. Furthermore he has constructed Ghostwheel, a vast, innovative, magic-powered computer complex (I kid you not) which is self-omnipotent in his service whenever it happens not to be sulking. I gave up at the end of the fourth volume – which strangely fails to be called *Forever Amber* – when, obviously feeling the lad Merlin to be lacking in worldly resources, Zelazny issues him with an enchanted ring controlling immense new powers and offensive weaponry. Just what he needed!

I forgot to mention the Jewel of Judgement, or the Corridor of Mirrors, or the add-on pack of nonstandard Trumps, or the extremely special swords Grayswandir and Werewindle, or . . . one could go on and on, and Zelazny does.

It seems rather difficult to provide this guy Merlin with any credible opposition, especially since he also has many sorcerous pals, sisters, cousins and aunts of awesome talent to help him out of tight spots. Even though the writing is inoffensive and even amusing, enlivened by the odd wisecrack, one's lack of interest in Merlin's perils is relentlessly fanned into a blaze of apathy by this wretched plethora of plot devices. The reader is warned.

Back in the real world, the strict Wellsian rule is not altogether viable. Writers plotting their way more than a few years into the future can no longer assume that a realistic background will remain technologically (let alone politically) stable in everything except their one 'permitted' addition, the amazing Doubletalk Ray or whatever. Information technology and genetic engineering are not going to stand still, and neither, unfortunately, will global resources.

In David Brin's *Earth* (1990), for example, there are whole thickets of perfectly legitimate extrapolative material which we can take on board as a mere part of consensus future number 12, subtype IV: eco-doom, UV hazards, extinctions, pollution overload, data-net hacking and the like. Along with this come the unexpected developments which are so much to be expected (if only as happy confirmation that those bland, 'surprise-free' scenarios beloved of futurologists are particularly unlikely to come true) – strange quirks like a bloody war fought in the name of Freedom of Information against Switzerland's too-secretive bankers. I wonder which side the British government was on?

Against this quite reasonably teeming background, our author duly slips in the one real Wellsian innovation, which would appear to be a glibly plausible extension of gravitational physics as we know it. Microscopic black holes, rather than suffering the quantum-thermodynamic decay predicted by dear old Stephen Hawking, can here be 'knotted' into a kind of stability and thus last long enough to threaten the Earth by nibbling at its core. On top of this is piled a (to say the least) highly unlikely theory of gravity lasers, whereby the hungry singularities can be manipulated by surface-mounted detectors or probes, with all manner of weird anti-gravitic side effects – such as portions of the landscape bounding into orbit with an accompaniment of visual effects by Industrial Light & Magic. This particular plot-line devolves into a sort of global ping-pong game as the good guys try to nudge the unpleasantness out into space while others, many of them anonymous, prefer to keep it in there for their own nefarious purposes.

All right. The story is indeed good clean fun, exciting to read. But meanwhile, in another part of the hypertext, a more familiar computer-net war is being fought. Here the climactic action comes when a revered ecological prophetess and Nobel laureate, hard pressed by both viral assault programs and gravitic mayhem, manages with her dying keypunches to download her entire personality (a thing never apparently done before) into ... well, I have neglected to mention that those orbiting singularities within the Earth had been leaving funny tracks behind them in the planetary mantle. From the book's description it's hard to believe that these could have anything like the connective complexity of an ordinary, dumb, personal computer, but nevertheless our lady of the Green (and/or *just possibly* the whole of the world data net) is electronically translated into them, becomes the formerly hypothetical Gaia, and assumes control over gravitational physics – being able by unexplained means to exercise veto power over whether or not the gravity-laser effect works. This includes using it to literally rip to shreds 'a few hundred' persons judged as Evil (no trial; no hope of appeal; organic, holistic Gaia knows best). Once again, metaphysics.

By this time the symptoms of sf indigestion are in full writhe. What, the Tunguska 'meteor' explosion of 1908 was in fact the arrival of an ultimately life-enhancing singularity? Too much, cries the bloated reader, too much. But the irresistibly readable David Brin still has his funnel down your throat and eases in one last little delicacy, like that final wafer-thin mint which detonates Mr Creosote in Monty Python's *The Meaning of Life*. Perhaps, he hints excitingly, this unlikely farrago of events was not mere chance, but was choreographed throughout by *aliens working amongst us for our own good*!

It is deeply worthy, it is ecologically sound, but a certain desperation seems to have set in when an author tries to smooth over an excess of coincidental developments by piling on such a new and all-encompassing one.

Sf gadgets and plot devices pose especial problems in series, since they can accumulate dismayingly as the series continues (an effect already seen in 'Amber', above) – unless the writer exercises the *Star Trek* option, whereby any inconvenient addition to human knowledge may be erased at will from history before the next episode. This is not thought wholly sporting on the printed page.

Larry Niven played by the rules and, after a good deal of colourful invention, more or less ran out of creative room in his popular 'Known Space' sequence. Its chronologically final book *Ringworld Engineers* (1980) seems to be largely an exercise in resolving earlier contradictions, at the cost of adding some new ones. For example, *Engineers* centres on an expedition to Ringworld motivated by interest in the transmutation machine that produced the implausibly strong material of which this giant artificial world had to be made. Later, the possibility of such a machine's existence is dismissed, implying that the Ringworld is constructed from 2×10^{27} kilograms of nonexistent stuff . . . But the book's most hilarious ploy involves organic superconductors. Ringworld civilisation fell apart when bacteria ate said superconductors. Now our heroes wander the world, reactivating ancient devices by connecting new lengths of superconductor between likely terminals! To relish this, imagine the vanishing of all silicon chips from our own technology, and the return to life of CD players or personal computers when kindly aliens connect little bars of silicon between terminals found on the outside of each device.

The most recent 'Xeelee' stories of Britain's very own Stephen Baxter are in several ways reminiscent of Niven, and are thickly studded with enigmatic alien artifacts. I always enjoy a good old enigmatic alien artifact myself, but Baxter has determinedly Thought Big about it all. As a result he's saddled himself with such a vast, sprawling, cosmological overplot (something to do with retrospectively landscaping the entire universe) that a god-like and disembodied point of view is required to explain all its complexities to the increasingly bemused reader – which duly happens in 'The Baryonic Lords' (in *Interzone*, 1991). Only Olaf Stapledon ever succeeded on this kind of scale, and Olaf Stapledon is dead.

Admittedly Dan Simmons, concluding his own miniseries in *The Fall of Hyperion*, makes a brave attempt at putting across *his* bizarre metaphysical rationale for everything that's been happening. Sensing that this stuff might read as excessively mindboggling or even ridiculous if delivered in clear, he filters it through a maddeningly quirky AI who talks a mixture of Zen koans and

Keats quotations, laid out as awful blank verse and festooned with funny symbols evocative of computer meeps
and bleeps. A special Signal To Noise Ratio Award is
surely merited here.

Orson Scott Card has been more cautiously parsimonious
when introducing new elements to his award-laden
'Ender' series ... at least until the latest volume, which
after a long, harrowing and genuinely impressive development suddenly goes bananas. It is a puzzle. The page
ripples and blurs at this point, to denote a flashback.

Ender's Game (1985) begins the sequence. Andrew
'Ender' Wiggin comes on stage at the tender age of six,
an all-round genius, destined to be humanity's military
leader against the unspeakable alien 'buggers'. (Almost
immediately, he kills a contemporary in unarmed combat.
Tougher school than mine.) A great deal of battle training
and war-gaming follows. Ender never loses, no matter
how overwhelmingly the odds are piled up against him.
(He kills a second comrade in the course of all this –
again, unarmed.) By the age of eleven he has wiped out
the alien race.

Which sounds like awful, jackbooted stuff; but in fact
Card manages to have it both ways. If you like rousing
descriptions of strategy, tactics and action on artificial
battlefields, these can be enjoyed for their own sake. If
not, the object of distaste is not our child hero but the
military types who (not without remorse of their own)
manipulate him: although definitely too gifted to be true,
Ender himself is a sympathetic character. His killings are
unintentional, in desperate self-defence. Even his genocide is unknowing, tackily forced on him in the guise of
training simulations. It is somewhat harder to believe the
parallel storyline which has his equally precocious Good
Sister (12) and Nasty Brother (14) more or less running
Earth through media manipulation by the time of the
climax, but on the whole the book works.

Plot devices: instantaneous communicator (Card bor-
rows Ursula Le Guin's name for it, the ansible. Did *you*

know it was an anagram of 'lesbian'?), slower-than-light interstellar craft, planet-busting disruption bomb, one surviving 'hive queen' of the insect-like aliens.

Speaker for the Dead (1986) heads off in a new direction, with a complex – though science-fictionally all too familiar – biological puzzle on Lusitania, a new planet of human colonists, intelligent native 'piggies', a weird animal/vegetable life cycle, a dread virus which makes AIDS look like a pussycat, and much inter-species incomprehension. Not bad at all, with some strong and emotive character interaction.

Plot devices: 'descolada' virus, sentient trees, a mysterious artificial intelligence called Jane, Ender's compassionate release of the hive queen to breed anew on Lusitania (perhaps not very logical with two intelligent species already in residence).

Xenocide (1991) marks the point where all the accumulated gimmicks and plot points reach a dangerous critical mass *even though* most of the book is compulsively readable and well written. As it has to be to keep all its crummy-sounding elements under control. Are you sitting comfortably? Then I'll begin.

Item: the descolada is constantly rearranging itself to overcome human medical defences, and might even be intelligent. Item: for the foregoing reason, at least one person feels strongly that 'xenocide' should not be committed even against the virus. (Later, this interesting point is quietly dropped.) Item: running scared, the human Hegemony has long since despatched a relativistic fleet carrying planet-busters to sterilise Lusitania . . . and here it comes. Item: Jane the AI, who mysteriously lives in the interstices of the ansible network, is able to cut off all fleet communications so that the fatal order cannot be given. Item: on a Hegemony world of super-geniuses kept under control by deliberate genetic crippling (giving them uncontrollable OCD, or obsessive-compulsive disorder), the very brilliant Qing-jao is hot on Jane's informational trail and will soon be able to kill or disable 'her'. Item: the hive queen with its new brood of workers has now developed spacecraft and generously offered them to the piggies should they (with their dread disease) wish to escape and infect the galaxy. Egged on by rogue sentient trees, some of them do wish it. Item: a counter-agent to the virus seems impossible to synthesise owing to impossible intermediate steps. Item: the nature of the descolada implies an author, in the form of yet another intelligent and nasty race (as yet unencountered) which has chosen this means to set its own seal on developing species – the piggies' evolution has been grossly tampered with.

Phew. There is more, but this covers most of the elements in Card's intractably knotted plot. It seems impossible that the book can end other than in major tragedy. Card hasn't shirked incredibly painful climaxes in the past. One pants at the edge of one's seat.

And then . . .

In a narrowly legalistic way, much of what follows can be sort of justified by the stipulated existence of the ansible. As implied earlier, trying to insert this device into a universe dominated by relativity (all those slower-than-light spacecraft, etc) does in principle bust the whole of physics wide open. One contradiction in a logical system means that anything whatever can 'logically' follow. A puzzled don once asked Bertrand Russell how the assumption that 1 equals 2 could possibly lead to the conclusion that, say, Russell was the Pope. It was perfectly simple, the philosopher explained. The Pope and he were two people; but it was now given that $2 = 1$; and so the Pope and he were one.

Just so, by fiddling around with the fake physics of the ansible, Card fudges up a justification for genuine, physical travel with the same instantaneous alacrity. Fair enough, although even this is something of a betrayal of the book's remorseless quality – this fearfully *sci-fi* rewriting of basic physics exactly at the eleventh hour. That door once opened, in comes the metaphysics. The instantaneous transit is achieved by, approximately, assuming that in a context of ansible 'Outspace', location and matter are mere functions of mind. So Jane the AI simply thinks you from A to unspeakably distant B. Moreover: 'Things can be created just by comprehending the pattern of them.'

Thus, merely by thinking about their molecular structure in the course of an eyeblink journey through space, a scientist creates, simultaneously, the impossible counter-agent to the descolada *and* a rapid viral cure for the genetically acquired OCD of Qing-jao's entire afflicted planet. (The latter takes some swallowing. Correcting the genes for the next generation, yes: but overcoming a lifetime's obsessive habits, just like that?) A tragically incurable cripple muses on his former, healthy body, and recreates it. (His personality somehow flips across, while the crippled remains crumble tidily into dust after the manner of Dracula.) Ender inadvertently thinks of his brother (long since dead of old age, owing to relativistic lags) and still-living sister, in such incredible detail as to create perfect clones of both as they'd been in youth. All evoked by Mind from nothingness. It is the Age of Miracles. It is too, too much.

And even though Card takes some care to bracket this miraculous excess with thoroughly effective tragedies – a piggy scientist dying nobly for the sake of research, Qing-jao lapsing into a kind of religious mania and refusing to accept her release from OCD – it remains too much.

There still seem to be a couple of loose ends (notably those hypothetical alien creators of the descolada), in addition to a huge spray of fresh possibilities. No doubt in a few years' time Card will bring us an award-winning sequel, confirming or denying my faint suspicion that this devout author's 'philotic' physics is meant to be taken metaphorically as bringing salvation through the love of God, through a very nearly literal *deus ex machina*.

As a contrast to that disappointing moment in *Xenocide* where almost everything suddenly comes too right too easily, I point the finger at Greg Bear's *Queen of Angels* (1990). This certainly doesn't limit itself to a single assumption. Like the 'consensus' parts of Brin's background, though, the Bear version of 2047 Los Angeles (City of Our Lady the Queen of the Angels) seems generally reasonable. Designer bodies and souls are available through genetic and psychological engineering, but accompanied by the right sort of real-world complexity and mess. The heroine's flashy skin job isn't quite perfect and she needs to take corrective vinegar baths. A new class system has automatically formed, with shabby, raw-state bodies and minds like yours or mine very much at the bottom of the heap. The psycho-twiddling techniques can be perverted to administer hitherto impossible torments; some terrifyingly idealistic vigilantes do precisely this to those they've defined as enemies of society.

Utopian city arcologies are featured, but appalling murders happen in them just the same. Nanotechnology (molecular-scale engineering, a recent flavour-of-the-month in hard sf) is all over the place, providing wonder-gadgets, 'perfect' fabricated components and even a kind of tortuous telepathy, with a dark side to every application – such as the detailed and impressively nasty speculations on what it would 'really' be like to contact and explore an insane mind. The most triumphant note of the book is the first coming-alive of an AI; yet it's a hard, cruel birth and a convincing price has been paid, with self-awareness born out of shattering disappointment.

The one thing we think we know for sure about the future is that it won't be easy. For this reason, Bear's highly mixed blessings carry conviction. Alas, the one other thing both he and we suspect about the future is that it's a different country and they will talk a different language there. The book's heavy larding of imagined 2047 slang and neologism does yield to patient study, but not, I fear, before our author had lost a fair percentage of the ever-fickle readership and, in due course, the 1991 Hugo Award for best novel.

Historical note: Brin's *Earth* and Simmons's *The Fall of Hyperion* were also shortlisted for this award, the winner being some piece of tomfoolery far less ambitious than any of them. So it goes.

It's an old and familiar story. Too many sf and fantasy authors entertain us with conflicts which turn on arbitrary pseudo-answers to pseudo-problems. (And why not? We are duly entertained, even if half an hour later we're hungry again.) Only a few seem to devise realistic, complex and involving problems, and then meet them with realistic and complex answers – which can of course include tragic acceptance of a dilemma's insolubility, although speaking as an optimist I rather hope not. Those who pose good strong problems and then shoo them away with a waft of imaginary physics: ahh, their hearts are doubtless in the right place, but once you've invoked spectres as grim as AIDS, genocide or global eco-disaster, is it kind or convincing to pretend these things will go away if only we pronounce the right words and clap our hands?

All together now . . .

Joe Protagoras is Alive and Living on Earth

and

The Name of the Game is Death

Philip K. Dick

Introduced by Paul Williams
Illustrated by Jim Burns

INTRODUCTION

Science fiction writers (and other genre writers, and I suppose
'serious literary' writers as well) have often made arrangements
with publishers whereby publisher advances author some
money on an unwritten novel based on an outline of the plot
of the proposed book (frequently there's also a sample chapter
or two). The late Philip K. Dick, one of relatively few American
novelists then or now to earn his living entirely by writing,
made many such deals during his writing career, despite the
fact that he did not actually use written outlines to write his
books. The sole purpose of the outline, then, was to hook a
publisher and get some money to buy catfood and other
necessities.

Dick, who published half-a-dozen fairly well-received sf
novels in the 1950s, found himself somewhat in demand as a
genre author after his novel *The Man in the High Castle* won the
1963 Hugo Award for Best SF Novel of the Year. He responded
with an amphetamine-fueled spurt of hyperactivity, producing
twelve novels in three years, late 1963 to late 1966. Some of his
best work was done during this period, including *The Three
Stigmata of Palmer Eldritch* and *UBIK*.

Every flood must ebb, however, and 1967 was a dry year for
PKD. His next novel after *UBIK*, *Galactic Pot-Healer*, was written
in early 1968. In April 1967, Dick sent fellow writer Avram
Davidson a plot outline, apparently in response to an expression
on Davidson's part of anguish at a 'writer's block' situation and

resultant lack of cash with which to buy catfood etc. Davidson
sent it back, and Dick replied on 27 April, 1967:

> I'm awfully sorry that my outline wasn't anything you
> could use. I sort of had it in mind that maybe you could
> send it off *qua* outline, more or less as it was, and maybe
> land an advance thereby. This is what I've done, now, by
> the way – sent it off as it stood, with that hope in mind. I'm
> sure, if you had wanted to write it up you could have done
> a wonderful job, certainly better than I could (or can, if the
> outline does sell).
>
> As to my end of things, I've been having a good deal of
> trouble, too. I started on a new book the other day (for
> which I've been making notes for four months straight), got
> 16 good pages done, and then – bam. Nothing. What
> followed was just awful. Naturally I blamed (one) the baby
> and (two) Nancy, with my own self a last (three), if at all.
>
> . . . It seemed to me on the phone when I talked to you
> that you already sounded better . . . I think every writer
> who is at all sensitive has one or more periods like you're
> going through. In fact I feel I'm going into one myself,
> soon. (I like to think of myself as sensitive.) There is
> nothing worse, I think, than the point you seem to be at. It
> will get better. God sees to that, as he sees to it that our
> digestive system keeps going no matter how badly we feel.
> The biological processes keep on: a signal that we're still
> alive.

'Joe Protagoras is Alive and Living on Earth (outline)' was
received by Dick's literary agent, Scott Meredith, on 1 May,
1967, and is presumably the piece Dick had sent to Davidson.
Three days later, on 4 May, Scott Meredith received another
outline from Dick, 'The Name of the Game is Death (outline for
a science fiction novel)'. This was followed two weeks later by
'additional material for the science fiction outline The Name of
the Game is Death'.

The Meredith Agency submitted the 'Joe Protagoras' proposal
to Doubleday and Avon, both of whom rejected it quickly, and
then to Berkeley Books, who held it for a year and a half before
giving Dick a contract and an advance on 31 January, 1969. Dick
got his revenge, however; he never wrote the novel. In October
1978, almost ten years later, Berkeley settled for a short story
collection instead, *The Golden Man*.

'The Name of the Game is Death' was submitted to Terry Carr
at Ace, who held it for five months and then declined it. It was
also considered and rejected by Avon and Lancer before
Meredith submitted it to Doubleday in May 1968. Doubleday
neither said yes nor no, presumably because they already had

an unwritten Philip K. Dick novel, *Deus Irae*, under contract
since 1964. Dick went ahead and wrote a novel in the fall of 1968
that represented some distant evolution of the ideas in 'The
Name of the Game is Death'; Doubleday bought it, and it was
published in 1970 as *A Maze of Death*.

The two 'outlines' you are about to read represent, as far as I
know, Philip K. Dick's sole writing output during the year 1967,
other than correspondence (certainly part of *Galactic Pot-Healer*
could have been written in 1967 – perhaps the sixteen pages
Dick refers to in his letter to Davidson are the start of the novel –
although it's more likely that Dick wrote all of *GPH* between
January and March of 1968).

In October of 1967 Roger Zelazny first expressed interest in
the possibility of writing a collaborative novel with PKD, and
Dick responded enthusiastically. In a letter dated 26 October,
1967, he says that he has an idea in mind. He explained that
Larry Ashmead at Doubleday saw 'a brief outline of the work'
(this would have been the 'Joe Protagoras' outline), 'and he said
he'd sign a contract on the basis of the outline except that they
signed a contract on a previous outline of mine, a novel from
which never emerged (*true*).' This is a reference to *Deus Irae*,
which Dick sold in chapter and outline form to Doubleday in
1964, which did in time become the project that Dick and
Zelazny wrote together. At this point, however, Dick is not
suggesting *Deus Irae* as their joint project.

Instead he includes in his letter a long paragraph in which the
'Joe Protagoras' outline and the 'Name of the Game' outline are
combined into a single project: '. . . Everyone's scheme is
brought down in a great crash when a *real* alternate present is
reached. The tyrant sets out to visit it – naturally. But it bears no
relation at all to their own world. It is a 'board-game' world,
with squares and the possibility of moving from one square to
the next. Each square is a sort of alternate world on its own,
with the characters themselves altering to fit into the Geist of
each square . . .'

Dick continues, 'I have half a novel, with no insight as to how
it will progress after their return from the mushroom world . . .
You can see I need someone to collaborate with me on this . . .
Can't you just picture it: the antagonisms and ambitions, hates
and loves of these people all worked out in this weird mushroom world?'

So by fall of 1967 the two proposed novels had become one, in
the mind of their creator, but this had brought him no closer to
being able to write them or it. Zelazny's response is not known,
but presumably he also drew a blank. Other correspondence
from 1967 provides clues to the genesis of some elements of
these outlines: Dick and his wife were taking part in a therapy
group 'for "well" people' in February of 1967. Dick is extremely

stressed out over the responsibility of being a father (his daughter Isa was born in March 1967) and is suffering from anxiety and depression. He makes mention in several letters of his fascination with *The Tibetan Book of the Dead* by Evans-Wentz, and notes the connection between 'the Bardol-Thodol existence (i.e. the period immediately following one's physical death)' and his own experience or experiences on LSD.

All of this is interesting (I hope); none of it is necessary or even especially relevant to an appreciation of these pieces of writing. They offer us a glimpse into the process of novel formation that went on in the conscious and unconscious mind of this gifted artist; but they also (I believe) have something more immediate to offer, something unrelated to context, something that may be of value to a reader who knows nothing about this writer and his other works.

This 'something' is (I suggest) a passionate spirit of inquiry, a need to know that is heartfelt and grandiose (this entire world may not be real; there may in fact be thousands of alternate worlds that also may or may not be real; and in PKD's vision an ordinary jerk out looking for a job cannot avoid being caught up in just these sorts of ontological issues), and that involves the emotions (fear, depression, desire) as well as the mind. Philip K. Dick, even when his immediate purpose is simply to get a deal from a publisher and to try to trap himself into having to write another novel, is a philosopher on a quest, a Parsifal determined to pierce the veil of this world's illusion. It's not a pretence for him. He lives it; and all of his experiences, and all of the experiences and feelings of his imagined characters, are at stake at every moment in the pages of his narrative. For him the simple act of perception – looking around and seeing the world, and, inevitably, questioning or feeling uncertain about what one sees – is a warrior's act. He doesn't try to romanticise it; more often he shows the pathos, the absurd humour of it all. But he never lets go of his genuine need to uncover the truth.

I realise my assertion that Dick did not actually write from outlines may seem to be contradicted by his statement 'I've been making notes for four months straight,' and by my own acknowledgement that these outlines do articulate the ideas that were gestating in Dick's head toward his next novel, the themes and characters and story-lines that were struggling to come into existence. What I am saying is that in most of his writing, while there would be a long period of gestation and meditation leading up to the start of the writing process, he did not follow a written plan. In fact, the power of his writing depends very much on his genuine lack of knowledge about what will happen on the next page. In a letter to Ray Brown at the Center for the Study of Popular Culture, 21 March, 1969, Dick describes 'the steps I go through in composing a novel'. A premise or idea pops into his head and he writes it down, and begins asking himself questions that follow from that premise. These are his notes, and when the premise is a fruitful one they may run to many pages and include major and minor details about the imagined world he is considering. When he has enough hand-written notes, he begins 'typing the notes into sequence *as the ideas occurred to me . . .* later thoughts, second thoughts, would replace earlier thoughts of lesser value.' Then the creation of the characters, and finally:

> The plot would come last, and I would do little work in outlining it before beginning the first draft. It is my practice to let the plot evolve out of (one) the premise, or society, and (two) the nature of the characters. I would go so far as to say that I plot in advance only the first chapter or so of the novel, and the further I go into it the more I tend to depend on the inspiration of the moment. The disadvantage to this method of working – i.e. developing the plot as you go along – is that you may be completely carried away from the original direction of the novel . . . I frequently find myself arriving at a point in the novel where, for example, the notes (and if there is an outline, then the outline) calls for the protagonist to say 'Yes,' where in fact he, being what he is, would say 'No,' so 'No' he says, and I must go on from there, stuck with the fact that that is the way he is . . . which fouls up the plot-line terribly. But I think a better novel comes out of this. Other writers would not only disagree with me; they would be horrified.

The title of 'Joe Protagoras', incidentally, is self-parody, Dick's protagonists typically being ordinary blokes (ordinary Joes, we say in the States) with names like Joe Chip. The irony, as you will see when you read the outline, is that Mr Protagoras is indeed alive and well at the end of the novel (according to Dick, and according to the novel as he imagines it now, which he knows will be nothing like any novel he might actually write), even though he is in fact the only person on Earth. Dick's stereotypical character is the ordinary guy who turns out to be at the very centre of the universe. Without being any the less ordinary. The author can identify.

So can the reader.

Paul Williams
November 1991

Joe Protagora⌐
and Living ⌐
(outline)

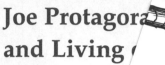

Philip K. ⌐

THEME: A revolution which has brought forth conditions less favorable than the dictator planned. He is asked to resign in favor of an aspirant who says he can do better. But a group opposed to the aspirant takes the dictator into an alternate Earth where the aspirant, not the dictator, has ruled. Conditions are much worse. In fact all the alternate worlds are worse. The aspirant ponders; he knows about this group and what they are doing. Solution: aspirant has a team cross into alternate world and create fake fakes here and there, very subtle in character, which, when dictator finds them, will convince him that this *whole* alternate world is faked. So far so good. But aspirant now goes too far: he plans out *entire* faked world (alternate Earth) where he rules superlatively. Aspirant knows that the dictator will be suspicious, will look for flaws, but aspirant is sure he can bring it off. Next step: what would group loyal to the dictator (the group who took him to real alternate worlds) do? They don't need to plant fake fakes in the 'good alternative' because it's already wholly faked!

PLOT: Joe Protagoras has a puny job – but in the overpopulated and economically malfunctioning socialist world of 2007 he is lucky to have any job at all. However, he has been saving up a sum of money by which to consult Mr Job. This peculiar entity, with tens of thousands of outlets throughout Earth and its planetary colonies, is virtually alive, although artificial, and is important to the lives of Earth's hordes of jobless and near-jobless citizens. Mr Job can tell Protagoras, after an analysis of his aptitudes and experience, where he can find a genuinely adequate career-appointment; Mr Job, through its network of multiple extensors, keeps computer-style tabs on all job-openings everywhere. But consulting Mr Job is expensive. Protagoras hasn't much *real* money saved up (i.e. metal coins in contrast with the nearly worthless inflationary scrip floated by the

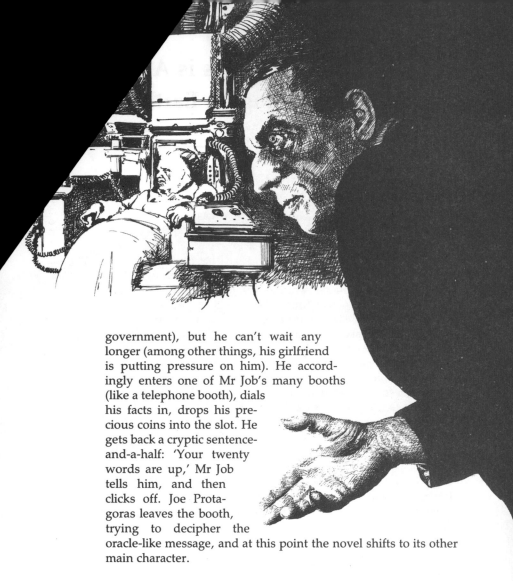

government), but he can't wait any longer (among other things, his girlfriend is putting pressure on him). He accordingly enters one of Mr Job's many booths (like a telephone booth), dials his facts in, drops his precious coins into the slot. He gets back a cryptic sentence-and-a-half: 'Your twenty words are up,' Mr Job tells him, and then clicks off. Joe Protagoras leaves the booth, trying to decipher the oracle-like message, and at this point the novel shifts to its other main character.

Simon Herrlich, the ancient, tottering despot, has kept himself alive by means of artificial organs for far too many years – and has kept himself in Earth's top office at the same time. He is ill-liked by his heir, an ambitious aspirant named Arthur Self. For years, Self has been trying to persuade the Old Man to bow out voluntarily and hence turn everything over to him, i.e. to the younger, more virile Art Self. It is Self's contention that if he had been ruling all this time, Earth would be in better shape economically, politically and socially – if not spiritually (i.e. ideologically, this being a totalitarian state).

From Self's viewpoint we learn about Project Almost, the breaking through to and investigation of alternate Earths. We learn about the scientist in charge of operating the inter-Earth project: Nick Edel, a close associate and good friend of Simon Herrlich – a man whom Self hates because it is Nick Edel who is, by means of his project, keeping Herrlich in office . . . inasmuch as all alternate Earths visited are worse than their own.

This section of the novel ends with Self conceiving the idea of sending his own teams across into one of the worst alternate worlds and planting 'simulated forgeries' – in other words fake fakes, with the idea of discrediting Edel's whole project by giving the alternate Earths the appearance of being phony. We see him visiting the REM Corporation, a huge industrial concern owned by the government (which of course owns every economic enterprise on Earth, this being a communist type society). We now meet Cynthia Stonemerchant, the director of REM Corporation, the elderly widow who manages this vast industrial cartel. She is quite hostile toward the old dictator; she is, in fact in favor of a noncommunist government, with industries privately owned, as in a capitalist society. Therefore, she is glad to have her factories produce the fake fakes which Self wants. Then, together, they hatch out the extraordinary idea of creating an entire fake alternate world: a world which Mrs Stonemerchant and her technical staff will plan.

Unknown to Self, Mrs Stonemerchant plans to construct a *capitalist* fake alternate world which is better than their own. She is not merely hostile toward Simon Herrlich; she is hostile toward Art Self as well. She is in fact hostile to their whole totalitarian society, and is doing this job for her own purposes.

We return to Joe Protagoras, who has managed – with the help of his girlfriend – to decypher the sentence-and-a-half which Mr Job gave him. It is telling him to go to REM Corporation's Los Angeles branch and apply for the job technically listed as 20538-AR . . . a designation which means absolutely nothing to him; he has no idea what the job, for which he will be applying, consists of. But Mr Job is never wrong, so Joe Protagoras quits the meagre job he has, gathers his few possessions together (he has only a rented room, adequate housing being years away, due to the faulty economics of the government). Going by second-class surface bus, he sets off for Los Angeles.

When he reaches REM Corporation's Los Angeles branch and applies for job 20538-AR he discovers what it is. Designing rides for what is called an 'amusement park,' something which he has never even heard of. The personnel manager of REM, however, assures him that he is the man for the job (Joe Protagoras has given the personnel manager the same resumé he gave Mr Job). 'You'll do just fine,' Mr Bean assures him, and leads him to his bright, modern, high-class office. He is to begin work right away. Historical texts and technical manuals dealing with amusement

parks are already in the office; Joe Protagoras begins to read, and we leave him. But before we return to the schemes of Art Self, we see Protagoras making an interesting inquiry. What is REM Corporation's product? What is his job *for*? He gets no answer from his new superiors; they know but won't tell him. 'Just design good, scary, fun rides,' he is told. 'Pay special attention to Mr Toad's Wild Ride from the twentieth century amusement park called Disneyland; that is your prototype. Update it and you'll be on your way.'

We of course know what REM Corporation is producing: the fake alternate world supposedly for Self's benefit, but actually for Mrs Stonemerchant's personal purposes. In any case, Protagoras, the 'little' protagonist, is now linked to Art Self, the 'big' protagonist, as well as Mrs Stonemerchant, the third force at work on the world-stage, or rather inter-worlds stage.

At this point all the characters will have been introduced. These are:

Elderly despot: Simon Herrlich
Aspirant: Arthur Self
Director of REM Corporation: Mrs Cynthia Stonemerchant
Craftsman 'little' protagonist: Joe Protagoras
Girlfriend of Protagoras: Abby Vercelli
Girl, party zealot for Simon Herrlich: Marleen Poole
Hatchetman thug for Herrlich: Patrick O'Connell

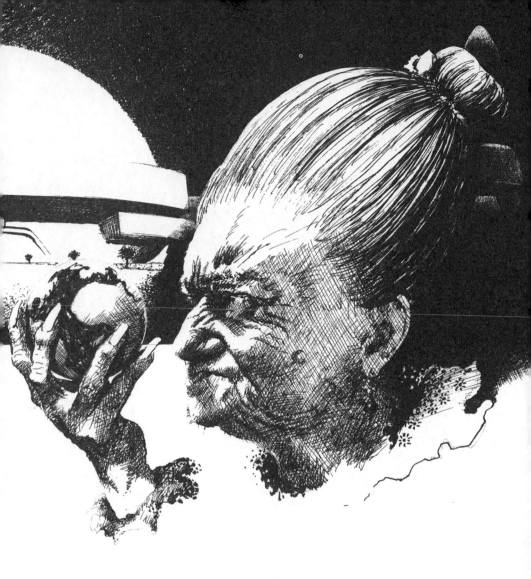

Tough goon for REM Corp: Mike Fox
Group of top officials loyal to Herrlich: Calvin Gold, Dan
    Hastings, Ian Kain
Spy and informer for Art Self: Demeter Troll
Wife (young) of Herrlich: Aulikki Mildmay

The plot continues as follows. Briefly, it's this: while REM
Corporation is building the fake capitalist alternate world, Nick
Edel's research workers *stumble onto a genuine capitalist alternate
world*. This pleases no one; that is, neither Art Self nor the old
despot (it would please Mrs Stonemerchant, of course, but both
Herrlich and Self keep this startling information top-secret). It is

a better world than any other alternative – including their own. This is one possibility that neither Self nor Herrlich anticipated; wrapped up in their communist ideology, they were absolutely certain that if a capitalist alternate world showed up (which in itself is considered by both of them unlikely) it would of course be awful.

Art Self crosses over to it, spends time there skulking about incognito, then returns to his own world. And, back in it, encounters almost at once a fake fake object!

What does this discovery mean? Two hypotheses are possible. (one) It – his own world – is real and someone has planted fake fakes there, as he himself has done in the alternate worlds; for instance, Mrs Stonemerchant, who may have learned about the real alternate capitalistic world. Or (two) His own world is entirely fake, and he has a false memory grafted into his brain by someone unknown to him but who is obviously out to destroy him. This someone could be either Herrlich's supporters in the party apparatus or Mrs Stonemerchant's technicians. Hard to tell.

The maximum host of perplexities is now at its peak; from hereon the plot will unravel.

(A) Protagoras is doing a strange sort of task for a purpose he does not know and for a corporation whose product is kept secret from him.

(B) Mrs Stonemerchant may or may not know about the discovery of an authentic capitalistic Earth. If she does find out, what will she do?

(C) Art Self has found what appear to be fake fakes in his own world. What does this mean? Who put them there and why? Or is *everything* fake?

(D) The old man, Simon Herrlich, has seen his hopes and dreams shattered, here at the end of his life, by the discovery that a capitalist world would have been – is, in fact – far better than anything he and his world-revolution takeover can come up with. What should he do now? Renounce his own totalitarian society and attempt to bring capitalism back – with Mrs Stonemerchant's help and that of other industrial directors who share her attitude?

The novel is resolved in this way. A team working for REM Corporation is discovered, by Self's personal police, planting fake fakes in his own world. That answers that. His world is real, and Mrs Stonemerchant has tried to do to him what he did to Herrlich. Self therefore has his thugs kill Mrs Stonemerchant (after a heavy-pitched battle with her company goons), since he knows for a certainty that she is, in totalitarian jargon, plotting against him, obviously with the idea of undermining their socialist state. However, Mrs Stonemerchant has made certain arrangements; the instant she dies, an automatic instrument goes into action; it drops into a mail slot many, many copies of a full statement of REM Corporation's activities, its creating of fake fakes at Self's command. This letter is addressed to every powerful official loyal to old Simon Herrlich, and within twenty-four hours the elderly despot learns what Self has been up to.

Self becomes, at once, a hunted criminal in a society where escape from the government police is impossible. He knows he can't escape Herrlich's agents, but at least he can take revenge vis-à-vis REM Corporation – which, he reasons, has brought about his downfall and certain death. He therefore, with all the resources he can muster, attacks REM Corporation's various branches, and, in a matter of hours, reduces most of them to rubble . . . killing the majority of the corporation's employees. Or so he thinks. Actually, Mrs Stonemerchant had anticipated exactly this; upon her death, REM Corporation's employees began passing across to the alternate capitalist world via a pirated duplicate of Nick Edel's mechanism.

Again the novel focuses on Protagoras, who believes himself safe in this capitalist alternate world. However, he very soon makes a hideous discovery. This is not the authentic alternate capitalist world at all. Something – at least in his case – went wrong. This is the mere partly-completed fake which REM Corporation was building for Self up to the time that Mrs Stonemerchant learned of the existence of the real one. Here he finds, for example, the not yet functioning 'rides' which he himself designed: a ghostly, lonely, echoing 'amusement park,' of which he is the sole patron; he is alone in this ersatz world, with no way to get back out.

The ending is not downbeat, however. REM Corporation has not removed its machinery, the autonomic building rigs by means of which they were constructing this 'world.' At the end of the book we find Joe Protagoras starting the great elaborate autonomic machines once more into action; if he can't leave this ersatz world, at least he can complete it – make it pleasant and habitable, including the building of ersatz 'people' to keep him company. He is emperor of an entire landscape, and he is happy. Of all the major characters, Joe Protagoras came out the best – which the reader will agree is as it should be.

In this ending, the question What is Real? What is illusion? is answered (or anyhow the attempt will be made within the context of the novel). Joe Protagoras has gone from a *real* but unsatisfying world into an *unreal* but satisfying alternate. The test will be purely pragmatic. If this half-completed ersatz world is capable of answering Joe Protagoras's needs, *then it is real* – in the sense that it provides the material out of which he can fashion a reasonably tolerable life. In fact the issue of *real* versus *unreal* is itself false; the authentic issue is: What will sustain life?

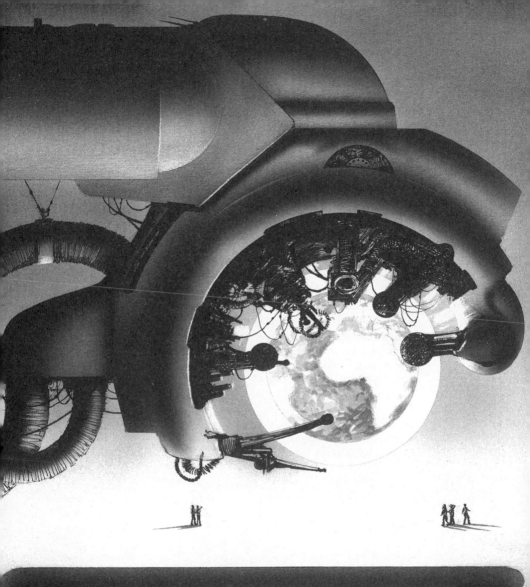

REPLICATION OVERVU
GENUINE PSEUDO-EARTH SIMULACRUM (FAKED
FACSIMILE OF DUPLICATED ANALOGUE) - ONGOING
MODEL
CURRENT STATUS @ PSEUDO GEO-STAB IMM
                @ PSEUDO MET-STAB IMM
INSERTION TO DENEB NODE IMM
AMPLIFICATION & CREW RETREAT T MINUS 5 G/HRS
SOLSPACE REC CELL IN PLACE
NOTE: THIS FAKE IS 5TH GEN FAKE OF ORIG FAKE

What will permit a living organism to function? In answer to this, the ersatz, half-completed world is advantageous, because, among other things, it gives Joe Protagoras a field in which to work creatively (i.e. as he personally completes it). Instead of a bureaucrat he is now an artist, and this ersatz world is the lump of clay out of which he will fashion his own, idiosyncratic reality. Which, we realise, is the finest reality of all.

The Name of the Game is Death

(outline for a science fiction novel)

Philip K. Dick

This is a game-board novel, like Brunner's *The Squares of the City*, or *The Fairy Chessmen*, or *Alice Through the Looking Glass*. The flaw in most game-board novels is that chess is always the game. This is bad because (one) it's been done to death and (two) chess is a game which every reader knows, and so he'll expect to find the characters moving as the knight moves, then as the bishop moves, etc.; in other words, as soon as he begins reading the book the reader already knows darn near most of what's going to happen.

In this novel, the game is not chess. It is not any game that we know, or that the characters – at least in the beginning – know or recognise. There are squares, however, or anyhow different areas or zones or vectors which the characters move along, and, as in *Alice*, the tone, mood, quality, whatever you want to call it, changes from one square to the next (although it's possible for a character to find himself back in a familiar square, as happens, say, in Monopoly). In a sense, each square is an alternate world with recognizable characteristics; certain elements *qua* elements are retained from one square to the next (e.g. the same house, the same business establishment, the same familiar girlfriend's apartment) but ah . . . the subtle and profound differences! (Cf Leiber's *Destiny Times Three* or my *Eye in the Sky*.)

Since this is not chess, not any game the reader knows, the theme of What Is This Game, For God's Sake? becomes major – rather than merely Who Is Moving Us? Of course, that is a vital issue, too; at least in this respect: the characters, to a certain degree, do not voluntarily move but are moved *From Above*. In addition, however, they take it upon themselves to make dangerous and important excursions – with a wide variety of consequences.

Added elements: the characters can be located, at a given time, in different squares, but all communicating with one another via

VERPA BOHEMIA

some sort of vid-intercom system. In other words, in terms of our world, the characters are from the future; so this is initially set in the year 2019, with a futuristic base built up before the game begins (i.e. before the Event which tumbles the characters onto the board). (The characters could know one another before the Event, or they could meet afterwards – e.g. they could all be aboard a particular rocket ship or some such accidental proximity-creating device.)

Possibly the move to the next square occurs when a character comes across a Latin word or words plastered onto or recorded into a constituent of the square he is already in (the words could turn up anywhere: on a cereal package, the label in a shirt, sculpted in bronze on a park monument, as headline in a newspaper). The words are such as these: *suillus albidipes, lactarius aurantiacus, dentinum umbilicatum, pholiota kauffmanii, verpa bohemia*. But what do these Latin words mean?

The reader can, of course, cheat at this point by flying to his dictionary. These are the formal names of mushrooms. Each square or zone (or whatever) is an expression of the diverse characteristics of a specific mushroom. For instance *amanita muscaria*. This mushroom is deadly poison, so all elements of its square world exude poison – in both the figurative as well as literal sense (e.g. someone tries to drink a milkshake while on this square; it kills him horribly, whereas a milkshake on the *clitocybe alba* square would cause hallucinations). So the characters (and especially the protagonist) pass from fetid, black, evil, toxic environments to a variety of other possibilities, ranging from benign to mildly nauseating to hallucinogenic to heaven-like joy, peace and beauty.

Also, the *shape* of elements within a given square shares the physical appearance of the mushroom involved; for example, on the inky cap square, the tops of buildings are turning into mushy black sludge. In another square, flies gather everywhere (this is the fly agaricus).

(For research purposes I have adequate textbooks on mycology; no problem there.)

Once the characters figure out the underlying logic of the make-up of the various squares, they would of course head for the morel square, since the morel is the finest and most tasty fungus known (with the exception of the French truffle). Now, at this point, a new phase of the novel can begin: Forces From Above impede their progress toward the morel square . . . or perhaps *one* of the Forces (i.e. game-players) impedes (the evil one) and the other (the benign one) facilitates – since, in most games, there are opposing players.

Then, too, there is the problem as to how the squares are laid out; in other words, just how *do* you get to the morel square?

An additional – in fact crucial –
factor is the sudden, shocking disappearance of one character after another as
they are 'lost' – at least this is the supposition
of the remaining characters. To save themselves
they must discover what causes this 'loss', this
abrupt and possibly irreversible disappearance of
person after person (in one way, however, this
'loss' factor could be of positive use: bad characters
could be 'lost' at critical moments, as when threatening the life of a good character, etc.).

Many conjectures will be made as to where they

go when they are 'lost', in addition to the question of why. At last a viewpoint character could be 'lost', and we could find out, first-hand, where they wind up when removed from the board (it is also possible that, unlike chess, a character could reappear, as in Monopoly when a house or hotel is traded in and then later brought back and replaced on the board). (The realm into which a character goes when removed from the board could be a sort of ultimate reality, a transcendental absolute realm beyond the lesser reality of the arbitrary board. Conceivably, one or more of the characters could crave an encounter with this ultimate world; he could deliberately strive to be 'lost'.)

Various other plot combinations are possible. For example, one or several of the characters could ally themselves with one of the Cosmic Game-Players; other characters could choose the opposing Player. The Game-Players could even manifest themselves, either directly or indirectly, on the board itself; hence the transcendent realm is not *necessarily* separate from the here-and-now, a property of ultimate reality which we, in our own lives, may have experienced.

There are other ways in which the two realms (i.e. the board and the Players) could merge. There could be this: one of the human characters could change progressively until he becomes unhuman – reveals himself as one of the Game-Players (either good or bad), rather than a 'pawn' merely. (*Vide* my Ace book, *The Cosmic Puppets*.)

As to characters. I suggest a slice-of-life motley clump of them, from university professor to car-hop, or rather futuristic versions thereof (in contrast to *Eye in the Sky*, where the characters were from our present-day world). Half the fun of writing – and reading – the novel will result from having the right cast of extreme-type characters, who offset one another, are proper foils for one another.

As to viewpoint. I intend a multiple viewpoint approach; i.e. more than one protagonist going. I would switch back and forth between two diverse types of men, or possibly three, or two men – say, one young, the other old – and a girl.

And I wish to keep the 'alternate worlds' (different squares) down to a few basic, radically different mushrooms: possibly four to six in all – then several returns to squares (i.e. mushrooms) formerly visited. 'Christ,' Ned expostulated testily, 'we're back on *amanita muscaria* again. Taste this orange juice; it's like hydrochloric acid.' Bob stared at him as if not believing his ears. '*Like* hydrochloric acid?' he said slowly. 'Not *like*, Ned. *Is*. For God's sake, drop that glass; it'll kill you!' And so forth.

The tone of the novel (humor, the ominous, lyrical, etc.) will alter from square to square. Hence the possibility of many varied approaches will be possible – in fact necessary. Which is good.

The Name of the Game is Death

Philip K. Dick

Be it known that *two* future societies will be shown in this novel: that of 2017 and that of 2118. The ten or so characters live in the earlier one, and are yanked from it into the future. These are the aspects of their own society (i.e. 2017):

Humans have evolved in relation to our own world of 1967, but the evolution is not physiological; there are no mutants with ESP powers. But learning processes have been stepped up so that each person makes use of more brain tissue than we do. It is a collective or communal society, but benign rather than feral, as for example the forced collective society of *1984*. Speech has been replaced by what is called 'speedch', a sort of oral shorthand which takes place at great velocity. All writing is done in a similar shorthand fashion; all data and knowledge are communicated at a fantastically rapid rate between persons and between a person and a computer. In addition, brain metabolism is controlled electrically. The natural state of these people is a polyencephalic existence: fused brains via complex electronic gadgets which everyone possesses and uses continually; there is no such thing as isolation or privacy – nor does anyone desire these 'antiquated' states.

In addition, these people know where they go when they die: a specific planet in another galaxy. Hence many are allowed to die voluntarily, when their work is done. Children are allowed to be born on a lottery basis; a couple 'wins' a child. Previous life of the baby is known via a retroscanner. Earth is regarded by these people as a punishment world along the ladder of repeated life (i.e. reincarnation – but this term will not be used). Because it is a punishment world there must of necessity be pain and boredom. (You file a petition to die, then wait to have it approved. If you kill yourself illegally, before your work is done, you devolve back to a worse world. The ultimate punishment doled out by the courts is a requirement to live for ever.)

Yet, this earlier world is regarded by the citizens of the later society (2118) as a golden era . . . because it was the last period in history when an individual could absorb all known information and hence have a unified worldview – in other words a picture of reality as a cosmos. The people of 2118 can't commu-

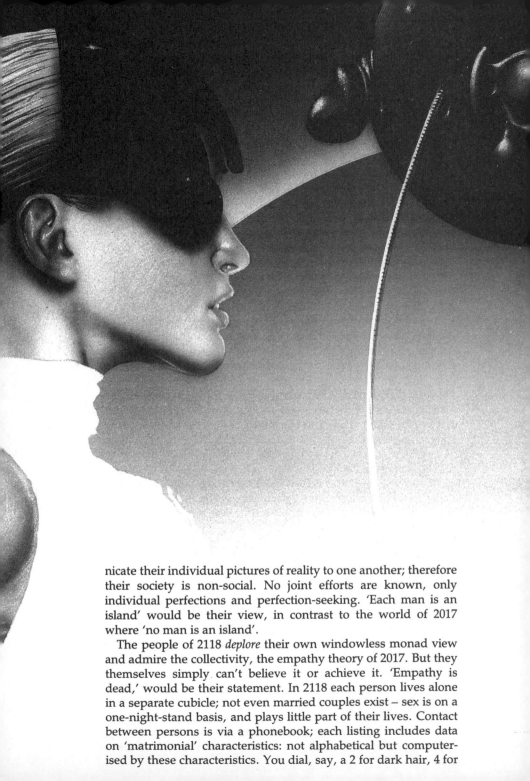

nicate their individual pictures of reality to one another; therefore their society is non-social. No joint efforts are known, only individual perfections and perfection-seeking. 'Each man is an island' would be their view, in contrast to the world of 2017 where 'no man is an island'.

The people of 2118 *deplore* their own windowless monad view and admire the collectivity, the empathy theory of 2017. But they themselves simply can't believe it or achieve it. 'Empathy is dead,' would be their statement. In 2118 each person lives alone in a separate cubicle; not even married couples exist – sex is on a one-night-stand basis, and plays little part of their lives. Contact between persons is via a phonebook; each listing includes data on 'matrimonial' characteristics: not alphabetical but computer-ised by these characteristics. You dial, say, a 2 for dark hair, 4 for

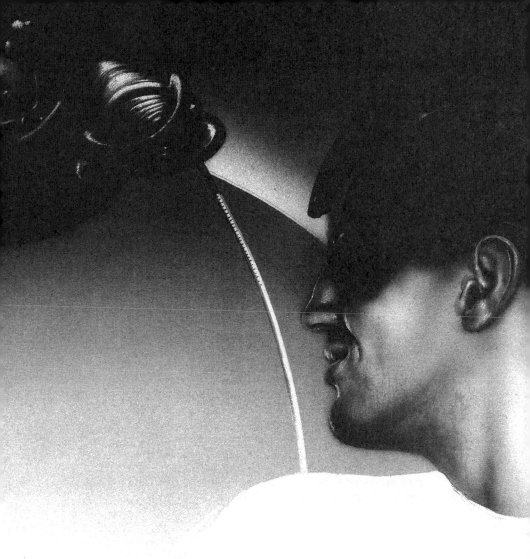

tall, 6 for slim, 12 for interest in golf, etc. The phonebook contains 3-D pics of each person, a pop-up pic that walks and talks on a full-size wall screen. Point of law: if you dial someone and want to go to bed with her, and she refuses, she must then show just cause in court; otherwise extra years are added to her life (this aspect has survived from 2017, this view of Earth as a punishment world).

The difference between these two societies, however, is very great. In 2017 up to 50 persons can tune in and merge mentalities as well as experience. The people of 2118 regard this experience as illusory, as for example the watching of a TV drama and identifying with the protagonist. They hold that Aristotle's theory of the universality of art is false; hence for them art itself does not exist. All that is left is the unique personal experience of each separate person. Billions of separate lives, billions of views which cannot be communicated . . . no wonder they long for the golden age of 2017!

In the world of 2118 communication is not achieved merely by 'speedch' but by displaying complex colors, smells and textures. When the ten persons from 2017 are transported there they find this quite fascinating; it is quite a different way of 'talking' to one another.

The group of ten characters know one another when the novel begins; they have assembled as representatives of ten corporations *supposedly* for the purpose of price-fixing on a new battery which provides enough power to drive a spaceship which the government buys for use as high speed pursuit vessel (i.e. for military use). In actuality, however, these people are cloistered in one room for an illegal purpose: for electronically amplified group-sex.

In 2017, group-sex is legal and common – but not when the sensations, the erotic stimuli, the ultimate orgasm are boosted to a vast pitch electronically. The meeting of these ten people constitutes what is legally described as unnatural sexual polymorphic fusion – unnatural because of the artificial amplification. The electronic device which they employ is in itself legal, but only for nonsexual polyencephalic merging; these ten people in this group have adapted it for this wicked purpose – and have been doing so for some time. (The feedback system of the device makes possible multiple simultaneous orgasms – prolonged electronically, too . . . but the government believes that this destroys brain tissue and nerve conduits. The protagonist has never participated in any kind of sexual activity but this popular group-sex; later, when put ahead to the society of 2118, he will experience individual sex; i.e. intercourse with one other person, a woman. And without any electronic amplification.)

Here is a breakdown of their group:

Grace Harrington. Age 21, huge and fat but pretty, nice skin and hair. Has malice toward all, but covertly.

Eddie Brandise. Age 38. Skinny, mentally disturbed, clever, fanatical, politically oriented. Likes to gossip.

Lynn Porter. Age 32. Extrovert, blond, noisy and loud, always talking, but good sense of humor. Not very pretty, and far too bossy. A career type woman who wears tweed.

Willard Greybo. Age 40. Sloppy, drinks beer, well-read but a bore. Has nutty occult theories, plus depressions of a near-paranoid nature. Bad temper. Always sullen.

Steven Afreikian. Age 35 but looks about 18. Small, kindly, like an elf. Draws quaint pictures. Introverted, saying little. Great sense of humor and very honest and good.

Alex Tree. Age 40. Energetic, dogmatic, educated, cultivated, ruthless and selfish, even cruel. Extremely brilliant.

Liz Roach. Age 55. Old maid type, timid and withdrawn, but has a fine, dry sense of humor. Firm, even rigid, in her views. Reliable, but exceptionally judgmental – and often offensively blunt. But her perceptions are almost always accurate.

Dave Percheron. The protagonist. Age 45. Powerful, intense, acute in his thinking, wry sense of humor but inclined to be pompous and to make speeches. Quick to act, however, in a crisis. Very decisive, but broods. Hates to hurt anyone but is fatalistic; people will get hurt: this is, after all, a punishment world.

Paula North. Age 50. Heavy-set, malicious, tries to look much younger than she is and fails. Holds grudges. Hates all other women. But inclined toward being a lesbian – in spite of her stated love for various men. Rather sick mentally, and not attractive physically, but has a bold artistic twist to her clothes; she makes little pretty flower arrangements, puppets, hats, god's eyes, etc.

These people are deliberately taken from their world of 2017 and brought to the world of 2118 by entities in 2118; these people have been selected because their meeting is illegal, hence no one will dare report their disappearance to the police. The purpose for which they have been brought to the year 2118: psychologists of 2118 wish to see how persons accustomed to communial interaction will react to a maze in which cooperation is impossible. Since some of the mushrooms are highly toxic, persons landing on such toxic squares will absorb the elan of death and destruction and will possibly wind up murdering those other persons who have been, for years, part of their interacting polyencephalic group-entity.

Various further plot considerations: In addition to being picked off due to, say, drinking orange juice on the amanita square, characters could murder one another in such fashions as this: by maneuvering each other onto toxic squares. Why would they want to do this? They have been given to understand that only a few of them, or perhaps merely one, can survive the game. What has happened is that a scrap of the 'rules' or 'instructions' for the game has fallen into their hands; on one square a computer exists by which the protagonist asks for and receives an initial segment of the rules – and then the computer is squashed from above. Better, however, would be this: the *computer* is above, and what he finds on the square is a contact station or info booth; he dials onto a line which momentarily hooks him up to the computer-in-the-sky – then the link is abolished from above. But he retains a valuable slice of the rules (which perhaps he keeps secret for a time). Could be like racehorses: first three to reach morel square win – and stay alive. And are returned to their own time.

Also, there could be a who-done-it theme; one (or more) of the group is murdering the others. Is it always the same person who commits the murder? Or is it whoever happens to be on the amanita square?

Could be (one) *another* character got a bit of the rules, too, a different bit; or (two) *all* got bits; assembly of the bits makes up a complete set of the rules, but each person has hidden his bit . . . then protagonist admits to his girlfriend and she, too, admits that she has a scrap of the rules in her possession. But he and she don't know that all others have bits, too (one denies he has last missing bit – they kill him, find bit in his possession, as suspected).

One of the most important themes in the book is the fact that

the natures of the characters alter according to which squares they are on. Therefore, when at last one or more of them get to the morel square, he or they achieve attitude and quality possessed by the Game-player Himself (saintly, beatific, etc. A metamorphosis into a higher state).

In view of this, if there is one static murderer among them, he would change radically once he had reached this final, winning square. Another factor: it takes time before a character acquires the quality underlying a square. If they have deduced that the murderer among them is he who is on the amanita square, they could head there, grab him and drag him off it before he commits another murder. (Murderer has operated this way: he briefly leaves his toadstool square, kills, then gets back before he has altered to a more benign view. Basically, it alters you 'only if you stay there too long').

Since the psychologists of the future are trying to determine if the empathic, polyencephalic, communal mind of this previous period can be broken down by such a situation as this gameboard – then leak of rule-info that 'only three can win' (i.e. survive) is *deliberately* arranged by them in order to sunder their collectiveness. Each of them being on different squares would facilitate this.

The protagonist could discover, at last, that 'rules' are merely a fake, deliberate leak and are actually part of the game (i.e. the maze is an experiment, and it isn't true that only three will be allowed to live). Discovery by the protagonist that 'rules' are part of the experiment is a vital turning point of the novel; if he can convince the others remaining alive, no more need die. But those on the malign squares are too feral (and paranoid) to back down; the info has come too late (did the future people – the research psychologists – plan this, too? To see if it will work at this late date?).

The transcendental Game-player is not merely one of the future people but a nonTerran entity who hopes and tries – contrarily toward the psychologists – to save and elevate them all (i.e. the whole group). Unknown to the psychologists, he has infiltrated his presence into the maze in order to save them. To him, the psychologists are evil – so here are the two antagonistic players, at last. He speaks in a 'still, small voice,' from within the board; for example, at the end of a roll of toilet paper, or on free-sample box of cereal.

The news that *all* can survive, not just three, could be leaked – not by the psychologists – but by the still, small voice of the benign entity.

One final point. The protagonist finds that individual sex, that is, with one other person rather than among a group, and *not* amplified electronically, is more satisfying. Much, much nicer.

Editor
NEW WORLDS (issues 142-20)

Michael Moorcock

The Last Word

Michael Moorcock

Only another editor can appreciate fully the extraordinary sense of luxury I enjoy as Consultant Editor. All a consultant editor has to do is make a few irrelevant observations about how things were when they were still able to read without glasses, murmur a few suggestions about general production and then sit back and enjoy the show. It gives me all the pleasure with none of the responsibility!

It was a very great pleasure to read these latest stories. The distinctive style of editorship which we saw in *Zenith* is now providing us with a steady supply of wonderful fiction. Everyone seems to be working at their best — the well-established writers like Aldiss or Watson, the newer authors like Baxter, Ings, McDonald, Di Filippo, Laidlaw and Hamilton and others of that talented company who, through *Interzone*, *Other Edens* and *Zenith*, have been making names for themselves, and brave new ones like Jack Deighton who makes an impressive debut here. What's more, with the addition of material like David Langford's and the Jim Burns-illustrated Philip K. Dick (thanks to Paul Williams), we're seeing a continuing expansion into less conventional areas.

David Garnett has already noted the disappointing lack of women writers and non-Anglophone writers here. Very few unsolicited manuscripts have been received from readers. Please send your work to NEW WORLDS — the rates are competitive and I speak from personal experience when I guarantee that David Garnett is a helpful and conscientious editor. Even his rejections are swift and relatively painless.

Personally, I'm sorry to see so little non-linear work. Given that non-linearity has never been more respectable in a whole variety of disciplines, it seems strange that *New Worlds*, which waved the flag of non-linearity for so many years, has acquired a distinctly linear tinge. Where are the authors who will go on doing for fiction what Mandelbrot did for mathematics? New tools are as important as new ideas — in fiction as in the sciences. Moreover, the arts and

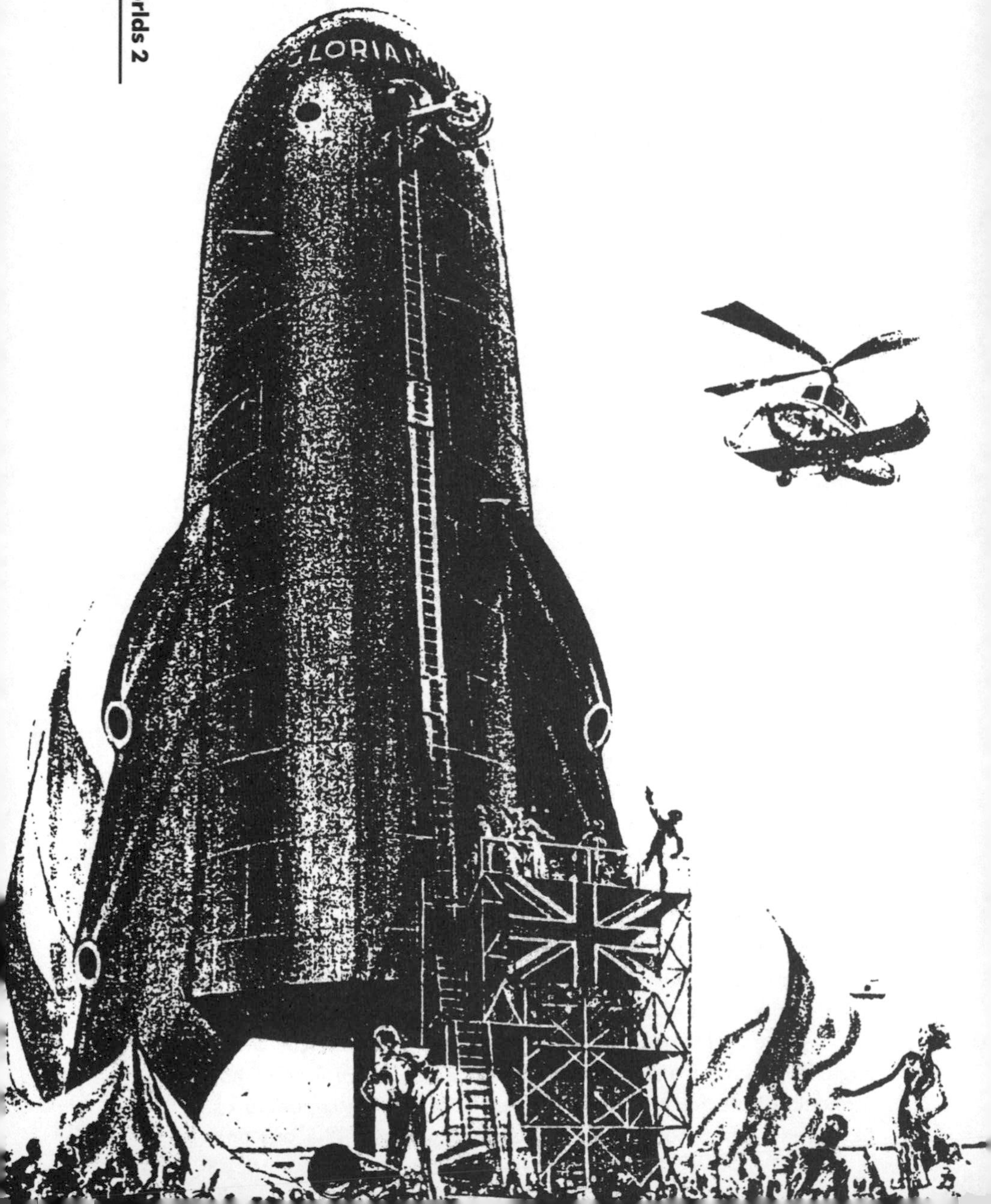
GLORIAN

sciences have never seemed closer, it would be nice to see more recognition – or perhaps even celebration – of this phenomenon.

I have personal reasons for welcoming Wick Colvin to these pages. The nephew of my old friend James Colvin, Warwick Colvin Jnr. was raised in Tangier. Parts of his uncle's library were shipped to him and Wick grew up reading the complete works of William Burroughs, E. E. 'Doc' Smith, W. Pett Ridge, J. G. Ballard, Frank Richards, Anthony Skene and George Meredith. He also received his uncle's pulp magazine collection and his lifetime subscription to *Scientific American*. James Colvin died (many still say he was murdered) in 1969 when his nephew was two years old. With David Garnett's support I prevailed upon Wick Colvin to let us publish a few extracts from his epic serial *Corsairs of the Second Ether*, and its slightly longer sequel *Lost Universe Buckaroos*, written before Colvin learned of the demise of THRILLING WONDER STORIES, an irony, he told me, of peculiar poignancy for him.

On 16th February 1992 Angela Carter and George MacBeth died. Both were enthusiastic readers of *New Worlds* and MacBeth published his longer poems regularly here. Both were people of enormous generosity and unique talent; both brought considerable originality to their imaginative fiction and were active in supporting other writers. Angela was fifty-two. George was sixty. Two other generous spirits associated with *New Worlds* were Sir Angus Wilson (who was our main supporter on the Arts Council) and Jack Trevor Story (who contributed 'The Wind in the Snottygobble Tree' to *New Worlds*). They died in 1991. A great deal of light has gone out of the lives of their friends.

The Authors

IAN McDONALD is the author of the novels *Desolation Road*, *Out on Blue Six* and *King of Morning, Queen of Day* (which won the 1992 Philip K. Dick Award) and the collection *Empire Dreams*. 1992 sees the publication of his most recent novel *Hearts, Hands and Voices*, the collection *Speaking in Tongues* and the graphic novel *Kling Klang Klatch*. His short fiction has appeared in various magazines and anthologies, including *New Worlds 1* and both volumes of *Zenith*. 'Innocents' is set against the same background as his next novel, *Necroville*, to be published in 1993.

PAUL DI FILIPPO is the author of the novels *Ciphers* and *Joe's Liver*. His short stories have been published in magazines such as *Fantasy and Science Fiction*, *Amazing* and *Interzone*, and anthologies such as *Synergy*, *Universe* and *New Worlds 1*. As well as fiction, he also writes reviews and criticism on subjects such as comics and rock music in publications as diverse as *The Washington Post* and *Reflex*. He lives in Providence, Rhode Island.

WARWICK COLVIN JNR is a nephew of James Colvin, whose novel *The Wrecks of Time* was serialised in *New Worlds* in 1965/6. All of his previous stories and novels have been written under a pseudonym — which he declines to reveal.

BRIAN W. ALDISS was first published in *New Worlds* in the fifties, and his most recent story appeared in the first of the new volumes. This was FOAM which has been reprinted by Gardner Dozois in his *Year's Best Science Fiction* anthology and also by Giles Gordon in his *Year's Best Short Stories* — which is *not* a science fiction series. Aldiss's latest novel *Remembrance Day* and a collection of poems *Home Life With Cats* will both be published during 1992. His next book will be the collection *A Tupolev Too Far*. 1992 also sees the publication by Borgo Press of *The Works of Brian W. Aldiss*, which is an annotated bibliography and complete checklist, by his wife Margaret Aldiss.

PETER F. HAMILTON lives in Rutland. His first novel *Mindstar Rising* will be published in 1993; and he has completed a second, provisionally entitled *The Nano Flower*. His first short fiction was an sf story published in *Fear*. More stories have since appeared in various small press magazines, as well as in the new anthology *In Dreams* edited by Kim Newman and Paul McAuley (also published by Gollancz). (Four other authors in this volume also have stories in *In Dreams*: Stephen Baxter, Marc Laidlaw, Ian McDonald and Ian Watson.)

MARC LAIDLAW is the author of two novels, *Dad's Nuke* and *Neon Lotus*, and his third, *Kalifornia* will be published in the spring of 1993. He lives in San Francisco. His stories have appeared in *Omni*, *Isaac Asimov's Science Fiction Magazine*, *The Magazine of Fantasy and Science Fiction* and elsewhere. He is now contributing a cartoon strip to *F&SF*: a 'Thinking Man's' series of revisions of sf and horror B-movies. As may be deduced from 'Great Breakthroughs in Darkness' and its accompanying illustration, he is strongly influenced by photography, and he is now working on a new novel, *The Secret World of Photographs*, co-written with Paul Di Filippo.

SIMON INGS is the author of the novel *Hot Head*; his next novel, *In the City of the Iron Fish*, is now completed and will be published in the fullness of time – as will the two stories he has sold to *Omni*. His short fiction has been published in *Interzone*, and the anthologies *Other Edens 3* and *Zenith 2*. His collaboration with Charles Stross appeared in the first volume of the new *New Worlds*, and he is now writing his third novel.

IAN WATSON first appeared in *New Worlds* in 1969, with his first ever story, 'Roof Garden Under Saturn'. (His photograph in this volume was taken in that year.) Since then he has published over a hundred stories and thirty books. His most recent novel is *The Flies of Memory*; his latest collection is *Stalin's Teardrops*. He is currently writing a two-volume epic sf novel entitled *Mana*. The first part, *Lucky's Harvest*, will be published in 1993. He has also been working on a film project with director Stanley Kubrick.

JACK DEIGHTON is the author of *Structural and Spectroscopic Investigations of Ylides and Bicyclic Compounds*, which was his doctoral thesis in chemistry at Glasgow University. He now lives in Fife, with his wife and two sons. 'The Face of the Waters' is his first published story, his name rhymes with 'lighten', and an ylide is a compound whose molecule has an *internal* pair of opposite charges on adjacent atoms.

STEPHEN BAXTER is the author of *Raft*, a nominee for the 1992 Arthur C. Clarke Award and the British Science Fiction Award. His second novel is *Timelike Infinity*, and three more novels (one of which is based on his story in *Zenith 2*) and a collection of short stories will follow. His short fiction has also appeared in *Interzone*, *Isaac Asimov's Science Fiction Magazine* and *Other Edens 3*. Born in Liverpool, he took his engineering doctorate in Southampton and now lives in Buckinghamshire.

DAVID LANGFORD had a story accepted in 1975 by *New Worlds Quarterly* which immediately ceased publication. He has since published many short stories, novels (including one sf title, *The Space Eater*) and non-fiction works. He is the editor of the legendary *Ansible*, for which he won one of his six Hugo Awards (the others have been as best fan writer). He has also won the British Science Fiction Award for his story 'Cube Root' and a share of the European Science Fiction Award for *The Science in Science Fiction*. Born in Wales, he now lives in Reading; in between, he studied at Oxford and worked as a nuclear physicist.

PAUL WILLIAMS was the publisher of *Crawdaddy!*, America's first rock magazine, when he was nineteen. He was in John Lennon's hotel room in Montreal in 1969 for the recording of 'Give Peace a Chance'; and he has written books such as *Bob Dylan, Performing Artist* and *Rock and Roll: The 100 Best Singles*. The author of *Only Apparently Real – The World of Philip K. Dick*, he first met Dick in September 1968 and remained friends until PKD's death. He wrote the famous profile of Dick for *Rolling Stone* in 1975, and is now the literary executor of PKD's estate and editor of *The Philip K. Dick Society Newsletter*. His latest book is *Heart of Gold* and, after five and a half years' work, he recently completed another book on Bob Dylan.

JIM BURNS spent eighteen months in the RAF 'but despite trying to hoodwink the instructors into believing that I was von Richthofen's reincarnation, there was no disguising the fact that I was a lousy pilot'. He is acknowledged as *the* British sf artist, won the Hugo Award for Best Professional Artist in 1987, and has also collected five British Science Fiction Awards as best artist (a record for any category). His illustrations attracted the attention of film director Ridley Scott, and in 1980 he spent ten weeks in Hollywood working on designs for the film *Blade Runner*. Born in Wales, he now lives in Wiltshire, with his wife, three daughters and one son.

PHILIP K. DICK was born in Chicago, December 1928 and died in California, March 1982. His first story was published in 1952. In 1953 he had thirty short stories published and wrote his first sf novel *The Cosmic Puppets*; in 1954 he had twenty-eight short stories published and sold his first novel *Solar Lottery* (published in 1955). He won the Hugo Award in 1963 for his novel *The Man in the High Castle*. The same year, he completed four sf novels; in 1964 he completed six. By the time of his death, he had written some fifty novels, of which thirty-four were published during his lifetime. (Many of the others, which were non-sf, have seen posthumous publication.) The films *Blade Runner* and *Total Recall* were both based on his works. A French film of *Confessions of a Crap Artist* will be released during 1992.

MICHAEL MOORCOCK became editor of *New Worlds* in 1964; he became 'consultant editor' in 1991, when the title reappeared after an absence of twelve years. His first *NW* story was published in 1959, a collaboration with Barrington J. Bayley; his most recent was 'Colour', in the first volume of the new series. The author of over eighty books, his new novel *Jerusalem Commands* is published in the same month as this volume of *New Worlds*.

DAVID GARNETT is currently the editor of *New Worlds*.

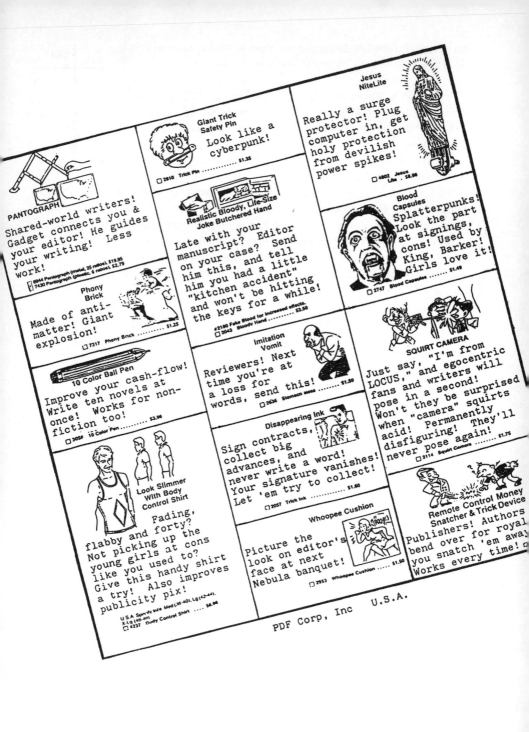

Manuscripts and letters to the editor should be sent to

New Worlds,
c/o Victor Gollancz Ltd,
14 Henrietta Street,
London WC2E 8QJ

SCIENCE FICTION · FANTASY · HORROR

84 SUFFOLK STREET, BIRMINGHAM, B1 1TA
Tel: 021-643 1999 Fax: 021-643 2001

In Dreams

Edited by Paul J. McAuley and Kim Newman

A celebration of the 7-inch single in all-original sf and horror fiction.

The vinyl record, and in particular the 7-inch single, are soon to become extinct as record companies stop manufacturing them in favour of the more resilient and profitable CDs. But it was on singles that we first heard Roy Orbison, Chuck Berry, Elvis Presley, The Beatles, The Rolling Stones, The Sex Pistols etc. The single was at the heart of the pop music revolution, but it was more than a pop culture artifact. It was a statement. It could carry the seeds of rebellion. It could get banned. Rapidly denigrated by sapphire needles, it was disposable and immediate.

Put together by hard sf writer Paul McAuley, and journalist and horror novelist Kim Newman, *In Dreams* transposes the subversive energies of the single into the printed word in a collection of outstanding stories by some of the best of sf, fantasy and horror writers including Jonathan Carroll, Ian McDonald, Lewis Shiner, Greg Egan, Ian McLeod, Ian Watson, Gwyneth Jones, Stephen Baxter, Graham Joyce and Christopher Fowler.

0 575 05201 5   £4.99 net

The Difference Engine

William Gibson & Bruce Sterling

Available for the first time in mass market format, Gollancz is pleased to present the highly acclaimed steampunk novel from the controversial pairing of two of science fiction's most exciting writers.

London, 1855, and the Industrial Revolution, supercharged by the development of steam-driven cybernetic engines, is in full swing. Greater Britain, with her calculating-cannons, steam dreadnoughts, spring-wound Colt machine pistols, and information technology, prepares to better the world's lot ...

'A visionary steam-powered heavy metal fantasy, Gibson and Sterling create a high-Victorian virtual reality of extraordinary richness and detail' – Ridley Scott, creator of *Alien*

'Stuffed with periodic detail, lovingly researched and polished. The deepest and raciest collaboration since Pohl and Kornbluth' – *The Guardian*

'A triumph' – *i–D*

0 575 05297 X   £4.99 net

Death Discs
**From ashes to smashes –
an account of fatality in the popular song**

Alan Clayson

Remember *Terry*, as sung by the inimitable Twinkle? Or the classic *Leader of the Pack*, in which a young lover accelerates into the night – and, tragically – a brick wall?

Death and rock'n'roll have always walked hand in hand. Once no playlist was complete without its DEATH DISC – that heady mix of music and morbidity that reached its dizziest heights in the golden age of the '50s and '60s.

Now 'the A.J.P. Taylor of pop', Alan Clayson, has written a timely account of death in the popular song, comas, heart attacks, industrial accidents, et al. From teenage trauma and traffic mishaps to tributes and real-life terminators, DEATH DISCS traces the history, themes and value of the phenomenon that left no gravestone unturntabled.

0 575 05475 1   £4.50 net

The Way to Babylon

Paul Kearney

Riven had been a successful writer of fantasy novels, until a climbing accident killed his beloved wife and left him physically and emotionally scarred. When he eventually returned to his remote cottage on Skye he was unsure that he would ever write again.

But then a stranger arrives, who takes Riven on a walk into the mountains — and a journey out of our world and into another: into Minginish, Riven's imaginary land, now as torn and troubled as its creator. Only he can save it from destruction — if he has the will.

Paul Kearney is a young Irish writer. *The Way to Babylon* is his impressive and moving first novel.

0 575 05309 7   £8.99 net
Also available in hardback

Still available . . . The first volume of NEW WORLDS

NEW WORLDS 1   FREE*

The first issue of the UK's best SF anthology

To get your copy send a cheque
or postal order (made out to
Victor Gollancz Ltd) for £2
to cover postage and packing to:

Sales Department
Victor Gollancz Ltd
New Worlds Offer
14 Henrietta Street
London
WC2E 8QJ

*plus postage and packing